STAY

a love story

TRACY EWENS

STAY

a love story

Book design by Maureen Cutajar
www.gopublished.com

ISBN: 978-1-7323216-7-0 (print)
ISBN: 978-1-7323216-6-3 (e-book)

For everyone who survived their childhood
and found a way to let go.

"I still have a lot to figure out, but the one thing I know is, wherever you are, that's where I belong. I'll never belong anywhere like I belong with you."

– EMILY HENRY (*People We Meet on Vacation*)

Chapter One

Clara Mar hated Paris. The city was magnificent, and the people were pleasant enough, but Paris was officially the backdrop against which most of the excrement of her life was thrown. The first time she'd lost focus during a performance? Paris. First champagne hangover? Paris. Awful first kiss? Paris. The "aggressive tongue incident," as she'd termed the experience, technically happened on a train from Versailles to Paris, but close enough.

Even the town car fender-bender that left her a scant fifteen minutes to warm up before performing Beethoven's Cello Sonata No. 3 for the first time in front of thousands of people occurred in Paris.

And the pièce de résistance? Her cheating fiancé, a man she barely liked, dumped *her* in front of nearly every contemporary she knew—and some she even respected—under the ubiquitous glitter of a New Year's performance in the preeminent City of Light. So, quoting *The Grinch* movie she'd watched on the plane from Charles de Gaulle last night while drinking an extra glass of wine with dinner, Clara's thoughts on Paris were *hate, hate, double hate,* and *loathe entirely*.

Bodega Bay already seemed like a much gentler place. Granted, she was standing at the bathroom sink of an inn she'd inherited from a grandfather she'd never known, but that would hopefully sort itself out later in the day. Staring at her reflection, Clara regretted both the extra glass of wine and skipping at least a cursory skin care routine before falling into the first bed she found and sleeping until noon.

She'd arrived at eight-thirty that morning, and she should have made the concoction that always worked for her jet lag, and she should have stayed awake. But there was nothing to do to keep her busy. No hotel restaurant, no other chatty musicians, not even a spa. So, after setting up her cello in the downstairs study, Clara caved, adjusted her phone alarm to ensure she was awake in time for the meeting with her mysterious grandfather's attorney, and crashed.

Mr. Norman Hill, Esq., would arrive in a little over an hour to "review the documents and explain the stipulations."

Clara normally left stipulations to other people, but fleeing Paris amidst protests from those who claimed to love her meant she was truly on her own. No staff, no representatives. She'd abandoned all of that in the city that shall no longer be named.

The escape was necessary to sort out her recent embarrassment and her parents' . . . lie? Misstep? Betrayal? She wasn't sure what to call it, but up until sometime before Thanksgiving when Mr. Hill had emailed Clara and called incessantly regarding her inheritance, she'd believed most of what her parents told her. She would have defended them to anyone as supportive, loyal, and trustworthy.

A small voice inside her argued they were still all those things, but in adult reality, Clara's mother was a liar, and her father, the man who raised her, called before she boarded the plane to ask if she'd consider talking things out with the amoral fiancé who'd ended things. Apparently cheating fell under the "men are complicated" clause, and the dumping-her bit was a "rash and unfortunate choice."

To say Clara was having a crisis of identity, that she was like a workhorse who'd removed her own blinders, was an understatement.

Splashing water one last time, she dried her face and studied her reflection again. At thirty-one, she was nearly ten years older than her newly discovered birth father was when he died. She never knew, would never know, either her grandfather or her father, but there she stood on the second floor of their family business.

Clara swallowed her handful of vitamins and supplements. She had no inkling about running an inn or, apparently, about family. Serums, eye cream, and moisturizer later, her phone lit with a giant letter M.

On a deep exhale, she answered.

"Darling." Bianca Mar's voice spilled, luxurious and mellow, from the other end, like expensive champagne.

"Mother. Shouldn't you be asleep? It's late in Paris." Clara didn't have the energy for anything more than cordial.

"Off to bed now. We've just finished a lovely evening with friends. What's this I hear about you hiding in shame?"

Setting the towel on the sink, Clara returned to the warm afternoon sun peeking through the sheer draperies in the adjacent bedroom. She sat on the bed. "I am not hiding. I . . . had some business to attend to."

A dramatic sigh rushed through the phone. "Sweetheart, Carter still cares for you, and I think you're both big enough to make it over this minor bump."

Clara closed her eyes. "Cheating on someone multiple times is not a *bump*."

"Those are ridiculous rumors," her mother insisted.

Clara wondered if her mother was drinking and medicated, or was simply unwilling to take her daughter's side, ever.

"I don't love Carter. I've never loved Carter. And I am not running. I'm . . . absorbing the impact of my bizarre new reality." *And your lies.* Clara left that part out. "Besides, Clara and Carter? We sounded more like a circus act."

"Pfft, *you* sound like a child. Carter is your best match."

Clara couldn't remember ever acting like a child, ever being given the space for anything as frivolous and safe as childhood. Leaning back on the bed, she said nothing. There was no need—her mother had always been deft at handling both sides of the conversation.

"You should consider what this outburst will cost your career. I know you're upset about the misunderstanding with your grandfather and all, but running from life's challenges is never the way to handle things."

"*Misunderstanding?* My father died."

Her mother was silent.

"And you never told me he existed. I had to find out from a *lawyer*." Her voice faltered with surprising emotion, which never played well with her mother, so Clara swallowed it back.

Another sigh. "Unfortunate, I admit, but you're a grown woman. And your father is the man who raised you."

"I know Burt raised me, but this"—Clara glanced around the white-wainscoted bedroom her mother would immediately dismiss as gauche—"is part of my history."

"Do *not* use your father's first name. It's disrespectful. And the idea of some dinky beach town playing any part in your history is utter nonsense."

Clara closed her eyes. "I have a family and roots you kept from me my entire life. That's not nonsense."

"Oh, please. He died, Clara. You were a baby."

"Well, I'm not a baby anymore." She opened her eyes, watching the wind strum the leaves of a tree branch outside. "I deserved to know."

"You are a world-renowned cellist, dear. The symphony is your home, your roots. Your dead grandfather and father change nothing about the glorious fiber of your making. Please do not belittle yourself by thinking you're going to become some impregnated innkeeper making pies, or some such absurdity."

Clara exhaled, the leaves through the window now still. There was no point in arguing. "I should go. I arrived early, and I need to get a practice in. You could think about an apology while I'm away." She braced for her mother's blast but doubled down, bolstered by their physical distance. "And . . . it's not nice to tell me to reconcile with a man who cheated on me and embarrassed me in front of my colleagues."

"Apologize?" Her mother practically spat the word. "I have nothing to apologize for. I was acting in your best interests. Christopher, your sperm donor, was a summer fling. Nothing more. I was already engaged to your father. When you were born, the man wanted to see you. And I, out of the kindness of my heart, schlepped all the way back down there." She sucked in more air. "That was the last time you had any contact with those people. We returned to Europe, and he died. There was no reason to scar you with useless information."

"Scar me?" Clara nearly laughed.

"Yes. You were born for greatness. Of that, I am certain. All anyone has to do is listen to you play. I would put nothing as banal as parental loss into your story."

The conversation was going nowhere. All these years Clara thought she'd had a good relationship with her parents, but now she wondered if it was only contingent on her obedience. Saying the right thing, never complaining or even thinking about escaping whatever hotel suite they'd tucked her into.

"What is the purpose of your call, Mother?" Clara asked, bravery and nausea rolling together through her empty stomach.

"You are part of the creative world we both live in, and for you to—"

"Purpose, Mother. What is the purpose?"

"To tell you to stop this nonsense and come home."

"I don't have a home," she nearly yelled. Clara had never raised her voice at her mother in her life.

The line was silent until her mother exhaled and said, "Young lady, you cannot—"

At the familiar and deprecating start to that sentence, Clara disconnected the call and told herself she would ignore any others that followed. She should block her mother. *But what if someone fell, or they needed her?* the small perfect child that lived in Clara's head asked. She tossed her phone on the bed.

Opening the only trunk she'd managed to haul upstairs upon her arrival, Clara wondered how she'd gotten things so wrong all these years and where to begin unraveling such a mess. She didn't have another performance scheduled until May. Her manager and her agent didn't like it but knew she was taking a break. Hopefully she could learn about these other members of her family and figure out a way forward.

She went down the worn, carpeted staircase, hand trailing along the polished wood, and dragged up another of her trunks. She needed to change her clothes and try to find something to eat before her meeting with Mr. Hill. The airplane biscotti she'd eaten when she'd woken up around ten o'clock before falling back to sleep certainly did not count as nourishment.

She would meet with the attorney like a grown woman who did this sort of thing all the time and do what she'd done her whole life—act confident when she wasn't, break things into practicable pieces, and deliver an outstanding performance.

Dylan Pace hated doctors and hospitals, which made no sense, given he'd spent his life surrounded by the medical profession. Working coast guard search-and-rescue and part-time for the fire department when he was off the water, Dylan had seen nearly everything. That didn't make sitting on the exam table in Dr. Marsh's office any easier, and he hoped like hell his orthopedic surgeon would be on time for once in his life.

Dylan checked his watch. He had a meeting with Mr. Levinson's lawyer, of all people, in an hour and a half. The man was so formal, he made Dylan's palms sweat. He couldn't be late. Levinson died months ago. His will and the Inn by the Bay had been in limbo while Mr. Hill tracked down Levinson's mysterious granddaughter.

According to town gossip, they'd found her, and she was arriving on a red-eye from Paris. Dylan wasn't sure when, but he guessed her arrival sparked settling the will, since Mr. Hill mentioned that Levinson had "bequeathed" something to Dylan.

He couldn't imagine what Levinson would leave him, but he hoped it wasn't the old man's prized and ancient blender. Although, the blender would be the perfect thing to leave behind, given how much crap Dylan used to give him about it. Maybe Levinson left him a book or a letter, something sentimental.

He scrubbed a hand over his face at his asinine thoughts. While Mr. Levinson leaned toward flowery language and ten-point words, he was never that way with Dylan. They had often enjoyed one another's company over the silence of a cup of coffee or deciding if the hedge lining the walkway to the inn needed trimming again.

Dylan glanced at the clock over the *Muscles Are Our Friends* poster. Fifteen minutes late. Leaning both hands on the exam table, he watched his dangling feet and tried to straighten his right knee. Better. It was better than it was when he'd blown it out by lunging into the helicopter when he should have waited until they'd ratcheted him and the woman pulling his hair—not in a good way—higher and through the cargo door.

The unforgiving fluorescent light of the office seemed to highlight the graveyard of scars up and down both legs. Lost in thought, Dylan pivoted to rest his knee on the exam table as Dr. Bob Marsh walked in, flipping papers in that way hurried doctors did to convey their importance, before setting the chart aside and washing his hands.

"Hey, Dylan. How's the knee?" He quickly glanced over his shoulder before returning to the sink.

"Better," Dylan said.

Next through the door was Dr. Chris Marsh, once a defensive lineman on their high school football team, now a doctor looking to join his father's practice. It must be nice having a father who paved a life path.

"So, it's healing, which means you'll continue to walk. You may need another surgery down the road, but I wanna see how it goes." Dr. Marsh dried his hands and tossed the paper towel.

"And you're not clearing me to return to duty, right?" Dylan asked.

Dr. Marsh leaned against the counter, one foot over the other with his arms crossed, before he sighed.

"Just give it to me straight."

"Straight?" Dr. Marsh said. "You want it straight?"

"I do."

"Doctor, want to give it a shot?" Marsh asked his son. "You've reviewed his case. You can tell Dylan what he needs to know."

"Okay." Chris looked back at the X-ray and met Dylan's eyes. "Your knee is shredded. Multiple repairs already, possibly another one in the future. It will always be a weakness. Your supervisor—"

"Captain."

"Whatever. He wants assurances you can return to strenuous duty. You can't. You're never going to be able to rely on this knee in the way search-and-rescue demands you rely on it." Chris looked at his father, who concurred.

Dr. Marsh the elder exhaled as if Dylan's broken body was a reflection of the guy's skill. "Straight enough for you?"

"Like an arrow. Well done." Dylan tipped his head at Chris.

"Sorry," said Chris. "My bedside manner is usually better, but you're a—"

"Pain in the ass," Dylan finished. "I know."

"Takes one to know one." Chris grinned, again reminding Dylan they'd once shared a football field.

"What about the fire department?" Dylan shifted on the exam table.

Dr. Marsh looked over from the laptop clamped to the wall. "It might be an option with PT. We'll have to see, down the road."

"Down the road? How am I supposed to pay my bills?" Dylan asked before recoiling at the question. No one cared how he paid his bills, and he wasn't some broken-ass man. "I'm kidding," he said, releasing his best fake laugh as he hopped off the exam table, jaw clenched at the shot of pain. "Well, I guess that's it, then."

"Hold on. We still need to examine your knee. Walking is the priority, remember? Get back up there." He pointed to the table.

Dylan obeyed, and Dr. Marsh handed the rest of the exam over to his son while he left to prep for surgery at the hospital in Santa Rosa.

Chris lifted Dylan's leg, carefully resting it on a rolled towel. "You and Annie still a thing?" he asked, eyes on the knee.

"Is that a professional question?" Dylan asked, briefly snapped out of his what-the-hell-now panic spiral.

"No, but I'm trying to get you to hold still for more than twenty seconds."

"And you thought bringing up the last woman to dump my ass would do the trick?"

Chris poked and prodded some more. "I didn't know she dumped you."

"Bullshit." Dylan closed his eyes as Mini Marsh manipulated his knee a little more. They were almost done. Dylan knew the steps of the exam in his sleep.

"Any idea how grueling a surgical residency is? I'm only recently coming up for air. Sorry if I've fallen out of the gossip ring."

"Yeah, well"—Dylan extended his leg again—"you're not missing much. Annie dumped me because I wasn't—ouch." Pain shot all the way to his toes.

Chris gave him a minute and typed more notes on the computer.

"She dumped me, and now she's a dentist somewhere." He exhaled.

"A dentist, huh?" Chris faced Dylan again. "Okay. So, you can move from the rigid brace to the soft hinge. Do you have one, or should I—"

Dylan shook his head. "I have them all."

"Perfect. So, take it easy"—he glanced at the file—"and you're all set up for physical therapy starting next week."

Dylan closed his eyes.

"Let me guess, you hate physical therapy?"

He nodded.

"I get it, but walking. Remember walking."

"I'm walking right now."

"You are, but as the body ages, it is—"

"Yeah, yeah." He made to get down again, but Chris held him off.

"So do you still think about her?"

Dylan furrowed his brow.

"Annie."

"It's been two years." He snatched the instructions from the doctor's hand and noticed "ice packs" in bold. He'd need to get more ice packs.

"There are a few other things we should go over," Chris said.

"About Annie or my knee?" Dylan scooted to the edge of the table.

"Your knee."

"I know the drill, Chris. I'll show up to PT and wear the brace. Hey, maybe you should date Annie, since you're so interested."

Chris met his eyes and handed him another form.

"Wait, *are* you dating her?" Dylan asked.

Chris said nothing.

"Seriously?"

"Nah." Chris patted him on the shoulder with the chart. "Just messin' with you."

Dylan shook his head. "Still an idiot."

Chris pointed with the chart this time, one hand on the exam room door. "Always fun catching up. You still have enough meds for inflammation?"

"Yeah."

"Okay, well, I'll update the *elder* Dr. Marsh, and like you said, you know the drill. Take it easy, go to PT, and we'll see you in a month."

"Got it." Dylan slid off the exam table, less badass this time. "Thanks."

"No problem." Chris peeked back in. "Oh, and do you still have Annie's number?" He grinned, evil and familiar, and was gone behind the door as Dylan flipped him off.

After grabbing a quick lunch, Dylan drove through the gated entrance of the Inn by the Bay, pulled his truck out of sight, and cut the engine. Reaching into the bag next to him, he peeled the wrapper off a Drumstick ice cream cone and ate the coveted snack of his youth in silence. Catching most of the chocolate-covered peanuts before they hit his white long-sleeve, Dylan tried to imagine the realities of life without his job.

Who was he if he wasn't grabbing coffee before shift, beating himself up, and returning home to a town that valued his bravery, his dedication?

Dylan recognized change. Hell, he'd dealt with it his whole life. Someone or something was always coming or going, but he'd thought he *was* his job. No matter what else swirled around him, he could count on his earned professional skills, the people he worked with, and even the bay of water that both taunted him and kept him sane.

There would be other jobs. He could work with Chance in the metal shop or see if the Branches needed help around their bed-and-breakfast. Dylan had practically grown up around Levinson's inn. He could dust off those skills and be of use somewhere else in town. Search-and-rescue was only part of his life, Dylan tried to assure his anxious mind. He'd get through this meeting, find a spot for Levinson's blender, and then figure out his bills for the month.

Having reached his self-reflection limit for the day, Dylan checked his watch and popped the best part of the Drumstick, the tip of the cone, into his mouth and started his truck.

He could be anything he set his mind to. His brother Tyler had preached those words at various stages of their life. Dylan wasn't sure what or who he wanted to be yet, but he would figure it out on his own. There was no need to bother anyone with his latest . . . challenge, but at thirty-two, he hoped there was still time for something new.

Chapter Two

The bookcase tilted hard, and Clara instantly regretted kicking the rock aside. She'd wandered the bottom floor of the inn, trying to stay awake through another wave of jet lag. The answers she wanted about her grandfather and about her father's death were most likely in that giant study somewhere, but Clara couldn't help feeling like an intruder, so she touched nothing. Instead, she'd gone onto the porch for a breath of cold air and found a bookcase, of all things, outside.

Eight shelves high, it stood filled with books on every subject, from crime to cooking. Clara ran a hand along the spines and pulled out a well-read mystery. While she was skimming the back cover, she noticed a rock wedged under the front corner of the bookcase. It was scratching the gorgeous wood of the porch, so she kicked it away.

Now, she'd dropped the mystery novel and was swaying with said bookcase, continuing her latest pattern of questionable decisions. Right as she imagined her mother extolling Clara's virtuous death-by-literature to their artsy friends, heavy footsteps approached from behind.

"You need some help with that?"

"No. I've almost got it," she called out, her voice muffled by the books.

Clara had maneuvered difficult situations before. Granted, when she was not inheriting inns from mysterious grandfathers, a staff of people handled her daily schedule and tasks, but the challenging pieces, personalities, and projects were still Clara's responsibility. Difficulty "built character," as her parents touted. This physical situation was a bit different because her straining arms were about to give up.

Adjusting the weight, she lost her footing. Two much larger and seemingly up-to-the-task arms joined her, instantly caging Clara in warmth while her face was still buried somewhere near *Pride and Prejudice*.

"Easy. I've got you," a deep male voice—baritone, possibly G2— said softly at her ear, the weight of the bookcase easing but still unsteady. "You've gotta"—the voice strained, and the body pressed firm at Clara's back—"keep this rock under the front corner," he finished.

Freeing her face from the books, she dropped her head and noticed the man's worn boot sliding the rock back under the corner of the bookcase.

Relief—at not having to explain any of this to the dozens of people waiting for her to fail—was instant, as was the awareness of her rescuer's body. On his next push, Clara stepped aside, prepared to thank some mountain man in plaid with a beard and maybe an axe.

Tucking her hair behind her ear, she brushed at the front of her clothes and decided black may not be the best color for a new inn owner. She glanced up.

His back, still to her, was nearly the width of the bookcase. No flannel and no axe. Instead, the man wore faded charcoal pants and a red jacket, collar high on his neck. His hair, shorn a couple of inches from his scalp on the sides, was longer on top, but not by much, and brown with flecks of time spent in the sun.

One more shove of the bookcase, and the man turned, dusting his hands together. Clara was about to thank him for the save, and then he met her eyes. Blue *and* brown, she noticed as he stepped forward. Because why bother with one eye color if you're a rescue hero, right?

His face was lovely. The angle of his jaw was out of balance with the fullness of his lips, as if some higher power decided his look was too intense, too Bach, so they sprinkled a little Debussy in there. It was a stunning combination, one that caught Clara off guard.

"You must be the granddaughter," he said, brushing at his own jacket now.

She froze like she was on a quiz show. *Yes, she was the granddaughter. Yes* would have been a perfectly acceptable answer, but good lord, this guy was potent. Not glossy-magazine or perched-behind-a-baby-grand-piano handsome. More visceral, windswept like those adventure shows on late-night TV. Clara had always been a sucker for all that Kevlar, but she needed to say something instead of ogling the poor man.

"Yes. Apologies. I am the granddaughter." She extended her hand. "Clara Mar."

He glanced at her outstretched greeting, and Clara wondered if she registered as overly formal. Normally astute at reading a room, she was again thrown. Clara had never been on a porch, so etiquette was anyone's guess.

Before she could rewind and try something else, he took her hand in his and the out-of-place gesture turned easy, almost intimate, as his fingers swiped the underside of her wrist before pulling away.

"Pleasure. Dylan."

Pleasure. One word, but a good one. Clara cleared her throat. "I hope you're not here to stay at the—" She pointed toward the front door of the inn, almost like she knew what she was doing. "The inn. We are closed until summer."

"I'm not a guest." He pushed a hand into his pocket and offered nothing more.

"Oh, apologies again. How can I help you?"

He grinned, almost like he couldn't help himself, and Clara tried not to notice his mouth, but there was only so much a woman could take on a few hours of sleep.

"I was told to meet Mr. Hill here at two."

"Oh." She tilted her head. "Are you an attorney?"

"No."

"Trust manager?"

He shook his head. A man of few words, this one.

Clara met his gaze. *Eye contact is the cornerstone of a confident and professional persona.* She could practically hear her father—or at least the man she'd thought was her father—drilling the lesson home when she was six.

"Should I know you, Dylan . . ."

"Pace. Not necessarily."

"But you know me?"

"I do."

Clara put a hand to her hip. "You're messing with me, right?"

He grinned. "Maybe a little, but I *was* told to meet Mr. Hill here in"—he glanced at his watch—"ten minutes. I'm early."

Her jet-lagged brain raced for an explanation he wasn't offering. "Well, can I invite you in?"

"Sure." Dylan wiped his feet on the front mat like he'd done it a million times and opened the front door.

Clara followed, about done with mysterious men. He'd gotten the time and the lawyer's name right for the meeting, so he must serve some purpose in her grandfather's estate.

They stood silently in the entryway.

"Any idea why there's a bookcase out there?" Clara finally asked, gesturing out the still-open front door.

"Lending library. After our town library caught fire years ago. They've rebuilt since, but your grandfather left it there." He glanced out one of the long windows framing the front door.

"You knew him, obviously?" she asked, oddly craving information. "My grandfather?"

"Yeah." Dylan met her eyes again.

"The library was a . . . gracious gesture." Clearly, she'd forgotten how to have an engaging conversation.

"It was."

"And you read?" What in the world? Had she seriously asked that?

"I do," he said, expression not annoyed, but something she couldn't decipher.

Clara tilted her head. "Well done, you. Okay." She clasped her hands together to keep from twisting the edge of her sweater. "Well, he sounds like a pleasant person, which is . . . a promising start."

"Pleasant? Yeah, I guess that's accurate," Dylan said, tone grounded in the familiarity of an inside joke or a story about a man Clara would never know. He shifted his weight again, studying her now. If her lack of family knowledge was confusing, he said nothing. No inquiry about why he'd never seen her around if she was close enough to receive her grandfather's inheritance, which was fine because Clara had no answers.

"What do you do for a living, Mr. Pace?" she asked, unsure where the question came from or why her cadence sounded so snooty against the welcoming entryway. Clara had spent her life around snooty, so perhaps she always sounded this way and just never noticed.

He narrowed his eyes. "I'm on leave at the moment. Why?"

"Oh, no reason. Just making conversation while we wait. On leave from where?" she asked, undeterred by his reluctance.

"Coast guard. Search-and-rescue."

Clara gave herself a mental checkmark for calling his career—rescue hero—even with her face smushed in a bookcase. "Makes sense."

Seemingly tired of standing there, Dylan hung his coat on the stand by the door, which left a long-sleeve white T-shirt pushed up his forearms and stretched across a chest Clara willed herself to not enjoy.

"What makes sense?" he asked, another expression she couldn't read. Cold? Unyielding, maybe?

"Nothing." She stopped twisting the edge of her sweater. "There's something about the way you—Never mind."

"The way I?" Dylan crossed his arms, leaning on the wall like part of the structure.

"Confidence." She gestured to his face. "I imagine it's part of search-and-rescue. Also, excellent eye contact. If I'm drowning in that water"—she pointed in a direction she hoped was the bay—"I would want someone like yourself to save me instead of, say . . . Paul Giamatti. That's what I meant."

"The actor?"

"Yes." Clara hoped a change of subject might reverse the bizarre turn she'd taken on their first encounter.

"Size rarely matters," Dylan said, straight face, no innuendo. "Paul may be an excellent swimmer, highly trained."

Clara wasn't bold enough to inform him size often mattered. She was only that brand of fearless behind her cello. Offstage, life was often more complex.

Dylan walked into one of the side rooms and sat on the couch. Was this guy the old innkeeper? Maintenance? He seemed awfully familiar with her grandfather's inn.

"Paul may be skilled," she said, following him. "But if I'm drowning, I'm clinging to assurances. I don't want to find out if he can swim." Clara stood in what looked like the living room, with a giant fireplace and framed pictures on the mantel she hadn't noticed before.

Dylan's grin was quick. She nearly missed it, but it was there and casual in a way Clara knew put people in distress at ease. She hadn't a clue about searching or rescuing, save those occasional late-night shows or YouTube videos people watched backstage between rehearsals, but she knew with certainty Dylan was good at both.

"Right. Well, let's keep you out of the bay then, because I'm out of commission, and if Hollywood dries up, Paul might be gunning for my job."

"Funny." Their eyes met again. "You're funny."

"Rarely." He glossed over all her odd questions effortlessly, which confirmed he dealt with tired and crazy all the time. It made Clara feel a bit handled. He didn't seem to care who she was beyond what he already knew, which was refreshing, given what she'd left behind for Bodega Bay.

"You never met your grandfather?" he asked.

The question was unexpected, and she scrambled before saying, "Nope." A casual response that would have summoned one of her instructors to correct her elocution while prodding her to stand up straighter. Clara crossed her own arms, wondering if Dylan's brand of aloof might work for her too.

Nope?

Yeah, he'd bet money she'd never used that word in her life. Not that "Pleasure. Dylan" was his usual introduction either. When Dylan was in junior high, Mr. Levinson had taught him "a greeting under pressure should be concise and professional," so it seemed fitting to serve Levinson's etiquette back to the proper and polished Ms. Mar. The granddaughter had an accent too. Not foreign exactly, but distant and out of town. Maybe that had him on his best behavior.

Despite Levinson's efforts, there was nothing proper or polished about Dylan. He *was* a gentleman—this town, the coast guard, and his brother Tyler had drilled those lessons in tight—but Dylan was Bodega Bay through and through. He rarely had time for formalities.

Clara looked exactly like the kind of woman he imagined arriving on a flight from Paris. Whereas most people who'd gone nearly twenty-four hours without sleep might present haggard, she was oddly luminous, like the lack of sleep had pinked her cheeks and made her eyes more attractive. She was in all black, from leggings to an expensive-looking sweater. Her dark blonde hair was tucked behind one ear, and she smelled good. Wood and herbs, something probably simple, organic, and overpriced too.

Clara Mar wasn't pretty. That was too easy. Words to describe her seemed beyond Dylan's pay grade. Refined? Nah, she was more like one of those paintings on school field trips. Encased in light, untouchable, and possibly a little sad.

Christ. Five minutes in her presence, and he was a poet now?

Whatever the adjective, Dylan knew one thing for sure. The granddaughter was sophisticated and cultured in a way that usually found "quaint" towns like Bodega Bay "charming" until they realized the nearest sushi joint was at least an hour away.

Why would Levinson, a beloved and longtime resident of Bodega Bay, leave his small-town inn to a woman like the one presently trying not to twist the edge of her sweater again? It made no sense unless she was his only option.

Dylan had a feeling she'd be gone by month's end, which kind of pissed him off. He had no investment in her staying, but Levinson died during the off-season last spring and instead of authorizing the repair of a small gas leak, Ms. Mar from afar decided to close the whole damn inn. Dylan looked around the living room. The place deserved better. Hell, their town deserved better than some stopover.

Dylan couldn't think of a time when the Inn by the Bay was closed when Levinson was still alive. *Shit.* What if she sold it to some big developer?

Unable to sit still, Dylan was back in the grand entryway now and felt oddly out of place. It was like he didn't belong in the space without Levinson emerging from the back kitchen in an apron, reading glasses perched, and cigar smoke trailing. It was strange, chillier without him.

"You need help with these . . . trunks? Are these actual trunks?" Dylan asked, surveying the luggage in the foyer.

"Yes," she said. "I mean, I do not need help, but yes, they're trunks. I recently came off tour, and all of this travels with me."

"So, not a light packer."

She grinned. "Not a day in my life."

"Huh. Well, are you staying upstairs, or in the innkeeper's quarters?" Dylan wasn't sure how he was suddenly friendly, but they were standing there, and unless he was going to wait outside like a child in trouble, he might as well find out how Ms. Mar and her multiple trunks were settling into lil' old Bodega Bay.

"I . . . slept upstairs in the first bed I found. Innkeeper's quarters?"

Dylan gestured toward the back of the inn. "Two rooms off the kitchen. I'd give you a tour, but we should probably wait for the professionals." He glanced at the study. "Cello? Is that your instrument?"

"Yes. How long have you known my grandfather?"

"My whole life. How long have you played the cello?"

"My whole life. Well, since I was six."

Dylan shoved a hand in his pocket. "Pretty big instrument. How'd you get that on the plane?"

"She gets her own seat."

"She?"

Her face flushed, and Dylan looked back at the cello. Human weaknesses like blushing made her seem real, which he did not need to notice. He understood snobs. They sauntered around Bodega Bay once the season started, but elegant *and* human was not a combination Dylan often witnessed.

"Yes. My cellos have always been female. I used to name them, so be glad you missed those years." She chuckled, tucking her hair behind her ear again.

"When did you stop naming them?"

She looked up, surprised.

"I . . . guess when I was thirteen. Evangeline was the last."

"Good cello name." Dylan kicked one boot against the other. "Weird, the stuff we leave behind once high school hits, right?"

She seemed confused, so he clarified. "Thirteen? Beginning of high school?"

"Oh, sure. Yes, high school. Yeah, weird."

And they were back to awkward. Dylan checked his watch. Hill was five minutes late. Hadn't Levinson always said timeliness was next to godliness? Apparently doctors and lawyers got a pass.

"So, if you're search-and-rescue, on leave or otherwise, what do you have to do with my grandfather's estate?"

"I am happy to shed some light on your question, Ms. Mar," Norman Hill, Esq., said, now pushing through the door to the inn.

Dylan had met Mr. Hill twice. Once when he was younger, trimming the hedge in front of the inn as Mr. Levinson walked his lawyer to the car. And again, shortly after Levinson's death, when Dylan helped coordinate the repair of the gas leak. Mr. Hill arrived in person and paid the gas company with a check, of all things. That was months ago, and the inn had sat vacant since. Waiting, Dylan imagined now, for the woman stepping aside and closing its glossy front door against a predictable afternoon wind.

Chapter Three

Thank heavens. Clara could have kissed the tall man, expertly manicured and dressed in an exquisite suit, as he removed and hung his jacket. His skin was dark and stunningly moisturized. She appreciated face products. His hair was short, and his bowtie was slightly askew, which Clara found charming over imperfect. Most importantly, Mr. Hill had rescued her from possibly the most uncomfortable conversation of her life, save the earlier one where she'd asked Dylan if he read books.

Clara had thought herself quite eloquent since about the age of seven, but not today.

"Mr. Pace. A pleasure to see you again." Mr. Hill extended his hand, and Dylan did the same.

"And Ms. Mar." He took Clara's hand in both of his. "A delight to finally meet you in person. How was your flight?"

"Uneventful. Thank you." Clara smiled.

After placing his scarf on the stand with his coat, Mr. Hill clapped his hands together, rubbing them presumably to warm up from the chill.

"Shall we?" he said, picking up the briefcase he'd set at his feet and gesturing toward the living room.

"I don't think Ms. Mar wants me here for all the details, so if you could just tell me what—"

"Join us, Mr. Pace," Mr. Hill insisted.

Dylan exhaled and followed Clara into the living room. When they were both seated, Clara on a giant cream-colored chair and Dylan on the patterned couch, Mr. Hill set his bag on the coffee table, pulled out two packets of paper, and handed one to each of them.

"I'm sorry. Is Mr. Pace part of my grandfather's team?" Clara asked the attorney, who had closed his case and scooted a high-backed chair over from the window.

Mr. Hill looked at Dylan. "No. Mr. Pace is in . . . rescue services, is it?"

Dylan smirked. "Sure. We'll go with that. But I'm retired as of this morning's physical."

Mr. Hill tilted his head. "Excellent timing." He glanced at Clara. "Your grandfather always had excellent timing."

Retired? Hadn't he said he was on leave? Clara realized she was jet-lagged, but she hoped someone would explain what was going on soon.

Clearing his throat, Mr. Hill flipped open his packet of papers. "Now, if you will both turn to the first page, I have simplified some of the legalese. Essentially, this explains that prior to his death, Mr. Levinson engaged Hill and Spaulding as executors of his will, which, among other things, includes this estate.

"The second page"—they all turned—"summarizes each section of the will." He moved to the next page. Clara and Dylan did too. "And here is how Mr. Levinson wished his belongings and properties to be distributed."

Clara scanned the page. *Clara Mar to receive $452,600.00 in cash inheritance. Clara Mar to receive personal effects described as follows.* Below was a list of a few items Clara assumed belonged to her grandmother. She paused on the page; the oddity of sitting in a home she'd never visited, being given things by people she'd never known, was acute.

Moving on, Clara began the next paragraph. *Clara Mar and Dylan Pace will—*

Dylan looked up. So did she.

"I don't understand," she said first.

"Which part?" Mr. Hill asked, crossing one leg over the other and leaning closer.

She turned to Dylan. "Using more than one word this time, who are you, exactly?"

"I . . ." Dylan muttered, his effortless charm, on full display moments ago, now gone.

"Mr. Pace was your grandfather's dear friend."

Dylan's face flushed, and Clara was suddenly aware of her heart in her chest, a thrumming in her ears.

"That's a stretch," Dylan managed.

Mr. Hill shook his head. "I don't think so, and obviously neither did Mr. Levinson." He gestured to the paperwork.

"So, he left the inn to both of us," Clara confirmed. "Fifty-fifty?"

"Yes."

"Why?" The question sounded harsh, but she was tired and feeling like a pawn on some small-town chessboard.

"Those were his wishes. Once we get through these initial pages, there's a letter I will read to both of you, but essentially his plan was for you two to take over the inn, hopefully learn to love it, and at a minimum get it ready for the seventy-fifth anniversary summer season."

"Why drag me into this?" Clara asked.

Mr. Hill's pleasant expression furrowed, lifting his glasses slightly above his eyebrows. "I hardly think this is dragging, Ms. Mar. When I got your call last week, you seemed quite eager to claim the inheritance—after a bit of a delay, I might add."

Clara squeezed the bridge of her nose. *Because my fiancé dumped me after I dared to question a black bra dangling from the back doorknob of his dressing room before our final holiday performance.*

"I have been touring nonstop, which, of course, is no one's issue but mine. I didn't realize this was a thing." She held up the stack of papers. "I was simply looking for a place to—That is, my assistant said there would be a key under the outside mat. It seemed simple. Easy. And there was a key, so thank you."

"Of course."

"But that's all I knew. This presents like a commitment, a project."

Dylan appeared to be in shock as he kept looking between the two of them and the paperwork.

Mr. Hill made to speak, but Clara continued.

"Why leave your estate to a woman you've never met *and* to such a close friend? Why not leave it all to Mr. Pace?"

"Your grandfather imagined he knew you."

Odd, since she barely knew herself these days. Clara snorted, then quickly covered her mouth. "I . . . did not mean to laugh."

"Sounded more like a snort," Dylan said, apparently finding his voice and his sarcasm.

She glanced over in mild horror. She'd been on red-eye flights before, but they'd never caused her to lose her composure. Mr. Hill nudged the bridge of his tortoiseshell glasses.

"Are there any other big reveals?" She raised a brow in defiance, which she hoped masked her own insecurity.

Mr. Hill cleared his throat. "As I said, you two will share ownership of the inn. Ms. Mar, you will also inherit the sum of money indicated in item two on the third page and several personal effects."

Clara stopped twisting the edge of her sweater and raised her hand this time.

"Question?"

"Yes. Well, more like two statements. First, I would like to apologize for my harsh response. I am not normally this agitated, but as I said, I am tired and . . . well, this is all a bit unexpected."

"No need to apologize. These things can be complicated."

"Second, I do not want the money."

Mr. Hill clicked his pen. "May I ask why?"

"I am not here for money. My interest is strictly unraveling the lie of my parentage and resting from a rather tumultuous start to

26

the new year. Can we put the money back into the inn, use it for supplies or something?"

Her grandfather's lawyer seemed in thought. "Half a million dollars is a lot of supplies, Ms. Mar."

Clara understood, but taking money felt opportunistic, given that she'd never met the man.

"A memorial, or a trust for the town. Education, something along those lines, maybe," she said.

"I can look into it and get back to you." He made a note on his copy and glanced up. "Right. Any other questions or statements, Ms. Mar?"

"No. Not at the moment."

"Mr. Pace?"

Clara's eyes cut to Dylan, who shook his head.

"Excellent. As I stated, the bulk of the personal effects, such as jewelry and heirlooms, go to Ms. Mar, save Mr. Levinson's watch, a Vacheron Constantin 222 Jumbo." Mr. Hill handed Dylan a polished wooden box. "Oh, and a blender. Mr. Levinson seemed to think you would understand the blender."

Dylan set the box on the coffee table and grinned. "I do."

"Excellent. The appliance is clean and in the kitchen for you," Mr. Hill confirmed.

"Thank you." Dylan leaned back on the couch, crossing his leg.

"Ms. Mar, your items are in the safe in the primary suite upstairs and listed on this page here." Mr. Hill held up his copy, seemingly to ensure Clara understood.

At her nod, he continued. "Everything else remains with the inn. The two of you must live in the inn until it opens for the summer season, which is in"—he glanced at his watch—"about six months. This should give Ms. Mar plenty of time to learn about her family lineage, and it is a stipulation of the inheritance." He scanned the document with his pen. "Oh, and Mr. Pace, Mr. Levinson hoped you could help his granddaughter by sharing memories and town history."

Dylan furrowed his brow. "I can share what I know. Some other people in town might be better at that."

"Mr. Levinson seemed to think you were the one to help."

Clara glanced at Dylan, who looked a bit cornered.

"Why six months?" he asked.

"The will stipulates you and Ms. Mar should pool your efforts and talents to prepare the inn for its seventy-fifth anniversary and a grand summer reopening." He splayed his hands like an old Hollywood director with a vision. "As you know, Mr. Levinson passed some months back, but it took us a bit to connect with Ms. Mar." He glanced at Clara, who felt oddly guilty. "So, six months it is." Mr. Hill returned to his paperwork.

"I know nothing about running an inn," Clara said.

"Understood. We have a few more items to get through before I read the letter, which will explain your grandfather's rationale."

They both nodded, and Clara wondered what Mr. Hill was saving for last that might explain a lifetime of divide. How a man she'd never met felt compelled to leave her half of an inn filled with memories she would never share and a safe full of ephemera she would never understand.

Must be some letter.

Dylan was still trying to get his head around what happened when Clara moved on to what-ifs. He didn't want to appear slow, but his mentor of sorts had left Dylan half of something so entrenched in their hometown that its façade was on T-shirts and coasters in every gift shop on Main Street.

The Inn by the Bay was an institution. A beacon built into the hill of a fishing town, glowing warm above cold winter nights and in full bloom every summer. It was inconceivable Dylan now owned a part of the place where nearly every couple in town, local and tourist, chose to have their wedding.

Mr. and Mrs. Levinson had been anchors throughout Dylan's life, and now they'd left him part of the town's future. Ignoring the nerves sloshing through his belly, Dylan tried to "seize the opportunity," as Levinson often advised.

"What if we don't get along? Or we disagree on how things should be . . . restored?" Clara asked, back to twisting the edge of her sweater.

"You are not restoring the inn, Ms. Mar. Look around. Apart from a small gas leak months ago, it is in excellent health."

Dylan scoffed.

Clara looked at him, narrowing her eyes. "What? What was that?"

He shrugged. "I'm just reliving that you shut down the whole inn over a tiny gas leak."

"What?" she scoffed right back, feeling a bit juvenile. "What are you talking about? How would I have closed down an inn I knew nothing about?"

Mr. Hill cleared his throat. "Perhaps I can help." He looked at Dylan. "As estate managers, in Ms. Mar's absence, we, specifically my firm and I, made the decision to close the inn until Ms. Mar was located."

Clara looked straight ahead but raised a brow. That was all the energy she had to hopefully convey that while Dylan Pace might know *of* her, he didn't know her as a person. Certainly not enough to be passing judgments.

"Neil, the manager, lost his job," Dylan said, nonplused by her annoyance, and homing in on Mr. Hill.

"I understand. We have since compensated all staff." Mr. Hill turned to the next page. "Now back to the tasks at hand. The letter will outline a few things your grandfather would like you and Mr. Pace to do as sort of a . . . thank-you for the inheritance and in trib-ute to the inn." He let out a slow breath before continuing. "Mr. Levinson asked for completion of all tasks prior to the new season. He imagined you and Mr. Pace would bring the inn into the next generation. Secure its best chance of survival."

"And then?" she asked.

"Then you can continue running the inn as a business, or you can sell, provided you allow my firm to perform due diligence on your buyer to ensure their intent is in the best interest of the inn. Aside from that, you are free to do as you wish."

"Can one of us buy the other out at the end of six months?" Dylan asked. He'd pegged Clara as temporary, but Dylan wasn't going anywhere, and he didn't want a technicality to mess things up.

"Yes," Mr. Hill confirmed.

Clara narrowed her eyes at Dylan before returning to her copy of the paperwork. He wasn't sure what made her tick yet, but he could tell his question hit a nerve. Was it offensive a man like Dylan might buy the inn right out from under a woman who could afford to turn down half a mil? *Welcome to Bodega Bay, sweetheart. We're all about sophistication.*

"So next, we will flip a coin," Mr. Hill said, pulling a quarter from his jacket.

Okay, so sophistication was a stretch, but Dylan wasn't letting outside attitude mess with his head.

"Per Mr. Levinson's instructions, whoever wins the coin toss gets first pick of the housing accommodations—the upstairs primary suite, or the innkeeper's quarters."

Dylan smiled. Levinson always was the best kind of pain in the ass.

"Housing accommodations? As in, we are living under the same roof. Together. For six months?"

"Yes." Mr. Hill pushed at his glasses again, thankfully not pausing for Clara to have another bewildered moment out loud. "The person with the last name closest to Levinson gets to choose first. So, Ms. Mar, heads or tails?"

She seemed stunned into silence for a minute. Probably at the thought of anything being decided by a coin toss, but then she called, "Heads."

Rookie move. Mr. Hill was holding the coin tails up. There was always a three percent greater chance of a coin landing on the side where it started.

Mr. Hill flipped the coin. "Tails."

"Boom," Dylan exclaimed before he could stop himself. Clara blinked at him. "Sorry. Competitive."

"Clearly," she said. "It was a coin toss."

Dylan tilted his head. "True, but the winner gets to pick rooms." He knew he sounded like a kid and didn't care. Christ, it felt good to be excited about something.

"Mr. Pace, which housing accommodation would you like?"

Dylan's heart raced a little. How had Levinson been there for him, offering purpose, an alternative path, even from the grave? "I'll take the innkeeper's quarters. Ms. Mar, er, Clara, is already upstairs."

"I'm happy to move. Please do not *accommodate* on my account. After all, you won the important coin toss." She was annoyed. More like sleep-deprived, hungry, and probably dehydrated too, if his assessment was correct.

"No accommodating," Dylan said. "I want the innkeeper's quarters. I'll give my roommates at my current place notice and move in tonight."

"Excellent. There is a fund allotment for any expenses incurred," Mr. Hill said.

"Sorry?" Dylan asked.

"Item seven. If either Ms. Mar or Mr. Pace have prior housing obligations, the estate will recompense."

"Wow. This is nuts." Dylan sat back, wondering if any minute someone would bust through the door and declare this all a joke.

"I could not agree more," Clara said. "I assume my grandfather had a sense of humor?"

"Yes," both Dylan and Mr. Hill said in concert.

"Good to know." She returned to the paperwork.

"There is also funding if you need to pay out a lease, Ms. Mar."

"I . . ." She looked around the living room. "I do not have any prior obligations."

She probably owned her home, or homes. Exactly how much did an internationally acclaimed cellist pocket in a year?

"Very well." Mr. Hill flipped his packet closed and pulled an envelope from his briefcase. "I will now read the letter per Mr. Levinson's instructions and then leave you to get settled." Mr. Hill adjusted his glasses and cleared his throat. "If emotion gets the better of me, I beg your forgiveness."

Dylan glanced at Clara. She glanced back at him, and Levinson's attorney started the letter.

Clara Mar and Dylan Pace,

If Mr. Hill is reading this to you, I am gone. Crossed to the other side, as my dear Edith liked to say. I am sure my will has you both intrigued and confused, so I will cut to the chase. The Inn by the Bay will turn seventy-five years old soon, and I want the two of you to bring her into the next seventy-five years with a grand celebration and reopening for the summer season.

Why did I choose the two of you? Fair question.

Dylan, I chose you because I've watched you grow into a wonderful young man. You had a rough start, but you've always shown up and wanted more. That's what makes a life worth living. I trust you with half of my inn because I know you will protect every brick and board. The inn gave you a place to land, a shelter from the storms of your adolescence and sometimes even as an adult. You know it's special because of what it means to you and our town. I could not be leaving our precious place in better hands.

Clara, I chose you because you are part of your father, my son.

Mr. Hill quickly swiped his eye and continued.

This may be painful, but use some time to sort through the history. We never knew your mother. She was passing through town, a girls' weekend, if memory serves. Christopher didn't know your mother was pregnant until he received a legal document asking him to sign over his parental rights. He didn't and asked to meet you instead. The request was granted, and we had you with us for less than an hour. You were and are beautiful, our only grandchild.

Your mother was on the next plane, and Topher—that's what we called him—was gone eight months later when a heart defect took him in his sleep.

After his funeral, our lives moved in a different direction—one of grief and healing. Your grandmother and I reached out years later, hoping to meet you, and were denied. We were told you were busy. There were a lot of years spent in anger, but we eventually came out on the other side.

Your father loved you, Clara. You may find it a silly thing to say because he'd only met you once, but you were his as much as your mother's. We loved you too. Instantly.

I will never know if you wanted us in your life or even knew about us until this letter. Maybe we should have tried harder, but I offer you half of this inn as a way to get to know us now. We shared a life between these walls, joy and sorrow. Perhaps it is even better you'll get the highlights and none of the boring day-to-day. I trust you will bring new and vibrant music from your world beyond Bodega Bay. You are immensely talented, my delightful young lady, and half of our life's work is yours now.

Mr. Hill cleared his throat.

So now that I've made myself teary at writing these words, let's get on with the show. Please see to the following:

The Study

Please create a system for all my boxes and scrapbooks in the study. When the inn reopens, I would like some of these things to tell our story. Guests should know who we were and what the inn meant to our family.

Mr. Hill read four other requests as Dylan and Clara listened. When he'd outlined everything Levinson wanted done, the attorney released a slow exhale and finished the letter.

Clara, I'm hoping you can take some time away from your performances, and Dylan, I know you work all the time, but try to slow down a bit. I'm sure this will be an inconvenience at first, but with your help, I know the Inn by the Bay will live on for many more generations. Good luck to you. Wherever my death and these challenges may find you, please know I believe in you both, and hopefully, if Pastor Mike is right, I'll be watching you from above.

With love and gratitude,
Cedric Theodore Levinson

Mr. Hill folded the letter, returned it to the envelope, and removed his glasses to dab quickly at his eyes. When he finished, he glanced up.

Dylan rarely cried, not because he was all that macho, but because crying wasn't a tool he was raised to rely on. Tears were weak, according to his dad after too many beers. By the time Dylan realized the opposite was true, he was an adult, and crying didn't come naturally.

But, listening to Mr. Hill read Levinson's letter, emotion welled in Dylan's chest as if Levinson himself was sitting in his living room, handing down a lesson or a quirky story.

Growing up, Dylan often tuned out during those chats or the man's penchant for going on and on about fine craftsmanship, specifically the damn blender. Like most things in life, Dylan hadn't absorbed every day or cherished every minute. But he would give his half of anything back for one more chat or an extra Sudoku puzzle argument with his friend. Since that wasn't possible, the next best thing was to honor his memory by ensuring the Inn by the Bay lived on. And that's exactly what Dylan intended to do.

Chapter Four

Nearly an hour later, after all the questions with answers had answers, Clara and Dylan walked Mr. Hill to the door. The rest, as her grandfather's attorney said in parting, was for the two of them to sort out.

Clara locked the door, and instead of standing in the entryway, as they had hours earlier, Dylan went straight for the living room, pulling a laptop from his backpack on the way. She wondered if she should get her own computer, but exhaustion won out, and she folded herself back into the giant chair instead and waited for her new roommate to speak first.

She hadn't had a roommate since she was nine and in junior orchestra. On tour, a city stopover for holidays, or an extended break, her parents always had their own suite. They "needed their alone time," which meant Clara spent much of her life, certainly her private life, alone.

No roommates, and certainly never one like Dylan Pace. As she was about to break the silence, Dylan stood.

"I'll be right back."

"What? Don't you think we should discuss—"

"Fifteen minutes. Why don't you put on some coffee?" He was

almost to the front door and turned. "Do you know how to make coffee?"

Clara scoffed. "Of course, I know how to make..." Her eyes drifted toward the antique rug. "Define make?"

"Don't worry about it." Dylan grabbed his coat. "I'll be right back."

To stay awake, Clara took in the living room—rich wood, bookcases, trinkets, yellow flowers on the couch and curtains . All of it spoke to a life spent in one place.

Standing, she carefully touched the framed pictures arranged on the mantel above the fireplace, as if contact might form connection. She didn't know any of these people, and yet the smiles and goofy faces were universal.

One picture in a shell frame was of her grandfather—Clara had googled him—and a younger man. She had never seen a picture of her father, but she knew it was him. Pulling the frame closer, she noticed he had the same eyes as hers, the same blond hair, and although he was more casual, more sun-kissed than she'd ever been, Clara saw herself in the faded image. With an exhausted sigh, she gently pushed the frame back into place. Such a strange thing, pictures. Generations frozen in time, preserved exactly as they were long before time slid past, leaving them behind.

Returning to her chair, Clara again wondered what on earth she was doing in Bodega Bay. These people had lifetimes of association, and yet her grandfather must have wanted her there, or he wouldn't have named her in his will. He could have given the inn to anyone, but he gave it to her. And to Dylan.

The sun was setting, and the house grew colder. Clara might have started a fire, but the only fireplace with which she was familiar had a switch on the wall. There were no switches, only a stack of wood in a large basket, so assuming it was the Girl Scout kind of fireplace, she grabbed the blanket off the back of the chair instead.

When she'd left Paris yesterday—or was it the day before?— she'd thought she would regroup at an inn by herself, which seemed quaint. Now that there were complications, the details of her left-behind life scrambled to attention. Did they deliver food here? Was there a dry cleaner? Coffee shop? Clara could surely live without those things but wasn't sure she wanted to for six months.

If she left now, she would give up her half of the inn but keep the inheritance, according to Mr. Hill. She didn't need the money. She didn't need half an inn either, but she wanted to know about the lives "between these walls," as her grandfather had written in his letter.

While his words had obviously touched Dylan and Mr. Hill, Clara searched for some connection. Would sorting through papers and talking to people who knew them bring her closer? Or would she always be on the outside? She wasn't sure it was worth knowing, even a little, about something she could never have.

For the first time in her life, Clara wanted to feel something other than music. Carter had called off the engagement backstage in front of the entire orchestra, with bonus points for being fully miked up and sharing the whole mess with an audience waiting patiently for the performance to begin. Clara was upset and humiliated, but she'd felt nothing close to love for Carter, so by the time the plane left the runway, she was left with only embarrassment.

Her engagement had been transactional, "an advantageous match," as her parents who were obviously enraptured with the Georgian period had surmised. Feelings were not a concern, and somehow Clara had gone along with it, but she didn't know he was cheating. All her peers, and most likely her parents, knew. She'd left mortified, and for that, she needed a minute.

So a mysterious inheritance in a barely-on-the-map fishing town was suddenly a perfect place to escape and uncover her parents' lie. But this had turned into something else. This was a project with a *partner*. Clara knew nothing about working with another person. She was a soloist, and while it wasn't her nature to be a pessimist, cohabitating with Dylan and attempting to prepare an inn seemed like an imminent disaster. The smart move was to think about how to return to her old life, but she wasn't ready to figure that out either.

Dylan returned in fifteen minutes as promised, put a large brown paper bag on the table, and sat on the couch.

"What's this?" she asked.

"Sandwiches, chips, and two brownies." He pulled open the staples at the top of the bag. "There's no food in this place, and you're already hangry, so I figured it was best to feed you."

"I am not . . . hangry." Clara sat up. "I am completely myself."

Dylan raised a brow and handed her a paper-wrapped sandwich. "Let's hope not."

"What's that supposed to mean?"

He pulled open a bag of chips. "Nothing. Travel is tough on the body, plus lack of sleep, and when was the last time you ate?"

Clara never did find that nourishment before their meeting. Her stomach growled. Dylan offered her the open bag of chips. Narrowing her eyes, she could have argued there was no way for him to know her habits in mere hours, but the smell of fresh bread grabbed Clara like a hug, and instead she said, "Thank you."

Taking some chips from the offered bag, she set them on the paper of her now-unwrapped sandwich. Clara normally avoided bread and sugar, but instead of rationalizing and rationing herself, she took a bite and fell into a memory of her own.

So much of this place felt like history, but not hers. Her past wasn't about running in the backyard sprinklers that had kicked on around ten that morning or sliding down the banister on her way to school.

Potato chips instead reminded Clara of sneaking junk food through room service to enhance the bland diet her mother insisted she follow while on tour. As a nod to her younger self, she thought about opening the sandwich and adding a few chips before smashing them under the top piece of bread. However, hangry or not, she managed a level of decorum, placing a paper napkin across her lap before continuing to eat the first proper food she'd had in days.

"They only had turkey this late. Hope you're not a vegetarian."

"I'm not," she said, closing her eyes and nearly moaning at the deliciousness. When she opened them again, Dylan's lip ticked up right before he sipped his water.

Ignoring his smug and completely accurate assessment, Clara ate a few chips before releasing a contented sigh and wiping her hands.

"Okay, so where should we start?" she asked, reaching for her bag on the floor to pull out a pen and her stack of papers from Mr. Hill. "Should we discuss living arrangements and coordinate schedules? Or review the list?"

"The arrangements seem set. You'll be upstairs, and I'll take the rooms off the kitchen."

"Okay. I'm not used to living with someone, so do we need to go over how to make coffee, or a grocery list?" Clara managed bites in between her rapid-fire questions, and her eyes grew heavier.

"Most of this will take care of itself as we go along. I'll show you the coffee in the morning, and we can go into town or order groceries. There are a few things outside of your grandfather's list we should consider before the season. I'm happy to do most of it, but I want to run things by you."

Dylan built a fire in the time it would have taken Clara to order a latte. She'd heard of the term "competence porn" but had not experienced the sensation until Dylan struck the match. Returning to the couch, he referenced his laptop, and Clara folded the blanket and rested her chin on her hand as he spoke about cleaning the storage room and installing new carpet on the stairs.

The inn was warm and smelled like a ski lodge. Clara had never been skiing, but the evening smelled like she imagined a ski lodge might—fire, wool, and spices. Dylan moved on to putting in supply orders and cross-promotion with something called Branch BnB.

Clara, for her part, fell asleep.

"Holy fucksicles, really?" Jules, Dylan's soon-to-be sister-in-law, said, always eager to use her favorite four-letter word in a creative new way.

"Yes," Tyler confirmed. "It's all there in black and white." He scanned the document Mr. Hill had given Dylan and emailed it to his lawyers. "This is a big deal."

Dylan agreed, still kind of stunned himself. When Clara fell asleep ten minutes into their first meeting, he'd brought his mounting mental list to his older brother.

Tyler set his phone aside as the three of them were gathered around the small table in the kitchen of the cottage home. Bella, Jules's daughter, was spending the night at a friend's house.

Over the years, Tyler's success had been profiled in nearly every financial magazine, but Dylan liked to keep it simple and tell people his brother was loaded. Tyler had recently purchased the Glass House across the bay. The architectural wonder had been untouchable when they were kids. Tyler spent much of his adult life undoing the filth of his and Dylan's childhood, but when he asked Jules to marry him, they agreed to live in Jules and Bella's modest new place, something about not leaving the strawberry plants behind.

The plan was to rent the Glass House as an additional wedding venue and for bigger events hosted by Branch BnB, which was run by Jules's parents, who also owned the Crab Shack. All part of her "hospitality empire," as Mrs. Branch announced over the holidays.

Dylan thought Tyler was nuts to give up such a phenomenal house, but love made people crazy. From an early age, he understood the dynamics of two different people navigating a life together, and that it often led to disaster. Dylan spent years taking risks at work, but Tyler was on his own when it came to offering up his heart.

"Any idea Levinson was going to leave you something like this? I know you two were close, but Inn by the Bay is an—"

"Institution, I know," Dylan said. "When the lawyer called, I honestly thought he'd left me a blender or something as a joke."

"He must have loved you," Jules said, wistful in a way that was rare for Bodega Bay's only female fishing captain.

Dylan winced. "Love is a reach. We were friends."

"Friends leave one another a check or a token gift, not an inn, Dylan." Tyler pushed his cup toward the pot in the center of the table and glanced at his phone.

"*Half* an inn," Dylan corrected.

Jules sipped her coffee. "That's right. The granddaughter. Kind of mysterious, right?"

Dylan shrugged. He wasn't sure "mysterious" was a word he'd used to describe Clara, but they'd certainly gotten off to an interesting start. "She's—"

"Beautiful?" Jules asked, sitting back in her chair.

Dylan was suddenly tired, probably coming down from the excitement of the day, or exhausted already thinking about Jules's twenty questions. "We need to bring the inn into the 'next generation,'" Dylan said to his brother.

Tyler quirked a brow as both he and his fiancée studied Dylan. "What?"

"No comment on the 'beautiful' descriptor?" Tyler asked.

"Descriptor? You really are from a different time, you know that?" Dylan sipped his now-cold coffee.

Shit. Here we go.

"She's tired. Curious about a grandfather and father she never knew, successful, not a light packer, and has no clue how to even begin co-running an inn."

Jules sighed. "The only interesting part of that total dodge of my question was 'not a light packer.' How do you know?"

"There must be seven trunks in the inn's entryway."

"Who the hell still packs a trunk?" Jules glanced at Tyler, who shrugged.

"No idea, but they look expensive."

She scoffed. "How does a trunk look expensive?"

"They've got those little LV symbols all over them and her last name stamped on the front."

Jules's eyes went wide. "Okay, expensive. Well, she's successful. So why not?"

"Seems like she's packed for the six months. Did she know about the fifty-fifty thing before she arrived?" Tyler asked.

Dylan shook his head. "She seemed to think the inn was hers alone, but when Mr. Hill told her about the money, she didn't want it. Told him we could put it back into the inn."

"Interesting." Tyler yawned. "I've got to get to bed."

Dylan checked his watch. It was already ten thirty. He stood and helped clean up the table.

"We still didn't tackle the 'beautiful' part," Jules said.

"I'm sure you'll google her. You can see for yourself what she looks—"

"Yup." Jules held up her phone to Tyler as they walked into the living room. "Beautiful."

Tyler widened his eyes.

Dylan grabbed his coat from the couch. "Beauty is subjective."

Jules snorted. "Ah-huh. You could take a picture of her in, like, everyday mode, instead of the splashy ones on her website. Drop them in the town chat."

"You're joking, right?" Dylan stared in amazement at her seriousness. "Even if I was creeper enough to take a stranger's picture, which I'm not, there's no way I'm 'dropping' anything in that town chat."

"Why not?" she asked.

"Because it's weird. There are like three dozen people on there. There's nothing I want to share with three dozen people. Ever."

"It is a central place to share important—"

"Gossip," Dylan and Tyler said at the same time.

Jules circled behind the couch to the entryway. "Well, I hope she's cool. We need more cool women in this town."

"Do we?" Dylan asked.

"She might stay. Could be the start of a promising business relationship," Tyler said.

"Or she'll sell me her half once the six months is over."

"Is that what you want?" Tyler's tired eyes lit with interest.

"This morning, I had a blown-out knee and was trying to figure out my next move." Dylan shrugged. "Levinson handed me one. Typical of him, really."

"You and Clara Mar might become more than business partners." Jules waggled her brows, sliding her phone into her back pocket.

"What has happened to you? You used to be so pleasantly cynical. Now it's like we have nothing in common."

Jules laughed and hugged him. "You're way worse than old me."

Dylan shook his head as she let go. "No one was worse than old you. You tortured this poor bastard."

She scoffed.

"She truly did," Tyler said, kissing his fiancée and opening the front door.

Dylan, who was still getting used to happy Tyler and, even more bizarre, happy Jules, zipped his jacket and walked out.

"Right," said Tyler. "So, I'll let you know if my legal team notices any loopholes or inconsistencies, but everything seems in order. Levinson left an inheritance and a few personal items to his grand-daughter and ownership of the inn to both of you," he recapped. "Oh, and he left you an insanely valuable watch."

Dylan held up his wrist. "I know. And a blender."

"You're going to wear that all the time?" Tyler furrowed his brow. "With those boots?"

Dylan looked down. "You're obsessed with my boots. I think you're jealous."

"I assure you I'm not. That's an expensive timepiece. An antique."

"More expensive than yours?"

"More expensive than . . . several of my watches, yes."

Dylan scoffed. "Levinson gave me the watch. I'm wearing it—with the boots."

"You do you, man. Have you discussed anything with Clara?"

"Not yet. I told you, she fell asleep. Jet lag. I'm sure we'll talk tomorrow."

"Over breakfast?"

Dylan shook his head. "Stop. I'm focused on the inn. That's it. I'm still shocked he thought to leave me half. It's kinda . . ."

"Touching?"

"Let's not be dramatic." Dylan exhaled. "I'm honored, I guess."

"It is an honor. Bring it in." His brother held his arms open like he was coming in for a hug.

Christ. Dylan stepped aside.

Tyler laughed. "The things on his list are optional. Levinson's attorney can't legally enforce those."

"How am I supposed to ignore a man's dying list?"

Tyler chuckled. "I see what you did there. Do you think Clara will make it six months?"

"She seems like she wants to lie low, learn about her dad. I would have guessed a couple weeks tops, but now she has to go six months if she wants her half."

"True."

"But she flew in from Paris. I'm guessing she'll fly right back as soon as she can."

Tyler stepped into the dark night with Dylan. "Paris is beautiful."

Dylan stared at his brother, puffs of cool night air between them. "Have fun painting pottery tomorrow."

"Precious days before Jules is back out on the water every morning." Tyler clapped his hands together, a big-ass grin on his face. "We'll talk tomorrow, yeah?"

"Yeah."

"Be safe out there," Tyler said.

Dylan shook his head. "I'm retired, remember? You don't need to say it anymore."

Tyler walked backward toward his front door. "Let's keep it. You're starting a new adventure."

"Not a dangerous one."

He shrugged. "We'll see."

Before Dylan could ask what the hell that ominous parting meant, Tyler closed the door.

Chapter Five

The surprising comfort of the couch was the first thought Clara had when she opened her eyes. It was dark, middle of the night most likely, and she somehow had a pillow under her head and a blanket. It took a few blinks to realize she'd fallen asleep on Dylan mid-conversation.

She'd wanted to discuss things, come up with a plan, but the deep timbre of his voice, the fire, and the delicious sandwich mixed with her jet lag, and Clara couldn't keep her eyes open. Sitting up now, she pushed her hair off her face and wondered how annoyed Dylan was by her less-than-stellar first impression. More importantly, she wondered if there were any more sandwiches.

Clara stood in the dark living room, bits of outside lights coming through the front windows, and wrapped the blanket at her shoulders. The brown bag he brought home earlier was full. Surely there was one sandwich left, half even.

She walked toward the kitchen, careful of her footfall and leaving the hall light off. She still didn't know exactly where the innkeeper's quarters were, and she didn't want to wake Dylan if he'd moved in already. Pushing through the kitchen door, she was startled to find Dylan, lit only by the open refrigerator. No shoes, no shirt, just his pants barely hanging on to a body she already appreciated fully clothed. *Dear lord.*

She must have sighed deeply because he turned, and while Clara wasn't often swayed by physical beauty, poems or at least a Taylor Swift song needed to be written about this man.

She held up a hand and pretended at least to divert her eyes. "Apologies."

"For what? You live here too."

"Barging in on you. It's late, and you're clearly . . . indisposed."

Dylan looked down. "Is that you-speak for I'm 'missing a shirt'?" Reaching across the counter, he flipped on the overhead light and closed the fridge. Easy and efficient movements, nearly as succinct as his words.

"Me-speak?" Clara asked.

"Yeah. Ten-point words when two will do? A lot like your grandfather."

"I don't do that. Did he do that?" She tightened the blanket around her shoulders, trying not to take offense.

"You do. He did."

"I meant this is your private space, and I should have—"

Dylan set his ice cream on the counter and buttoned the previously undone top button of his pants. "It's a kitchen, Mar, not my private space."

"I meant the innkeeper's quarters are apparently right there, and it's dark and"—he took a bite of ice cream, then pulled the large spoon from his mouth, and Clara told herself not to stare—"I'm aware this is a kitchen. Why are you using my surname?"

He furrowed his brow, finishing another spoonful. "Your surname? I'm not sure. It just felt right."

"Oh, well, please refrain."

He smiled, his eyes glistening for a second before returning to the contents of his midnight snack as if he'd caught himself flirting.

"This one is mine." He put the lid on the container and held it up. "I marked it with a D," he said, putting the ice cream away. "There's a Sharpie on the top of the fridge for you to mark your food."

"Why would I need to mark my food?"

"So we don't get things mixed up."

"I doubt that will happen," Clara said.

"Why not? Roommates claim their food all the time."

"I don't eat what you eat."

"You don't eat ice cream?"

She exhaled, anticipating his sarcasm. "I do not."

Dylan leaned on the counter, crossed one leg over the other, and Clara imagined the entire scene might be a jet-lag dream. After a brief silence, he shrugged and tossed his spoon into the sink. "I guess you're right, then. No Sharpie needed."

"I didn't mean to be . . ." *A snotty bitch?* Clara blinked her tired eyes. "I will keep the Sharpie in mind and label my food."

"Your call," Dylan said, not nearly as enthusiastic or as charming as before.

It was possible Clara had hurt his feelings, but she doubted it.

"It's after midnight. Why are you up?" he asked.

"I was going up to bed. Thank you for moving me to the couch, and for the blanket, by the way."

"It was on the back of the couch. No effort."

"Right. Well, I was on my way and thought there might be another sandwich, but I will—"

Dylan opened the fridge and tossed her a paper-wrapped roll. Clara miraculously caught it. Glancing down, she noticed the letter C scrawled in Sharpie and smiled.

"Sold," she said, going to the opposite counter and opening the sandwich. "Your Sharpie system is brilliant."

"Thought you'd see it my way." He made to leave but turned back. "Oh, before I forget." He pulled out his phone. "I want to give you my number and get yours so we can be in touch when we're not together."

Clara chewed and tried not to imagine the state of her hair after sleeping on the couch for several hours or Dylan moving her to the couch. Hopefully she hadn't drooled. Or snored. Although whatever her state, she was sure he'd seen worse.

"How are you so animated this late?" she asked, after wiping her mouth.

"A lifetime of night shifts," he said, crossing his arms. Still no shirt.

"Ah." Clara took another bite.

"You're in entertainment. I'm sure you're used to late nights."

She swallowed. No one had ever described her profession in those terms, but she supposed she was an entertainer. "True, but I'm usually in bed by midnight." She swiped the screen of her phone and typed in the number he gave before texting a smiling emoji back, so he had her number too. It was a perfectly normal exchange between co-owners until she began humming and must have said aloud, "Call me maybe."

When she glanced up, Dylan was grinning. "Okay."

She shook her head. "It's a song. Carly Rae Jepsen."

"You listen to Carly Rae Jepsen?"

"Of course. I mean, I did. The song was everywhere. Catchy too."

"I thought you music types only listened to highbrow stuff."

Again, she wasn't sure whether to be insulted or impressed by the endless synonyms Dylan had for a classical musician. "Know a lot of *music types*, do you?"

He shrugged.

"I'll have you know I am well-versed in the pop music genre."

He held up his hands in surrender. "Noted."

Their eyes met, and a new familiarity passed as Clara rewrapped the piece of sandwich she couldn't finish.

"Anyway." Dylan pushed off the counter. "I did just meet you, and our situation is 'crazy,' so—"

Clara smiled, more comfortable and still tired. "You've got my number. So text me maybe."

Dylan shook his head.

"Oh, since you're wide awake, could you give me a quick run-down of the services in Bodega Bay?"

A grin spread across his lips. "What kind of . . . services?"

She'd walked right into that one. Clara had never been good at flirting—if he was even flirting. She imagined charm and quick wit were in the DNA of men like Dylan. Everything was chill and effortless.

At her silence, he raised a brow, and every inch of her body offered suggestions.

"I don't . . . nothing like that," she said, as if anything in his middle-of-the-night eyes wouldn't be exquisite.

His expression deepened. "Nothing like what?"

"You're messing with me again."

"You asked about services. Bodega is a small town. I'm trying to get more information. What did you think I—" Realization dawned, and Clara wanted to pull the blanket over her head. He grinned. Of course he did.

"Oh, yeah, no. I was legit looking for info."

"I didn't—I don't need that either." What was wrong with her? How was she a perfectly capable woman when she was not in the kitchen with a half-naked man? On an exhale, she tried again, chalking her misread up to the number of men she'd been anywhere with. "I was inquiring about dry cleaning, a nail salon, things of that nature."

Dylan pushed off the wall, startling Clara out of her mortification. "I'll text you Emily's number for the nail and hair salon, and Sam picks up dry cleaning twice a week, although I don't think you'll need much dry cleaned around here."

"Thank you."

"I asked Rusty, the town handyman, to bring by some carts from the library and extra boxes. I figured we could start by clearing things out of the study and then put them back once we come up with a system."

"That's a great idea," Clara said, happy to be moving on to another topic. "We can sort through how much history we want to share with new guests."

"I'll help fill in the blanks about your grandfather. I never met your dad, but I'll help where I can."

"Thank you."

"For what?" he asked.

"I'm not sure. For being . . . pleasant."

"I'm always pleasant." There it was again—hot and cold. Clara wondered if he even knew he switched so quickly.

"Would your friends agree? Your family?" she asked, again for no logical reason.

"Probably not." He walked toward the doorway she assumed led to his rooms. "Rusty will be here at noon tomorrow." He patted on the doorjamb.

"Wonderful." Clara stood to put the rest of her sandwich in the fridge.

He turned back, one hand anchored on the wall. "Oh, and Clara?"

She met his eyes.

"I'm pretty sure we all need 'that.'" One air quote, and he was gone.

As Clara made to leave, her phone vibrated on the counter.

She debated whether to answer and would bet her recent inheritance her mother or father or agent had not bothered to check the time change. It was early morning in Paris, so it must be early morning everywhere else. Deciding to ignore the call, Clara grabbed her phone. She must have swiped the screen by mistake because the full force of her irate mother's voice barged into the peace of the empty kitchen.

"Clara Hildegard Mar, we need to—"

Scrambling, Clara cut the call.

"Hildegard, huh?" Dylan was back. "Forgot my phone." He found it on the other counter.

Determined not to be ruffled again in the same twenty-four hours, and uninterested in explaining how her middle name honored one of the most prominent women in classical music, Clara slipped her phone into her pocket.

"Aren't mothers a treat?" she said, now at the opposite kitchen entry.

"Yeah, I wouldn't know. Night." With that, Dylan was gone. Clara turned off the light. As she climbed the stairs, she hoped, like music, this would all improve with practice.

Dylan had never had to navigate life with another adult outside of work. He knew his part on a crew, but his longest personal relationship, save his barely-there roommates at his old place, had lasted a little over a year.

Clara wasn't a personal relationship, but damn. Living with a woman and running into her in the middle of the night made for a strange working relationship. Which was fine too, he decided as he dressed early the next morning.

Pulling on a T-shirt, he remembered Clara's response to his appearance in the kitchen last night, which was a first. Women rarely looked away when he was shirtless. The knowledge wasn't arrogance, more a fact. His body was a by-product of his job, and one that women seemed to enjoy. But maybe now that he'd busted his knee and woke up early to look at carpet swatches online, he was losing his edge.

Or Dylan's unrefined attire offended Ms. Clara Mar. The pompous thought almost made him smile. Either way, he didn't care. Sure, he had to get along with her for the next six months, but what she thought of him was irrelevant and none of his business.

Business. That's what this was about, and Dylan would focus and make it work. He'd spent most of his life working around the property and chasing odd jobs from the minute Levinson taught him how to earn his first five-dollar bill. Owning anything was never in Dylan's cards, but since the opportunity had presented itself, he found he wanted the inn for himself and his town.

So, he would help Clara fill in the blanks regarding her family, and then they'd go their separate ways. If Dylan was lucky, buying her half would fall somewhere between what he'd already saved and what the bank would lend him. He knew Tyler would jump at the chance to help, but Dylan wanted to do this on his own.

He'd never imagined a wealthy family member, no matter how distant, having to share anything with some scrappy kid caught snooping around the inn's property. Even if said kid grew up to be a man who introduced the old guy to the deliciousness of Drumsticks and encouraged him to get enough exercise.

"Expect nothing" was practically Dylan's credo, but Levinson was right. Dylan had showed up and learned the workings of the inn. The inn had been a refuge, and he would be forever grateful.

Now that he and Levinson's granddaughter were settling in and Dylan had convincingly ignored how attractive she was, he was certain she'd leave. Dry cleaners, a nail salon? Yeah, six months to the day, she'd sell her half and be gone. He was counting on it.

He assumed Clara was still sleeping when he entered the empty kitchen and grabbed his keys. So he drove into town, scored two breakfast sandwiches from the Roastery, and settled into one of the frilly chairs at Swept Away Books, the romance-only bookstore owned by Nikki, his Auntie N.

"So," Nikki said, joining him in the opposite chair with the cup of tea that seemed eternally in her hand.

"So," he repeated back.

"How are things?"

He glanced up at her. "You know how things are. Probably better than I do."

"You sure?" She sipped her tea.

"I am, but let's cut to the chase anyway. Levinson's granddaughter has arrived. Her name is Clara Mar. And he left the inn to both of us in his will."

Nikki didn't even try to tamp down her excitement. "I know. Plot twist if I've ever seen one." She set her tea down. "Are you excited to co-own the inn with the enchanting Ms. Clara Mar who flew in from the City of Lights?"

Dylan sighed. "To what extent have you stalked her?"

Nikki held up two fingers to show a small amount. "Haven't you? Jules was hoping you'd take a picture, but when you declined, I did some searching and found two shots of Clara at a charity event. Very little makeup. I sent them to Jules and Millie. We agree she's beautiful in real life."

"Excellent. Thank you for that." Finishing the last breakfast sandwich, he balled up the paper and tossed it into the trash. "Rusty will be at the inn to drop some things off by noon, so I'd better get started on your bookcase." Dylan could feel Nikki winding up for Twenty Questions and knew the easiest way out of her line of fire was to stay busy.

He'd given up trying to keep his private life private a long time ago. No matter how little he revealed, the people of Bodega Bay had always found him, which was annoying when he was young and swiping extra candy from the bowl at the market, but Tyler always assured him their meddling was rooted in love.

"So, you're officially retired from search-and-rescue and the half-owner of a gorgeous inn with a beautiful-without-makeup and supremely talented co-owner."

"I am." Dylan stood and grabbed the measuring tape Nikki had left on the counter by the register. "How many versions of these life summary declarations do you have?"

"A few. The bookcase can wait."

Dylan grunted and measured the space anyway. When he was sure the bookcase waiting in the alley would fit, he set the tape measure on the counter and took the dolly from her storage closet.

"I'm not discussing the co-owner," he said, a little guilty about being the reluctant player in Nikki's sunshine show. He returned and slid the bookcase into place.

"It's perfect, right?" She poured him a glass of water.

"Yeah, it's good. I like the color. What are you putting on this one?" Dylan asked.

Nikki unfolded herself from her chair. "Books." She held out her arms in excitement. "Specifically, I'm starting a monthly theme feature. This month is 'new beginnings' because it's—"

"January. Got it." He took a rag from behind the register and dusted the shelves.

"It's perfect. Thank you." She squeezed his arm.

"No problem," he said.

"According to Bernice down at the courthouse"—she scooted a box toward the new bookcase—"you two have your work cut out for you getting the inn ready for its anniversary season. Going through all of Levinson's stuff in the study should be an exciting history lesson."

"Unbelievable." Dylan joined her back at the chairs.

"I know. I'm sure there's a ton of stuff in there. You know, forced proximity is a popular trope in a lot of romance novels." She gestured to the bookshelves lining her store.

"I meant it's unbelievable that Bernice, a clerk of the court, is in your pocket too."

Nikki laughed. "Oh, stop. In my pocket. You're silly." She sipped her tea. "Although, I kind of like the idea of people being in my pocket. Makes me sound powerful."

"You are." Dylan smiled.

"That might be the kindest thing you've ever said to me." She propped a leg on the pink puffy thing by her chair. "I guess I kind of am." Nikki tipped her head, letting her reading glasses drop to her nose. They both laughed.

"I'm sure she'll sell after the six months," he said.

"And you'll buy her out?"

"That's the plan." He exhaled slowly.

Nikki eyed him. "You taking over the inn would be special. The way you loved Levinson and all."

"What's with everyone and the love? We—"

"Understood one another?"

"Sure. That works."

"He lost a son," Nikki said. "And struggled for years after." She tilted her head in a way Dylan recognized as remorse. "Shapes a person, don't you think?"

"What?" he asked.

"Tragedy."

"I guess." Dylan stood, done with gossip and Nikki's not-so-subtle shelf-help wisdom. Putting the rag back behind the register, he checked the bookshelf one last time. This one was yellow. Dylan thought it belonged more in a kitchen but didn't say.

"Have you chatted further with Clara yet, or just at the will reading?" Nikki offered him more water. "Even her name sounds elegant."

"A little last night." Dylan held out his glass, cursing himself for entertaining any of her questions.

"And?"

"And she's jet-lagged and totally out of sorts."

"Does she have an accent with all the world-traveling?"

"A little. She's formal."

"Is she married?"

"Not sure," Dylan said, stunned it had taken Nikki so long to ask.

"Hmm. No ring?"

"Didn't look." Dylan stood, grabbing his bag. "I should get going."

"Alrighty. Well, I can tell you she is not married. Town intelligence says Clara Mar *was* engaged to a fancy conductor."

He said nothing.

Nikki sipped her tea. "*Was*, you ask?"

"I did not ask." He shook his head.

"Yes, Dylan, said fiancé broke off the engagement in a spectacular enough way to make one of the hoity-toity gossip magazines. It's all there on the internet. Poor dear." Nikki pouted as the perfect ending to her gossip declaration.

"Who are we talking about again?"

She swatted his arm. "The granddaughter, Clara."

"Oh, right." He grinned. "See? You *do* have more intel than me. Never fails."

"So, she's single."

"Great for her. Wow, look at the time. I need to get back before—" Dylan pointed to the cuckoo clock over the front door. It hadn't worked for years, but there was a bear reading a book, so Nikki kept it. "I'm a business owner now. No time for idle chitchat."

Nikki scoffed. "Is she nice?" The woman was practically rubbing her hands together. "Delightful?"

Dylan waved one hand overhead as a goodbye and opened the door with the other. "No comment."

"Too late. You already commented."

"I did not. I should go. The knee really acts up in this weather." He limped for effect.

"Faker." Nikki put a hand on her hip. "It's lovely out today."

As the door closed behind him, Dylan could hear Auntie N laughing. He climbed into his truck and sat in peace, having escaped, at least for now.

New people in town always shook things up. Everyone acted weirder than usual. Especially Nikki, who was forever recruiting unsuspecting singles into her matchmaking game. The key to staying out of her grasp was to share as little as possible, which was one of Dylan's core talents. Usually. He'd opened up a little more than normal and was sure it would come back to bite him later.

Probably because this time, the Queen of Romance in their little town was right. Clara Mar didn't just *sound* elegant; she was. As her new business partner, Dylan hoped she was more than cashmere and her giant trunks, so she could help him get the inn ready for the season. If she couldn't or wouldn't, he'd do it himself. Never expect, never be disappointed.

Dylan arrived back at the inn and heard Clara as soon as he got out of his truck. Nikki was right. It was turning into a near perfect day. Blue sky with a few giant clouds, the whole thing framed by the massive oak trees on the property. Closing his eyes, Dylan took in the warmth and the sound of music.

He had never heard a cello before, or at least he didn't think he had. It was possible there was a cello mixed into some of the classical music Levinson or occasionally Tyler listened to, but Dylan could never pick out a specific instrument. Solo, the cello was distinct, kind of like a moan or a voice, even.

He opened his eyes but stayed put, listening until she stopped and began something new. Dropping the tailgate of his truck, Dylan sat as the music seemed to grow closer, louder. It was like singing. Up and down, soft and harsh, slow, and then impossibly fast.

Grateful for the outdoor concert, compliments of Clara Mar and the inn's old windows, Dylan lay back, folding one arm under his head. The beginning of another day over a familiar bay, but different with the music and, he supposed, the woman playing it. Each note seemed to wrap itself around the branches and skim along the surface of the water until something as recognizable as his own name was new, changed by the accompaniment.

Dylan sat up. He didn't have time for this, but Christ, she was good. He knew next to nothing about classical music, but if the endgame was to make a person think about life or feel an odd sense of possibility, no wonder Clara Mar was, if the internet and town gossip could be trusted, world-renowned.

Chapter Six

*C*lara set her bow aside and took a sip of water. The acoustics in the small room where she'd moved her cello to that morning weren't great, but the old windows allowed a lovely bay breeze into the space, and she decided it was a fair trade. With the weight of performance lifted, Clara found she was open to loosening her practice routine too. She could play whatever and wherever she wanted while she was in Bodega Bay, and that alone was worth the trip.

She had intended to rise early, but jet lag had won out, and she'd slept in. On her way to the shower, she'd noticed her trunks on the landing. Dylan must have hauled them up for her either out of kindness or because he was tired of them in the foyer. Either way, it was a pleasant surprise, and no small feat, given she hadn't heard a thing.

Despite the size of the primary suite, Clara couldn't fit everything, so she stored the trunks in what was now her practice room. Satisfied with her space and that she'd practiced for over an hour, Clara felt a sense of accomplishment she had not experienced since arriving.

Before going downstairs for coffee, she opened the safe in her room and pulled out the first item her hand touched. She'd decided to open one item at a time rather than taking everything out at once. She hoped that would give her some space to absorb each piece on its own.

Taking the small embroidered box to the bed, Clara carefully lifted the lid. Atop a small blue velvet cushion sat a delicate hair clip in the familiar shape of a treble clef. Dotted with diamonds and sapphires, the clip was stunning and crafted in a way things rarely were anymore, with a gold edge and a decorative clasp.

Never one to wear music-themed jewelry, mostly because her mother had declared it tacky and juvenile as far back as Clara could remember, she loved this clip. Setting it back on its cushion, she gently traced the sparkle and noticed a yellowed slip of paper tucked at the edge of the box.

She pulled it free and read.

> *For Edith my love, in celebration of one of your many passions on our 50th! I am grateful every day I was so wrong the first time. I love you, Cedric.*

After admiring the twirls of her grandfather's script, Clara carefully tucked the paper back into the box and found she felt less like an intruder and more like an invited guest.

Her grandfather left her the inn with intention, not as a last resort or because he wanted to mess with her life. Quite the contrary, his words were elegant, heartfelt, and bursting with love for the people in his life and, by association, the love extended to her. She simply needed time to explore without judgment.

Fastening her grandmother's clip into her hair, she wondered if Edith Levinson played music or merely loved to listen. Did she and her husband go to concerts? Was her instrument somewhere in the house? And what did he mean about being wrong the first time?

Clara would ask Dylan, or she might uncover the answers when they started digging into the study that afternoon. Admiring the beauty clipped and shimmering in her still-damp hair, Clara remembered her mother's call last night, and the bit in her grandfather's letter about her keeping them from Clara. All of it was so senseless and unsettling. She would never get a straight answer from her mother, which threatened to upset her all over again. Clara didn't have room for more anger where her parents were concerned, so she pushed it aside.

This experience was challenging her to stay in the present. Throughout her life, she'd read books on mindfulness and being in the moment but had never incorporated it much into her hectic schedule. Now, with her professional life on pause, she could take time for things she'd rushed by in the past. Hopefully when it was time to return to her life, she would have the strength to make her own decisions.

It was funny how the smallest bit of history, her grandmother's clip, had already strengthened Clara's spine. Instead of being pushed front and center as she'd been her whole life, she now had people who had gone before. She certainly wasn't going to run an inn, but she could learn things, and maybe leave her own mark on the legacy.

Clara walked downstairs, steadying herself this time for more Dylan. As a soloist, she wasn't big on collaboration, but for the next six months, she was half of a business duo with the man presently in the living room, at his laptop again.

Dylan glanced over his shoulder, and she took in the morning version of him—mussed up like he'd lost a fight with the pillow last night and still unnervingly sexy.

"Morning," Dylan said. "Coffee's fresh. I made another pot." He raised his mug.

"Good morning. Thank you." Clara went into the kitchen, poured her coffee, and noticed two small brown bags on the counter. They both had a large C in Sharpie. She smiled, again surprised the same man who rarely offered more than two words had thought to bring her breakfast. Grabbing a napkin, Clara joined him in the living room, this time sitting on the couch, determined to pay attention to whatever was on his laptop.

"Thank you," she said, removing one scone from the bag. "You didn't need to—" He met her eyes, and she didn't want to seem ungrateful, so she started over. "I appreciate you getting me breakfast."

"This is weird, right?" Dylan said.

"A little." She took a bite and wiped her mouth. "But so far, it's not complete torture co-owning an inn with you."

"Well, that's a start." He glanced at his screen. "Wore my shirt and everything today."

"I noticed. Thank you." She smiled. Not wanting to launch her fully rested energy at him before noon, she started slow. "Also, thank you for bringing my trunks upstairs."

"No problem." Dylan typed something else and sat back.

"Have you already been out this morning?" she asked.

He nodded, typing something. "I had things to do in town."

Fueled by three sips of coffee and a few bites of a delicious scone, Clara was ready to get started. "So, since we will be cohabitating for some time, can we talk about our setup?"

Dylan blinked in quick succession like he might need more caffeine. "How do you mean?"

"I'm not sure. Do we need a master shopping list, a meal delivery service, if that's a thing here, or do you always have takeaway breakfast? Are you a coffee pot man or a French press guy?"

He raised a brow. Sipped his coffee.

"Right. Okay. So, no French press," she replied. "I'm simply saying if you want me to get the takeaway sometimes, I'm happy to help."

Dylan lifted his mug in agreement with a barely-there grin.

"Is something funny?" she asked, slightly annoyed at the feeling they were going in circles.

He shook his head. "I'm listening. Takeaway?"

"What do you call it?"

"Grabbing breakfast."

She shrugged. "Same thing. I like . . . having a plan."

"I can tell. Nice hair clip." He reached out like he might touch it but seemed to change his mind. "It was your grandmother's, right?"

"Yes."

Going with his change of subject, Clara asked a flood of questions that revealed Edith Levinson *was* a big music fan, classical and jazz mostly. Besides concerts in the area and San Francisco, Clara's grandparents went to New York every year to attend Broadway shows.

"What did the note mean by 'being wrong the first time'? Did he ask my grandmother to marry him twice?"

"Legend has it Levinson built this inn for his first fiancée," Dylan said. "She took a pass. They broke up, and he moved in alone. Three years later he met Edith, and the rest is history."

"Seriously?"

"Would I lie about something like that? Women can be fickle."

Clara chose not to take offense. "What *would* you lie about?" she asked, stunned by her candor and pleased at the same time at her growing comfort.

Dylan stopped, coffee cup hovering in his hand. "Not sure," he said, before taking a sip and returning to his laptop.

"That's it? Your response to my impromptu philosophical question is 'not sure'?"

He shrugged. "I've never thought about what I would lie about, and I'm not coming up with something right now. We've got a day ahead of us and a study to get through."

"You're right." Clara sipped her coffee and offered Dylan the other scone. He declined, so she tucked it away for later. "Anything you want to ask me?"

He met her eyes. "About?"

"About me . . . or philosophical."

"The lying question was not philosophical," he said.

"Not the point." Clara wiped her mouth and waited him out.

"All right, fine. What did your parents say about the will?"

Surprised by the question, Clara almost forgot Dylan had witnessed her mother's rant in the middle of the night. She could give him the glossy version of her family or the truth. Still recovering from a slew of family fabrications, Clara chose reality.

"My mother is married to Burt. Until a couple of months ago, I thought he was my biological father."

Dylan looked up from his computer and faced her.

"When I told my parents . . . let's see. Well, Burt laughed at first and then offered some schmaltzy life quote. He's famous for his schmaltz." She let out a slow breath, unsure how to explain her mother and Burt objectively.

Although she hadn't met Dylan's parents yet, she imagined they were nothing like hers. Or maybe his parents were gone. She should probably ask. Did she need to know these things about her business partner?

"My mother," Clara continued, "saw no reason for me to know about my 'sperm donor,' since he was dead." She sighed. "So that's my world."

Dylan exhaled, and she felt the weight of her answer. For a minute, she wondered if it made her less interesting in his eyes. Clara's life had always shown more melodic in bold strokes. The details, the challenging notes in between, that's where things often fell apart for the Mar family.

"Huh." Dylan nodded, and Clara hoped to God he had more of a response. Had he asked to test the likelihood of her bailing or out of genuine interest?

"Well, you're here now," he said. "And parents can suck."

"They certainly can." She exhaled. "Well put."

Dylan bowed his head for a second at the praise, but when their eyes met, his expression was serious, like he understood or could relate.

"All right." She sipped her coffee. "We've got a study to sort. Maybe we'll uncover some exciting things in there."

"Anything is possible." He grinned.

"You're less intimidating with the dimple."

His brow knit. "I don't have a dimple."

"Oh, but you do." She brushed the crumbs from her hands and reached over, stopping short of touching the side of his mouth.

"That's a smirk," he clarified, not budging a muscle.

"No." She shook her head, putting her hand back in her lap. "That's a dimple. It doesn't flash all the time, but it's there. It is not a smirk. A smirk is sinister."

"Exactly." He smiled, returning to his laptop.

"Well, if you're so sinister, you might want to stop buying me breakfast."

"Purely business strategy."

"Interesting. How so?"

"You're in a better mood when you eat." Dylan slid the laptop toward her. "Okay, so here's a quick database my obscenely organized brother put together. We can start by cataloging everything and designating in this column whether we're keeping it out or putting it in storage."

Clara listened attentively as Dylan explained his thoughts on organizing the study. She had some ideas of her own but found rather than quickly offering her suggestions or modifications, she enjoyed his enthusiasm. He was so relaxed when they focused on the inn.

She imagined it was rooted in his affection for her grandfather and their town. Something less ugly than jealousy at the simplicity of those allegiances bloomed in Clara's chest, and she hoped with time she might feel a similar definitive direction with her life.

Russell "Rusty" O'Leary was in the middle of telling Dylan about running late because his dog "tossed its cookies" into the bathtub last night. Dylan sensed Clara's confusion as Rusty rambled on, but she kept smiling.

"Do they have bathtubs in Paris?" Rusty asked.

"They . . . um." Clara blinked at him as if trying to find his frequency.

Good luck, Dylan thought.

"Yes." She cleared her throat. "They do have bathtubs, though they're quite small."

"Figures." Rusty unloaded three library carts from the back of his truck. "They're tiny people." At Clara's apparent confusion, he clarified. "The French. They're tiny, right? Like Napoleon?"

Dylan almost laughed at her expression. Despite her always appropriate demeanor, she seemed to be left speechless by Rusty.

"I guess that's silly." He pulled a stack of file boxes. "I'm sure we all come in the same shapes and sizes, right?"

"There are some very tall French people," Clara confirmed.

"I believe it." Rusty formally greeted Clara and assured her if they—meaning her and Dylan—needed anything, he was a mere phone call away.

"Thanks," Dylan said, rescuing Clara. Rusty was best enjoyed in small doses. "Do you have the tile Levinson ordered for the kitchen, or would that be Gus?"

Rusty scrunched his face, the same pencil tucked behind his ear. "Not sure. Lemme ask Gus, and I'll text you later."

Dylan tipped his head.

"Other than the tile, you good for now?"

"I think so." Dylan began wheeling everything toward the porch when Clara took one cart and the boxes.

"All right, you two. I'll be back next month to deliver the firewood and help get some things organized in the shed if you're gonna be a working inn again."

"Sounds good," Dylan said.

"Absolutely. Exciting things happening, am I right?"

"You are. Thanks. And don't forget about the tile."

Rusty tapped his head and then bowed with a flourish toward Clara. "Ms. Mar, it was a pleasure to meet you."

"You as well, Rusty. Thank you."

"Anytime. Welcome to Bodega Bay!" he called out before honking his horn and driving off in a cloud of gravel dust.

Once everything was on the porch and in the front door, Dylan stood back, grateful Clara had helped. He shouldn't be surprised. She had as much invested in this first part of Levinson's list as Dylan did.

Dylan set the boxes against the wall and opened one, ready to get started.

"If I may?" she said, pushing the sleeves of her sweater up to her elbows and walking to the large shelves in the study. "I think we sort by boxes with labels, boxes without, and loose papers or photographs. Those could be the initial categories for the database. We can move everything into the dining room, alphabetize the boxes with labels, and take a quick inventory. Then we move on to the boxes without labels, inventory those, and create labels. Which leaves sorting the loose papers and photographs for filing into the new boxes."

Dylan stood, box in hand, and said nothing.

"What?" Clara ran a hand along the smooth wood of her grandfather's desk.

"Nothing. I'm impressed."

"That I can organize boxes?"

"No, that you think the way you do. Sorting what you know and then figuring out the rest. You don't seem practical on first impression."

Clara stood taller. "Oh, well, I am quite practical."

She wasn't, at least not Dylan's kind of practical, but it seemed there was more to her than those trunks he'd hauled upstairs.

"Is it a music thing?" he asked.

"Sorting?"

"Yeah."

Clara appeared to think about it for a minute. "I suppose so. Taking on a piece of music is a lot like these shelves. Some of it jumps right out, and other parts are less obvious. It requires work. So yes, I suppose sorting is part of my background."

"Well, it's a good idea. How about you gather up the loose stuff, and I'll start moving the rest?"

Clara took the box from him. "Deal."

They worked in silence for nearly three hours, Dylan bringing boxes to the dining room and Clara at Levinson's desk among stacks of stuff. On one of his trips back to the study, she was humming.

He stood in the doorway, watching a new version of his business partner. She looked up and immediately stopped.

"Did you get a good night's sleep or something?" he asked.

"I did, thank you. Why do you ask?"

He shrugged. "You've got more energy."

Clara stood. "You're evaluating me?" Her eyes narrowed. "Is it because you heard my middle name is Hildegard last night, or that

I shared about my awful parents? I mean, they're not completely awful." She bowed her head as if the guilt of being honest about her parents was too much.

Dylan wondered what kind of world she came from.

"Assessing," he said. "Not evaluating. And no. I like Hildegard."

"Assessing? Like I'm someone on a trolley thing or in an ambulance?" She shifted her weight, leaning on the desk.

Dylan smiled. "The *trolley thing* is a gurney, and most of my work was on the water, so helicopters."

He should get back to the boxes, but he liked seeing things from her perspective. She was not as she first presented. Dylan found talking with her was something he *wanted* to do rather than something required to get the job done. There was more to her, and he wasn't exactly interested, but he *was* intrigued. A little.

"You know what I mean. You're assessing like I'm a person in distress."

"Okay. So?"

"Well, I am not in distress. I'm absolutely in control of my faculties today." Clara touched her finger to her nose and walked along the edge of the study rug.

Dylan knew it was condescending and would never say it out loud, but there was something oddly adorable about a woman who could play the cello the way he knew she could, miming around with her hair clipped off to the side. Maybe she'd had too much coffee.

She stopped, and Dylan did his best to keep a straight face.

"Good to know you're sober at"—he looked at his watch—"two fifteen in the afternoon."

"If we're going to be owners—"

"Co-owners."

"Isn't it the same thing?"

Dylan shrugged. "Sort of, but I like the sound of co-owners."

"Fine. If we are going to be co-owners and living together, I can't have you assessing me all the time. I've lived enough of my life under a microscope. If this experience is going to be judged, perhaps I should—"

"Look for another inn to inherit?" Dylan asked.

"Yes. Exactly." She pointed at him, smiling now. Levinson's study seemed to agree with her, made her more comfortable in her skin.

Dylan crossed his arms. They were different people, for sure. Probably not even compatible as friends, let alone partners. *Business partners*, he reminded himself.

"Find anything good yet?" he asked.

Clara exhaled. "I'm not even looking, just sorting. There's so much stuff." She dropped back into the chair behind the desk in obvious frustration. "I don't know what I'm even looking for, or if any of this will help me know them better."

"Okay." Dylan sat in the chair opposite Levinson's desk. "Let's take a break. No papers, no boxes. I can answer some simple questions."

Clara's eyes sparked with renewed interest, dialing up the already brilliant blue. "I do have a few questions."

"Excellent. Shoot."

"You said you've known my grandfather your whole life, so you were obviously born in Bodega Bay?"

"Oh, questions about me." He exhaled. "Okay."

"You know things about me. Or at least it seems like you know things and I . . ." She shook her head. "You know what? Forget it. There's no reason—"

"Right. Well, Clara Hildegard, yes, I was born here," he said. Simple. Easy.

"So, your family lives here too?"

"Yes." Dylan shifted in the chair, which suddenly felt smaller.

She leaned forward. "And you have one 'obscenely organized brother.' Any other siblings?"

"Nope."

"You are . . . restrained. I'll give you that."

"What else do you want to know?"

"More than this. I'm trying to cohabitate, and you're . . . not. What are your parents like? If you were writing a bio for a résumé, what would you include?"

"Not my parents." He stood. It was time to get back to work.

She sighed. "Do you have social media?"

"No."

"Why not?"

"No one cares." Dylan grabbed a few more boxes and set them on the cart.

"Oh my god. You're impossible."

"Are we having our first fight?" He stacked a few more.

"No. Forget it." Clara returned to her piles.

Turning from the shelf, he faced her. It was easier with them both on the same side of the desk, less interview-like, until she stood. Those wide, searching eyes and the scent of her in a small space caught him off guard, and for the first time in his life, Dylan felt compelled to explain himself. "I'm not great at talking about personal things," he said.

She lifted her chin, clearly assessing him this time. He didn't want to care what she saw when she looked at him or whether she approved, but he did.

"I'm inquisitive," she said, eyes searching his.

She might as well have said, "Let's get naked," by the way his body reacted. What was it with this woman?

"To a fault, sometimes," she continued. "I'm aware not everyone shares or welcomes the intrusion." She looked away, and Dylan would have sworn she felt foolish. For what? Being herself? After hearing her mother on the phone last night, he wondered if she often felt diminished. Why the hell he cared was anyone's guess.

"I'm interested," he said. There it was again, the incessant urge to help her see things as they were instead of the sadness of her assumptions.

Her eyes flew to him.

"Interested in your life too," he quickly added, because what the hell was he doing? "We're kind of stuck together and—whatever. Point is, I'm not trying to be difficult. Sharing is not my thing."

"Noted," she said, with a smile at mimicking his earlier response. Dylan grabbed a couple more boxes, one marked "fun stuff," and returned to the other side of Levinson's desk, where he belonged.

Chapter Seven

Three weeks went by in a frenzied effort. The boxes were now color-coded—Dylan's idea. Clara continued sorting the loose documents and pictures while Dylan and Rusty built additional shelves in the outside storage area. She and Dylan had narrowed down which boxes and scrapbooks were pertinent to the story of the inn and her family.

They'd also fallen into a routine—breakfast standing in the kitchen most mornings and takeaway most nights. A few days ago, they'd had lunch at Clara's now-favorite sandwich shop in town, and Dylan introduced her to his brother Tyler and to Drake, Tyler's business partner. They gave her a quick tour of BP Glassworks, and she purchased a stunning vase for the inn's entryway table. After meeting Nikki at Swept Away Books, they'd stopped by the farmers' market for a massive bouquet of camellia to put in the vase.

Clara liked Bodega Bay and its people. Being in town showed a side of her grandparents, and even her father, that she needed to feel. Not every answer sat among the birth certificates and greeting cards. The people who remembered her father's first bike or how her grandfather liked his grilled cheese filled in the cracks of a story Clara was only beginning to understand.

She came from a place where people greeted with propriety instead of hugs and handshakes. A world where what you'd achieved meant more than who you were. She had no inkling of the favorite colors of anyone she knew, save Carter, who always wore a red T-shirt under his black sweater before performances. She'd never asked but always assumed red must be his favorite color. Why hadn't she asked?

"Most people are jealous," her mother had said when Clara was only seven. "They want what you have. Always keep an eye out."

Clara had unlearned that bit of advice, but the world of professional performance, especially as a soloist, gave her the challenging pieces others in the orchestra wanted but had been denied. She wasn't part of the whole, even in music, which often crafted an outer chill. Her time in Bodega Bay had already softened that part of her.

Had her grandfather known? Had he seen pictures of her and known a life less . . . structured might have been a happier life? What were the chances a stranger armed with only newspaper clippings and interviews on television knew what she needed, wanted, loved?

The research had given her a welcomed sense of direction. As she continued updating the database and tweaking their system, she had set aside a few pictures and documents she hoped to frame and hang in the study. One night over Chinese food, she and Dylan had gone through the scrapbook titled "Our Inn." Behind the leather cover were construction pictures and accompanying writeups on the history and design elements. It was clear her grandfather had meticulously planned every part of the Inn by the Bay.

Last week while Dylan was at physical therapy, Clara learned the inn was a Monterey Colonial. The knowledge led her to her laptop, where she promptly went down a rabbit hole of house styles and which ones had an upper-level wraparound porch versus a lower-level porch. She filled Dylan in when he got back, and they decided to turn the finished study into a place for historical research and possibly an area for guests to work remotely. The inn had always been a fixture in their town, and now it would welcome locals to celebrate Bodega Bay's rich history.

Standing in her practice room now, Clara realized it was the last day of January and she'd been in Bodega Bay for nearly a month already. She couldn't remember the last time she was in one place for more than a few days, let alone months. Her agent had already emailed two performances she hoped Clara would reconsider with orchestras close to Bodega Bay. One was a one-night-only performance in San Francisco. Clara didn't reject the idea outright but replied that she would decide by the end of next month.

When she was a child, being onstage was a magic playground, a place she could finally have fun once all the practice, discipline, and starch brought her to the spotlight. She and her cello were a pair, as Clara discovered the joy of entwining an audience in the soft melodic pulls and bold release of music. The power of performing was delightful when Clara was a young girl, but as she grew older, the same talent kept her from the rest of the world.

Many of her early friends and fellow musicians had gone on to permanent positions within prominent orchestras or parlayed their experience into teaching. They'd touched enough success and happily settled into a peaceful rhythm, which often included homes and family.

The few times Clara proposed slowing down, possibly starting a life with people who loved *her* instead of a performance, her parents swiftly exalted her remarkable talent. It would be "such a waste to step away," and "she was in her prime." Clara wondered, having now seen a picture of her grandmother at eighty in a waterfall, at the absurdity of only one prime phase in an entire lifetime.

She would always need music, always want to perform, but there was more to life than being "brilliant." Brilliant was for special occasions. Taken off the shelf and put away. Brilliant never belonged with the simple joys of everyday life.

Learning about her grandparents and a framework of her father's early years, Clara was often overwhelmed. Some days it seemed like every detail or event they uncovered was one more she'd missed, which ached like regret. On those days, she clung to her routine, her music, and spending time with Dylan. She tried to remember he was temporary, that this whole thing was just a stopover, but with each day, that too felt like a lie.

Clara combed her fingers through her wet hair and took a seat next to her instrument. Wearing a T-shirt and jeans, squishing her bare feet in the plush rug, she could feel the disapproval of her previous instructors and her parents as she stared at the cello, resting regal at her side.

Her mother always preached Clara ought to be "performance-ready" even for practice. From the time she was seven, she'd never once sat to play without at least pulling her hair back and wearing earrings.

Your posture will be off, a voice whispered as Clara sipped her water.

You will never sit properly in those jeans, another warned.

What will people think? yet another shrilled as Clara tucked her hair behind an ear.

You are a disgrace to your gift, the final voice bellowed before she gently took her cello by the neck and placed it between her knees.

"You're fine," she whispered to the empty room before running a hand along the smooth polish of the upper bout. It was always her favorite curve of the instrument, but especially on this Polstein & White 2016 design. The pale gold wood was lighter than her last cello, and Clara loved the four-inch knot on the lower treble side. It reminded her of a dancing stick figure.

All the cellos she'd had the privilege to play throughout her career, some ancient and others modern, were works of art. But her personal instrument was always her favorite—there was a tested and built-upon relationship.

Clara knew it sounded silly, but she had learned most of what she knew about partnerships from her instruments. Respect for both beauty and imperfections, allowing room for growth and discovering new things, even communication—it was all there. Clara had few human relationships in her life so tactile and honest, but she always had her cello.

The instruments never cared if she wore heels, nor did they notice when she had a blemish or a bad hair day. Too often Clara had listened to others, which at times helped her career but jeopardized her sense of self. Maybe she would emerge from her time in Bodega Bay with a similar sense of kinship offstage.

Practice, she told herself. It all came down to practice. With the criticism in her head silenced for now, Clara cradled her knees around her instrument, picked up her bow, and played.

Dylan's physical therapy was working, which was annoying because it meant he had to keep going. Clara had proven to be a mixture of contrary and complicated characteristics. She was work, and sometimes pretty moody, and yet there he was, driving back to the inn, trying to convince himself he hadn't enjoyed spending nearly every day with her, somehow isolated in the world of Levinson's history. They'd even ventured out recently, and she seemed to fit in town too.

As the gate opened, Dylan tried to convince himself it was because Clara played the cello. He'd never met a musician, save Bella and her elementary jazz band. It was possible that explained the attraction. Maybe it was out-of-town intrigue and nothing more.

When Dylan came through the front door, Clara was in the living room on her laptop, papers on the coffee table. She glanced over the couch, fire already going, and he laughed as she splayed her hand to present her newly mastered fire-building skills. Hanging up his coat, he had the strangest sense of belonging.

Dylan had never understood the phrase "feels like home." His home growing up was chaos, and he'd been on the go since. He supposed Bodega Bay was home, but walking through the door of the inn to Clara on the couch, Dylan suddenly understood the appeal. He hoped it had everything to do with the inn, and things would feel the same once she left, but he needed to keep his head on straight just in case. There was no sense in getting used to something or someone if the loss could ruin everything.

"If it's the seventy-fifth anniversary, the inn was completed in 1948, right?" she asked when he walked closer. Now that they were putting things back in the study, Clara wanted to redo the "Our Inn" scrapbook to better preserve some of the pictures.

"That sounds right." Dylan leaned over the back of the couch.

"So, why does the sign out front say 'established in 1925'?"

"No idea."

"He was *born* in 1925. I pulled out his birth certificate again just to confirm." She pointed. "Construction started in 1947 and ended in 1948 while he was engaged to Miss Crabtree, the first fiancée."

Dylan took the large leather book to have a closer look. "Huh. I guess we'll need a new sign. I wonder how that happened?" He turned the page to find she'd remounted the photograph of a young Levinson standing on the site with only the inn's framework in the background.

"Maybe it wasn't a mistake. Perhaps he felt like the inn was his rebirth?"

Dylan narrowed his eyes.

"What? He could have seen it as a renaissance of sorts after Miss Crabtree broke his heart."

"Do we know she broke his heart?"

She pursed her lips. "I suppose we don't."

He shrugged. "I mean, they were engaged. People who are engaged are usually in love."

"You'd be surprised," Clara said.

Dylan smiled. "That's right, I forgot you were engaged. Wanna talk about it?"

"Absolutely not." She took back the scrapbook.

He laughed, kicking off his boots and leaving them near the door. He wasn't fishing for information, but he wondered why she never discussed that part of her life.

"I still can't believe he was younger than we are when he built this place," Dylan said, joining her on the couch.

"I know." As she closed the scrapbook and set it aside, they sat quietly looking around the living room at the rich wood floors, simple white molding, and intricate textiles. The images of the inn being built from the ground up were some of Dylan's favorites. That

Levinson had the drive to build something so permanent at his age was fascinating.

"I know you said you've known my grandfather all your life, but how old were you when you first met him?" she asked.

"I'm not sure." Dylan took out his phone, swallowing back emotion. "Dinner?" he asked.

"Pizza's on the way." She checked her phone and returned to scanning her laptop.

He leaned forward, surveying the open scrapbooks and searching for a better answer to her question. "I can't remember when your grandfather wasn't around, or I didn't know about him. We probably met for the first time when I got in trouble for snooping around the grounds. I was like eight or nine."

"So, he was seventy-five when you knew him." She glanced at the ceiling like she was calculating. "And then he died at ninety-eight?"

"Yeah. He was ninety-eight."

Clara looked up, and Dylan realized his voice had again hitched on a memory.

He cleared his throat. "What'd you get on the pizza?"

"It's the special."

"Which is?" he asked, getting up to grab a beer.

"I'm not sure. I had to call in the order, and there was a lot of background noise. I could have asked him to repeat it, but I didn't want to sound like . . ."

He stopped on his way to the kitchen. "Like?"

"Like a snobby tourist."

Dylan smiled. "Beer?"

"Yes, please," she said, her attention back on her laptop.

"Did you know about my father?" she asked when Dylan returned.

"I knew they had a son, and he died. We never talked about it."

At the knock on the door, Dylan answered and listened to Pete from Dough Bird recap his favorite shot of last night's hockey game before Dylan tipped him and returned to Clara with the pizza. They ate amid the quiet crackle of the fire, Clara on her computer searching an ancestry website for an image of Edith's sister, and Dylan looking over the other open scrapbooks on the coffee table.

She closed her laptop. "One minute I have questions, and other times I'm convinced I'm too late, so why bother."

Dylan didn't have a chance to respond before she stood and went to the kitchen. Returning with an ice pack and a glass for her beer, she set down the glass and grabbed a pillow from the couch.

"Scoot up," she said.

"You don't need to—"

She tucked the pillow behind his back and handed him the ice pack.

"Thank you," he said, setting it on his knee.

"You're welcome. How was physical therapy?"

Dylan shrugged. "Annoying."

Clara smiled. "I sprained my wrist once."

"Yeah? Playing the cello?"

She nodded.

"Wow. I was joking. Is that common?"

"Not sure," she said. "It was only minor, but I was religious about the ice."

Clara poured her beer into the glass at an angle like a pro, and Dylan wondered if caring came naturally to her or if she did things out of enforced obligation. Her parents didn't seem like a loving bunch, but there she was, caring for him seemingly on instinct. She'd charmed Tyler and Drake. Nikki was already in love, and yet nothing about Clara's outside logically fit with any of them, save maybe Tyler.

"Anyway, back to all of this." She spread her hands across the coffee table. "I'm not sure I'm ever going to catch up, and even if I do, they're gone, so again, what's the point?"

"It's a weird situation, no question."

Clara was all over the place tonight, and he wondered if there was such a thing as too much family history. She seemed a little on edge, so he tried to help.

"Maybe let's stop searching and take a break," Dylan suggested, as he did any time she seemed to spin too much in the past. Clara turned to him on the couch, tucking a pillow behind her back.

"Your grandmother baked pies," he said, hoping to give her something more than dates and old photos. "She sold them at the market."

"Interesting," Clara said.

"Yup. She had a pie case. I used to make runs to the grocery store for her, and when I got back, the smell was everywhere." Dylan looked around the whole of the living room again and tried to transfer the memory.

"How old were you?"

"Twelve or thirteen."

"Delivering groceries?" she asked.

"Easier than chopping wood."

"He made you chop wood?" Clara wiped her hands on a paper towel.

"No. He taught me to chop wood and then paid me a good wage. He was fair."

"You always speak so fondly of him."

"Not much in my life was reliable, outside of my brother. Your grandfather was steady. I enjoyed coming here, working and being busy."

She sipped her beer.

"He wasn't warm and fuzzy, which worked for me because neither was I, back then."

"And you are now?" She smiled teasingly, which seemed to get easier as the weeks wore on.

"Funny." Dylan rested his leg on the coffee table.

They ate for a few more minutes in silence.

"What was he like after Edith died?"

"I was in high school by then. He didn't talk as much. He was kind of the same. Eggs, bacon, toast every morning. Coffee black. He'd sit out on the back patio, eat, and read the paper."

"Did he ever invite you for breakfast?"

"Once."

Clara seemed poised for what he knew were another dozen questions, but he held up his hand. "Story for another day." Dylan wasn't ready to share that much of himself yet. Or ever.

"Fair enough. So, it sounds like you two were perfect for one another."

"I guess we were."

Dylan wiped his hands and eyed some of the newspaper clippings in one scrapbook. He picked the largest one, highlighting a full picture of Clara, younger and so serious.

"'Any performance of Clara Mar's is brilliance personified,'" he read. "'In her hands, the most predictable, ordinary piece blooms radiant, as if she is reflecting the composer's soul rather than their notes. Her mastery of the music is breathtaking and an opportunity of a lifetime for any music connoisseur.'" Dylan glanced over at her.

She seemed to squirm under the words.

"That's some review, right?"

"I'm not always sure who they're talking about in those things." She sat back, pulling one leg underneath.

"You. This"—he looked at the clipping again—"Michael Ing of the *New York Times* is using all his ten-point words on you."

"Yes, well, he's entitled to his opinion." Clara took the clipping, slid it back, and closed the scrapbook.

Dylan said nothing, still sensing a storm.

"What?" she asked at his silence.

"I would think you'd be used to all this praise by now."

"Praise is isolating." Clara went to the kitchen and returned with two more beers. "Praise puts you on a level of adoration. I've only ever wanted the music. I started playing to please my parents, then I played because everyone said I couldn't stop, and then finally I started for myself, I think."

"And you're unbelievably talented."

Their eyes held.

Clara handed him a bottle and poured the other into her glass. "You've never heard me play. Unless you've stalked me on Google. According to Nikki, googling is common practice here in Bodega Bay."

"I've heard you play."

"When?"

"The afternoon before Rusty dropped off the carts." Dylan adjusted the ice pack on his knee.

"That was practice."

He smiled. "Yeah, well, your practice was like an outdoor concert. I haven't heard you play since, though. Don't world-famous musicians have to practice all the time?"

"We do. I usually play when you're gone."

"Why?"

"Because I have a routine, and I practice alone." She sipped her beer. "I played this afternoon while you were at physical therapy. It wasn't great."

"Why not?"

She shrugged. "I'm not sure. Some days are better than others."

"Okay." He wasn't sure what to do with her obvious disappointment, or maybe it was anger, so he changed the subject. "Well, apparently your grandfather followed your career." He gestured to the scrapbook.

"Apparently." Clara exhaled.

"He did love music," Dylan said.

"Great. That's . . . perfect, isn't it?" she spat out the words before standing to gather the scrapbooks.

Dylan got up to help, but she held him off.

"It's wonderful everyone in this town knew him, and he left me all this stuff"—her hands splayed, almost dropping everything—"and no one ever bothered to call me or get to know me except for what they put in this goddamn scrapbook. Kept me on a shelf like everyone else in my life."

"I thought the letter said he tried?"

"Yeah, well, he should have tried harder."

She left, and Dylan heard the books slap to the dining room table.

He followed her. "You're right. I'm sure he—" Dylan lost his words when she turned, tears in her eyes.

"He what?" she asked, her expression pained. "He couldn't get past my terrifying mother? The family dynamic was too much? I was his granddaughter. I was a *child*." Clara's voice grew louder, frustration spilling off her. "My whole life has been in movement from one place to the next. I'm not complaining, but it would have been nice"—she wiped at her eyes—"to know someone cared. To know all of this existed."

Dylan stepped back. Never one for conflict or yelling, he thought about giving her some space, but she seemed so alone, so lost, he stayed.

"I'm sorry." God, he hated it when people said that, but there he was, standing in Levinson's dining room with nothing but those two useless words to offer a woman who clearly needed more. Unsure what else to do, he pulled her into his arms and let her cry.

Moments later, Clara sniffed, pulled away, and there it was again—embarrassment.

"I am so sorry. This isn't your—I need to collect myself. My apologies." She tucked her hair off her face and stood taller. "You're right. It was a lovely review, and I am grateful for my career. I adore performing, but those articles never show a full person." She swallowed. "I can be obsessive, difficult, and awkward. All of it disappears when I play, but I'm not just a handful of pretty words."

"Believe me, I know." Dylan hoped to Christ she laughed.

She did, wiping at her eyes one last time. "I'm not a product."

"No one thinks you are."

"Everyone in my world *knows* I am." Her gorgeous mouth, normally flying a mile a minute with her latest observation or idea, straightened into a tight line.

"Well, I don't think you're a product," Dylan said, taking her hand.

The air between them sparked with something new, as if another layer of who they were before they ended up in this situation fell away. While Dylan was glad to be there for her, even happy to share some of his memories, he needed to forget how she felt in his arms and remember there was no scenario where whatever was coursing through his body didn't explode in his face.

Letting go of her hand, Dylan walked back to the living room and picked up the only book left on the table, hoping to change the subject. He didn't want her to end the evening upset. Her grandparents were such a source of stability for him. He suddenly needed her to leave Bodega Bay with a sense of that gift instead of a swirling collection of what-ifs.

Once they returned to their spots on the couch, Dylan read the cover of the book. "*One Question a Day for You and Me.*" He met Clara's eyes.

She shrugged. "From the inscription inside, they started answering those on their thirtieth wedding anniversary."

"Seriously?" Dylan flipped through the pages. "Wow. I did not know they were so—"

"In love?"

"No. I knew that. You could see it in the way they were. I just never took Levinson for a talker or Q&A kind of guy." Dylan stopped on one page and found insight into a man he thought he knew.

"'Did you have an imaginary friend?'" he read.

Clara slid her laptop into the bag on the floor. "Strange, right? Seems like a first-date question, or at least something you'd discover in the first month of knowing someone."

Dylan tilted his head. "Can't say I've ever asked a date about her imaginary friend. Sounds like you really go all out." He smiled, but she didn't. *Shit!*

"I—" She seemed to steel herself before glancing at the fire. "I'm not a big dater."

"Well, according to this, your grandmother had an imaginary friend named Kimberly until she was seven," Dylan said, hopefully shifting to a lighter subject.

Clara smiled, and Dylan felt the world right again.

"But no imaginary friend for Levinson." He set the book back on the table. "How about you?" he asked. "Have you ever had an imaginary friend?"

"No," she said. "You?"

"Nope."

"Would you tell me if you did?" she asked.

"Nope."

Clara laughed and stood, putting her bag over one shoulder like a woman used to packing up and moving on.

"I need a shower, and I haven't oiled my cuticles all week." She made to leave.

"Uh-oh," he said sarcastically. But she glared, and he held up his hands.

"Thank you." She stood at the base of the stairs.

Dylan didn't ask what for this time. He knew and didn't want her to have to explain.

"Night, Hildegard."

She smiled. "Good night."

Clearing their mess and extinguishing the last breath of the fireplace under the glinting glass of the photographs on the mantel, he picked up one of Levinson. Unlike so many of the younger photos they'd seen over the last few weeks, this one was from his ninetieth birthday. Dylan had been at the party. He knew the man in this photo well and could practically hear him say, "Are you flirting with my granddaughter, young man?"

Dylan set the photo back and turned off the lights. Later in bed, he lay staring up at the ceiling. He wasn't flirting with anyone. "You're the one who left the book, old man," he whispered to no one before finally falling asleep.

Chapter Eight

Clara spent Saturday putting the finishing touches on the study and backing up their now-searchable database. Between Tyler's technical expertise and Dylan managing to make her laugh even through the difficult bits, Clara had grown less uneasy with each passing day.

She'd developed a sense of purpose outside herself, and lining up the new boxes and color-coded labels behind her grandfather's desk, she realized the first item on the list was a lovely collaboration. She may still be outside the experiences reflected in the photographs, but by pushing through, she'd become a curator, a protector of someone else's life.

Taking in the day and a sense of accomplishment, Clara nearly missed the dark sedan parked next to Rusty's truck, but when the hairs on the back of her neck stood up, she somehow knew exactly who had arrived. Running to the entryway, she nearly knocked over her coffee cup. When she opened the door, Carter Sterling stood at the base of the steps to the porch. Not quite close enough to poison things, but way too close for Clara's liking.

"Darling." He extended his arms like a long-lost . . . piece of crap. Clara contemplated running back inside and locking the door, but instead marched down the steps, forcing him to move back. Close to his smug face now, the only saving grace was Clara knew her parents would never take the time to also arrive unannounced. They'd sent him instead.

"Carter, what are you doing here?"

Sliding his hands into his pockets, he took in her appearance and said, "Your mother is worried sick, and apparently you haven't been answering her calls. I promised to swing by before hopping a flight to NYC this evening. So"—his lip curled—"how are things?"

After a sharp intake of breath, Clara stood taller, as if preparing for battle. Somehow one of her ugliest yesterdays had slipped into her delightful now like a photograph in the wrong book. She imagined he wouldn't go quietly, but she would try her damnedest.

"How kind of you to make time for my parents' errand, but it was unnecessary. As you can see, I am perfectly fine."

He looked her up and down. "Clearly open for interpretation, darling. Should I take a picture of this ensemble and add it to your online portfolio? Do you have a barrette in your hair? Good lord, pack your things. I'm saving you from yourself."

Clara resisted the urge to touch her grandmother's clip, to protect it. She had dealt with Carter most of her adult life, but this little performance was some of his best work. Perhaps he sensed her joy and volunteered to step on it before anyone else could.

"You're doing no such thing. I don't need saving. I'm taking some time for myself. You're free to catch your plane."

"Taking time for yourself?" He looked up at the inn. "Here? What is this place?" He sniffed the air. "A farm?"

"Yes, here. And no, it is an inn." Clara channeled Dylan's brevity, offering nothing more for Carter to use against her.

"Listen"—he made to put his arm around her, and Clara stepped back—"if you're going into some kind of heartbreak spiral because I've moved on, as your friend before your fiancé, I'm here to snap you out of it." The man snapped his fingers, and Clara nearly laughed.

"I'm fine, Carter. I appreciate your concern, but you can tell my parents I am a grown woman, capable of taking care of myself."

"Oh, come on." He glanced around the front of the inn, and despite herself, she felt smaller under his gaze.

Dylan came around the side of the house, pushing a wheelbarrow of firewood, shirt stuck to his chest by sweat despite the breeze.

Clara held up a hand to Carter. "Would you excuse me a moment?"

Not waiting for an answer, she ran over to Dylan before he got too close to the grime of her poor choices.

He set the wheelbarrow down and pulled his sunglasses off his face to wipe his forehead. Clara put a hand on his shoulder, more familiar than was their norm. "I need to kiss you," she said before she lost her nerve.

"What?" Dylan furrowed his brow, turning to look in Carter's direction.

Clara took his chin in her hand and stepped closer. "That man over there is Carter, my ex who, fueled by my insane mother, has arrived to slap me on the wrist and drag me back to where I belong. I've asked him to leave, and I could keep trying. There are certainly less childish ways of dealing with people, and you are not obligated to help me, but—"

"Clara, when you're done speaking with the help, can we resume?" Carter tapped his watch. "I'm on a tight schedule."

Dylan took her hand from his face, looking over her shoulder at Carter and then back at her. He closed his eyes and opened them after a deep exhale. Clara sighed. This was absurd. She needed to go over there and—

Without another word, Dylan wrapped an arm around her waist, hoisting her off her feet so fast it pushed the breath straight out of her body. He met her eyes briefly before resting his other hand on the back of her neck and kissing her. Not a quick brush of lips or even a first-date goodnight kiss—no, this was a large, warm hand gripping into her side, lips pulling kind of kiss. Exactly what one would expect to find on the warning label for a man like Dylan. It was glorious—warm tongues, tug-and-release glorious. Clara could have sworn she heard music or birds, she wasn't sure, but she realized something cinematic had occurred moments later when he set her down, held her for a beat longer to make sure she was steady, and then returned to the wood in his wheelbarrow.

Leaning back into her, he dipped his head into the hollow of her neck and whispered, "You owe me one." Hesitating a beat, his breath tickling at her ear, he kissed her there too.

"Morning, Carver." Dylan waved, grinning right up to his stunning eyes.

Clara held both hands to her mouth to squash her laughter.

"It's Carter," her ex corrected.

"Yeah. Doesn't matter," Dylan said with one hand overhead as he dumped the wood and pushed the now-empty wheelbarrow back where he came from.

As Clara returned to the front of the inn, Carter looked like he might have a seizure, disgust seething from him like one of those ominous overtures he loved so much.

Clara stood tall, letting out a slow breath as she approached.

"What in the hell are you—"

"Safe trip home, *Carver*," she said, walking up the porch steps before he could say another nasty word. Most people who'd traveled a couple of hours to speak with someone would follow to the front door, knock, even.

Clara knew Carter, and he was not most people. After her performance with Dylan, he would huff into the black leather of his rented Mercedes, call her parents on his way back into the city to let them know she was "slumming" or some other awful phrase, but he would never reduce himself to following her anywhere.

Carter was a prick in expensive clothes, and while she should have shared those words, she took the easy way out for once in her life. Dylan's help had maximum impact and left Clara less vulnerable to Carter's venom. It was the best choice, and yet as she closed the front door and walked toward the back patio, her knees were weak. People kissed all the time, she reminded herself. Dylan probably kissed women on the regular, but she still touched her lips before opening the back door and, for an instant, pretended she too kissed lovely men all the time.

"Hey, you two are a thing?" Rusty asked as soon as Clara stepped out back.

"No." Dylan pointed to Rusty as he stomped up the back patio. "We are absolutely *not* a thing."

"Sure seemed like a thing."

Dylan shook his head. "I met the woman a month ago. Do I seem like the guy to hook up with my business partner?"

Rusty shrugged. "I dunno, but you were there, and she was there"—he pointed to the side of the yard—"and that kiss definitely wasn't business." Rusty stuck out his tongue and swirled it around in what Clara assumed was an exaggerated kiss. She held in a laugh as Dylan pulled her back into the house.

Once in the kitchen, Dylan leaned on the counter. "Okay, so I'm not sure what happened out there, but I'm not used to spontaneous performances." He was a little out of breath.

"I apologize, I know it was—"

"So, if you have any other exes you need to scare off by kissing the shit out of me, I need to know ahead of time."

"Only the one ex."

"Great."

"Some kiss." Clara couldn't help but smile.

He met her eyes, his expression again unreadable.

"I mean, for someone unaccustomed to performance. I can honestly say no one's ever lifted me off my feet with such . . . enthusiasm."

"Could be because you hang out with guys like him." Dylan took off his work gloves. "Did he fucking call me the help?"

"He did."

"So that's the kind of guy who gets you musician types going, huh?"

Clara swallowed, suddenly not ready to discuss her decisions. "I . . . have known Carter most of my life."

"Lucky you. I can see why you fell in love."

"I wasn't in love with him."

Dylan furrowed his brow. "But you were set to marry him?"

Clara looked away. "It's complicated."

"Like arranged-marriage complicated?"

"Kind of, yes, but without the contract." She exhaled slowly. "It was understood I would secure a certain marriage, but he cheated on me one too many times."

Dylan said nothing for a beat, shoving a hand through his hair. "That's screwed up, Clara. You know that, right?"

Something in her wanted to argue. Tell him he didn't understand the pressures of her professional life or the societal constraints she came from, but all those things she used to rationalize suddenly revealed themselves for the mess they were. Clara knew most parents didn't push their daughter into a marriage of professional alliance. She also realized now how pathetic accepting his proposal despite not loving him had been. And, how *screwed up*, as Dylan had put it, her situation had been for her to be even a little embarrassed when Carter dumped her.

She knew all of it now, given some distance and fresh air, but it didn't make the deep and ingrained bits of her life any easier to swallow. She could have made a million excuses to push back and protect her polished image, but instead she simply nodded and enjoyed the freedom of self-acceptance.

What in the hell just happened? One minute Dylan was ready to walk away from her absurd request, and the next he couldn't leave her to fend off some asshole on her own.

There were a dozen ways he could have helped, including having the guy removed from their property. But she hadn't asked for any of those options—no, she'd asked him to kiss her. It would be easy to say kissing Clara was like kissing a cousin or a platonic friend, but Dylan always tried to at least be honest with himself.

There was no denying he was attracted to Clara. She was a beautiful, smart, and surprising woman. More reasons *not* to kiss her.

Ever. And why the hell had he lifted her, like he was one of those guys on the covers in Nikki's store window?

He'd done some stupid stuff in his life, but kissing Clara Mar, her arms wrapped around him while he swallowed the moan on her lips, was death-wish stuff. Nothing in Clara's eyes before he took her mouth matched her delicate stature. He imagined much of her refinement came from spending time in theaters or wherever musicians hung out. But there was nothing subtle about the way she kissed.

Dylan's phone buzzed.

It was Tyler. *Perfect.*

"Hey." Dylan's heart was still racing.

"Some random thoughts in no particular order," his brother said, seconds before the image of him riding his stationary bike on his patio appeared on Dylan's screen.

Hoping he appeared neutral, Dylan leaned against the side of the inn. Tyler lived life as if everything, including technology, took too long, which was crazy, considering he'd waited years for Jules.

"Okay," Dylan said. "Let's have 'em."

"Instead of just providing food for guests, you could eventually add a small restaurant. Limited seating, exclusive menu for tourists, give them a glimpse of the inn and create interest in booking a full return stay. Also, thoughts on a dock off the private beach? You could set up a place for water—Crap!"

"You all right?" Dylan asked, when the image on the screen jumbled.

"Yeah, dropped my phone. Hang on."

After some scrambling, Tyler returned to the screen. "The rest of my notes are things I'm sure you've already thought of—updating the Wi-Fi, possibly pet-friendly, and Jules mentioned muffins."

"Muffins?" Dylan moved out of the way as Rusty brought another pile of firewood.

"Yeah, she's all about food."

"We just finished the study, and you're already on to a restaurant?" Dylan ran a hand through his hair. "Slow your roll. I have a business partner, remember?"

"The restaurant isn't a right-now thing. I'm brainstorming. Besides, I've spoken with your partner a few times. She loves me already. *And* my ideas." Tyler sat back on his bike and wiped his face with a towel.

"Your brainstorming is another man's nervous breakdown. I need to get back to work."

"Looks like you've been working," Tyler said. "How's everything going?"

"Good. Yeah, things are fine." Dylan lied because he sure as hell wasn't telling his brother he'd just kissed everyone's favorite new out-of-towner. "How's everything with you?"

"Excellent." He climbed off his bike, towel at his neck. "Please tell Clara I said hello."

"I'll relay the message."

Tyler smiled. "Okay. Well, I'll get back to work too." He took a swig of his water bottle. "I'm psyched about this. You?"

"Don't get too psyched. We still have five months and the rest of the list."

"What kind of attitude—"

"Gotta go." He disconnected, not ready for another one of his brother's pep talks.

Grateful Clara wasn't in the kitchen as he walked back into the house and made a beeline for his room, Dylan pulled off his sweaty clothes and hoped like hell a hot shower would erase the last hour.

Dylan was rarely surprised. He'd even convinced himself around eighteen he didn't like surprises, when Tyler was away at school and their dad had forgotten Dylan's birthday. He had made the mistake of assuming a father would remember his son's milestone birthday. The years without Tyler at home made it even harder to imagine their family ever being normal, so Dylan learned to manage his expectations.

After kissing Clara, he might change his mind on surprises. The cluster of beauty marks at the left curve of her long neck, her normally polished shoulder-length blond hair that was wavy now and pulled to the side with her grandmother's clip. And when his mouth took hers, she responded like someone who not only knew how to kiss but enjoyed it. He'd enjoyed kissing her too, and that was the problem.

Dylan knew from experience women like Clara Mar didn't belong in his world. They were passing through, and she hadn't technically kissed him. She'd used him to get out of a difficult situation. All of it was a break for her—the talking, the dinners, learning about her past, the kiss. It was all part of one big difficult situation. His body still humming as he stepped under the water, Dylan closed his eyes and wondered what the hell he was thinking when he told her she "owed him one."

Kitchen

The kitchen is the heart of the inn. So many happy memories live there, but it gets a lot of traffic, so spruce it up before the reopening. Please retile the kitchen, but find the existing tile (we liked it a lot). Please deliver the attached glassware order to BP Glassworks. Do what you like with the rest of the kitchen, so long as it stays a place for friends, family, and guests to gather for laughter and sustenance.

Chapter Nine

Clara thought about calling her mother to discuss the Carter visit but, in the end, chose silence. If she called, it would only end with her mother cast as righteous, concerned, and abandoned, and Clara as selfish, mean-spirited, and horrible. Talking would accomplish nothing, so she stayed quiet and shifted her attention to the kitchen.

Replaying the Carter incident, she tried not to recall the taste of Dylan's mouth—smooth, warm, and minty, with a hint of coffee. The kiss was delicious, but the lift was next-level. Who lifted a woman with one arm and kissed her breathless? A peck would have been enough to send Carter's ego running. Her own curiosity might have imagined a bit more, even a quick brush of Dylan's tongue, but what happened was more than she could have ever conjured up on such short notice.

His hand at her neck, the pull of his lips, and *that lift* made keeping Dylan in the business-partner box much more difficult. It might not have been the best idea to kiss him, but she'd let Carter's audacity rile her up, and there Dylan was, sweaty and helpful, genuine, and so tangible. It had been a long time since she'd made a decision on her own. She couldn't remember the last time someone hadn't arranged things for her, complete with "Ms. Mar must have" and "Please ensure Ms. Mar" nonsense. And now Dylan was avoiding her.

Up early and working late, he and Rusty were making progress pulling up the old tile in the sunroom portion of the kitchen. She'd stayed out of their way. There were a couple of notes left behind regarding what was next up to move or cautioning wet grout, but the routine she and Dylan had while working on the study was gone. It had been two days since they kissed, and ignoring her was his prerogative, she told herself, opening both cabinets under the kitchen sink and wondering how many trash bags one older couple needed.

She and Dylan were business partners. Clara had crossed the line, which entitled him to some space. At the same time, she certainly hadn't attacked him. He seemed caught off guard, but his tongue felt like it was having a good time, so that helped assuage her guilt at adding a complication to their otherwise pleasant cohabitation.

Since they'd finished the study, Clara wondered if they would ever get back to talking and sharing their stories. She missed him. Missed his outlook on things and their comfortable banter. She also wondered if he was going to buy more ice cream, but under the circumstances added it to her own list for Monday.

When she heard the shower in the innkeeper's quarters turn on, she wondered how the hell he'd returned to his room from outside without a sound. Clara sat back on her heels, content she'd cleared everything out from under the sink. Standing, she made a list of the appliances so once Dylan emerged, she could talk with him about which ones to keep and what needed to be replaced prior to reopening the inn.

Resting on the counter, she heard the shower stop, and fresh heat crept up her body as her mind replayed the darn kiss again. This was absurd. She'd asked for a favor, and he'd helped her out. There was no reason for either of them to be uncomfortable.

Christ, what was he doing in there? Dylan had probably taken dozens of showers since they'd lived under the same roof, but the scent of this one slid right under her skin as it wafted into the kitchen. If this was their new normal, she needed to get ahold of her senses. Awareness led to visuals of steam, soap, and his body in—

"Hey."

Clara jumped, turning to find him fully clothed. A relief and a disappointment.

"I'm going to the hardware store and then to a meeting. Do we need anything other than the order we put in last week?"

"I . . ." Clara watched Dylan dry his hair with a towel, droplets of water at his neck disappearing into the gray of his T-shirt.

Dylan shook his head. "Don't do that."

"What?" Clara glanced over her shoulder in mocked exaggeration. "I'm not doing anything."

"You're looking at me weird like . . ."

She furrowed her brow. "Like what? I'm listening to you and noticing you fresh out of the shower."

"Fresh out of the shower? Cut it out, Clara."

She blinked away the lust. "I am not doing anything. You're the one who's making this a thing. You shower. I shower." She held up both hands. "No problem. There are no problems here."

Dylan shook his head and then threw the towel at her. "Nothing from the store?"

"Nope." A solid answer, considering she wanted to put the towel to her nose like a silly teenager. She hadn't been this ridiculous when she *was* a teenager. Clara set the towel on the kitchen table. "I do have a few things to discuss if you have a minute later," she called out, as he left the kitchen.

Aware that the front door had not closed, she waited for a response.

"I'll be back around five."

"Sounds good," she called back.

"Takeaway?" he asked, and Clara smiled like a fool.

They'd get past this, she decided, before offering to order and listening to the door close behind him, but she begged her mind to show up as the grown woman she was instead of some lustful—wait, why couldn't she be lustful?

Because they were business partners, not *partner* partners, cried the sensible side of her brain. If she was going to get through the next few months on task, she needed to redirect her thoughts from exploring the absolute pleasure Dylan's body promised, and ignore that her heart settled a little more in her chest every day they spent together.

The last thing she needed to do was ruin either of their chances by feeling things. "Emotions belong on the stage during a performance, and nowhere else," Carter Sterling, dick of the century, had once said.

She liked Dylan, that was all. He was physically attractive, which was pleasant, and liking him would make things much easier in the coming months. It wasn't crazy to think they would even part as friends once he had the inn and she returned to her music.

Managing her response to others was a practiced skill. She might lack experience reading a group and weaving into its fabric, like a member of an orchestra, but a solo required a different kind of restraint. She could apply some of those skills to her current situation.

Or she would learn that she was a complete lunatic offstage and spend the next five months in a constant state of frustration. While the second scenario was the more likely, Clara chose to have faith in herself at least through the weekend.

Deep into assembling the shelves for under the sink, Clara almost missed the knock at the front door.

"Open," she called out, getting more comfortable with the comings and goings of the inn. "I'm in the kitchen."

"Morning, Clara. Sorry to bother you on the weekend, but I want to check if the tile we laid yesterday is setting all right. Only be a minute."

When she pulled her head out from under the sink, Rusty stood in the kitchen, kneepads strapped over his jeans and what she thought was a coffee stain on his T-shirt.

"Go right ahead. I was—" She turned to her mess now spread all over the floor.

Rusty's eyes went wide. "How's it going?"

"Good." She smiled, standing to take a break.

"Moved onto the kitchen, I see."

"Yes. We have checked the study off the list, and I think we have a marvelous story to tell future guests and town historians. Thank you again for helping with all the storage."

"You bet." Rusty tapped his worn baseball cap. "I love this stuff." He stooped to look at the area of tile. "You know when we were building the back deck"—he pointed for emphasis—"your grandfather used to invite me in for a brandy on Wednesday nights. Don't mind saying the study was kinda intimidating in those days."

Clara washed her hands. "I think it's the giant desk."

Rusty laughed and stood, dusting his hands. "You might be right. Looks friendlier now."

"Thank you," Clara said, accomplishment welling in her chest. "So, you and my grandfather were friends?"

He tilted his head. "I'm not sure he would call me a friend. He was more friendly with my dad." Rusty shrugged. "Eh, he might've called me a friend. Back then I was a contractor. We were client friendly. Your grandfather liked to talk about details."

"Having gone through most of his paper, I believe you."

"Yeah, he would ask about which wiring we were using or innovations in insulation. He wanted to chat up the things he knew and learn more. The man was always learning."

Clara nodded, more comfortable with the parts she'd missed now. They stood for a few beats, nothing between them but the sun slipping through the window above the sink, and the barely-there sound of the Vivaldi Clara had turned on when Dylan left.

"Okay. Well, so far, so good." Rusty glanced again at the section of new tile.

Clara loved the fresh look already. The new tiles were the same as the original yellow-and-blue wreath-shaped flowers, just more vibrant. She imagined her grandfather picking out tile for the kitchen not yet knowing Edith, a woman who would light up his world in a few short years. There'd been little in her and Dylan's findings about Miss Crabtree, the first fiancée, but Clara liked to imagine, for the sake of her grandfather's heart, that he'd never cared all that much about her anyway. Her grandmother had been the great love of his life, and if the pictures were any indication, they'd spent countless moments in the kitchen where Clara and Rusty now stood.

"They look great. I'm excited to refresh this space."

"I know you play the fiddle, but do you have any DIY experience? You're pretty handy around here. Can't say I expected that."

Clara smiled. "Nope. Just learning from the best and lots of practice."

"All right, now you're just fluffin' my feathers." He grinned. "I'll let you get back to your work now." He made to leave but turned back. "Oh, almost forgot. How're you and Dylan getting on?"

Clara blinked, not sure what he was referencing, but not wanting to appear suspicious. "Sorry?"

"You two still good? I mean, after the hubbub the other day?"

"I . . . Yes, we are still good. To my knowledge."

Rusty scratched his head. "Glad to hear it."

Following an awkward silence in which it seemed he had more to ask but changed his mind, Rusty clapped his hands together. "*Anywho*, I'm off."

"Okay. Enjoy the rest of your weekend." Clara returned to her project, hoping she appeared collected, because if her instincts were right, Rusty was fishing for information. When he'd gone, Clara turned up her music and relaxed back into the solitude of her project.

Dylan was absolutely thinking about kissing her again when she'd nearly devoured him with her eyes in the kitchen. Honestly, he'd wanted to kiss her again the minute he pulled her into the kitchen after their little performance for her ex.

He'd done his best to stay away but was still losing his damn mind. The first kiss, while unexpected, was a one-off and nothing more. They'd order pizza tonight and be over it by the time they'd both gone to bed. In *separate* beds, he told his suddenly overactive imagination. Kissing Clara again was not an option. If they went there, it might lead to longer and deeper until he was unable to stop himself from asking her if he could hoist her up on the —

"Hard as a rock. This thing can pound any nail, right?" Gus from the hardware store startled Dylan out of his fantasy. Hell, he'd forgotten he was even in the store. Was this some kind of withdrawal thing? Had he been out of the dating game so long a kiss threw him into a tailspin? And fantasies? Dylan didn't have fantasies. His feet were firmly in reality.

Nodding his approval at the hammer Gus kept hitting into the palm of his hand, Dylan made small talk with Gus while he wrapped up Rusty's "tool replenishing" order. Once the tile was done, there were two cabinets Dylan wanted fixed before they moved on to appliances.

Dylan left the store determined to clear all non-business partner memories of Clara Mar from his mind and body. She was Levinson's granddaughter, he told himself, tossing the bag in his truck before locking it again. She was a co-owner.

There would be no more kissing, touching, and dear god, no more moaning. Dylan was a sucker for a soft moan, and Clara, it appeared, had talents beyond the cello. So, when he got back to the inn, he would be cordial, helpful even, but distance was vital if he was going to make it to the end of June. Clara Mar was a guaranteed goodbye. He needed to remember that too.

Walking down Main Street, Dylan convinced himself things were fine. Rusty had seen the kiss, and so far, it seemed he'd kept his mouth shut. If not, there would be questions. It was only a matter of time, but before any town-gossip triage, Dylan needed to focus on his most pressing issue, which thankfully had nothing to do with Clara Mar.

His father had texted him for a "chat." Dylan had ignored him last week, but since he was at the hardware store anyway, he'd agreed to give his dad fifteen minutes. Relieved his father suggested the Roastery instead of a bar, Dylan grabbed a latte and took a table in the corner of the coffee shop as his father and a group of people walked out of the back room.

Sipping his drink, Dylan realized the group was his dad's AA meeting, and he wondered how long those would last. It had been a few months since Tyler dragged their sad excuse for a parent to a rehab clinic, which had, of course, failed miserably. Tyler, the family fixer, had finally given up and left their father with an AA schedule. To everyone's surprise, he'd picked himself up the next morning and went.

Dylan had no clue what went on behind the back door, but his father emerged now looking nothing like the man who used to send him to the kitchen with a "get your old man another round, will ya, kid?"

Now in a coffee shop instead of a bar, some guy in a Jimmy Buffett T-shirt patted his dad's shoulder, and Dylan stood as his father broke from the crowd and walked over. He didn't know why he stood. Habit? Nerves? He wasn't sure, but there he was.

"Do you want a—" His dad looked at the cup on the table.

"I've got one."

"K, let me grab a refill." He turned toward the counter and then back. "You want a muffin? They're good, and they serve them until closing."

Dylan's stomach growled at the warm-sugar smell of the place but he shook his head. His father got in line. He'd put on some weight. Was he working out? Dylan scoffed. His father didn't work out, unless lifting a beer constituted weight training.

A few sips of latte later, his dad returned with his own mug and two muffins. Setting both bags in the center of the table, he took a seat and opened one for himself. Dylan left the second bag sitting in the center, steam and cinnamon slipping again, tempting his hunger.

"I need to get back, so I've only got"—he checked his watch—"fifteen. What's this about?"

His father swallowed, sipped his coffee. Never one to rush and always up for building the tension, he set down his cup.

"I'm sorry," he said, barely above a whisper.

"For? Christ, Dad, what happened now?"

His father winced, hands shaking as he lifted the cup again. "Nothing. Nothing's happened. I wanted to have coffee to apologize." His voice was clear now.

"You're sorry?"

Their eyes met. His father's were less bloodshot than they used to be, softened at the edges. Dylan realized he was apologizing for *everything*. This was a blanket apology for being a bad dad, a drunk.

Dylan took a sip of his drink, hoping it would melt the steel of his jaw so he could speak. He had to say something, right? What was he supposed to do with this? Tell him it was okay?

"You don't need to say anything."

"That's good," Dylan managed, not intending the sarcasm, but not sorry for it either.

His father looked at his hands, both wrapped around the cup now. "Part of my process"—he looked Dylan straight in the eyes—"part of getting clean is making amends with those I have hurt with my . . . with my . . ."

"Drinking?"

He confirmed, dipping his chin, and despite years of hating the man across the table, Dylan felt the tiniest stretch along the layers of scar tissue surrounding his heart.

"I'm sorry I couldn't be the dad you and your brother needed."

"Wouldn't."

"Couldn't." His lips trembled. "I had—I *have* a problem."

"True."

"And I'm trying to fix myself, or heal, or I don't know, but whatever it is, it is working and I'm sober. My mind is getting better."

Dylan almost laughed, but he wasn't cruel. The man genuinely seemed to believe a weekly meeting at a coffee shop would keep him from the bar, which was asinine even for a guy who'd once showed up to their school in nothing but boots and a blanket. Dylan's father had never once tried to improve his mind, and he'd never put down the bottle, save the three days he spent in the fancy place Tyler sent him. But if all small-town accounts were true, he'd been sober for months. The accomplishment was enough to keep Dylan's laughter at bay.

"So, these Wednesday meetings are working?" he asked.

His father nodded. "Wednesdays are local, and my sponsor is at this one, which helps. Mondays are in Salmon Creek. Tuesdays and

Thursdays are online. Your brother bought me that fancy laptop for those, and Friday is usually at the Denny's in Santa Rosa, but we move around some. The weekend meetings are smaller, which I like because, you know, I'm not—" He trailed off, and Dylan knew his mouth was open. He closed it.

"What?" his father asked, defensive.

"You go to meetings every day?"

He blinked. "Well, yeah. I'm a drunk, son. What'd you think, Wednesday coffee and a muffin was gonna fix that?"

Dylan did laugh that time, and his father smiled, meeting his eyes again. Eye contact must be part of sobriety too, because his father had looked him in the eye more in the past five minutes than he had most of his life.

Sliding over the other bag from the center of the table, Dylan tore into the muffin before taking a bite. He closed his eyes and let the cinnamon transport him somewhere less tangled.

"They're good, right?" his father said, as if he'd just discovered a place the whole town already adored.

Eyes still closed, Dylan confirmed approval with a thumbs-up.

"How's things going at the inn? Tyler tells me Levinson left you half."

Dylan opened his eyes, reminding himself he was still with his father, and as much as he wanted to believe the man would stay clean, there was little history to support that expectation.

"It's good. Fine. We're getting ready for the season."

His dad seemed to relax, balling up his paper bag and settling further into the chair. "Great. You happy to be trying something new?"

"I don't know," he said, resting a hand on his knee.

His dad winced. "Tough break with the knee."

"Yeah. Retired now, so the inn was good timing," Dylan said, not wanting to share much else. Old habits.

"Change is good," his father said, seemingly out of nowhere.

"Is it?"

"I think so." He patted the table.

"Okay." Dylan shoved another piece of muffin into his mouth and washed it down with lukewarm latte.

"I bought a plant for the kitchen. I'm into plants right now. Learning about sunlight and stuff."

Dylan nearly choked.

His father laughed. "I know. Lame."

He shook his head, trying to swallow. "No. Not lame. Plants are great."

"I'm trying."

"I see that."

He looked up. "Yeah?"

"Yeah." Something like hope swelled in Dylan's chest, scaring the hell out of him. Plants or not, he had history with this man. Ugly, neglectful history.

"I should go." Dylan stood, the scrape of the chair jarring against the jazzy background music. His father stood quickly too.

"I'm assuming you've talked to Tyler about this?" Dylan asked. "He's really the one you should—"

"I have." His dad's eyes welled.

Shit.

"Good. Well." Dylan looked everywhere, anywhere else but at his father. "I'm glad things are better and you're . . . working on yourself."

His dad reached for his arm, and Dylan instinctively pulled away. Their father had never physically taken anything out on Dylan or Tyler. He'd never been violent, just a void.

"I'm sorry," his dad said.

Dylan nodded and left the Roastery without looking back. Unlike Nikki, Dylan didn't live in a Harlequin. A cozy coffee shop scene didn't erase years of emptiness, and Dylan wasn't a hero in anyone's story but his own. As if the whole of Bodega Bay could read his thoughts, he checked his phone and found six text messages.

Son of a bitch.

Chapter Ten

*H*aving found the cabinet with the cookbooks, Clara pulled everything out, including the loose recipes. Flipping through the yellowed pages, she thought it might be lovely to incorporate some of her grandparents' recipes into their offerings for new guests. Edith's banana bread or Cedric's chili would be a fantastic way to keep their spirit alive. She would share that idea with Dylan over takeaway later.

Clara opened one cookbook to find the quote "You, as the cook, must bring soul to the recipe," written in her grandfather's now-familiar script. Or maybe he gave the cookbook to Edith as a gift, and the words were his own. Closing the cookbook and dusting the spine, she again missed these people she'd never know. There was a distinct energy in the kitchen. The more time she spent in the space, the more Clara imagined them milling about or rushing out the door with breakfast in hand. She wondered if they sat in the formal dining room for dinner or sat, as she and Dylan did, on the couch by the fire. Wherever they spent their meals, cooking and their kitchen seemed to play an important role.

Clara had once sat in a hotel kitchen after a performance. The manager was a fan of her music and offered a tour. After giving her a behind-the-scenes, the chef made her a crème brûlée. She remembered thinking he was giving her a gift by cooking for her. Watching someone else make dessert was the extent of Clara's cooking experience. She liked food, but she'd never known it to have a soul. Deciding not to dwell on what she could turn into another of her shortcomings, she moved on to another cabinet.

Reaching for a binder and two books toward the back, Clara nearly hit her head when the front door slammed.

"Clara?"

"In here." She finally reached the last book and pulled it close.

"We have a small problem," she heard Dylan say, behind her now.

"Well." She pulled her head from the cabinet to find him tense, arms folded. "I have figured out a way to scan these recipes, so I'm in a problem-solving mood, as long as it doesn't involve more paper or endless rolls of paper towels. Seriously, did they have a fear of running low on paper towels?"

Dylan rolled his neck. "Are you finished? Because we have a real problem."

Clara furrowed her brow. "You know when a man has been avoiding their business partner, it's not best to lead with grumpy." She set the books on the counter. "And you said we had a *small* problem. Should I order takeaway?"

He shook his head. "Everyone knows."

It took Clara a minute to shift from recipes to Dylan's declaration, but then she remembered. "Our kiss?"

"Yeah."

"How is that possible? It's been—"

Dylan held on to the counter opposite her. "Tyler texted me, asking us to have dinner tonight."

"Is that—"

"At the Branches' place." Dylan sounded far from the casual guy he'd been up until then, and Clara wondered if he was overreacting.

"Who are the Branches? Are they significant?"

"Are the Branches significant?" Dylan scoffed. "Christ, where to start? I should have never—" Instead of finishing with what Clara read as regret, he pulled a beer from the fridge, took a sip, and leaned on the opposite counter like he was about to relay a battle strategy.

"Pay close attention, because they're expecting us for dinner in a half hour." He grabbed a few paper towels and pulled the cap off their refrigerator Sharpie. "When I say these people will eat you alive, I'm not exaggerating."

"Your family?"

"Yes," he said, nearly done with his diagram. "They're the best, but it's . . ."

"Complicated?" Clara asked, trying not to smile.

Dylan pushed the paper towels in front of her and stood at her back, one arm on either side of her, as he started at the top.

"My brother is Tyler Pace. You met him."

"And Drake Branch, his business partner," she confirmed. "He's Iron Man because of his prothesis."

"Right. Tyler's engaged to Jules Bartlett." He pointed. "Jules has a daughter named Bella from her first marriage."

Clara nodded. "She plays the trumpet. I think Rusty mentioned her."

"Drake is Jules's brother. He's married to Millie Hart, who's a romance author." Dylan dragged a finger down to another box he'd connected with a dotted line, and she tried not to notice the flex of his arms or that he smelled like pastries.

Focus, Clara. He'd helped her out with Carter, and this dinner or fallout from the kiss was clearly important to him.

"Which brings us to Nikki," he said.

"Met her too," Clara said.

"We all call her Auntie N, like *The Wizard of Oz.*"

"Isn't it—" Clara made to correct.

"Yeah, but we put our own spin on it."

"Good to know." Clara looked over her shoulder at him. "These are excellent details." Her eyes found him, hoping her confidence would ease his obvious tension.

Dylan cleared his throat. "Auntie N, as you know, owns Swept Away Books."

"Been there." She made a check in the air.

"Yeah," he said, obviously not a big romance fan himself. "Moving on. Nikki is best friends with Drake and Jules's mom, Muriel Branch, and their father is Chuck Branch."

"Got it."

"You do?"

"So far."

"Drake and Jules have a younger sister, Sistine." He pointed to the boxes on the edge of the paper. "She's married to Cade, who owns a brewery with his brothers. Sistine runs a knitting store in Petaluma. They just had a baby."

"Sweet."

"Sweet? This is serious, Clara. In a few minutes, they're going to—"

"Eat me alive. Understood. Question: will they all be there? At once?"

"Not Sistine and Cade, but the rest? Yeah. It's going to be like an interrogation, and you're not—"

Clara stood. "So, the small-town adage about news traveling fast is accurate."

"Afraid so." Dylan ran a hand over his face and checked his watch.

"How much time do we have?"

"We need to leave in fifteen."

"Right. Let me quickly change my top and grab some lip balm." She went to the stairs.

Dylan followed. "Clara, I'm not sure you know what's about to—"

She turned, two steps up and nearly eye-to-eye with him, and set a hand to his shoulder. "Deep breath."

Despite the impending doom of his expression, Dylan closed his eyes and did as she asked. When he opened them, she was grateful her existing skill set meant she could handle one dinner with the nosy people in his life. Clara brushed aside the hair at his forehead.

"I've thanked you for the Carter thing, right?"

"You have." His jaw clenched.

She exhaled because the man was beautiful. "Now, I'm sure your people are intimidating, but believe me, I have this."

Dylan made to speak, but she held up a hand.

"Trust me. I learned word association as a child specifically to remember first my parents' important friends and then the people who traveled in my circles. I've been to countless events to schmooze people and help fund the arts."

"Yeah, but you've—"

She put a finger to his lips. "Trust me," she said softly, before running upstairs.

When she returned, she grabbed the book from the table. "Before we go, let's check in with Cedric and Edith."

"Clara, we don't have time. You don't understand. They know I kissed you, they smell blood, and they're going to—"

"Eat me alive. Yes, so you said, but did you know—" She flipped through the pages. "Oh, here's a good one." She handed him the book, hoping a change of subject would ease his tension.

"Is there an instrument you would love to play?" He met Clara's eyes. "You're hilarious."

She gestured to the book, and he kept reading to himself.

"The French horn?" he said moments later. "I had no idea Edith played an instrument."

"And my grandfather didn't want to play anything," Clara added.

"'Listening is enough.'" Dylan held up the book. "Levinson's answer, right there."

"I saw," she said, thrilled to be back spending time with Dylan. She would analyze or tamp down on that feeling stuff later.

"Is there an instrument you would love to play, Clara?" he asked, as was their practice after reading her grandparents' answers, a smile still on his lovely face.

"Why, yes," Clara said, batting her lashes. "I actually play the cello and a little piano, but not well."

"I play a little piano myself," Dylan said, seemingly more relaxed. She smiled. "Do you, now?"

Dylan gave an animated nod like a kid, and there on the edges, his playfulness returned. "'Chopsticks' and I go way back." He carefully closed the book.

"'The Celebrated Chop Waltz.' A classic," Clara said.

"And here I thought it was 'Chopsticks.'"

She shook her head. "Euphemia Allen composed it when she was sixteen in eighteen . . . seventy-six or seven, under a male pen name, of course. It was the only piece she ever composed."

"Huh. Well, it's a mic drop. Why bother with anything else, right?"

Clara agreed.

"And I played the recorder in sixth grade," Dylan added, leaning against the doorjamb now. "There aren't a lot of musical paths to take in a small town unless you're going to leave."

"And you never wanted to leave?" Clara asked, knowing she was asking more than the prompt in her grandparents' book and ready for Dylan to deflect.

"I've left. Nearly two months in New Jersey for bootcamp. A couple of vacations."

Clara nodded.

"There's a lot to see and do out there, but I like living here," he continued. "It's always felt like the right place to be. Speaking of, we need to get going."

"Feel better?" Clara slipped into the coat he held out for her.

"Oddly, yeah." Dylan wrapped a scarf around his neck.

"Edith and Cedric illuminate the journey every time." Clara tied the belt of her coat, realizing it was heady to finally be prepared for something in this town. She couldn't wait to meet the famous Branch family and anyone else who helped shape Dylan.

Trust her? This had nothing to do with trust. He sure as hell hoped she knew what she was doing, because he'd successfully ridden under the town-gossip radar for years for a reason. Closing Clara into his truck, Dylan tried not to think about the way her long black sweater barely hung off one shoulder. He ran a hand over his face and rounded the truck to the driver's side with a sigh, because he really didn't need her bare shoulder right now. Going through Levinson's stuff and working on the inn was one thing, but in a few minutes, she would be in his world. Everything suddenly felt too close.

"You good?" he croaked. The small space of his truck was again in stark contrast to the expanse of the inn. The air between them was unpredictable inside the inn, possibly explosive in evening air.

Clara nodded. "Let's do this."

An hour later, Dylan realized he really needed to stop underestimating her. Clara had asked a few more questions on the drive over, and when they sat down with nearly all his family by blood and friendship at the Crab Shack, she was incredible.

Mr. and Mrs. Branch popped over occasionally when they weren't serving the dinner rush. Clara shook hands, made jokes about owning the inn with Dylan, and kissed cheeks like a politician. She remembered everyone's name and even asked after Sistine and Cade.

Auntie N was an instant believer in Clara's retelling how she and Dylan ended up kissing. Nikki sighed and declared Clara had taken things into her own hands and made herself "the heroine of her own story." Clara complimented the food, talked with Bella about her trumpet, and shared some of her favorite cities with Tyler. Even with her air of formality, she was warm and relatable, and Dylan couldn't take his eyes off her.

"Where were you born, Clara?" Nikki asked.

"Well, I've recently learned I was a love child conceived one summer night in Bodega Bay when my mother was engaged to my... non-birth father. As far as I know, she discovered she was pregnant, and they decided to raise me as their own. I was born in Germany."

"No shit," Jules said.

She nodded. "Dresden, to be exact. My father, or at least the man I thought was my father, is a conductor."

Nikki's eyes widened. "Like your—"

"Very ex-fiancé, yes," Clara said, knowing they'd all googled her anyway.

"Have we covered him yet?" Mrs. Branch asked.

"No," Dylan said.

"Should we—" Dylan cut Jules a look, narrowing his eyes at all of them as if that might hold them off for at least one night.

"Anyway," Clara said. "My non-birth father led several concerts during Dresden's music festival."

"Where does your birth fit into this?" Tyler asked.

"I've strayed from the question. Apologies." Clara straightened as if the mention of her parents alone brought tension. "My mom went into labor two weeks early. I was born in room 304 at the Bü-low Palais."

At their confusion, Tyler added, "It's a hotel."

"You were born in a hotel during a German music festival?" Nikki asked.

"I was."

"Wow, and I thought it was cool that my birthday was on Easter one year," Bella said.

Clara smiled, so relaxed that Dylan almost imagined she be-longed right where they were. "I love Easter," she said.

"Me too." Bella beamed.

"I was born in between performances. My father loves to say I was even an accommodating baby."

"My word." Nikki looked at Mrs. Branch.

"Where did you go to school?" Drake asked.

Clara sighed. "None of my answers are going to be normal."

He shrugged. "Like I'm normal." He held up his prosthetic arm. "Normal's boring."

"You go first," she said.

"That's easy. Bayview Elementary, Eldman Junior High, and Bay-side High School, home of the Dolphins." He pumped his fist in the air. "Your turn."

"My parents were usually on tour or on vacation. I had tutors un-til I was fifteen, and I took a test for my high school diploma."

"Wow." Drake nodded. "Different but cool."

Drake put it perfectly. Dylan's and Clara's lives were different. Beyond what instrument they played or if they had imaginary friends. They were not Cedric and Edith, but he would admit, at least to himself, he wanted her to like him as a person, wanted her to know the people important in his life. It seemed like she felt the same, which was ridiculous and dangerous, given those same differences.

"Go ahead. Tell me how sheltered and odd I am," Clara said, bumping his shoulder like she had dozens of times on the living room couch. The familiarity suddenly had everyone's attention.

Dylan shrugged. "You were homeschooled. Not sheltered."

She met his eyes, held there for a beat longer than co-owners might. "Yes. Exactly."

"Cool," Bella said.

"Well, we're happy to have you here in Bodega Bay," Tyler said, as Dylan moved off to the side of the outdoor seating to get some air.

"So, what's the deal?" Jules asked, coming to stand at his shoulder.

Dylan always liked Jules, even before she and Tyler got together, but the woman was a force.

"Deal?" Dylan looked straight out to the bay.

She exhaled, shoved her hands into her coat, and waited him out.

"There's no deal. We are business partners. Her ex-fiancé arrived at the inn. Clara kissed me as a screw-off to him. She told you all the story."

She shook her head.

Dylan looked over. "Clara didn't kiss me? Okay, we can go with your version."

"No. I'm sure she did, but something's up," she said, and Dylan almost laughed.

"Any idea what it is?"

"No." Jules shook her head, dark ponytail swishing along her shoulders. "Do you think Levinson knew you and Clara would hit it off?"

"We're not . . . hitting anything off."

"Sure, but something's up. Right?" She glanced at Millie, who was now at Dylan's other side. *Unbelievable.*

"Whatever it is, I'm here for it," Millie said, bumping his shoulder.

"Something's definitely up," Drake added, standing next to his wife.

"Okay, what are we doing here, circling the wagons?" Dylan moved back toward the table and found Clara.

"Time to go," he whispered close.

Clara grabbed her bag.

"We are co-owners of the inn. That's it," he announced to the group. "We are not an arranged marriage, secret lovers, or any other weird-ass stuff you people can come up with."

"One question." Nikki raised her hand. Dylan sighed. "Is there perchance only one bed?"

"It's an inn! There are lots of beds," Dylan said.

Clara laughed.

"You'd be surprised," Nikki said. "Sometimes rooms, beds, things disappear. Clara?"

"I can assure you there are multiple beds, and we are not sharing any of them."

Nikki harrumphed. "Now that's a shame."

"Wow. Thank you all. This was a perfect deep dive into our town. She now knows who to steer clear of."

Clara shook her head. "Not true. You were all lovely. Funny and lovely."

"We're leaving now," Dylan announced.

"You and your business partner?" Jules asked.

"Yup." He made to put an arm around Clara but caught himself before anyone noticed.

"Let's have dinner soon," she said to the group. "At the inn, once the tile is finished."

"Have you lost your mind?" Dylan said.

"We'll be there," they all called out in concert before he could rescind the offer.

They drove back in silence. Dylan didn't know what to say. A woman he'd met a little over a month ago had now charmed the hell out of his family. They knew little about each other, and somehow he was impressed and proud to have her with him, which was nuts. He glanced over, and she was smiling.

"I think it went quite well. They're all charming people." Clara pulled her coat tighter.

"They can be. You were . . . not bad."

"Why, thank you, man of many words." She warmed her hands. "Like I said, lots of practice. And they were fun." She glanced out the window and then at him. "I had fun."

Dylan nodded as they parked in front of the inn. "Yeah. Me too."

Why the hell did this suddenly feel like a date? They were co-owners and now part of the town gossip mill. If he'd refused dinner, it would have made things worse. They faced it head-on, and now everyone knew Clara. It was simple, completely professional. Walking her to the door under those circumstances did not qualify as a date. And still, there they were, standing on a dimly lit porch, making small talk.

Before giving himself a chance to notice the moonlight and Clara in the same breath, he opened the door and followed her inside.

"If you're not tired," she said, locking the door, "do you want to go over my thoughts on the appliances and some amazing recipes I found?"

"Sure." Dylan pulled off his gloves and stuffed them in the pocket of his coat. Nervous? He was nervous now?

Clara took off her coat, revealing her damn shoulder again.

"Could you start a fire?" She smiled.

"Bored already with your new hobby?"

"You're faster." She folded her arms.

Dylan exhaled. Christ, she was breathtaking, pink cheeks and hair windblown. "Yeah, fire. I'm on it." He went into the living room.

Clara brought her laptop, sat on the couch, and there they were again.

He'd managed two whole days away from their routine, and now, as he joined her on the couch, Dylan said, "You asked me about my parents." He didn't know why he was speaking, but there was something in the way she shared herself. It was like a gift she offered without strings. Dylan had never met anyone, even those closest to him, who compelled him to share, but shutting himself off from Clara was starting to feel selfish. "Parents drank a lot when I was young. My mom left. My father was, or is, or could be again, a drunk. He's in my life on a limited basis, and as of tonight, you've met everyone who is truly important to me." He exhaled. "And that's all I've got."

"Thank you." She met his eyes. "Sometimes parents suck," she repeated his words back to him. "But seriously, thank you. I'm sure it's because we're uncovering these things about my family, but sometimes it's like I'm the only naked person in the room."

Dylan raised a brow, willing his feeble mind not to go anywhere near a naked Clara imagining.

She closed her eyes. "Poor choice of words."

"Debatable."

She laughed, handing him two sheets of paper, and pulling up something on her laptop. They spent the rest of the evening talking about shelf liners and curtains. When Dylan finally went to bed, he decided if in another world he had been on a date with Clara Mar, he'd had a great time.

Chapter Eleven

lara lay staring out her bedroom window at the iridescent moon over the bay. It was so quiet. No sirens, no muted parties in the next room. She read an article once about a celebrity who carried the noise of the city on her phone to help her sleep when she was away from home. The noise of any city was part of the allure—high-up windows, blaring horns, and blinding light muted behind heavy curtains—but Clara had never been anywhere as quiet as Bodega Bay. There was beauty in removing oneself from things, she thought before falling asleep.

Waking the next morning to the distant sound of birds, Clara realized she'd always connected with sound. Where New York and London were cacophonies, the music of Bodega Bay built much like a solo amid the orchestra. Subtle at first, the sounds grew throughout the day until, before she knew it, the delightful noise swelled all around. She loved so much about this town, and yet her happiness seemed to tick on an imaginary clock toward the end of June.

Clara had always led a solitary life. Alone wasn't lonely, she often told herself, but until recently, she never realized loneliness was born of longing. There had been a constant flow of other musicians, assistants, and audiences in and out over the years, but those people were part of her job, not her life.

Maybe alone was never lonely because she had never longed to be somewhere, or with someone. As the sunlight tiptoed across her freshly made bed, Clara felt certain if she walked away from Bodega Bay in June, she would know true loneliness.

She'd had such a wonderful time with Dylan, his friends, and his family last night. Somehow, the pain of her own world before arriving in Bodega was acute by comparison. Holding tight to her black cardigan as a breeze from the open window swayed the silk of her pajama bottoms, Clara again slipped out of her be-present mindset and wondered now at the approaching finale.

She'd left Paris determined to uncover the truth about her family. Clara never believed in sweeping things under the rug. She pulled things apart for a living, notes and melodies from people long before her time. She faced things and asked questions. That characteristic put her on an airplane and agreed to her grandfather's project, but somehow her reliable old life, lies and all, felt easier than the unknown of the happier one her heart had started to compose.

Clara cared about this inn, the people of this town, and the man downstairs most likely making coffee. What was she supposed to do with all of that caring at the end of June? She certainly couldn't swallow it all back and climb under some warm duvet in another glamorous city. It was too late, wasn't it? She was already changed, and she still had months to learn more, grow closer. Perhaps she'd always thought of herself as facing things because nothing she'd ever faced felt like this.

Having dressed, Clara pulled a green silk envelope from the safe in her room. Opening the delicate basket-shaped button on the front, she emptied a red enamel pin in the shape of a tomato. She touched the bright green leaves at the top and wondered how her grandmother chose this one or if it too was a gift from her grandfather. Upon closer inspection, there was a small gold chain attached to a tiny strawberry. It reminded Clara of the pincushions seamstresses used backstage to repair dresses or costumes, but instead of functional, this was, like the hairpin, delicate and darling.

Swapping out her black cardigan for a yellow one she'd found in the closet of her practice room, Clara pinned the tomato in place and decided she liked her grandmother based solely on her taste in clothes, her treasures, and that waterfall picture which now sat framed on the dresser in Clara's room.

Bonus points to Edith wanting to play the French horn, Clara thought, as she descended the stairs for another day. Halfway down, she realized she was still in slippers and didn't care.

Catching her reflection in the entryway mirror, she liked what she saw. Yellow suited her, although her hair was longer than usual. Reaching up, Clara braided the front of her hair and tucked it behind her ear. She would be cleaning out the kitchen today, so she had returned Edith's treble clef to the safe for now. Having skipped her morning skin-care routine, Clara had opted instead to splash water on her face before applying only moisturizer and sunscreen. Closer to the mirror now, she touched her face, holding her chin higher before turning away to head down the narrow hallway that led to the kitchen.

As she shuffled through the doors, she stopped short again at the sight of Dylan, this time in an apron.

"Is that your grandmother's sweater?" he asked, looking up from the large silver bowl resting at his elbow as he stirred.

Clara nodded. "It's incredible what's in those closets."

"Looks good on you."

"Thank you." She twirled before pouring herself some coffee and sitting at the counter across from him. Dylan scanned the paper in front of him and grabbed a pan from the cabinet over the stove, one Clara had yet to organize.

"So . . . some early morning baking?" she joked.

"I liked your idea about the recipes and wanted to try some out. And when I grabbed coffee at the Roastery they had overripe bananas they were getting rid of, so this"—he poured the contents of the bowl into a narrow pan—"is Edith's banana bread. Well, at least I hope it is."

Clara leaned forward. "Looks delicious."

"Right? Wait until I bake it." Dylan put his creation in the oven.

"I didn't know you could bake," she said, sipping her coffee.

"Firehouse. We make all the food ourselves, including baking."

"I'm sorry"—Clara tilted her head—"are you telling me all fire-fighters, the rescue-hero people in the red and navy, also bake?"

Dylan grinned. "Most of them, yeah. Although we all kind of have our specialty. Some make delicious salsa or spaghetti sauce. It depends."

"I am stunned."

"I can tell." Dylan laughed and set the timer.

"I thought you were coast guard search-and-rescue."

"I've done both." He hung a towel over his shoulder.

He was the picture of domestic bliss, and Clara was grateful she was sitting down.

"The fire department here is pretty small, and I'm only one of two paramedics, so I picked up shifts when I could."

She studied him while he washed up. "This is a whole different thing for you," she said.

Dylan shrugged. "I guess. Some of it's the same. Less adrena-line."

"Do you miss it?"

His brow creased. "Sometimes."

"Are you worried the inn won't be successful? Once it opens, I mean."

He shook his head.

"That's it? Just, no?"

"I watched your grandparents run it. I know the town, the tour-ist market. It won't fail."

Clara sipped her coffee as the smell of sugar and bananas filled the kitchen.

"You like banana bread?"

"I do. Warmed, with butter."

"Seriously?"

She nodded, and Dylan took the butter from the refrigerator.

"Are you making the chili next?"

"I thought we could make it together."

"We, as in *me?*"

Dylan laughed. "Don't look so scared. You're the one who invited half the town over for dinner once the tile's done. We can make it then."

"Oh, like in a few weeks." Relief was instant. Clara didn't cook and certainly wasn't quite ready to learn yet another new thing. She preferred to bask in the victory with his family and spend more time watching Dylan in the kitchen.

"We could do a practice run before then," he said.

"You know, I'm really enjoying takeaway."

He laughed.

Once it was out of the oven and cooled enough to slice, Clara ate two pieces of banana bread with butter and found another reason to appreciate her business partner.

Dylan stopped by the coast guard station later in the day to clear out his old locker. Having enlisted a year after high school, this job and the fire department were the only real work he'd ever know. There were the reason he went to bed on time and got up early.

Leaving was inevitable at some point, and sure, there were days the job sucked, but most days were challenging in a way nothing else could match. The routine and adrenaline were so much a part of who he was, and even though he felt secure about the inn, as he packed up his stuff, something deep in his chest pulled toward who he was before everything changed.

"Got your doctor's report," Captain Brett Vance said, standing in the locker-room doorway.

Dylan zipped his bag and met the man's eyes. "Yeah, well, we knew this day was coming."

"I suppose we did, but I always imagined I'd convince you that a desk job wasn't such a scary option."

Dylan laughed.

"We'll miss you." His captain was rarely emotional, but like so many of the people in Dylan's life, they had history, and Dylan had been putting off coming in because he knew signing off for good would be rough.

"I'm not going anywhere. I just won't be out there anymore."

"I know, but you're the best to come out of here in a while."

"I appreciate that, even if it's a lie."

Both men laughed, as their usual banter kept them from facing the swell of change.

"Congrats on the inn," Brett said.

"Thanks. It's coming along."

"I'm sure you'll bring it back better than ever. You've always gone after what you wanted."

"Yeah?"

His captain nodded. "Looking forward to seeing it reopened, but if you get tired of making muffins, I'm not filling the desk position for a few months. I'll wait for you."

"What's with everyone and muffins?" Dylan shook his head. "Banana bread. I made banana bread this morning. Get with it."

"Oh, well, forgive me." He held up a hand in mock defense.

"I'm not desk material. You know that." Dylan hoisted his bag, his knee feeling stronger every day. "Fill the position. Someone needs to keep this place in line."

"Don't tell me what to do, kid." Brett grinned, and Dylan realized the man had been one of many fathers throughout his life. "See you at Movie in the Park once this weather warms up?"

"I'll be there," Dylan said, tripping over his words. He'd almost said "we," "we'll be there." What the hell? "I'll need my popcorn fix by then."

"You got it. I'll let Patsy know. She'll be elbow-deep in caramel corn next month."

"Can't wait." Dylan swallowed and adjusted his bag, unsure how to end things.

As always, his captain took the lead. "Don't be a stranger," he said, patting Dylan on the back before heading back to his office.

"Never." Dylan waved overhead, the weight of his gear—and the press of what used to be—squeezing his chest.

"Change is good," his dad had said. Dylan knew in theory he was right, but goodbyes always sucked in practice.

Back at the inn and unsure what to do with his gear bag yet, Dylan left it in the truck. Standing in the entryway, he noticed the staircase carpet was done, but no Rusty. After checking the kitchen, he looked at his watch. It was only three, but maybe Rusty had another job.

Clara had changed the flowers in the vase, purple now. Grabbing an apple out of the new bowl in the kitchen, he then checked out back and in the study for Clara. Nothing. He was about to call upstairs when he heard the music and smiled.

There she is. He'd thought about getting his laptop to review some quotes for new appliances. He could do that while she practiced. The music grew, and the urge to see her pulled Dylan to the foot of the stairs.

"I practice alone," she'd said, and Dylan wondered if that was by choice or simply because no one was ever there to watch unless she was under a spotlight.

Quietly climbing to the second floor, and grateful for the new carpet to soften his footfall, Dylan told himself if the door was closed, he would leave her alone. He wasn't sure which room she'd made her practice room, so he followed the music, which sounded at first like the low moan of a house settling at the change of season. As he got closer, the sound opened up with a hint of sadness he now knew was part of the cello's distinct sound. The door at the end of the hall was open, and Dylan leaned against the wall where he could watch Clara and her instrument.

Eyes soft and nearly closed, her body seemed almost molded around the cello. One hand sat high near her face, gliding and sliding through the strings, while the other hand holding a bow, he learned from her weeks ago, moved back and forth. The rhythm was at first so intimate and private Dylan looked away, but not for long.

Peeking in the room again, he wondered if audiences were mesmerized every time they saw her perform. When Dylan was in high school, Tyler took him into the city to see the symphony. They were performing music from all the *Star Wars* movies, and it was a great experience, but he didn't know anyone on stage that night. He knew they were talented, but knowing a person and then watching them perform was different.

Her fingers paused at one string and then another along the giant curve of wood. The expression in her hooded eyes seemed like a moment of ecstasy with enough charge to power the whole inn. Her playing spilled into the hall and wrapped itself around Dylan like a spell. Transfixed, he could not look away from her body, the strain and release.

He found her fascinating when she was propped on a stool in the kitchen, wearing her grandmother's clothes. This was next-level, and so not what he needed in his effort to maintain distance.

A pang of something like envy crept up his spine. Dylan had never wanted to play an instrument in his life. He agreed with Levinson—listening was enough. But watching Clara consumed by something she clearly adored, it was no wonder music was her escape. She seemed so comfortable, safe.

Dylan was so enraptured—and slightly turned on, if he were honest—he hadn't realized she'd stopped playing and was now looking at him.

"Is everything okay?" she asked softly.

We're business partners, and you're absolutely leaving this small town the minute the first guest walks through our doors, but I'd like to kiss every inch of you on the small frilly bed right there. No, Dylan thought, things are definitely not okay.

He cleared his throat. "Yeah. Everything's fine." He stepped into the room as Clara set her cello aside, pulled on the yellow sweater, and walked toward him. There was a small red pin he hadn't noticed before at her collarbone, and he knew it was another treasure Edith left behind. Why did everything from the past look good on her? More urgently, why did everything about her mess with his head?

"How did it go?" she asked, inches from him now.

Dylan couldn't speak.

"Cleaning out your locker?"

"It was fine," he managed, breath and pure desire doing battle for balance. She met his eyes, and despite everything he knew about women passing through and opposites not attracting no matter what the stuff Nikki peddled in her shop said, Dylan wanted her, and God help them both, she seemed to want him too.

He closed the last bit of distance between them and realized his captain was right: Dylan often went after what he wanted. Not the best trait to have, considering his want at the moment came with a slew of complications, but ignoring every warning siren in his head, Dylan gently touched the side of her face. Clara closed her eyes, and when she opened them again, meeting his, they stood on that sharp edge between one and more.

He could walk out right now. Blame it on watching her play or on a tough day saying goodbye to his old life. She would understand. They could order egg rolls for dinner and keep things the same, but every time he made to step away, pure want kept him right there holding her gorgeous face.

"Can you do me a favor?" he asked.

"Sure," she said, eyes warm but alert, like she was ready for anything.

"Tell me you look at everyone the way you look at me." Dylan took in a slow breath, his thumb gently brushing her cheek. She was made of so many things he would never be, but when he looked at her, there was so much that fit. He'd never felt so noticed, understood, like he did when he was with her, and that had him swallowing what felt like fear. "Or that wanting to kiss you again is some . . . side effect of working together, your family history, anything."

Clara smiled, bringing her hand to rest on his.

"Tell me you don't feel this," he demanded, less than a breath from her lips. "It's all me, and I'm losing my mind."

Inhale. Exhale. She put her other hand on his chest.

"Clara? Help a guy out here."

She shook her head. "I'm sorry."

"Excellent." Dylan let go and stepped back. Arms at his sides now, there should have been more space between them, but somehow, she was still right there. "I'm sorry is a perfect start. Good."

Clara laughed and returned to him, draping her arms around his neck. "I would love to help, but I'm afraid I can't this time."

Dylan met her eyes. The room was darker than most of the inn, making the sparkle of her blue deeper, the heat between them more desperate.

"Shit." He looked to the ceiling as if that would transport them back to where he thought of her as Levinson's granddaughter and his one-word answers got under her skin. Somewhere less close, less dangerous.

"But if you think this is a side effect, I'm willing to control—"

Before Clara could remove her arms from his neck, Dylan pulled her close, hoping to squash any doubt his hesitancy might have sparked in her.

"Now may be a good time to point out the last time you kissed me you said I'd owe you one." Her hands caressed his neck. "Will I owe you two now?"

"Technically"—he leaned in, trailing his mouth along the curve of her neck—"if I *need* to kiss you this time, we're even."

Clara let her head fall to the side, giving him more access before she whispered, "If you *need* to kiss me?"

Nodding as he moved along her collarbone, Dylan returned to her mouth and—

"Knock, knock. Anyone home?" Rusty called up the staircase.

Dylan's heart jumped like someone had doused him with freezing water, and Clara flew back so fast she nearly knocked over her cello.

Rusty called out again, and they were both left standing in a room much larger than it felt a moment ago. Clara was on one side, Dylan on the other, and every reason why almost kissing her was a bad idea sat between them like weighted boxes.

"Be right down," Dylan called out.

"You two aren't canoodling up there, are ya?"

Clara laughed before putting a hand to her mouth.

Dylan shook his head. "The man is an idiot."

"He's lovely. Eccentric, maybe." She pulled the sweater around her body.

Turning to leave, he looked back. "Probably best we didn't—I mean it's not—"

Clara said nothing for a beat and then barely nodded as things grew uncomfortable and complicated.

Dylan grabbed the doorjamb to leave as if anchoring himself to keep from changing his mind and kissing her despite Rusty, despite everything.

"Hey, Dylan." He turned, her voice sounding like his own. "I still owe you one."

Jesus Christ, he needed to go.

"Jiminy Christmas, could one of you love birds get down here? I need a thumbs-up on this carpet."

Dylan chuckled. He couldn't help it. The man was ridiculous.

"You better get down there." She turned back to her instrument.

"Sorry to interrupt your, um . . . practice."

"Really? That's your line to roll this whole thing back?" She shook her head. "Get out of here." She smiled, and he was gone, the longing still there, but the logical part of his brain, the part responsible for survival, gave a deep sigh of relief.

He'd been able to convince himself it was physical, but Dylan knew Clara now, knew what her details meant for his heart. A safe distance had always been his MO, but she had a way of sidestepping his sarcasm and getting him to share more than he had with anyone else.

They were stuck together for a few more months. All the more reason to keep things as they were. If he kissed her, he would want to do it again. Want and women were not parts of life Dylan paired. Ever. As his father used to say after their mother left and Dylan or Tyler had tucked his drunk ass into bed, "the one who cares most always loses."

So, while Dylan would admit to having fun with Clara and wanting to kiss her again, all of it stopped in June. He saw no other scenario. The bricks and mortar of the inn were solid, his tangible next step. Clara had a million places to be, options to take, and he knew she would take all of them the second she was ready.

Dylan had one shot to stay in the town he loved, tend to a legacy he was proud to continue. Losing that chance because of a temporary distraction was not an option. Not even if that distraction was a woman who played so beautifully, Dylan almost imagined he could have it all.

Chapter Twelve

"Why is there so much *stuff*?" Clara asked an empty kitchen, her head buried again, this time in the cabinet next to the pantry. She'd saved this one for last because it was filled with board games, a wooden box, and a piñata that looked like it was from the 1970s.

"Intriguing nostalgia, Grandfather, but what exactly does one do with an old piñata?" she said to herself before yanking with both hands. The paper sculpture ripped free as Dylan and Rusty wheeled in the new refrigerator. Clara flew back, nearly colliding with them.

"Whoa." Rusty steadied her with one hand while the other remained on the fridge Dylan had tilted on the dolly.

"Oh, god. I'm so sorry." Clara straightened, awkward in her overalls, the latest fashion find from her grandmother's closet.

"Mornin', dungarees," Rusty said with a big smile.

Clara must have looked confused, because he pointed to her overalls.

"Oh." She set the mangled piñata on the counter and glanced down. "Is that what you call these?"

"Sure. That's what they are," Rusty said, helping Dylan ease the new appliance off the dolly. "What do you call 'em?"

"Overalls," Dylan said, walking behind Rusty with an armful of plastic. He stopped and took in Clara's outfit but didn't meet her eyes, which was helpful since they were back to co-owner status after their almost-kiss in her practice room. Dylan wasn't avoiding her this time, and they still had their routine, but they were definitely dancing around their attraction, Dylan seemingly trying to ignore it, and Clara no longer willing to entertain it alone.

"Nice," Dylan said, stuffing the plastic into the trash.

"Thanks." Clara finished wiping down the shelves and closed the cabinet.

Dylan and Rusty had finished the tile while Clara coordinated repurposing the old appliances, save the antique gas stove, which was staying, and, of course, the blender. Bodega Bay's police department had picked up the microwave yesterday, and a moving company was due to arrive shortly to pick up the old refrigerator for the elementary school's teacher breakroom. Clara had ordered a rug for the kitchen floor and new curtains for the window above the sink.

"Did you know Cedric and Edith had a spoon collection?" she asked, stacking the board games on the new table in the sunroom area so she could go through them later.

"I did not," Rusty and Dylan both said together.

"It's pretty extensive." Clara leaned back on the counter, sinking her hands into the deep pockets of her overalls. She'd never worn anything so comfortable, save pajamas.

"I see the piñata didn't make it," Dylan said, glancing at the counter.

"Clean-out casualty."

"Probably just as well," he said, their eyes holding again in that way Clara was learning to accept as normal.

She held up the mangled piñata by one foot, and they both laughed at the sad creature before she stuffed it into the trash bin.

"Well, aren't you two a couple of gigglemugs today. Any updates on non-business things you'd like to share?"

Dylan groaned. "You gotta stop with this stuff, man. First dungarees and now the giggle-thing? It's not even noon," he said, expertly avoiding the inquiry.

Rusty swatted his shoulder. "Smart-ass. Clara, have you ever heard of a gigglemug?"

"I have not, but it is an interesting word," she said, continually amused by what she and Dylan had started calling "Rustyisms."

"See?" He gestured victory. "Clara thinks I'm interesting."

Dylan shook his head. "She's being polite."

"Nah. I'm fascinating." With a chuckle, Rusty pulled some remaining tape off the new refrigerator.

Having never thought about appliances until recently, let alone shopped for them, Clara was back to learning a lot and enjoyed being part of the kitchen refresh with its bright tiles and new stainless-steel shine.

"Hey, speaking of business info, I hear you have a performance coming up," Rusty said.

Clara had turned to wash her hands and tried not to stiffen at the mention of anything outside Bodega Bay. "I just confirmed today. How did you—" She dried her hands and turned.

"Small towns," they said in unison.

"But I didn't tell anyone." Clara searched her mind and landed on a conversation she'd had with Griff at the Roastery that morning when she'd picked up breakfast. He and his brother were originally from San Francisco. Clara complimented their new morning buns, and he mentioned they'd "borrowed" the recipe from a great bakery in the city. Somewhere in the conversation, she *had* mentioned briefly returning to San Francisco for a performance.

"Griff?" she asked.

Rusty nodded.

"Unbelievable." She leaned against the counter.

"It's fun to have someone else in town to gossip about," Rusty said.

Clara shook her head. "I'm happy to help. Your intel is correct. I'm performing one night with the San Francisco Orchestra for charity in a few weeks."

Dylan nodded like she was adding something to the grocery list.

"Well, that's great. Getting back in the saddle, so to speak," Rusty said.

"Something like that." She smiled.

Clara obviously hadn't told Dylan about her performance. She hadn't told anyone, and despite a twinge of something like guilt, she knew she wasn't obligated to share anything with him. She'd told him so much already, but her professional life was different.

"All right, enough flirting with your client," Dylan said. "Or I'll have to start a rumor."

"Yeah, the day that happens." Rusty snorted.

Both men left the kitchen, and Clara, suddenly wanting to ground herself in the work, slid the old refrigerator from its spot and stared in surprise, as Dylan returned with a giant wrench.

She pointed to the wall, and Dylan stepped forward to peek behind the fridge.

"Huh, it's still there."

"How did it get there?" she asked, as they stepped back from craning to look in the small space.

"I helped your grandfather install this fridge years ago when your grandmother decided she wanted an automatic ice maker." He set the wrench down, seemingly enjoying the memory. "She scheduled the cleaning people. He handled the delivery, so things overlapped, and they were 'at odds,' as he put it."

Clara grinned at the image of the couple, whom she now knew better than she knew her own parents, bickering. Her grandfather was right, the kitchen must be the heart of the inn, because unlike the study, which was filled with vacations and achievement, these cabinets and corners seemed to house details of everyday life.

"He told me to pull off the packing, plug it in, and throw everything out while he took a call in the other room. Before he left, he handed me ten dollars and said, 'Leave no trace. This kitchen needs to look like you were never here. We have guests arriving later,'" Dylan continued, having affected a distinguished older gentleman's voice. "I was sixteen." He shrugged. "And full of myself, so I—"

"Wrote your name behind the refrigerator," Clara said, still smiling at the *Dylan was Here* scrawled on the back wall.

"Technically no trace. Not visible, anyway." Dylan went behind the refrigerator with the wrench, emerged moments later, and pulled the old fridge free.

"No trace, but still there," Clara said, watching him.

"I guess." He met her eyes. "You make it sound deep."

"There's some symbolism there."

"It's a wall." Dylan looked away, but not before she saw a flash of the teenager he might have been.

Rusty returned to the kitchen, and he and Dylan went back to work, while Clara opened the wooden box she'd found with the board games. It was empty except for a VHS tape. No label. Grateful they hadn't yet donated the old TV and video equipment from the study, Clara brought the box to her grandfather's desk.

A mystery for another day, she decided, mostly because the chances of anything about her father or grandfather being on a tape, forgotten in a cabinet with a sad-looking piñata, were slim.

Returning to the kitchen, Clara tackled one more drawer brimming with birthday candles and patterned paper napkins before sorting through the board games.

Later over pizza, Dylan suggested they take a break from questions, answers, and the past to play cards with one of the six decks she found with in the kitchen cabinet.

Sitting crisscross on the floor by the fire with her now-favorite blanket and him with his back against the giant chair and his knee extended, Clara tossed a throw pillow off the couch, and Dylan instinctively tucked it under his knee before dealing the cards.

They were nearly back to comfortable now, as if the almost-second kiss had never happened. Clara supposed it was for the best. She would rather spend the next few months with him like this than complicate things, even if the words he'd whispered into her neck that afternoon still played on a loop when she was alone in her room.

Despite their mutual attraction, they *were* friends. They knew things about one another, shared things. Clara supposed it was inevitable living in the same space, but sometimes it felt like much more. She was used to being alone, so it was surprising to find she enjoyed having someone with whom she could share her day, her stories. Specifically, she enjoyed the someone presently concealing his cards like a professional poker player.

Maybe they had been thrown together for a reason other than the inn. People met and started a life all the time, didn't they? Sorting her cards and taking her turn, Clara decided she was being ridiculous. The last time she'd had a genuine friend, one who hadn't wanted her solo, her seat, or her talent, she was nine. Since then, her relationships, romantic or otherwise, were transactional.

It was possible she wasn't built for the collaboration of a proper relationship, and she certainly had no experience in the certainty of her growing feelings for Dylan. Nothing in her life offstage had ever been this joyful, this easy. Even if these months with him were the exception, it was more likely he was fighting his attraction because he wanted the inn, and not her.

He might want her in his bed, but that wasn't a relationship. Studying him now, the fire highlighting his furrowed brow as he plotted his next move, Clara didn't think she could have sex and leave it there. Even if he offered, she knew him too well, cared more than she should already.

Dylan put down a card. Clara tried to concentrate on winning instead of crawling across the floor into his lap and kissing him until the sense of sadness at missing out again dulled to a whisper.

Dylan cleared his throat. Their eyes held, and she realized it was her turn.

"Problem?" He raised a brow.

She shook her head and scanned the cards. "No. Sorry, I was distracted."

"By?"

"No comment." Clara placed four cards on the rug in front of her.

"Interesting." Dylan grinned, eyeing her cards.

"Not really." She met his eyes again, her want thankfully back to simmer, and dropped her last card. "Gin."

Dylan tossed his remaining cards on the pile, shaking his head. "That's three in a row. You could at least let me win one."

"Not a chance," Clara said, gathering the cards.

"This is—"

"Humbling? Enlightening?" she asked, eyes wide as she shuffled.

"Humiliating." He leaned back on his hands.

"Another?" she asked.

He narrowed his eyes at her and then resumed his posture. "Yeah. Why not? This time, I'm totally kicking your ass."

She smiled. "Pretty sure you said that last game."

Removing the pillow from under his knee and tossing it aside, Dylan leaned over the cards with newfound determination. Clara beat him twice more before heading up to bed with game night and their shared laughter confusing her even more.

Dylan stretched out on the couch, not ready to go to bed and still replaying the fierce look in her eyes right before she kicked his ass for the fifth time in a row. The woman pulled him closer without even trying.

Business and nothing more. Dylan's new mantra scrambled for purchase amid another night with Clara. He reminded himself she had other priorities, bigger things like a scheduled performance she hadn't bothered to mention. People on a break or looking to make a change didn't schedule performances. No matter how she looked at him or how much he wanted to skip the kiss and ask her to bed, she was leaving. Eventually. He needed to focus, torture himself for a few more months, and get on with his life.

Dylan closed his eyes and pretended he couldn't still smell her in the room. Opening them seconds later, unable to stop thinking about her, he marveled at how being adored all the time might be a bad thing. Clara was the definition of world-renowned. He'd heard the phrase a few times in his life, usually people hyping up their bowling prowess or a cake they'd baked, but Clara was the real deal. She wasn't a celebrity. She was world-renowned, highly respected in her profession. Women didn't walk away from high-profile careers to run an inn. And why was he even entertaining this crap?

When she first arrived, she seemed in pain among the boxes and memories she'd missed, but now she was becoming part of the space. Levinson would have loved her, Dylan thought with a touch of sadness. Clara seemed truly alone in her life, but maybe she liked it that way. After all, if she wanted to be around people, Dylan was sure there were plenty waiting in line. He never imagined when he'd met her fighting with a bookcase that he would not only be interested in her life, but would care.

Was he a little pissed she hadn't told him about her performance?

"Get a damn grip, man," he mumbled, turning off the living room lights and going to his room. Moments later, a knock hit his door. When he opened it, Clara stood in the small hallway in blue pajama bottoms and a T-shirt with "Cell-O" across the front.

"Would you like some ice cream?" she asked.

"Nice shirt."

She looked down. "Thank you. Jules and Bella dropped it off while you and Rusty were picking up the refrigerator. Ice cream?"

"No. I'm good." No way in hell he was eating ice cream with her in pajamas without his head on straight.

"Suit yourself." She took a few steps toward the kitchen and turned back. "Is something wrong?"

"No." Dylan shook his head, deciding he was acting like an idiot. "I'm up for ice cream." He followed her into the kitchen.

"Chocolate chip or mint chocolate chip?" Clara asked, holding two pints up while still facing the open freezer.

"Whose is whose?" he asked, not looking at her ass. He was not looking at her ass.

"I bought them today. They're unclaimed."

"Thought you didn't eat ice cream."

"And I thought you were more agreeable at night." She shook both pints overhead.

"You pick."

"We're sharing?" she asked.

"You want your own?"

"I might." She held both pints, still indecisive.

"Celebrating your win?" Dylan asked, still not deciding.

"Wins. You meant to say wins, right?" She set one pint on the counter and took down two bowls from the orderly cabinet next to the shiny new refrigerator. "I've dragged you into the kitchen at midnight because I wanted to say I'm—" She glanced over from scooping the ice cream, eyes on his chest before she shook her head.

Dylan looked down. "I was going to bed."

"So was I. I thought you'd grab a shirt."

"I don't sleep in pajamas."

"Do you sleep completely . . ." She handed him his bowl.

Dylan grabbed spoons and gave one over. "Naked? No. I don't sleep naked. Well, sometimes." He took a bite of mint chocolate chip. "It depends," he said, over a mouthful.

"On?" She met his eyes.

Dylan took another bite. "Wow. This is good."

Clara laughed. "I'll assume you're pleading the Fifth."

He nodded and kept eating.

"Anyway, I think I caught you off guard by not telling you about my upcoming performance."

"It was not on the color-coded calendar you insisted we create," he mocked. "Just saying." He took another bite.

"It's one night."

Dylan shrugged. "You still have a life, Clara. One I'm sure you're eager to get back to. No need to explain." He hoped like hell he sounded convincing.

"Right. But . . . I wanted to explain," she said, moving the ice cream around in her bowl with the spoon.

"Why?" he asked. "Because we are . . . friends?"

She paused mid-bite before finishing the ice cream on her spoon. "I suppose we are. Friends." She hung on the last word, held his gaze, and there it was again. Except this time the look in her eyes had the added benefit of ice cream on her lips and absolutely no bra. What in the hell was he supposed to do with that? Ice cream or no ice cream, he could not be friends with this woman. There was no way.

Clara set her bowl on the counter.

"Where are you going?" Dylan asked.

She walked into his room and returned to toss him his T-shirt.

His spoon clinked in the bowl, but he still caught the shirt. Laughing, Dylan set his bowl down, and put both arms through the fabric.

Clara's eyes were in her bowl.

"You're safe now," he announced. "Fully clothed."

"Good. Helpful." She looked up. "Thank you, *friend*."

Dylan resumed eating his ice cream, a grin still teasing his lips at the realization it had never been about not liking his body.

"What? If I were standing here without a shirt on, are you telling me you wouldn't be distracted?"

He met her eyes and said the stupidest thing a man trying to avoid the obvious heat between them would say. "If you were standing here without a shirt on, I wouldn't be eating ice cream."

"Are you saying if I had my shirt off it would be an invitation, because that's—"

"I'd be too busy begging." Yeah, he should have never left his room.

Clara snorted. "Shut up."

"No? I thought it was a pretty good line."

"You're ridiculous."

"True." He extended his bowl when Clara returned to the freezer. She gave them both another scoop.

Once again, they stood in the still of night, nothing but the wind through the trees out back.

"You don't need to apologize," he said after a while.

Clara eyed him. "I know I don't *need* to, but I—"

"Your business is your business."

She nodded, seeming like she wanted to say more but changed her mind.

He had no right to care about her work or when she planned to return, but the whispers of late night screwed with him, and he needed to stop meeting her in the kitchen like this.

"Great. Well, that's settled." He took both their bowls and rinsed them in the sink. "Schedule flexibility, that's what co-owners are for."

"Friends, you mean," she said barely above a whisper as she followed him out. Dylan turned to face her in the hallway outside his room. The light from his bedside peeked under the door, barely highlighting their features.

"I should have never . . . When you were practicing the other day, I got wrapped up in your playing," he said, suddenly needing to clarify.

"Occupational hazard," she said, a touch of pain in her voice as she cleared her throat. "I'm told my performances have that effect on people. Again, I'm sorry for crossing the line with—"

"Don't be sorry. I was happy or . . . willing to help but—"

"But we have a job to do and we're—"

"Different." Dylan swallowed. She was too close, nothing but the sweet smell of mint and chocolate between them.

"Exactly." She brushed past him to the staircase.

Once again in the clear, Dylan thought. And then she stopped.

"You know, I've been thinking," she said, back still to him.

"Okay." He wondered if she had another idea for the inn.

She stood in front of him again. "I don't want to be your friend."

"Thank Christ." Dylan took her mouth so fast he forgot all the reasons why he'd vowed to keep his distance.

Scrambling to finally touch in all the ways they'd been denied, he took the kiss deeper. Swallowing her moan like the best midnight dessert, Dylan lifted her closer, one hand cradling her face.

As his back thunked against the wall, Clara eased away, lifting his shirt over his head before trailing soft, open-mouthed kisses along his collar bone and making her way back to his mouth.

She gripped his neck, holding on and kissing him like she would never have enough of him. Hand at the edge of her T-shirt, Dylan found the soft skin of her stomach right as the goddamn fire alarm shrilled from somewhere in the house. His mouth still on her, Dylan put his fist to the smoke detector overhead, irrationally hoping to pound the whole system into silence. When that didn't work and the alarm grew louder, he remembered Inn by the Bay had a direct connect to the fire department. He needed to figure out where the alarm tripped and turn it off, or Bodega Bay's finest would be at the door in minutes.

When he made to pull back, Clara would not let go, moving to his neck.

"We need to—" He was having difficulty forming sentences as her hands moved to his ass.

Clara pulled away, her back to the opposite wall. "Oh holy hell," she called out over the shrill of the alarm, and Dylan couldn't help laughing. He reached for her, but she held him off. "How is this happening?" She closed her eyes. "I am *inches* from your bed."

Dylan pulled his bottom lip between his teeth, understanding the frustration, but trying to keep a straight face at her lust-filled fury. "I need to check. There might be a problem somewhere," he said.

She opened her eyes. "Isn't there always a problem? An interruption, or just stupid life."

He reached for her again, fairly certain by now that the alarm was the result of Rusty screwing around with the electrical in the kitchen yesterday, but acutely aware he was running out of time to hold off the fire department. Clara grabbed him, kissing him one last time before pulling away on a frustrated growl and running upstairs.

Chapter Thirteen

*C*lara lay on the bed, staring at the ceiling, her body still humming like a newly tuned instrument. Dylan must have silenced the alarm, but at the pounding on the front door, she realized she'd wasted the Bodega Bay fire department's time because she couldn't keep her hands off Dylan once he pulled her into a kiss she'd waited months to taste.

Not prone to superstition, Clara wondered if all of this was a sign. Seriously, what were the odds she and Dylan finally stopped circling one another and a freaking fire alarm starts blaring at one o'clock in the morning?

So instead of getting naked with her co-owner, friend, whatever the heck he wanted to call them, she was again alone in her own bed. Frustration had her stomping up the stairs like a petulant child, but it had been silent for a while now. Clara was sure the fire department was gone, and still no Dylan at her door.

Rolling over, she nearly screamed into her pillow. She knew they were right back where they started. His brain probably kicked on—hers was already offering ideas of omens and signs they would never be together—and he'd stayed downstairs. She wanted him. He seemed to want her too, but every time they got close to exploring more, something got in the way.

She understood Dylan's hesitancy and the inherent complications of mixing business with pleasure all too well, but they were preparing an inn for summer, not negotiating a corporate merger. Eventually falling off to sleep, she wondered why it seemed like everything was stacked against them.

When she woke the next morning, Clara skipped their usual morning routine. She dressed quickly and stayed away from the kitchen. Dylan might have thought she was asleep by the time the fire department left. He may have had to do some work to fix the alarm and that's what kept him from coming for her after the fiasco was over. Clara didn't care what the reason, but she knew she would run screaming from the inn if she had to walk into that kitchen one more time to find him with that look-don't-touch expression on his face.

She was in no mood to roll back the memory of his tongue in her mouth or her hands on his ass in favor of Dylan discussing his latest baking adventure. Unable to take any of it anymore, Clara grabbed her coat, ate breakfast at the Roastery, and picked up the new yellow kitchen curtains she'd ordered from the hardware store.

Gus rang up her purchase, and Clara learned he was looking to buy a bigger bed. Last week, when she'd picked up paint for Rusty while they finished the kitchen baseboards, Gus shared that he and his wife Regina rescued another puppy and Regina insisted on letting it sleep on their bed, so today's conversation was predictably about bigger bed options.

Clara didn't have the heart to tell Gus she'd never owned a bed and had spent most of her life in hotels because he would probably look at her like she was from another planet. Maybe not, but she was already feeling out of sorts and didn't need more rejection, so she shared her preferences based on hotel beds.

Small towns were different in a way Clara had once thought she would never enjoy. The way movies and television depicted them seemed so far removed from her reality that she'd never imagined being on a Main Street, let alone becoming a regular.

Everything in Bodega Bay presented as rooted, permanent. Not some long layover or an extra weekend on tour. It was giant trees, picket fences, and carved in concrete forever.

After grabbing one more latte, Clara tucked her wallet back into her bag and realized starting her day at the hardware store with Gus had chased away her foul mood. Amid all the things going on in her life and her maddening circles with Dylan, Clara found she cared whether Gus went with the Sleep Number or the Tempur-Pedic. She hoped they'd pick a name for the new puppy soon and already looked forward to an update when she visited his store again.

Taking in a deep breath of sea air, Clara again tried to stay in the present.

"Psst."

She turned to find Nikki gesturing for her to come inside Swept Away Books. She pointed at her drink cup.

Nikki shrugged. "Bring it along."

For a second, Clara thought she might feign urgency or even receive an imaginary call to escape the situation. Nikki was a notorious matchmaker who already had her eye on Clara and Dylan's story. Superfluous details like Clara's eventual return to performing or Dylan's dogged focus wouldn't deter someone like Nikki. She was probably the only person who would ever believe Clara and Dylan would have enough in common for conversation over dinner, let alone a lifetime.

Not that Clara was looking for a lifetime. Was she? Suddenly the idea of unloading half of her grandparents' inn before flying back to her life was embarrassing. What kind of person sold their past?

"You coming?" Nikki asked.

Clara nodded, finished her latte, and stepped into the romantic heart of Bodega Bay. The door jingled as it closed behind them. Clara tossed her now-empty latte cup in the bin.

"Tea?" Nikki asked.

"I"—Clara looked as if she might need an emergency exit—"should probably get back. I want to see if these curtains will work."

"Yellow is perfect for the window over the kitchen sink."

Clara must have looked surprised.

Nikki laughed. "Gus is the only man in our book club. You put a mimosa in him, and lord, the details he shares."

"I see." Clara set her bag down. "I would love some tea."

Checking her jeans for any remnants of the hardware store before sitting in one of Nikki's gorgeous chairs, Clara hoped she didn't have *I kissed the crap out of Dylan Pace again* written all over her face.

Nikki served them both before plopping herself down in the chair opposite.

"So." She stirred her tea with equal parts confidante and meddling aunt.

"So," Clara said before carefully sipping her tea. She knew this game. Keeping things superficial and polite was in her DNA. Although, the warmth of the bookshop probably had people spilling their dark secrets all the time. Not that Clara had any secrets the town didn't know already.

"Hard work at the inn, I hear."

"We have a few things we're adding in addition to my grandfather's list," she said. "The kitchen is nearly done."

"I've heard. Looks like your grandfather knew what he was doing. You two make a great team. Any chance you'll stay past the opening in June?" Nikki asked.

Clara wasn't sure what to say. Did Nikki want Clara to leave? Was she checking to see if Dylan would own the whole inn instead of some outsider? Did they still see Clara that way? She thought they liked her, but she'd thought a lot of things in her life, and she'd been wrong.

"I'm not sure." Clara sipped her tea. "I'm taking things one step at a time. Dylan gave me that advice when I arrived, and it's working so far."

"Excellent advice."

They sipped more in silence.

"You know, I remember a romance years ago. I'm almost certain it was a Nora."

"The title is 'A Nora?'" Clara asked.

Nikki chuckled. "No, dear. The author is Nora Roberts."

At Clara's blank expression, Nikki let out a deep and patient exhale before standing and going to her shelves. They were floor-to-ceiling, with multiple coats of white paint making them look like they had their own story. Nikki tilted a book and then put it back. She repeated this process a few more times.

"I think it was *Taming Natasha*."

Clara nearly spit her tea across her lap.

"You okay?" Nikki asked, rejoining her with a book.

She nodded and wiped her mouth with one of the paper napkins on the table.

Convinced Clara was all right, Nikki scanned the book's back cover. "Oh, that's right, Spence is a composer, and Natasha is a ballet dancer." She set the book down. "For some reason, I thought he played the cello like you," Nikki said, as if to herself.

Clara smiled. The woman obviously loved her store and its stories.

"Are they hired for the same production or something?"

Nikki bit into a cookie and shook her head while she chewed. "No." She swallowed. "Natasha moves to town to open a toy store."

"The ballerina?"

Nikki sipped her tea. "Spence is a single dad, a professor, and a composer."

"Wow." Clara hoped she didn't come across as humoring, but she knew a few composers, and in her experience, they didn't make swoon-worthy heroes.

"I know." She finished her cookie. "Nora spins exquisite tales." Nikki picked up the book again. "This one is old." She laughed. "Funny how we now define things over twenty years as old, isn't it?"

"Well-written music is never old. It improves through new performances." Clara met Nikki's eyes.

She smiled. "Same with romance. Everyone always nods to the literary classics, but romance has staying power too."

"I'm sure." Clara took an offered cookie.

"Do you read?" Nikki asked.

"I do."

"Romance?"

"I'm afraid not," Clara said.

Nikki furrowed her brow.

"I don't have anything against romance," Clara explained. "I've just never read one. I like murder and mystery mostly."

Nikki laughed, and Clara decided she wanted more of that sound in her life. The woman was joyful in a way life didn't always allow in people. Everyone had problems, sure, but Clara could tell Nikki was on the glass-half-full side of things.

"You probably give your heart to your music." Nikki set her teacup on the table.

"I suppose I do." Clara smiled.

"Would you play for us?"

Clara set her cup down with a clatter. Nikki didn't seem to mind, and Clara glanced up to confirm she didn't expect her to pull out her cello right there.

"My book club. It's my turn to choose this month's book, and I'm thinking." She appeared off in her romantic mind again. "I'll pick *Taming Natasha* and—if you agree, of course—I would love for you to play during our social hour before the discussion."

In her entire life, Clara had never been asked to play in such a casual and delightful way. She'd had schedules, detailed discussions about set lists and lighting, rigorous practices behind closed doors. Since she'd been old enough to hold a bow, no one had ever said, "Clara, play something for us." That's what Nikki was doing, wasn't she?

"Oh, I'm sorry. You're certainly not some musician for hire," Nikki added into the silence.

Clara blinked. "Actually, I am a musician for hire, and I would love to play for your book club social."

Nikki clapped her hands together. "Excellent. I'm excited already. Last month we read *Beach Read* by Emily—oh, never mind, you won't know her either. Anyway, Ruth brought in little buckets and shovels, and we drank umbrella drinks. I'm hoping to top her this month. Not that we're competitive."

Clara stood, collecting her bag. "Of course not."

Nikki walked her to the door. "I like you, Clara Mar."

"Thank you. I like you too."

"See you at the carnival tomorrow?" Nikki called, once they were back on the street.

"I am looking forward to it," Clara said, counting herself lucky to have spent time at Swept Away Books.

"'Please order three new glass panels for the china cabinet and all-new glassware. The inn should have the following on hand—'" Drake looked up from the list Mr. Levinson left in his will. "This is a lot." He handed the list to Tyler, who was sitting in the BP Glassworks studio, expensive shoes propped on his desk.

"Nice." Tyler sat up. "Strange he's ordering glassware postmortem for an inn he'll no longer run, but I appreciate the business." Tyler looked to Drake, who nodded. "Any idea when he wants this?" Tyler asked Dylan.

"He's dead."

Tyler looked confused. "So?" He held up the list. "This is unconventional already. I thought he'd give us a deadline too." Tyler scoffed. "What's up with you?"

Dylan crossed his arms. "Nothing's up with me. Can you guys do it, and how long will it take?"

Drake reviewed the list with Esteban, his glass-blowing master, who asked about Dylan's "new project" and grumbled about his daughter Hazel's new "college boyfriend."

"Give me two weeks for the cabinet panels, and the rest in . . ." Drake looked at Esteban again. "A month."

"You sure?" Dylan asked.

"Yeah, we'll make it work." Drake gave the list to Tyler, who handled all their invoicing.

"I like the stickers." Dylan gestured to the arm prosthesis Drake had sported since a motorcycle accident nearly killed him several years ago. The thing was sleek and state-of-the-art, save the two glitter flowers now near the wrist joint.

"Thanks." Drake looked at his hardware. "Bella."

"She told him he needs to get used to stickers in case Millie has a girl." Tyler grinned.

"Or a boy," Drake said. "The kid will glitter bomb anyone we welcome to the family."

"Hold the hell on, Millie's pregnant?" Dylan looked at both men.

"I told you," Tyler said.

"You did not."

"He did," Drake said. "I was there."

Dylan shook his head. "I would have remembered."

Drake put his arm on Dylan's shoulder. "Could be you're distracted."

Tyler waggled his eyebrows and Dylan shrugged off Drake.

"Whatever. Congratulations, man. That's exciting."

Drake beamed. "Thanks. Early days, but we're pretty psyched."

"Apparently, so is Bella," Dylan said, patting Drake's shoulder.

"Speaking of psyched," Drake said, looking between Tyler and Dylan. "How's the inn?"

Dylan shrugged. He knew they'd both been way too quiet. "Good. It's . . . We're almost done with the kitchen."

Both men nodded.

"Heard the fire alarm went off last night," Tyler started.

"They do that," Dylan said. He tried not to replay exactly where he and Clara were headed before the alarm because it only added to his frustration.

"At one in the morning?" Drake asked.

Dylan laughed. "Just stop. You two are bad at this. Rusty replaced some overhead lights, left something loose, we're all good. We're still on schedule for the reopening."

"And then?" Drake asked. "Once you reopen?"

Dylan shrugged, ignoring the turn in his chest. "Not sure. I'm hoping Clara sells me her half. She likes it here, but she's not exactly Bodega Bay material."

"I don't know about that. Rumor has it she's playing her cello for Nikki's book club."

Dylan furrowed his brow. "Is this in the town chat thing? How the hell do you know? I don't even know, and we live together."

Tyler held up his phone.

"Nikki posted it five minutes ago," Drake said. "Town chat is a valuable tool."

"Let's circle back to the living together bit," Tyler said. "How's that going?"

"Seriously?" Dylan sighed. "Didn't we cover this already? We're co-owners."

"Huh. Okay, so no more kissing." Drake took out a twenty-dollar bill and handed it to Tyler.

"What the fuck? You're betting on me?"

Tyler shrugged. "Not specifically you, but Drake was convinced you two were more than business partners."

"We are . . ."

Tyler and Drake looked up like it was Christmas morning.

"Not. We are not anything more than co-owners."

They both deflated, and Tyler slid the money into his wallet. "Told you. If they were doing anything more than sorting boxes, he'd tell me."

Why the hell had Dylan kissed her again? Like the first one for her ex wasn't enough to keep him up most nights. Now he had last night in the hallway, his hand sliding up her—

"Dylan?"

He glanced at Tyler, who sported the all-knowing brother face that annoyed the crap out of Dylan on a good day. This was not a good day. "There is nothing here. You're wasting your precious gossip time. She's a solid goodbye."

"Damn. You could write country songs," Drake said.

"Just being realistic."

"Do you care about her?" he asked.

Dylan scoffed. "I . . . sure. But it's not what you think. She's trying to find her past, and she's not some snob from Paris. She's funny and—" *Safe. Warm. And surprisingly caring. She's talented and wants to learn, which is such a cool combination.* Dylan cleared his throat. "I'm helping her get through the next few months so we can transition this thing."

"Have you heard her play?" Tyler asked.

"I have."

They were both back to watching him.

"She's brilliant. But I'm not lured in by her music, if that's what you're thinking."

"Siren reference, nice," Tyler said.

"Did you say siren?" Jules clomped into the studio in full fishing gear.

"Right on cue, Jules," Dylan said.

She flipped him off and sipped her giant thermos of coffee before leaning to kiss Tyler.

"You know, our dad used to talk about sirens a lot." Dylan held his eyes wide, hoping to piss her off. "Luring men until they crashed on the rocks and died. It's Greek."

"I know what sirens are." Jules swatted him with the stack of papers in her hand. "Has anyone ever thought to consider why sirens are evil? They're not human, and they lure their prey with song."

Speaking of, Dylan thought, his brother looked at Jules like she was in a ball gown instead of smelly waders.

"The angler fish," Jules continued. "Fun fact, it lures its prey by pretending to be the prey, like a spy, and then bam"—she clapped her hands together—"it turns into the killer. No one's writing about those guys and scaring people."

"Sirens kill men," Dylan clarified.

"And there you have it." She pointed at him. "Enchanting women singing alluring songs to trap their prey. Pure evil. And yet, jumping spiders have mouths that morph into the head of an ant to confuse unsuspecting ants. Why the hell didn't Homer write about those guys?"

Tyler grinned and raised his hand. "Quick question. Where is this deluge of knowledge on predatory creatures coming from? Has Bella finally picked a science project?"

"She did. Dressed to Kill," Jules said, spreading her hands wide.

"Nice," Tyler said as Bella came into the studio.

"We're going to be late." She hugged Tyler before stopping in front of Dylan, who lowered his head to offer his cheek. She kissed him and hiked her backpack. "Your business friend is playing cello at Auntie N's book club. It's going to be epic."

"I just heard." Dylan smiled despite his crappy mood.

She glanced at him quizzically. "Is she your girlfriend yet?"

Dylan shook his head.

Bella nodded. "Did you strike out?"

"Not even up to bat. We're friends."

"She's nice and pretty," Bella said. "And we need more musicians around here. I like her."

"Me too," Dylan said as Bella left to say hello to Esteban at one of the back work benches.

When he looked up, Drake, Tyler, and Jules were staring at him. Jules sipped her coffee.

"What?"

"You like her. I knew it." Jules held out a hand to Tyler and Drake.

Dylan rolled his eyes. "What the hell did *you* bet?"

"That you weren't just co-owners, and you liked her."

"Yes. I like her as a person."

"The 'as a person' is always interesting, don't you think?" Drake asked.

"Absolutely," Tyler said, coming to stand by his fiancée. The three of them were locked in a death stare Dylan wasn't sure how to escape until Bella, excellent kid and now savior, called from the front door. Jules gestured with two fingers to her eyes and back at Dylan to indicate she was watching him. Eyes narrow, she was almost funny.

"I love you." She kissed Tyler.

"I love *you*." He kissed her back, and Dylan looked away.

"One more time." Tyler pulled her close, and Jules laughed.

"So needy." She put her arms around his neck.

Dylan glanced at Drake, who shook his head. They'd both known pre-love Tyler and Jules. While they were happy to see them finally figure things out, their making up for lost time was sometimes tough to take.

"I love you." She kissed him. "I love you." She kissed him again.

"Mom!" Bella called from the door.

"All right, all right." One more kiss, and she was gone.

Propped against Tyler's desk, Dylan watched until his brother finally realized there were other people in the room.

"She loves me," he said, face flushed. No one flustered Tyler. He'd gone toe-to-toe with the school principal when he was only thirteen and Dylan was twelve. The guy was born into shit and had made himself the most confident man Dylan knew, but Jules undid him in seconds.

"Ya think?" Drake grinned at his dopey friend.

Tyler cleared his throat and pulled at the cuffs of his shirt. "Okay. We need to get back to work." He hugged Dylan and slid past to sit at his desk. "I'll get you numbers on this order mid-next week."

"Sounds good." Dylan bumped fists with Drake and Esteban, who had joined them when Bella left.

"Tell your delightful lady friend we all said hello," Esteban called out as Dylan walked to the door.

Dylan feigned pain and put a hand to his chest. "You too, man?"

Laughter erupted as Dylan slid the giant metal door of the studio closed. Esteban was happily married with nearly grown daughters. Millie was going to have a baby. Tyler and Jules were deep into their own happily ever after. Climbing into his truck, Dylan realized he was happy for anyone who found the love they deserved.

Dylan liked being alone. Solo, as Clara had confirmed, was easier. It was second nature to people like Dylan and his co-business owner and now twice-kissed friend. *Shit.* Their titles were getting more complicated every day.

He hadn't gone upstairs after the fire alarm because he had nothing to offer Clara, not anything to compete with what she already had, and it was too late to just take her to bed. Besides, they had three months left, and then everything would go back to the way it was before she arrived.

Chapter Fourteen

Rusty called Clara into the kitchen to show her the new wallpaper now in the sunroom while Dylan was at BP Glassworks. Clara had worked with Gus to create wallpaper from another one of her grandmother's treasures—a brooch with a miniature painting of a duck.

The piece was adorable, and standing in the kitchen with Rusty, she knew her instincts had been right—it made delightful wallpaper. Something new from something treasured. She stood in the kitchen alone, hoping her grandparents would have been proud.

After a couple of spoonfuls of chocolate chip ice cream, Clara ignored the pull to memories of Dylan and took the red-and-black flyer off the fridge. The Santori Brothers, a.k.a. the amazing sandwich guys, hosted a carnival every year. The last Saturday in March was a chance to *celebrate community and raise money for the following year's art programs at the local schools*, Clara read, as she brought the flyer into the study to put it in one of the blank scrapbooks she'd purchased to record the future of the Inn by the Bay. There was promise in a blank book, she thought, setting it aside on her grandfather's desk.

Clara was playing for Nikki's book club in two weeks, *and* she'd agreed to a one-night-only solo performance with the San Francisco

Orchestra next month. She confirmed through her manager that all proceeds from the event, including Clara's performance fee, would go to St. Jude's Hospital. She hadn't spoken to her parents, and while her agent and manager were "encouraged" by her scheduled performance, Clara did not want to discuss any further dates.

She wasn't ready to commit to anything scheduled for after the inn reopened in June, but she felt a part of things in Bodega Bay and still hoped to compose a bit more of the legacy, even if she moved on.

Clara had spent a few nights online researching best practices for inn management and had a new running list of ideas to share with Dylan. Not that they'd done much more than nod at one another in passing since they'd last kissed.

With still an hour to go before the carnival, Clara opened the wooden box she'd rescued from the kitchen clean-out and wheeled the TV and VHS player over to a plug. Sitting on the floor, she inserted the tape. As the screen turned to black-and-white fuzz, she checked the box for any sign as to the contents of the tape. When she looked up again, the small TV screen filled with an image of the inn's kitchen and a man she now recognized as her father standing at the counter. He was in a jean shirt, hair pushed to one side and still fighting to fall into his eyes. He was so handsome. Rugged like someone in an outdoor catalog.

A younger version of the grandfather she'd only seen in pictures stepped into the frame as he walked away from the camera, occasionally stopping to stoop down, probably checking to make sure it was on and in focus.

Moments later, a younger version of her grandmother joined them. Edith's hair was brown, dusted with gray, and cut chin-length. She kissed Clara's father on the cheek before sliding a slightly lopsided chocolate cake in front of him and lighting the candles with a match. There were twenty-two, Clara counted, before she reached up to turn the volume knob.

The study filled with a scratchy, hilariously out-of-tune version of "Happy Birthday" as her father mock-conducted his parents with his hands and joined in singing.

Clara didn't realize she was crying until tears slid to her neck. Her father was turning twenty-two right before her eyes on a grainy screen barely bigger than the new iPad. She wiped her tears as they finished the song on a shrilling crescendo.

Her father blew out the candles to cheers and applause. He wouldn't live to see his twenty-third birthday. She remembered that from the scrapbook in the study. The one she and Dylan decided to keep on the shelf, save for one picture of her father they removed and framed for the wall.

He grinned now through a whisper of blown-candle smoke. Clara pressed pause, as if she could stop things exactly as they were, be with all of them in that room for even a second. Pushing play again, she brushed her tears, caught up in the dance of a mother, a father, and their son.

"Okay, Toph, do you want to keep your candles?" Edith asked, grabbing a knife and pulling the cake plate over for cutting.

He shook his head, laughing. "I don't get it. What am I supposed to do with the candles if I keep them, Ma? Put 'em in a box?"

"You could show them to dates like 'Come look at all my birthday candles through the years.'" Her grandfather laughed, and her father howled as Edith shook her head and plucked the candles from the cake.

"Can we shut that off now, Cedric?" Her grandmother turned toward the camera. "Let's enjoy our time."

"Fine," her grandfather said. "Can you give Toph a kiss on the cheek first?"

With exaggerated lips, Edith kissed her son all over his face. Christopher Levinson, Clara's father, laughed as he said, "Okay. Okay."

Her grandmother was beaming when she turned back to the camera. "Enough, Cedric. Let's have cake."

He must have obliged, because the screen went to static. Clara sat on the floor of the study, staring at the old television screen, the tripping bits of black and gray, the sound of white noise. They were happy. Surely they had problems like everyone else, but they were joyful and real, so real it nearly broke her heart.

Clara was struck by how unstaged everything was, the empty box of candles still on the table, a wad of paper towels to the left. They were a family celebrating, not a group of people performing or creating an image for friends to envy. It was like someone opened the windows. Like being transferred in a time machine to a happier place. A better life.

Prior to arriving in Bodega Bay, Clara was never one to dwell on the past, or even visit it regularly. She liked moving forward, and now still staring at the static, she wondered if that was because this, what she'd watched in muted colors, was nothing like her past. She was raised to be perfect, polite, on time, and in tune. She'd never once mocked her parents, let her hair go, licked even a finger of frosting. Clara had never known she could.

"Christ." She lay back on the rug, staring up at the white crown molding before crossing her arms over her face. On a sob, Clara Mar, the granddaughter of Cedric and Edith Levinson, the daughter of "Topher" Levinson, let the swell of a life song she would never know by heart, no matter how many scrapbooks she reviewed, take her under.

Dylan poked his head into the study, prepared to once again pretend kissing Clara had barely phased him. Instead, he found her lying on the floor.

"Hey. You ready?"

She sniffed and quickly sat up, clearly crying. When Dylan stepped closer, he noticed Levinson's old TV was on. She looked at him, and her chest pulsed with tears she was obviously trying to contain.

Sitting on the floor, he pulled her into his arms. "Your dad?" he asked softly, brushing the hair off her neck. Clara nodded and sniffed again as she pulled away.

When she stood, he reached over and turned off the television. "I'll need a few minutes to get ready."

Standing, Dylan gently held her shoulders. "Do you want to talk about it?"

She shook her head. "There's nothing to talk about," she said, mouth in a tight line. "Just when I think I've gone through all of it, I find something else." She gestured to the VHS tape. "It was in that wood box behind the piñata. It's his twenty-second birthday." She held her eyes closed for a beat before opening them again. "I'm fine. Sometimes it's just so . . . incredibly sad. You know?" She sniffed.

Dylan nodded. "Twenty-two. His last—"

"Yes." She twisted the edge of her sweatshirt.

"I'm sorry." There were those damn words again. Dylan had expressed sympathy more in the last three months than he had most of his life. He marveled again at Levinson thinking Dylan could help her through all of this.

"Anyway." She straightened and stepped back. "I have cried twice on your shoulder now. Co-owner or friend, twice is enough."

He knew the chill in her tone was meant to push him away because of the way he handled the other night. Dylan was really getting tired of screwing things up.

"I thought you didn't want to be friends," he said, hoping to lighten the mood and let her know she could cry in front of him anytime.

Her brow furrowed. "I will never understand you."

"Makes two of us."

"I'm serious. One minute you're attracted to me, the next minute you're not."

"No. I am always attracted to you. I'm doing my best to ignore that because as much fun as falling into bed with you sounds, we need to get through the next few months on speaking terms."

"And if we have sex, we'll stop speaking?"

"That is my prediction."

"Why?"

"Because we know each other, Clara. Come on, you've gotta see that sex would complicate things. We're not together, and you don't strike me as the kind of woman who takes sex lightly."

"What? You think I'll want to settle down and have babies?"

Her words were clipped, and while Dylan wanted to rewind and pretend with her, one of them needed to face the reality of their situation.

"No. I think it will create problems for our working relationship."

"Our *working* relationship?" She rubbed the bridge of her nose.

He shrugged, sensing he was about to see another, less enjoyable, version of Clara.

"You're ridiculous." She shook her head and walked out of the study. "Go to the carnival without me. I'll catch up later."

"Clara, we don't have to—"

She groaned halfway up the stairs. "Oh god, Dylan. Please stop trying to play the good guy *and* the asshole. Polyphony is only interesting in music. In men, it's annoying. Pick one and stick to it."

He thought about yelling after her that things were already complicated just *talking* about sex, but he grabbed his coat instead, not even bothering to ask what the hell polyphony was or if she realized musical terminology didn't pack the badass punch she thought it did.

He was an asshole now? *Perfect.* Thrumming his hands on the wheel as he drove into town, he tried, as he had for weeks now, to figure out when he would lose interest. Clara was different every time he saw her. Tired, rested, hair clipped back, eating ice cream, and now pissed and kicking him out. Christ, there seemed to be endless variations, and he kept waiting for the one that wasn't funny or fascinating.

He was desperate for Predictable Clara, Boring Clara, or even Snobby, Entitled Clara. Given her life and privilege, she should be able to nail that one. He just needed one thing, any reason to kill the need to know her more, touch her again, or worse, offer her some foolish scenario beyond June. Nothing about this co-owner arrangement was going to plan.

Despite their obvious physical attraction, Dylan should have lost interest or slept with her by now. He should be ready and willing to have some fun for a while, kiss her goodbye, and start his next adventure as full owner of the Inn by the Bay. It was sex. He liked sex, if memory served. She wanted him, and he wanted her. They could knock this out in bed or anywhere else.

In her anger, Clara had gotten one thing wrong. He wasn't worried she would want something more. What woman who lived her enviable life wouldn't want to return at the first opportunity? There was no threat of her staying in Bodega Bay. This arrangement was the gold standard of temporary hook-up. So what the hell was his problem?

The sun was setting as Dylan pulled into the parking lot of the Santori family estate. Built into a cove, their home sat nestled deep into nearly three acres of wooded garden. There were blooms, Japanese maples, and cherry trees, all caged between massive redwoods. Walking through the gates, Dylan followed the glimmering stringed lights overhead welcoming guests toward Rex and the Roosters, Bodega's resident live band.

Dylan loved most events in his hometown, but the Santoris' carnival had been his favorite for a long time. When he was a kid, he and Tyler would save their money for months so they'd have enough to play all the carnival games at least once. There was something about the wildness of the woods and the painted faces. Back then it was magic, mystery, and a window into things beyond the stained couch in their living room.

Now, it was an escape, an echo of laughter, and a place for his town to take a break from their adult lives. Over the years, Bodega Bay had grown as a tourist town, but at its heart, it was a fishing town, a working town. Levinson was a wealthy man, a landowner and innkeeper, but he was the exception. Most of their town was made up of people on a schedule and a budget. Noticing Tyler and Jules in the crowd, Dylan walked toward his brother and realized for at least one night, Clara's polish would fit right in under the stars of the Santoris' carnival.

"What the hell is wrong with you?" Jules handed him a beer.

Dylan bumped shoulders with Tyler. "Seems to be the million-dollar question tonight. What specifically are we talking about?" They clinked bottles.

"Nikki is bringing Clara. You couldn't even drive your friend to the carnival?"

Dylan took a pull of his beer and considered his response. Telling Jules Clara kicked him out of the inn would lead to questions Dylan was in no mood to answer. Leaving Clara to fend for herself under any other circumstances made him an asshole. In keeping with the theme, he chose the latter.

"She wasn't ready and"—he shrugged for effect—"she knows people now."

At Jules's silence, he looked over, and she laughed, slapping him on the back. "Nice try. You two have a fight?"

Dylan shook his head and looked around. "Carnival looks good this year. You play any games yet?"

"Not yet. We just got here. Bella ran off with Drake and Millie to find the guy on stilts." Tyler sipped his beer.

"Fire-breather here this year?" Dylan asked.

"I believe he's down on the beach." Tyler looked at Jules who confirmed but was still staring at Dylan.

"What is your deal?" he asked.

She held up a hand. "No deal. I'm simply trying to figure things out."

"Yeah, well, give it a rest. There's nothing to figure out."

"Fine, fine." Jules glanced up at the trees overhead.

"You know, I get why you're not romantic," Tyler said, as if in mid-conversation with himself, and Dylan nearly spit out his beer.

It had taken his brother all of five minutes to mention the topic of love. A long stretch for him these days. Lately, the guy would not shut up about the benefits of coupledom.

"Who says I'm not romantic?" Dylan waved at two of his old roommates as they walked by. "Just because I'm not floating on a cloud and picking out overpriced flowers doesn't mean I'm against romance. I'm . . . wise. Like Gandalf."

Tyler cocked his head. "You're the Gandalf of love?"

"Exactly."

His brother laughed, and they clinked bottles again.

"You'll fall in love someday."

"Please stop."

"Why? It's good to discuss feelings, isn't it?" Tyler glanced at Jules.

"I love feelings," she said with a big grin.

He narrowed his eyes, and she stuck out her tongue.

"I prefer when we grunt at each other," Dylan said.

"We've never grunted at one another."

"We should start."

"It's too late now."

"Fine." Dylan exhaled. "But there's nothing to talk about right now. I'm not unromantic. I'm busy, and I don't"—he looked between his brother and Jules—"connect like you two."

"You connect with people all the time," Jules said. "Until a few months ago, you saved lives."

"*Because* I don't connect," Dylan clarified. "I can think rationally and do what I'm trained to do because I don't see them as people."

"I disagree," Tyler said.

"What a surprise." Dylan looked down the path toward the games and the smell of fried food. "Should we go in now? I'm hungry."

"In a minute. I think you're—"

"Look, I'd rather observe." Dylan tossed his empty bottle in the can near the ticket booth. "You and Jules are your own fairy tale. And it is romantic how you followed her around like a puppy and she finally stopped ignoring you. It's . . . touching."

"Aw, thanks, man. She didn't exactly ignore me. We were friends."

Dylan quirked a brow.

Tyler looked at Jules, who kissed him and left to find Bella. "Fine. Maybe the puppy part is accurate."

"Either way, it worked out. You two are an Auntie N-approved blissfully ever after." He batted his eyelashes. "I'm happy for you. Truly. But I'm not you."

"I know. But you could have your own story."

"I don't want my own story. I mean, I do, but it's not a love story. I've dated. It's fun for a while, and then the other person wants something I can't give or—"

"Leaves?"

"Do not start," Dylan said, wondering how they'd gotten on this topic.

"Have you talked to someone about this?" Tyler asked.

"You mean like a shrink?"

Tyler nodded.

"No. I don't need to pay someone hundreds of dollars an hour to tell me Mom and Dad were unstable, codependent, toxic drunks or whatever other label you want to throw at it. Or I don't share my feelings because I don't feel safe." He shook his head. "Let's get tickets."

They walked to the ticket booth, and Dylan would have gladly discussed anything other than the current topic. Purchasing his tickets and putting an extra twenty in the donation box, he stepped aside for Tyler, who did the same, except his donation was a lot more.

"That's pretty good," Tyler said, folding the tickets into a stack.

"I know. I'm all self-helped up. Instagram."

"You have Instagram?"

"No. Kathy's kid is a dancer. She was always showing me clips from their dance studio on Instagram."

"Your friend at the fire department with the"—Tyler gestured up his arm—"dragon tattoo?"

"Yeah." Dylan rolled the strip of tickets around his finger like he'd done when he was a kid and tried to pretend he didn't miss Clara, hadn't looked forward to going with her to the carnival.

"Instagram has mental health clips?" Tyler asked.

"Kind of. They're more like quotes and 'did you know' things. She used to tell me things I needed to work on."

They stopped near the food stalls.

"She was the therapist I never had," Dylan mocked.

Tyler seemed intrigued. "Isn't she divorced?"

"She is, and she's been dating Emily from the hair salon for almost a year. They live together."

"Huh. Too bad." Tyler got in line for barbecue.

"It's not. It's great. Besides, isn't it bad practice to date your therapist or someone from work?" Dylan flinched, remembering his argument with Clara.

"That only applies if you're not tasked with finding your soulmate in a town with exactly five single people."

Dylan laughed and changed the subject as Jules and Bella joined them in line. *Soulmates.* He didn't believe in those. The topic had come up several times before with Nikki, and Dylan still didn't buy the idea of souls searching for and finding their other half. "This stuff is best left to the fictional fairies," he'd declared several months back. Nikki had rolled her eyes and banned him from her bookstore for an entire weekend.

Dylan believed in love. He just didn't believe "fated mates " was anything more than one of the scripted signs in Auntie N's store. Genuine love required effort and sacrifices Dylan wasn't willing to make, which put him squarely in the single category. A single inn owner, attracted to a cellist playing at being an inn owner. People had to be made of the same stuff to be soulmates, two parts of a whole, right? If that was the case, he and Clara were about as far away from soulmates as two people could get.

Chapter Fifteen

*C*lara stood under stringed lights and giant trees with a handful of paper tickets while Nikki and Mrs. Branch chatted with some people Clara recognized from town and others she had never seen before. Tucked behind a blanket of clouds was a nearly full moon, and Clara wondered if it might rain. It hadn't rained once since she'd arrived, but she imagined something kept everything green in Bodega Bay. The carnival woke her stomach with smells of butter, sugar, and barbecue. Turning toward the arched entry, Clara was reminded of Narnia or *A Midsummer Night's Dream*. It was spectacular. Especially since she'd never imagined small towns with anything more elaborate than a pop-up tent. Reaching to touch the vibrant ribbons hanging from a tree near the ticket booth, Clara wondered how much more Bodega Bay would teach her about places she'd missed while she was busy touring the world.

Leaving Nikki and Mrs. Branch to socialize, Clara milled about the illuminated wooden food stalls, her stomach growling at the promising smells of firewood and spices. As she walked further onto the property, the path wove around several red-and-black tents resembling those Clara had once seen on a book cover in an airport. Each tent housed a game—floating rubber ducks, targets, bean bags, rings, and a spinning figurine. It was hard to take everything in, let alone make sense of a place and event she'd never experienced before. Wadding the tickets Nikki had given her into the outer pocket of her bag, Clara found a bench tucked under a tree and took a seat.

She shouldn't have called Dylan an asshole. Her language and demeanor were not appropriate, and she'd replayed the whole thing after she'd all but kicked him out of an inn he half-owned. It wasn't professional, but the push and pull of whatever coursed between them was maddening. One minute it seemed like he wanted her, the irrationality of their situation be damned, and the next he was looking at her like she was aimless and so far from the realities of his world that even if he wanted to touch her, he couldn't reach.

Dylan was right about one thing. Sex between the two of them would never be "just sex." They did know each other. They cared, and Clara knew from experience "just" anything was far easier without caring. It was possible this whole thing had nothing to do with sex, and the feelings they were juggling meant more than anything physical.

Maybe the inn with Dylan was something she'd longed for her whole life. Warm fires, stability, a sense of belonging. Somewhere along the way, contentment had settled in her chest alongside a man who'd been a stranger mere months ago. It made little sense, but no matter how much they tried to ignore or rationalize things away, it was the most real thing she'd ever experienced.

Clara understood performance. She'd lived most of her life beneath a spotlight. What she and Dylan had was not a performance. There was still a small chance it was temporary attraction, lust even. Maybe they were lonely and searching for something, although she found it hard to believe Dylan needed anything he didn't already have.

The band stopped playing somewhere in the distance. Clara tightened her coat to the breeze as it hummed through the trees. When she looked up, Dylan carried two large rainbow puffs of cotton candy as he parted a crowd in line to play a game.

They could have been anywhere—at a ball in a romantic city,

queued up for a sold-out show, or waiting for the best bagel. Surrounded by sounds and flashes, she was suspended in an unimaginable moment with a man she could never in a million years have composed.

He handed her a cotton candy and sat on the bench, and warm soap and sugar played with her senses as he rested back, his shoulder to hers.

"Rumor has it cotton candy is a superfood."

She glanced over as he pulled a piece of pure sugar and put it in his mouth like a kid.

"Wow." She eyed her own cone. "That is simply not true."

Clara looked up through the trees, pinching the top of her rainbow cloud until she could feel the sugar granules.

"Not a cotton candy fan?" Dylan pulled another piece from his cone and held it out.

"I can't say I've tried it."

Dylan put the offered piece in his mouth. "No one snuck this up with the butler or something when you were little?"

She laughed. "I did not have a butler."

He shoved another piece into his mouth. "Doorman?"

"Sometimes."

"Concierge?"

"There you go. And yes, sugary treats were forbidden when I was a child." Their eyes met. "And I rarely partake as an adult."

"You eat ice cream," he said, immediately ushering in new memories of their late-night kitchen meetings.

"That is . . . new." She swallowed.

"So, you're open to trying new things." He held another piece in front of her.

Clara shook her head. At his pleading eyes, she opened her mouth. The confection dissolved instantly on her tongue. Releasing his fingers, she licked her bottom lip.

"There. Happy?"

"Yeah, I am. I didn't know I needed that image until this moment. If the whole brilliant cellist thing doesn't work out, you should consider candy porn."

She smacked at his shoulder, and they both laughed until their eyes held, his dimple teasing like a mischievous child.

"You still pissed?" he asked.

She shook her head.

"I'm not trying to be an asshole or poly-whatever."

"Polyphony. The coinciding combination of two or more tones or melodic lines. Comes from the Greek word meaning 'many sounds.'"

"And you thought you'd break that out for our first fight?"

Clara rubbed the bridge of her nose. "Weak, I know."

"More like a power move. Your grandfather would be proud. Do you know any other Greek?"

"Μου λείπεις"

"Is that an insult?"

She shook her head. "It's how they say 'I miss you.' It's the name of a piece I once played. The translation is more like 'you are missing from me.' I thought it was beautiful."

"The piece or the words?"

"Both," she said.

At Dylan's silence, she glanced back at the animated crowd. "Is this an annual carnival?"

"It is."

"What other annual events does Bodega Bay offer?"

He sat back, legs crossed at the ankles. "Well, let's see. There's the Fishing Festival that kicks off the season. Easter Egg Hunt. A couple of music festivals—maybe three now?" He ate a few more pulls of cotton candy, looking up as if trying to remember. "Christmas Concert and Shopping Village," he continued. "Bread and Butter Days, which is an event we do with Petaluma. That one's a big draw. Everyone dresses up like dairy. Your grandfather sponsored a float every year."

"You dressed up like dairy?" Clara asked, imagining a younger Dylan.

"He sure did," Nikki said, standing in front of them with an older man whom Clara knew immediately was Dylan's father.

Dylan stood, nearly dropping his cotton candy.

Dylan had never wanted anything he cared about to be anywhere near his dad, so watching him greet and then take a seat next to Clara was surreal. The urge to snatch her up or hide something precious was only a dull roar in the back of Dylan's mind, left over from his childhood.

Precious. The realization had Dylan stepping back. Clara was precious, which meant nothing other than he recognized her as a person. Christ, he was starting to sound asinine even to himself.

She was important to him. He could admit that. He had feelings he wasn't ready to sort out, and at the moment, his father was sober and polite, and Clara seemed to be enjoying herself. Glancing over his shoulder, Dylan found Tyler monitoring things too. His brother raised a brow in question, and Dylan shrugged. For the first time in either of their lives, their father was at a community event acting like any other part of the community.

Nikki laughed, snapping Dylan back to the conversation.

"Oh, I'm sorry. Did you two want to—" Clara made to stand.

"Don't be sorry," his father said in a gruff tone Dylan imagined was a stark contrast to the careful and melodic way Clara was used to being addressed upon meeting new people. "Stay," his father said. Clara remained seated and scooted over to make room for Nikki.

Dylan felt like he'd been punched. How was it so easy for a man who had drowned his feelings in a bottle most of his life to ask a woman so far out of his world to stay with him? Dylan should have said something, but he stood staring at the three of them as if watching a carnival show.

"Have you heard this story, Dylan?" his father asked.

Clara glanced over, laughter making her eyes even more welcoming.

Dylan swallowed and stepped closer. "Which story?"

"Ms. Mar just finished telling me about the time a goat ran onstage during a concert at Carnegie Hall," his father said, still chuckling.

Dylan's eyes went wide. "Actually?"

"I was there," Clara said, still smiling as she pulled a piece of cotton candy and ate it like a pro.

"Darn thing was part of a—what'd you say it was again?" his dad asked.

"Performance art."

"Right. Some guy dancing around with paint and goats. You believe that?"

Dylan rested a hand on the back of the bench. "I think I do."

Clara glanced up at him.

"It's too weird to be made up," Dylan added.

Nikki laughed. "I think I'd like to see some of this performance art."

What the hell? Was he trapped in a sitcom, or the movie where the kids switch parents?

"You two seem like a good match," his father said, out of nowhere.

Dylan tried not to react, because Nikki was smiling.

"I mean like business—a good business match," his dad said, trying to backtrack, which Dylan appreciated.

"We are finding our way," Clara said, and instantly the suggestion of them as a match elevated to something formal.

"Good to hear." His father glanced at Nikki, who patted Clara's hand. "I like her."

Dylan wanted to say he didn't give a shit whether or not he liked her, but again, the man sat there so earnest and so damn sober, Dylan couldn't quite access his usual anger or indifference. Right when he made to search deeper for something dismissive to say, his father and Nikki stood. "Welp, it's been nice talkin' with you, Ms. Mar."

"Clara, please."

"I like the sound of Ms. Mar, but your first name is pretty too. Clara," he said, like he was learning a new language. "Yeah, that's pretty."

"Okay." Dylan patted the back of the bench, handing his cotton candy to Nikki. "You two are off then?"

"We are," his dad said. "Off to read a couple of magic stories to the kids over near the rose garden."

Clara's eyes lit with interest.

Dylan furrowed his brow. "You're reading? To children?"

His father chuckled at the obvious shock. "Yeah. Tyler's got me volunteering at the library weekdays so the librarian can have a lunch break. They're sponsoring story time for the carnival."

"And *you're* Story Time?" Dylan clarified.

His dad nodded.

"They like how he reads all the different voices," Nikki said.

When the hell had these two become buddies? Dylan wondered.

"Well, don't want to be late." Dylan's dad made to put his hand on Dylan's shoulder but changed his mind. Good, Dylan thought, but then felt guilty.

He was struggling to understand this version of his dad. Hell, Dylan was struggling to understand everything these days.

At his silence, Nikki kissed his cheek and did the same to Clara.

Dylan extended his hand to his father. He would replay the moment later and never understand why he'd done it. His dad seemed stunned at first but quickly gripped it with his own.

"Good seeing you too, son."

"Yeah, don't get in trouble."

His father sniffed. "I'll do my best." Squeezing Dylan's hand once more, he waved to Clara, and both he and Nikki walked off.

Dylan joined Clara on the bench. She offered him some of her cotton candy. When he shook his head, she paused as if trying to convince herself it was okay to break the rules and put another piece in her mouth. Dylan found the contemplation intriguing.

Glancing over, she licked her thumb, and Dylan recognized the mischief dancing in her eyes. It was the thrill of any new experience, any first time. It was intriguing how a woman so worldly—Dylan knew for certain she would leave his ass in the dust navigating any international airport—could seem to relish something as simple as sugar at a small-town event.

"Have you ever been to a carnival?" Dylan asked.

"I have been to . . . Mardi Gras." She tossed the rest of the cotton candy in the trash as they both stood. "Does that count?"

"Yeah, I think so. I heard Mardi Gras is off the hook. When were you there?" he asked, as they walked toward the crowds of people.

Clara looked around. "Well, I had a performance. Technically I was working, but my room had a balcony, and I watched the revelry."

Revelry? Christ, this woman needed a deep-fried Oreo, stat.

"Okay. Well, if you're interested in continuing your cotton candy string of bad behavior, I recommend we hit the photo booth, make some faces, and then eat fried food."

"Why the photo booth?" Clara asked.

"It's . . . a thing people do. They go to carnivals, take pictures, and throw them up on the fridge."

"Before the inn, did you have photo booth pictures on your refrigerator?"

"No."

"Why not?"

"Because I'm not into it." Dylan hadn't grown up in a magnets-on-the-fridge house, but he still saw the value in funny faces.

"Oh, well, me neither." She grinned and walked away.

Dylan shook his head. "Fried food? I'm into that. You?"

Clara turned, walking backward into a crowd of people like a small-town pro, her hand to her stomach. "How fried?"

Dylan laughed. "Gas-inducing grease."

She scrunched her face as he fell in step beside her. "That's not a good idea."

Taking her hand, Dylan had a better idea. "I have a plan. Do you trust me?"

"To get me into trouble? Absolutely."

"Excellent. Follow my lead." He pulled her toward the cove.

Crossing the grass, Clara took off her shoes as Dylan showed her how to slide down the sand embankment on her ass. Taking her hand again, they walked to the water's edge. They could still hear the muted sounds of the carnival in the distance, and the water was calm despite the blanket of clouds now covering the stars. Dylan scanned the dinghies parked at the Santoris' dock. As they walked closer, he explained how owners of the larger boats used the smaller boats as transport around the bay.

Locals and tourists usually chained their dinghies up to deter exactly what Dylan was proposing, but there were a few, like the one on the end, who trusted the honest people of Bodega Bay.

Mistake. Dylan smiled and guided Clara down the dock. Climbing into the dinghy, he held out a hand to her. She hesitated.

"Is this yours?"

He shook his head.

"Define trouble. I have a performance next month."

"I know." He flicked his hand again.

"Responsibilities. I know I'm all fun and games right now."

Dylan snorted, still waggling his hand and hoping she'd take it before someone caught them.

"I committed to the orchestra. Do you know what happens if I —"

"I do, Clara. Get in."

She closed her eyes and took a deep breath. Opening them, she finally took his hand. "I can't get arrested, Dylan."

He laughed as they pulled off the dock, following the line of the cove and into the larger bay. The motor purred as they cut through the water, and Clara noted the phosphorescent glow along the boat's small wake.

Dylan slowed the motor and pointed out a few town markers on shore. Clara didn't seem frightened of the water or the small boat.

She smiled, eyes skimming the water and the lights onshore. She let out a slow breath. "God, it is gorgeous here."

Dylan sighed. "Yeah, it is. Do you swim?"

"No." She looked at him, tightening her jacket around her body as if he might ask her to jump in. "I mean, I can swim, but I don't."

"Why not?" The wind picked up, and Dylan started heading back.

"Insurance, mostly. I avoid things that might lead to injury."

"But you fly?"

"I didn't say it made sense, but 'be careful' has been my life mantra. So, I can't hurt myself. And I should avoid getting arrested."

Dylan laughed as they approached the cove. "We're not going to get—"

The lights of the harbor patrol boat lit up the night sky. Dylan slowed the dinghy and glanced over his shoulder as Shane pulled to their starboard side.

Clara had her face in her hands, and he was pretty sure she was laughing. He hoped she was laughing.

"Evening, Dylan." Shane came to the edge of his boat. "Ms. Mar."

Clara held up a hand in an informal greeting so unlike her it made Dylan smile.

"Evening, Shane," Dylan said, holding back laughter.

"Everyone okay?" he asked.

"Yeah." Dylan glanced around the little boat like he owned it. "Yeah, we're good."

"Wanna tell me why you're in Mr. Eggert's dinghy?"

"Long story or short?" Dylan scratched the back of his head.

Clara looked up, trying to keep a straight face and failing. He had a feeling she was thinking of movies she'd seen or stories she'd been told about law enforcement. It occurred to him she'd probably never even been to a principal's office.

"End of my shift," Shane said. "I'll take the short."

"We were just fucking around," Dylan said.

Shane nodded with awareness anyone who grew up in Bodega Bay would possess. The fact that Shane was thirty-three with kids and a wife, and Dylan, only a year younger, was decorated and well-respected, didn't matter. In that moment, they were two locals assessing a screwup and figuring out a fix.

"Fair enough. Well, Eggert's got a sensor on his boat, tracks it with his iPhone. He's pissed and wants me to 'catch the rascals who stole his property.'"

"Borrowed," Dylan said.

"Sure, I know, but Shelly made lasagna tonight, homemade sauce and everything. If I have to fill out a report, I'll be late getting home."

"No one likes cold lasagna," Clara said.

"Exactly, Ms. Mar." Shane homed back in on Dylan. "You know what you've gotta do."

Dylan dipped his head. "I'll bring it back and drop off a six-pack of ginger ale for Mr. Eggert when I apologize."

"You got it." Shane grinned. "Sucks being an adult, right?"

"It has its ups and downs." Dylan bumped fists with his old friend across the two boats. Shane tilted his hat to Clara, bid her a good night, and was gone.

She bowed her head to Shane before looking at Dylan, her face still glowing with laughter as they pulled away. "Is there anyone you don't know?"

"A few people on the hill." Dylan steered the boat, grinning that he'd given her a true local experience. And that they'd gotten into a little trouble.

"That was surprisingly fun." She pushed her hair out of her face as the wind picked up and they pulled back to the dock. Cutting the engine, Dylan hopped off and tied the dinghy back where it belonged before helping Clara off.

Not quite adjusted to her sea legs yet, she faltered, and Dylan caught her around the waist. Gripping his arm, she smiled up at him like she could stay right where she was, swimming in his eyes for miles. He couldn't look away, couldn't let go. Why, after a lifetime of keeping his feelings to himself, was it so easy to let her close enough to see even the broken parts he never shared?

Clara's expression grew serious. On a quick intake of breath, she stepped out of his arms, and the joy splashed across her cheeks moments ago was gone.

"Why ginger ale?" she asked, refastening her coat.

It was obvious the change of subject was meant to push him back, and it worked. He figured turnabout was fair. "Mr. Eggert is a sucker for the stuff." Dylan exhaled slowly, hoping to calm his racing heart. "Do you want to meet him, or should I drop you back at the inn?"

"I was a co-participant in the troublemaking." She stood tall as if being caught stealing a dinghy was an achievement she might put with her other accolades. "It's only fair that we share in the penance."

"Lots of sharing going on in this relationship, Ms. Mar," Dylan said, as they approached the dock.

"Agreed. Looks like we're stuck together."

Dylan smiled, allowing himself to imagine if that were true. What life would be like spending every day in her laughter, curiosity, and brilliance. He would make her coffee in the morning, and she would fill their house with music.

He might not be romantic by Tyler's definition, but Dylan had always been able to spin a tale, a what-if, and let his mind imagine. These fantasies of a life with Clara were no different. Little wants he let wander before tucking them safely away from reality where he could protect them from disappointment.

Mr. Eggert forgave them for stealing his dinghy and when Clara promised to share some of her grandparents' recipes, he gave her a loaf of his "famous" zucchini bread to take back. It was raining when Dylan pulled up to the inn. Clara was asleep next to him, her features in shadow from the lights on the dash. When he'd seen her sitting on the sidelines at the carnival, he had wanted to show her a good time, give her some of the youthful fun that seemed missing from her childhood stories.

Dylan never thought of his childhood as idyllic, but despite neglect and addiction, he and Tyler had each other. They found the humor in shitty circumstances.

When he turned off the truck, Clara opened her eyes, her lips somehow remembering the smile she'd fallen asleep wearing.

"Home," he said, surprising himself.

She turned, head still resting against the seat, her eyes finding his in the darkness before she looked out the window. "How is it even more beautiful in the rain?" she said, wiping at the glass and glancing up at the inn.

Dylan's stupid heart pressed against his ribcage as if it could make all his imagining real. As if it could solve all their differences and make her—

"I had a terrific time," Clara said, pulling her bag into her lap. "I am officially a troublemaker. Looks like you're a bad—"

He raised a brow.

She swatted his shoulder. "Stop."

"Stop what?"

"The eye thing. Stop making things dirty."

Dylan laughed. "I like that."

"Making things dirty? I know." She laughed.

"No. That you *think* I make things dirty."

"I was going to say you're a bad influence."

"No doubt," Dylan said, as their late-night laughter and growing collection of moments like these swirled around the cab of his truck, writing a story they might someday tell. Suddenly, Dylan didn't want a short story. He wanted walls and bookcases full of stories with her.

Clara touched his hand, threading her fingers with his in as much of an invitation as she was probably willing to extend, given their history. It never occurred to Dylan that it was too late. That no matter how hard he tried, they would never go back to not wanting one another.

Clara squeezed his hand, freeing Dylan of his doubts.

"Ready?" She pulled up the collar of her jacket.

"Yeah." He let go of her hand and rounded the front of the truck in the rain, the smack of cold doing nothing to slow things down as need crept up Dylan's spine and his heart whispered, *Maybe just take it slow.*

Chapter Sixteen

*C*lara had never been in trouble as a child or an adult. She'd never once stepped out of line, save staying up all night watching television in a hotel suite after a performance when she was fourteen. She wasn't caught, but she had dozed off during brunch the following day, much to the dismay of her mother and her entourage.

Her evening with Dylan was exhilarating, more than simply getting away with something. It was getting in trouble *with* someone, and that had made all the difference. Water pooled in the gravel drive as Clara stepped out of the truck. Before she had a chance to discover how her leather boots would fare, Dylan lifted her just like he had the first time they'd kissed. She wondered if this was some sort of rescue maneuver because it seemed second nature to him. Once they were out of the rain, he set her down at the front door.

Under the shelter of the covered porch, Clara thought one of them ought to get a key, open the door, but Dylan didn't move, and she didn't either. They stood there like neither of them were ready for what was on the other side of the door. Clara pushed the wet hair off her face. When she reached to do the same for Dylan, he took her hand and drew her closer, nothing but his suddenly urgent puffs of breath between them.

Clara swallowed. "You don't want this."

"You're right."

"We're right back where we started this afternoon." Her heart was racing, and he was still holding her wrist. "You not knowing which side to pick. Remember—"

"Good guy or asshole. I remember."

"We are co-owners. We need to be on speaking terms."

"Yeah." He wiped the rain from his face with the hand not holding hers. "I said that too."

"Then what are we doing?"

"No idea, but if I don't kiss you again, if I don't take you inside and to my bed, I'm going to lose my damn mind."

Clara barely got out an "Oh" before he lifted her into his arms and, in a move right off the pages of Swept Away Books, Clara wrapped her legs at his waist, relishing the desperate tangle of their bodies. He was so warm, even in the rain, and when his tongue swept into her mouth, Clara didn't care about any performance, past or future. She would have taken him right there on the porch, but resting her against the now-infamous bookcase, Dylan managed to unlock the door.

After hoisting her once more, he kicked the door closed as she held on, kissing his damp and delicious lips, tasting the rain, unable to stop herself. Dylan carried her down the hallway toward his room, and Clara had a fleeting thought she was about to break her own heart.

Wrestling free of her coat, she pulled her sweater over her head, letting it drop to the floor. Dylan tugged off his shirt and turned on the bedside lamp. He swallowed as his eyes combed over her body like he was still aware what they were risking and drew her back into him anyway.

Clara was used to guiding her pleasure, but for the second time that night she understood the benefits of an accomplished partner. Dylan whispered her name, lips trailing kisses along her collarbone until she was in such a state, she nearly ripped the rest of her clothes off to give him more room to explore.

"And you're sure about this?" he asked, hands feathering along the outline of her bra.

She nodded, and he continued touching her in a way that spoke more to the mystery in his eyes than the broad set of his shoulders. His hands were careful as he cupped her breast, lips tangling with hers, urgent and retreating as if needing something he was afraid she'd deny. How anyone could deny a man like Dylan Pace was beyond her, but when he hesitated at her zipper and met her eyes, Clara's self-doubt got the best of her.

"Are *you* sure about this?" she asked. "Because you're the first person. Not ever. God, definitely not ever. I have, believe me, I've been with a lot—"

Dylan cleared his throat, a wicked grin at the edge of his well-kissed lips.

"Not a lot." Clara groaned. "My god, just come here." She pulled him to her, relishing the crush of lips and the pleasure of his body before her words, his words, or anything else kept them apart.

Dylan ran a hand down her neck, between her breasts, as she arched back over his arm, and he carefully lowered her to the bed. Her eyes barely opened, she pulled him down with her until he lay resting on his forearms.

Christ, she was beautiful. He said her name like a promise his heart had no idea how to keep, before kissing her again until a moan slipped from her lips, fueling an already raging fire inside him.

After taking his time with each breast, he made his way down her stomach, mouth tugging, his hands grasping at her hips, and then her thighs. Dylan unzipped her jeans and, through his need, found her eyes.

"Is this okay?" he asked.

She took both sides of his face and brought him back to her mouth, her tongue gliding along his neck like she needed to taste him.

TRACY EWENS

"I want you first," she whispered, nudging him onto his back.

Dylan realized he'd banked a few fantasies involving Clara, but somehow, they were nothing compared to the reality of her in his bed. Sliding on top of his body, she kissed her way down one arm and across his stomach, her tongue teasing, asking. The way she watched for his reaction and the hum of *her* pleasure at pleasuring him was nearly as erotic as sex, and he could barely breathe.

"Clara," he called in a rush of air.

She murmured a response somewhere along his body. Pure need pulsed through Dylan, so intense if she didn't stop, he was going to lose more than his mind. When he called her name again, she looked up, hair tousled around her face, lips swollen, and her pale skin flushed. No matter when she left him, Dylan knew the memory of her like this would live in his heart forever.

"Come here." He sat up, taking her with his mouth until she slid up his body and straddled his hips.

"You're killing me," Dylan whispered.

"And you are beautiful," she murmured, fingers feathering across his chest.

"I think that's my line." Dylan cupped her body and pulled her closer. When he took her into his mouth, her head dropped back on a prayer.

Pulling her underneath him, Dylan froze at the realization he didn't have a condom. With more control than he knew he had, he slowed down and prepared for one more thing to keep them apart.

"In my purse. I bought some today," she said, as if reading his mind. Slipping from beneath him, she grabbed her purse by the door, and Dylan thanked every god he knew, Greek and otherwise. Clara returned to bed, still gloriously naked and carrying a string of silver-and-black packets. Ripping one free, she tossed the others on the nightstand.

Her smile playful and wicked, she took her time protecting them both. Dylan liked to think of himself as a take-charge kind of guy. He knew how to please a woman, but he'd never had a woman thoroughly love him like this, and he wanted inside her, to please her, more than he'd ever wanted anything.

184

"My turn," he said softly before catching her mouth in a driving kiss as his hand slipped between her legs. Clara moaned, straining against his hand as he teased her like she had him, finding new clues to her pleasure.

"Do you like that?" he asked, hands working deeper until she pulled on her bottom lip and cried out his name.

"Hmm." He hummed into her neck, gliding faster now as her nails dug into his back.

"I—" Her breath hitched, seemingly desperate for more.

"I'm right here." He kissed her again, cherishing every stroke of her tongue, every whisper from her lips.

"Oh, god," she cried as her hands tightened in his hair and she arched, carried by ecstasy to her release.

Dylan rested his weight on his arms and kissed her neck, hoping to set her back down carefully. Clara smiled, eyes fluttering open as he continued softly stroking her, his own need near the breaking point. She caressed his shoulders, his back, and when she reached over to take hold of him, Dylan let out a strangled growl as she again guided him where she wanted him.

Cradling her face, he took her mouth, and slowly slid into her body. Sensation crashed around him as she drew him into silk and heat, enveloping him in a rhythm that seemed made for him.

Clara's hips lifted, meeting his pressure, and she swallowed his moan this time in a rush of pleasure as the last bit of his control drifted away. Hips pulsing again and again, she was every song he'd ever loved, every summer day, and when she closed her eyes, lips parted, her body melting into his, Dylan would have sold his soul to stay right there forever.

"It's so . . ." He mumbled incoherently into her neck.

Clara pulled him closer as his thrusts grew frantic, meeting her push for pull until she tightened around him, crying his name. Bowing his head into the refuge of her delicate neck one last time, his heart raced as they both gave themselves over to pleasure.

The last thought Dylan had before she fell asleep across his chest was if he were a sailor and Clara a siren, she could have him. All of him, jagged rocks be damned. He kissed her forehead and wondered if Jules was right about misunderstood sirens.

Maybe they *were* doing what they needed to do to survive, longing as humans sometimes did for the illusion of a soulmate. Dylan closed his eyes, his hand trailing along the curve of her body. "You are missing from me," he whispered, Clara's earlier translation circling like an unwelcome prophecy as the rain continued outside and the night pulled him to sleep.

Clara woke a few hours later, starving and in an empty bed. Wrapping herself in a blanket, she walked into the kitchen to find Dylan, jeans slung low beneath a bare chest. She meant what she said earlier in the throes of passion. He was beautiful. When he turned from the microwave, and she realized he was reheating last night's Chinese, she made love to him again in the living room—after they finished the leftovers, of course.

As they lay in front of the fire, breathless and looking up at the ceiling Dylan and Rusty had touched up last week, Clara thought about saying something witty to lighten the mood, because what they'd shared wasn't just sex, it was sensational sex. No telling where they might get to with consistent practice, but the thought of anything past exactly where they were was not somewhere Clara allowed herself to go.

"Well," she finally said and noticed Dylan turn to look at her.

"Well," he said.

She faced him, unable to contain a smile. "That was . . ."

"Pretty good," he said.

She laughed. There were no right words or rules to follow when she was with him. Clara had never felt so at ease with another person in her entire life. She wasn't sure what that said about her life thus far, but she was grateful for him now.

"Where do you think the idea for crown molding came from?" he asked, as if checking to make sure they were still the same people, capable of the same conversations.

"Cake decorators," she said, eyes back on the ceiling.

"Interesting theory." He tucked one arm behind his head. "Go on."

"They grew tired of decorating cakes only to have them eaten and then gone," Clara continued. "One day, they went to the head of construction in the land."

Dylan snorted.

"And offered their services."

"But they demanded their work be on the ceiling," Dylan added.

"Because it's preserved and appreciated forever up there," Clara said.

"By lovers."

She glanced over again at the tenderness in his voice.

"And they were right. I mean, who doesn't love crown molding?" Dylan asked, adjusting the blanket covering them.

"No one," Clara confirmed.

"Cake makers." Dylan laughed. "I like it."

She nodded, facing him. "What were you like as a kid?"

Turning on his side and resting on one arm, he seemed to consider the question.

"I was curious. Busy. Tyler used to laugh at a lot of my ideas."

"Like?" Clara hoped she wasn't pushing, but even after what they'd just shared, she wanted more of him.

"Like . . . one year we learned about birds in school. Specifically, mother birds prefer tight spaces when building nests. I was obsessed and started making birdhouses out of the junk in our backyard."

She smiled, reaching out, needing to touch his face. He kissed her palm.

"I went around the neighborhood trying to sell them in time for spring."

"Entrepreneurial."

"I didn't do too bad. Your grandfather bought one, but I never saw it again, so he may have tossed it."

"I doubt it. If that piñata made it, I'm guessing we will find your birdhouse eventually."

"I doubt it. But . . ." Dylan trailed a finger along her neck, as if touching her would bring him back to their present. "You were, this was . . . more than incredible." He kissed her shoulder. "What's a ten-point word for incredible?"

Her whole body relit from that one gesture, and she pulled her bottom lip between her teeth as if it might keep her from kissing him again, asking him for more than he'd already given. "Remarkable, astonishing, extraordinary," she offered.

He smiled, seemingly waiting for her to go on.

"Tremendous? Or . . . keep it simple and go with amazing."

Dylan pulled her closer, kissing first her mouth and then her nose before saying, "Amazing works. Hell, they all work. After some sleep, we could—"

"Practice?" Clara asked.

"I'm told it makes perfect." Dylan stood, offering her his hand.

"Is there such a thing as too much practice?" she asked playfully as they shuffled off to bed, wrapped in the same blanket.

"Nah." He lifted her into his arms, leaving the blanket with her and carrying her back to bed stark-ass naked.

"Hey, Dylan," she whispered moments later as they lay spooned, with his warm body at her back.

"Hmm?"

"Thank you." She looked over her shoulder, needing to see his eyes.

"For what?"

"For making me feel . . . normal. And so adored at the same time. I've never felt like this. Normal, I mean. It's . . ." Even in the dark, she lost her words, or her nerve.

His breath seemed to catch, and she wondered, not for the first time in her life, if she was too much. If she was feeling too much. But he rolled her body to face him.

"There is nothing wrong with you, Clara." He kissed her, soft and lazy, until her toes curled. "And you are so damn easy to adore."

They stayed in each other's eyes, surrounded by the pin-quiet darkness of her favorite night so far. Clara tried not to hope for more, tried to ignore the feeling that every morning and night she had with him would only lead to wanting another, and another.

She fell asleep knowing it was sex. She was of above-average intelligence. Her mind knew things, and yet her heart often prevailed. It knew she loved Dylan Pace, and even if she would never be able to stay past June, for the rest of her life, he would be a part of her, a lilting melody her heart would remember even when the clamor of her real life returned.

Fountain

We had the fountain commissioned by tile artisans from Catalina Island when Christopher was born. He splashed in that thing every summer like a little bird when he was little. As he grew older, there were a lot of dreams and discussions at the table near the fountain. When he died, we turned it off and never turned it on again. The pain was too acute. But the inn would not be complete without his spirit, so please fix the plumbing, and retile too if you like.

Chapter Seventeen

The only romantic images Clara ever conjured involved music, but waking in Dylan's bed had her rethinking those small-town romance novels Nikki kept suggesting. Mind looping on every moment from last night, Clara exhaled slowly. No panic, second-guessing, nor even a whisper from the ingrained voices of appropriateness and judgment. She, Clara Mar, was simply a naked and completely satisfied woman, stretching in the tangle of the inn-keeper's covers.

Sitting up, she slipped into a T-shirt tossed over the chair by the bed and pulled on the pajama bottoms she'd managed to grab from her room while Dylan made another batch of banana bread. The man's internal clock was still on search-and-rescue time. Not that Clara was complaining. She loved everything about him, from his unrelenting confidence in himself and his ability to try new things to his penchant for late-night snacks.

"There is definitely something wrong with him," her mother murmured somewhere in the part of Clara's mind trained to believe the worst lurked outside any hotel suite. "Men are capricious, and women will *always* envy you," she'd said when Clara was nineteen and asked about taking some time off to go to college. "Time spent coddling friends or cleaning up after some man is valuable practice time you cannot afford to lose."

Clara swallowed and tried to redirect her mind away from what she'd learned was nonsense. Focusing on the last of the rain clinging to the window and sparkling in the morning sun, she pushed away disappointment at waking up alone. Despite her surroundings, this wasn't a love story. She was a grown woman, and what she and Dylan shared last night was . . . An effortless smile spread across her lips. It was, as they'd decided last night, amazing and incredible.

The reckless freedom of an evening at a carnival, giggling like kids in the dinghy, and how well their bodies worked well together. It was strange knowing someone, the familiarity of a partner. Clara knew quick collaborations, she even knew the occasional dalliance, but the way Dylan looked at her was unlike anything she'd ever experienced. It was like she was silly *and* fascinating, like he couldn't care less what she did for a living or how many venues she filled. He liked her in overalls or a ballgown.

Clara caught her reflection in the mirror as she walked into the kitchen, and smiled. "Well, this is a new look," she said, tucking her hair behind her ear. Deciding to change nothing, she wondered if Dylan was disheveled too. Where the hell was he?

Her bare feet on the new kitchen tile, Clara decided she loved the new wallpaper before noticing the now-familiar paper bag from the Roastery with a large C in Sharpie. Peeking inside, she found a still-warm cinnamon roll, icing melting in all the right places. Next to it was a new French press, a pound of coffee, and a note.

Griff said you like the French press. I guess coffee isn't just coffee.
Now you can use the new hot water maker. Up early to pick up the supplies for the fountain.
Be back soon. Dylan

Dear lord, she was in trouble. Standing alone in the kitchen, the heart of the inn, Clara reconfirmed what she'd felt last night. She loved this man. Beyond his résumé and life plans, she discovered new things about him every day—what made him really laugh, nearly pull his hair out, or whisper her name in the dark. It was new, thrilling, and as out of control as she'd ever been.

"Easy, Clara," she whispered to the empty kitchen. She needed to get a handle on things before her heart overflowed and ruined everything. She had a professional life and would be returning to a career that didn't afford her the luxury of wallowing in the pieces of a broken heart. As much as she cared about Dylan, she needed to remember this thing was over in June, and while he was wonderful, he never promised a relationship.

Maybe Clara wasn't relationship material. Regardless, now was not the time to be fawning over anyone. She needed to play it safe, to look out for herself so she was not once again left humiliated. But for now, for the time it would take her to eat breakfast, she allowed the knowledge of loving someone for the first time in her life to rest easy in her chest.

Wrestling between the habit of "making herself presentable" every day and wanting to eat the cinnamon roll while it was still warm, Clara gave in to her morning bliss, made coffee, and ate breakfast on the back patio in her pajamas.

Her father's fountain, now surrounded by new spring grass and washed from last night's rain, seemed somehow less alone. Biting into the cinnamon roll and washing it down with coffee, Clara thought about how much her father had missed—mornings like this, friends, and family. On the video, he seemed to take up space, making his parents laugh, and was so alive that the memory of just the tape was painful. Months later, he was gone. She couldn't imagine the pain her grandparents endured or how they ever smiled again under the weight of such a tragedy.

Clara's relationship with loss was, like most things in her life, professional. She'd missed out on a couple of opportunities, lost her way in a few performances that didn't turn out the way she'd imagined, but until Mr. Hill's phone call, she had never experienced personal loss. The brief glimpses her grandfather left, and the blanks Dylan had helped fill in, taught Clara that loss seemed like a web that people never really escaped. From the moment her father was gone, her grandparents' pictures changed; their notes and even the way they ran the inn were more forthright, less joyful. It was sad, but at the same time, there was something so life-affirming about two people eternally changed but continuing in the best way they knew how.

They'd turned off the fountain because it reminded them of their son, and yet they hadn't torn it down; it still sat pride of place in their backyard. Clara took another bite and noticed something glinting in the sunlight to the right of the fountain. Wiping her hands, she rolled the legs of her pajama bottoms and made her way across the damp grass for a better look as her phone vibrated on the outside table. Kelly, her agent.

Clara had gone months without contact, but she had agreed to a performance. Kelly preferred text and email, so if she was calling, it might be something important. Besides, Clara wasn't a child, and she wasn't hiding.

"Good morning, Kelly."

"Clara." Her voice jumped in surprise. "I thought for sure I would have to leave a voicemail."

"Well, you hate unanswered calls."

She exhaled dramatically. "You know me so well. How are things, my favorite cellist?"

"Unless things have changed, I am your only cellist."

"True, but even if I had other clients who played the cello, you would be my favorite."

Clara knew the flattering small talk was leading somewhere. She wished Kelly would just get on with it so Clara could figure out what was sparkling in the tree. "Are you just checking in, or is there something—"

"I have sensational news."

"Okay." Clara stepped onto the grass, hoping her phone signal would hold as she walked toward the back of the yard.

"Your Saturday performance sold out in less than twenty-four hours."

"That's wonderful for St. Jude's."

"That's wonderful for you. People still love you, still want to hear you play."

Clara stopped halfway into the yard, brow furrowed. "Were we concerned they wouldn't? It's only been a few months. During the off-season."

"I know, but audiences are fickle."

Clara wondered if there was something in the fresh air of Bodega Bay, because it was suddenly clear to her she was being manipulated. Not in the mood to argue, she said nothing and took a few steps closer to the tree.

"Anyway," Kelly continued, "the San Francisco Orchestra would like to open up the Friday prior as a perk for patrons who missed out on Saturday's tickets."

Even standing barefoot in the grass, Clara's mind immediately shifted from the mysterious sparkling ahead to her career, her calendar. She knew she had something Friday and then remembered the book club meeting.

"I told them you were thrilled at the honor of an extension, but I'd need to confirm with you and then we could—"

"I don't think that will work." She should have said she had something, a prior booking, but Kelly knew her professional schedule. Some people were incapable of understanding small or precious things, experiences. Clara had worked with Kelly for years. The woman outsourced thank-you notes and replaced her couch with one that was more "on trend" nearly every year. She would not value Swept Away, nor would she understand a book club performance, so Clara stayed vague.

"Oh, come on." Kelly was practically whining. "You've been away long enough. I have so many people wanting you for the next season. Let's just put this whole thing aside and get you back in the spotlight."

Clara reached the tree. Hand on the bark, she went up on her toes to get a closer look.

"Clara? Did I lose you?"

Smiling, she realized exactly what was hanging on the lowest branch and rested back on her heels. "I can't," she said, walking around the back of the tree.

"Okay, how about this? Let's think about it. Pour yourself a large glass of wine."

"It's eight in the morning."

"Whatever. Give it a good think, and I will stall."

Clara glanced at her father's fountain, ran a hand along the new hammock, and then returned to the branch. In a way, it all made sense.

"Deal?" Kelly asked, a new strain in her voice.

"Sure," Clara said, no longer listening. "I have to go."

"You'll let me know tomorrow? The next day at the latest?"

"Sure." Clara disconnected and put her phone into the pocket of her pajamas before Kelly persisted.

Cursing herself for answering the phone, entertaining the ridiculous notion audiences were losing interest, and taking the call in her pajamas, Clara instead focused on the tree and her father and hoped Dylan would return soon.

When Dylan walked outside to the back patio to drop off the supplies, Clara was on the grass near the giant corner tree in his T-shirt and her pajama bottoms. He'd stayed in bed with her until Rusty had texted that Gus was opening early and had their order. Even then he'd stayed a few more minutes, wrapped around her. When he'd opened his eyes, he knew right where he was and who was with him. What should have felt like a line crossed or a mistake in the heat of things was anything but.

Leaning on the post of the wooden patio cover, he watched her, engrossed in whatever she'd found. When she saw him, she smiled. Dylan walked toward her for a second, unsure what to say, how to move forward from last night in the daylight, but when she threaded her arms around his neck, he remembered there was no right way with Clara. She was herself, which was a gift that some-how allowed him to be the same. He kissed her, soft at first and then deeper, her hands at his hair as Dylan held her closer, tighter, and tasted the coffee and cinnamon from her lips.

"Hey," he said.

"Hello." She kissed him again, the morning mist in her hair. So much for awkward, Dylan thought, before her tongue erased all rational thought.

"Look at this," she said, gesturing toward the tree once they eased apart.

Dylan scanned in the direction of her pointing and walked over to touch the glinting metal braided into an old branch of the giant tree.

"I knew we'd find it." She came to his side, held his arm.

"Holy shit," Dylan said softly, tracing the edge of the birdhouse he made as a kid, now a part of the giant tree.

"It's not going anywhere," she said. When he looked at her, Clara added, "Looks like my grandfather was a fan of your work too."

Dylan was once again grateful for this new version of her as she stood in the morning blue in her pajamas, giving him another story.

"Thank you," Dylan murmured, touching the branch. "For finding it."

Clara wrapped her arms around herself and asked, "Did you love him?"

"I didn't love anyone back then," he said, still entranced by the tree.

"And now?"

"And now, what?" He met her eyes.

"Do you love people now?" She must have caught herself being "too much," as she'd put it, because she looked away.

Dylan wanted to have these conversations with her, but he'd never been around someone who shared so much of themselves or broke him down so quickly. She was so accessible, he was having a hard time keeping up. Weren't musicians supposed to be reserved? He wondered if all the discovery of her grandparents, their past, emboldened her, or if even back in the city she opened herself to people.

"I do," he said. "Yeah, I love people. You've met most of them."

Her gaze held his as if again searching for a further explanation he didn't have. At his silence, she walked back toward the patio.

He followed. "Breakfast on the patio, huh? A sure sign of spring."

Clara smiled, took her seat, and offered him some coffee.

"I'm good. Why don't you finish your breakfast? I'll get the stuff out of my truck, and we can start figuring out a plan for your dad's fountain."

"Good idea." She kissed him, and Dylan wanted to take her back to bed, but he left it at a kiss. They had a fountain to restore, an inn to open. Being with Clara was—what were the words they'd come up with last night?—amazing *and* incredible. But Dylan needed to get a grip, or he would dive headlong into a relationship destined to fall apart.

Being with Clara satisfied some need. It could be he craved a rush, since he was no longer putting himself in rescue situations. Or, after years of constantly moving, he didn't know how to slow down. There had to be a reason; something in this new version of himself was drawn to a woman who couldn't, and he knew wouldn't, stay. Whatever it was, he'd decided on the way home, was harmless. He was a distraction for her. A place away from her real life. And being with her was a new kind of adrenaline rush for him.

Finally, a completely rational explanation for his attraction to Clara. Understood and controlled. Hell, he was so together, he might even make her dinner on the patio tomorrow night, once Rusty finished putting up the lights. Maybe they could make her grandmother's chili. Not like a date, of course; more like testing out recipes for the inn. *Business.* Yeah, to quote another Rustyism, Dylan was a special kind of idiot.

Chapter Eighteen

*H*aving finally found a company to convert her father's last birthday VHS recording to a digital copy, Clara packed up the tape and handed it to the postman when he arrived the following morning.

While Dylan was out back removing the loose tiles from the fountain and taking pictures of the broken ones, Rusty reached out to one of the only tile artisans left on Catalina Island and received an email back that he and his apprentice would love to recreate or repair any of the tiles needed. They had a plan, Clara thought, watching Dylan and Rusty from the kitchen window and trying not to dwell on either her upcoming performance or the fact that they were nearly to the end of her grandfather's list. In less than two months, the inn would reopen, and Clara would be—where? Glancing up at her grandmother's needlepoint that she'd framed and hung in the kitchen, Clara again searched for a through line, an ending point to this whole thing.

After lunch with Dylan and Rusty, Clara spent the afternoon messaging Tyler back and forth regarding the inn's new Instagram content and the draft of their marketing plan for the coming season. So much of this was in Clara's "wheelhouse," as Rusty put it. It was the same attention to detail she had with her performance pieces, and she'd mastered networking, often with people she didn't even like. She knew how to make concessions and found she enjoyed the challenge of learning new things, from which plants were dog-friendly for the back garden to the best hotel linens. Mr. Hill had approved the use of Clara's cash portion of the inheritance for the kitchen appliances, patio furniture, and a hammock for the spot under the trees near her father's fountain. After glimpses of his life through pictures and the video, she imagined he would have loved the hammock.

For the first time in her life, plans were not solely about her or her "talent." Nothing about the inn was a solo effort. It was a collaboration, which meant shared expectation and pressure. Drake and Esteban were finishing up the glassware. Nikki promoted Bodega Bay as a potential location for future romance-book signings, which would be co-sponsored by the inn. And Dylan—Dylan was everywhere. Or, more likely, she noticed him every time he walked into a room. Every night when they collapsed on the couch with takeaway or one of his latest recipe attempts, it was like the world reset. And when he took her to bed or right there on the couch, Clara imagined they could stay like this forever. She would simply shelve her career and spend the rest of her life running the Inn by the Bay with Dylan and become a Bodega Bay local. They could be her family of choice and all live happily ever after.

When she was not melting under Dylan's body or caressing his warm skin while he slept, Clara knew things never fell into place quite so easily. She recognized she was living in a bubble on course to break come summer, but she'd always had a stellar imagination.

Her agent, on the other hand, had none, so Clara replied that she could not honor the additional request but looked forward to Saturday evening's performance, before tossing her phone into her bag to avoid the fallout of not being accommodating.

It was possible to continue as a professional musician, tour occasionally even, and have a life in Bodega. It might be a complicated mixture of two worlds that on the surface might not belong, but

Clara knew how to dissect complicated. She knew how to pull the extraordinary out of the most creative labyrinth. She'd been doing it to the delight of audiences all her life.

Forgoing practice a bit longer, Clara went into town. She walked out of Happy Cone with a double scoop, and she sat on the bench overlooking the bay.

"Hi, Clara," Millie said, standing next to her. Her pregnancy was showing more now, another indicator time was moving too fast.

Clara stood and hugged Millie.

"Mind if I join you?" She held up her own cone, and Clara patted the seat next to her.

Millie scooted herself onto the bench. "My god, sometimes it's like backing up a truck."

Both women laughed.

"Will you be at book club on Friday?"

"I'm afraid not." Millie licked her cone. "I've committed to a short book tour for my new release so I'm off to . . . Tulsa, I think. Then my friend and agent Jade is moving from San Francisco to Los Angeles. I'm helping her move in—well, I'm moral support and ice cream buddy while her full-service moving company unpacks and places her things."

Clara nodded. "She sounds like a great agent and friend."

"She is. Are you close with your agent?"

"No." Clara licked her cone. "I've never met anyone who liked their agent. Mine was chosen for me when I was young." She smiled.

"Oh, I'm sorry."

"It's fine. That's exciting. For her and for you. Can you fly? I mean, being pregnant."

She smiled. "I'm only twenty weeks, so I have a few more months. I'll be gone for three nights on the tour and then three with Jade."

"Wow."

"You of all people should understand travel."

"Oh, I do. I just don't know how you manage travel and . . ." She glanced at Millie's belly.

"It takes practice, but I find I enjoy the travel more when I have a different life to come home to."

"Really? They don't conflict?"

"I'm sure things will get more complicated once the baby is here, but Drake's already making a play area in his studio, so I'm sure we'll be fighting over who gets the baby."

Clara had never imagined a life like this and a big career.

"I'm sure your writing has slowed."

"The opposite, actually. There's something about the air here that makes me productive."

"And the romance."

"That too. Speaking of romance, how are things at the inn?"

Clara knew she blushed but didn't care. If anyone knew about love, it was Millie.

"We are . . . things are good."

They finished their cones and talked town gossip and the upcoming movie night. After they hugged and went opposite ways on Main Street, Clara again realized how narrow her worldview had been before arriving in Bodega Bay. Women didn't have to choose career or family, city or small town. Life was a range of sounds and sights Clara had only begun to discover.

When she got back to the inn, she told herself that heading straight to her practice room instead of looking at planter boxes for the backyard was not done out of misplaced obligation or self-reproach, but it was. No matter how many carnivals she attended, Clara's default would always be to follow the rules. Setting her glass of water on the table by her cello, she sat, pulled her instrument close, and played.

The endless possibilities filled her head as her arms began to ache, but those possibilities were quickly squashed by the voice that told her Millie was a writer, not a performer, and "You're different, dear. Exceptional." She closed her eyes and played harder until the doubt diminished. After another sip of water, Clara switched to some of the pieces she imagined Nikki's book club crowd might request. Sweet, hopeful melodies, much like the town.

Once again, Dylan heard Clara before he saw her. He'd had to leave early to help Rusty finalize the tile order. He hadn't planned on sleeping in her bed. He clearly wasn't planning most things these days, but there he was, climbing the stairs, hoping to lure Clara away from her music to have lunch. As he approached, the song—or piece, as Clara had informed him—drew him closer. Rhythmic and lighter than he'd heard from her instrument so far.

Dylan watched as she pulled the bow through the last note. Music seemed to set everything right for Clara, like a treasure she held close, something she needed more than anything else. He wondered if playing in a small bedroom brought her the same joy as a symphony hall or if she needed an audience. Was an audience of one or a small town enough to feed a talent like Clara Mar? *No. In fact, absolutely not, you idiot.* Dylan absorbed his answer as he stood silently in the doorway to see if she had more to play before he barged into the room.

"That one sounds familiar," Dylan said, once she'd set her bow aside.

"Weddings," she said, looking up at him, a smile already on her lips. He wondered if it was for him or her music. Either way, she took his breath away in a sweatshirt, leggings, and bare feet.

"It's called *Weddings*?" He stepped into the room.

She shook her head, stepping out from behind her instrument. "No. It sounds familiar because it's a popular wedding piece."

"Ah. What's it called?"

"Cello Suite No. 1 in G Major. The bit you heard is called 'Prélude.'"

"Huh. So, it's old?"

"Bach wrote in the seventeen hundreds, so yes," she said, now inches from him.

"It's beautiful." Dylan pulled her close and softly kissed her lips. When he opened his eyes, Clara's were still closed.

"It's the composition," she whispered, reaching to kiss him again. "Nearly flawless and the rolling chords."

"I'll take your word for it." He touched her neck, her face. "Do you perform it a lot?"

Clara opened her eyes. "Do you remember when we talked about Carly Rae?"

"How could I forget," he said, distracted as her hand moved under the hem of his shirt, her fingers drawing lazy circles.

"When her song came out, you couldn't get away from it," she said.

"Right." Dylan kissed her neck, unable to stop touching her.

"'Prélude' is a bit like 'Call Me Maybe.' People love it, but every prolific cellist has done it a million times across the globe."

"So, you're saying Bach has some other great songs, but this is the one everyone wants to hear?"

She smiled into his next kiss. "Kind of, and as a musician, you want to play something different, progressively more challenging."

"To see if you still have what it takes?"

She laughed. "Probably."

"Why were you playing it now, then?" He ran his hands up her arms and suddenly didn't care what they were having for dinner or if he ever ate again.

"I'm practicing for book club." As if reading his mind, she threaded her hand with his and led them toward the door.

"Why?" Dylan pulled her into the hall and to her bedroom, locking the door behind them.

"I always practice." Clara stepped out of her clothes, and Dylan thanked Bach and every other composer for the passion they ignited in her.

They made love, this time slow and familiar. He'd memorized parts of her pleasure now, but there were still so many surprises. Dylan had been in a fog all morning, grinning when he wouldn't normally. He realized now, kissing down her back as they lay in bed on a weekday in the early evening, he'd been wanting her again from the moment he woke up.

"Favorite cellist?" he asked later that evening as they lay in the new hammock under the stars.

"Female or male?" Clara asked.

"Female," he said.

"Can I have two?"

He grinned, putting one arm under his head. "Sure."

"Tina Guo because she's strong and fervent. Think the Beyoncé of cellists. And she dances with the cello when she plays. So, her and . . . hmm, hard to choose. I'll go with Alisa Weilerstein because she's bold but also patient."

"Patient?"

Clara nodded. "She takes her time with the notes. Lets them develop without having to show off. It takes courage to not force things."

Dylan pointed to a shooting star and kissed the side of her head, trying to remember a more perfect night.

"Also, they're both lovely people," she added.

"Even though they're the competition?" he asked.

She shook her head. "Colleagues, not competition."

"Says the woman with all the accolades."

"Favorite search-and-rescue person?" she asked playfully, once again dismissing her accomplishments.

"That's not really a thing," he said.

"No? Okay, favorite comic-book character."

He narrowed his eyes as she rolled to rest her chin on his chest.

"What? Is there something too personal about comic books? I'd like to remind you we've been naked."

"I do not need to be reminded." He grinned.

"I'm assuming someone who has a tattoo of a comic-book character on his body is a fan."

Dylan held his arm out, the ink barely visible at the edge of his T-shirt sleeve. It was a representation of the Joker's first appearance in Batman.

"So, Joker is your favorite?"

"Hero or villain?" Dylan asked, putting his arm back behind his head.

"One of each."

"Batman for the struggle, and Green Goblin because he's an OG."

"Quick answer." She returned to looking at the stars. "Have you always loved comic books?"

"Tyler and I collect. Not as much as we used to, but it was an escape when we were kids."

"Me too."

She must have caught his surprise out of the corner of her eye and clarified. "With Bach. Music was my refuge growing up. An escape too. Still is." She smiled. "We have that in common."

"Bach and Batman." He looked at her. "I guess we do."

"I mean, I've never read a comic book, but it's close." She faced him too.

"I'm sure you've seen the movies."

Clara scrunched her face.

"Seriously? Not even *The Dark Knight?*"

She shook her head.

"What are you watching in all those hotel rooms?"

"I like rescue shows."

He raised a brow.

"You know, like people lost at sea, burning buildings, that sort of thing."

"Unbelievable." Dylan shook his head.

"It's like we were destined to meet, right?" Clara laughed.

Dylan did too, but the truth of her words hit him in the center of his chest. He wanted to believe she was his soulmate. That Levinson's will brought together two outwardly mismatched people to this point under the stars to discover they weren't so different after all. He wanted to believe in spun stories of magic, but he didn't.

Whatever the reason, as much as he enjoyed Clara, and he definitely enjoyed everything about her, a fog he couldn't explain obscured any imagined path beyond their six months.

"Not one Batman movie?" Dylan put one leg over the edge of the hammock and stood. "This is an emergency."

Heat flared in Clara's expression.

"Not that kind of emergency." Dylan rolled his eyes. "God, quit objectifying me."

She laughed. "I didn't want to ask before, but maybe you could put on some of your gear later?"

"Yeah? Like walk around the living room in it?"

"Or the bedroom."

"Ms. Mar, I had no idea you were into rescue services," he said, in his best Mr. Hill voice.

Clara stood and put her arms around his neck. "I will admit to having a thing for rescue services, but I'm also extremely into your apron from the other day." She kissed him. "And yesterday when you were outside and all sweaty, that was alluring too."

"Alluring. Another first." Dylan closed his eyes, laughter rumbling through his chest as she continued touching him. "I'm taking you to bed."

"I thought you would never ask."

"Grab your laptop. I'll get the popcorn."

"We just ate. And why do we need my laptop?"

"*The Dark Knight.*"

"You're taking me to bed to watch *The Dark Knight?*"

"Yeah. Why did you think I was taking you to bed?" At Dylan's feigned confusion, Clara whispered her answer in his ear, and heat raced up his spine. This game was fun, and he tried not to seem flustered, but the woman had a way with words.

"Right. *The Dark Knight* can wait." He snatched her by the waist and pulled her over his shoulder. Clara laughed hysterically. "Please try to keep calm, ma'am. We'll have you off this—What was it again?"

"Burning boat. Burning building," she offered through peals of laughter. "Any of them will work."

"Got it. Let's get you off this burning boat and into the bedroom so I can take off your clothes and fully assess the situation." When they got to the bedroom, he set Clara down, cracking himself up now, only to find she was biting her bottom lip.

"Seriously?"

"Oh, absolutely." She pushed him onto the bed and crawled on top of him, laughter turning serious as she lifted her T-shirt and tossed it aside.

Not once in all his years of search-and-rescue did Dylan ever imagine a woman like the polished and proper Clara Mar getting hot over the purely fictional version of his work, but when she undressed and took control, he'd never been more grateful he knew how to play along.

Chapter Nineteen

*C*lara had performed at nearly every concert hall and theatre of note in the world. Some version of that line appeared in her bio year after year and sat in prominent position on her résumé now. In all those venues, in front of all those people, she had never felt more appreciated than she did the following evening at Swept Away Books.

From the embroidered cushion of the folding chair Nikki had put out for her to the handmade sign in the front display window with musician-themed romance novels and a sign reading "Romance Strings You Along," everything about the evening felt personal, like the difference between copy paper and parchment. Clara loved performing for a large audience, but this book club was special.

Sipping punch mixed with Sprite, Clara wondered if she would have appreciated the experience years ago before she discovered her father grew up here, as did the man in her bed last night, or that someday her grandparents would trust her with their story.

Would she have cared enough back then to fear a broken heart? Clara's life had been a fairy tale. She knew wealth and opportunity mixed with the privilege of her birth, circumstances, and race gave her little to complain about. She wasn't mocking or disparaging any of it, but there was celebration and sadness in every life.

Rolling over that morning to find Dylan asleep, arms wrapped around a pillow, Clara thought of Vivaldi and the Byrds. Perhaps life, like a year, had seasons, and she was moving into something new, like owning a bed or a vintage blender. She could rescue a cat, grow herbs, even share her life with someone who didn't have a vested interest in her next performance.

Clara knew it was extravagant to ask for any more than she already had, but with the varnish of her glossy life stripped away, she was tired and alone. Lonely.

She might not have recognized it before, but there, under the track lighting, the hum of joyful laughter and a hysterical argument about the crab puffs Nikki put out for her book club guests, Clara's heart strained for more.

"Are you ready, dear?" Nikki asked.

"I am." Clara glanced at the chair, unsure how to say what needed to be said without sounding rude.

"Something wrong?"

"I . . . love this cushion. Did you make it?"

"I did. Do you see the cello? I had to google a few different angles, but it was fun. Such a gorgeous instrument."

"I love the blue birds," she said, touching the fabric.

"Thank you, honey. It turned out nicely."

"Do you mind if I move it to my chair? I want to give my best performance for you and your guests, and the chances are better if I use my practice chair."

"Sure." She handed Clara the cushion and folded up the chair. "You don't even need to use the—"

Clara touched her hand. "I love the cushion, and I will use it all the time. It's not that at all, I'm just . . . a creature of habit," she said, relying on a Rustyism.

"Well, I hear you on that front." Nikki set the folded chair aside. "Cheerios every morning. Three squares of chocolate every night before bed. Dark chocolate since Tyler told me about the antioxidants."

She patted Clara's hand. "Your hands are like ice. Are you okay, dear?"

"I am great, and so touched you invited me," she said.

"Okay. Well, enough of my jabbering. When you're ready, you can start. We'll be milling around before the meeting starts."

"Got it." Clara unfolded her chair and unzipped her cello to the oohs and aahs of the ladies and Gus. After quickly explaining the difference between a cello and a bass, she put her new cushion on her chair and sat to play, starting with the "Call Me Maybe" of classical pieces—Bach's Cello Suite No. 1 in G Major, "Prélude," as predictably requested by many of the book club members.

After nearly two hours of book club discussion, and all the standard favorites, Gus surprised Clara with his *Thunderstruck* by AC/DC request. He mentioned he'd watched 2CELLOS on YouTube, and with the help of Nikki's bucket, Clara gave it her best shot. She could practically hear her parents' lectures, but promptly drowned them out with some raucous thumping. The book club members were on their feet, and it was a blast being seen as fun instead of highbrow.

Gus drove Clara and her cello back to the inn. The bay was calm, and the air warmer. According to Nikki, tourist season was right around the corner. She was putting in new orders and "freshening up her shelves." When she had walked Clara out, Nikki asked if Bodega Bay "felt like home yet." Clara supposed it did, since she too was sensing the weather and even the changes in the bay as the months went on.

Music was a collection of notes, moments, and beats. It could captivate, turn chaotic, and fill a room with promise. Clara wondered if music was the only home she'd ever known. If it was possible to have the same sense of place offstage as she did on.

"Did you know Christopher Levinson?" Dylan asked his dad, during what was becoming a regular Friday night thing.

"We all know everyone here, don't we? We used to smoke pot and read nudie magazines on Butler Hill."

Dylan blinked. "Wow."

"What? Everyone does that in high school."

"You sure?"

"Whatever." His father smiled before sipping his coffee, and Dylan felt a pain in his chest. His dad's eyes were crystal-clear and so alert it was hard to see the man behind the madness of his youth and not wonder why he and his brother were never enough for their dad to get clean.

"Topher and his dad fought some. The usual stuff. He wanted to start a band, his dad wanted him to cut his hair." His father shrugged. "Then he died. I'm sure it messed with the old man."

"Look at you go. Practically a town historian."

His father rolled his eyes. "Zip it. I'm sure it's one of the reasons he took you under his wing."

Dylan said nothing, still trying to reconcile his father in recovery.

"You with your broken dad and him losing his son. Makes sense," he said, as if it was the most normal thing in the world to accept a substitute when you couldn't show up for your kids.

"That's an . . . evolved way to put it."

He shrugged. "Yeah, well, I gotta clean out my entire closet with this thing. I'm grateful for Levinson, all the people you and Tyler had growing up. I've told them so. Well, not Levinson, obviously."

Unlike many people, Dylan knew he was screwed up. He acknowledged, at least to himself, things from his childhood left a mark like a stained shirt or a smudge on his face. He knew it and moved on. There was no sense in trying to fix something if it wasn't broken. He was an adult now. He had control over what and who he let into his life. Lately he'd been lax in letting Clara close, but they were over in June, and when she left, he could run the inn on his own. On his own terms. No one knew this town better than he did, or respected Levinson more, plus Dylan had experience working with people. He would be all set, come June.

"How's Clara?" his improved and annoyingly insightful father asked.

Dylan sipped his coffee. Over the years, they'd had tons of conversations similar to this one. He and Tyler called it "throwing out bait." When their dad was drinking, their answer sometimes led to yelling, but mostly it was their father's way of pretending to be interested. Dylan knew how to act in this space. He'd wait him out and the question would go away.

"Do you love her, or is it all about getting the inn?"

Holy shit. What were they teaching in these meetings? Dylan's brow creased.

"What? It's a reasonable question."

"Since when are you asking reasonable questions?"

"I don't know. My mind isn't foggy much these days, and I think. So?"

"No comment."

"Oh, that's rich."

Dylan folded the edge of the napkin on the table. "I care about her."

"Good. Caring helps in a relationship."

He met his father's eyes. "Please do not give me advice on relationships."

"Never dream of it." His dad twisted the plastic stirrer. "Mine were all a mess. I'm in no place to give advice."

"Again. No comment."

"But I've done some work on myself and learned some things."

"Good."

"And I'm gonna share something with you that I read. It's not advice. More like information."

At his silence, Dylan's father cleared his throat and continued. "When a child's abandoned by a parent, either emotionally or physically, they detach."

His father held eye contact, like he expected Dylan to get up and leave. He didn't.

"It's like the pain of being left is so hard, the kid's brain says, 'I never want to feel this way again.'"

Dylan listened, understood, and wrestled down memories of the past. If their new coffee chats were going to continue, he needed to stay in the right-now with his dad. "Is that it?"

"Yeah."

"Interesting." Dylan's chest tightened. He wanted to pass it off as strain from working on the backyard at the inn, but it was deep, like something he'd taken for granted was shifting. As if all the boxes where he'd put things away were being emptied and rearranged.

He wondered if Clara felt that way going through Levinson's study. Only Dylan's life wasn't filled with birthdays and family vacations. He'd tucked things away to avoid looking at them, to release the disappointment. His mother was gone. Good riddance. His father was a drunk. Who cared? He and his brother had one another. That was his family, his loyalty.

The pain of his mother leaving, or his dad's addiction, weren't things Dylan ever examined past a soundbite on Instagram to get Tyler, or anyone else who inquired, off his back. Dylan never saw the point in rehashing pain, so these kids his father was talking about were smart to detach.

"Sounds like survival," Dylan said.

"It is." His dad nodded. "For a while."

"If the kid survives, that's success, right? Mission accomplished?"

"Yeah." His dad sat back in his chair, exhaled, and looked at his coffee cup. "Are you two going to run the inn together?" he asked, changing the subject after a few beats.

This new sense that his dad understood his life made Dylan uneasy. It was becoming difficult to keep his father's voice out of his head.

"Not thinking about it right now," Dylan said.

"Fair enough."

They fell into silence.

"Only a couple of months left, right?" his father asked.

"Yup."

"And then what?"

"It's getting . . . complicated."

"Sure." He nodded. "Complicated. I get it. Well, if you need anything."

He met his father's eyes. *Seriously?*

"Like, if you want me to build something for the reopening party or even help set things up, I've got my workshop running again."

"Yeah?" Dylan asked, happy to shift the focus off Clara.

"Cleaned up and getting started, at least. I can always count on Nikki needing another bookcase."

Dylan laughed and noticed his father's eyes were the same color as his own. The same blend of blue and brown. Tyler's were browner and a little darker. Dylan spent years looking to his brother for guidance and avoiding the drunk aimless stare of their dad. It had taken years to pack away the memories of his mother who abandoned them for a better life with some realtor, and then his neglectful and self-absorbed father.

Dylan had never wanted his father near anything of importance in his life. He threw away school calendars and football schedules and made excuses for both of his parents during parent-teacher week. It was different in a small town because half the teachers had gone to school with Dylan's dad, but they knew him too, knew his reputation, and let things be.

Now, sitting there, the coffee shop and their town about to close up for the night, it was like the clouds of shame were clearing, and Dylan acknowledged his father's place in their history. He was still reluctant to share his thoughts but had questions too. Did his dad know their mom, his wife, would leave? Were there signs blaring she was never all that into him anyway? Dylan knew his parents' marriage was a casualty of addiction, but maybe there were salvageable lessons somewhere, warnings he could use in his own life.

Was he going to suddenly share feelings and plans with his dad over decaf? Hell no.

"I gotta go." Dylan stood.

His father did too. "Okay, sure. I've got this." He picked up the trash, and they faced each other like two people stuck between a damn gale of a past and a future neither of them knew how to navigate.

"See you around," he said, patting Dylan on the shoulder.

"Yup. Thanks for coffee."

"You bet." His dad walked toward the bathrooms, and Dylan walked out.

It was warmer tonight. Summer was on the way. He normally looked forward to the change of seasons. Change was good, his father had said. Dylan wasn't so sure.

Chapter Twenty

Makeup-free and in her favorite pajamas, Clara started a fire like a pro and pulled up *The Dark Knight* on her laptop. The inn had televisions in all nine rooms, but not in the common rooms, save the small one they'd bought for the kitchen. Dylan was out with his dad, and she wondered if she should wait for him, but intrigued by the synopsis online, she grabbed a bag of popcorn from the kitchen. Propping the laptop up on some pillows, Clara had barely met Bruce Wayne when her phone vibrated. She swiped the screen and put it on speaker before she realized it was her father.

"Hello?"

"Clara Bell, can you hear me?"

Clara immediately sat up straighter, nearly knocking her laptop to the floor. "Yes, Father. Everything okay?"

"Of course. Why wouldn't everything be all right?"

Clara did a quick calculation. "It must be . . . five o'clock in the morning there."

"I couldn't sleep. I'm working on a film score."

"Ah, explains why we haven't spoken in almost a year," Clara joked, forgetting for a moment whom she was speaking with.

Her father sighed. "Let's not be petty. You've been busy."

Her father had a way of making everything someone else's fault. She didn't bother arguing. "True. To what do I owe the pleasure of your morning call?"

"There, that is a much more enthusiastic greeting," he said, voice laced with condescension. "Your mother asked me to call."

Clara closed her eyes, letting her head fall against the back of the couch. "Of course she did."

"She's concerned."

"She's always concerned." *And never when it matters.* Clara left the last part off. "I have been here for months now. What specifically is her concern this time?"

"Well." Clara heard her father light his pipe, puffing a few times before continuing. "She thinks you are cavorting with some local . . . person and jeopardizing your career. She advised I call as your father. So here I am calling. Are you cavorting with people on the farm, Clara dear?"

She almost laughed at the prescriptive way her father dealt with everything, specifically feelings, but then she remembered Carter's visit and his use of the "farm" descriptor. She should have said something, told off her father even, but instead, Clara acquiesced. She was already rebelling in everyone's eyes. There was no point in poking the bear, as Rusty was fond of saying.

"I am not on a farm. It is an inn."

"Please don't bore me with semantics," he scoffed.

"Okay, well, I am an adult, so my cavorting is no one's business but mine. I am taking some time, learning about my . . . birth father, and please assure Mother my career will be just fine."

"Thank you for clarifying. *I* am your father."

Clara said nothing, not out of cruelty, but because everything felt damaged, ruined. "You and Mother lied," she finally said, her voice annoyingly meek.

"We thought it was best."

"You were wrong. When were you going to tell me my father, birth father, died?"

"Never." He puffed on his pipe. "We never had any intention of telling you."

"Unbelievable."

"Why is it so unbelievable? Your father passed, and you had no contact with his family. Your mother never imagined your grandfather would reach out."

"But he did reach out, multiple times."

He moaned. "Dear god, his lawyer told you that too?"

Clara wrestled between wanting to hang up and needing confirmation. "Did either of you think I might deserve to know about my father? The man who died shortly after my birth? He's part of my history. My roots."

"Oh, sweetheart. That little place is seeping into your perfect pores. Performing is your life, your roots, as you call them."

"Not anymore."

He chuckled. "What utter nonsense."

"It's not nonsense. I am making changes."

"Such as?"

Clara exhaled. "I am still formulating things, but I will not return to the life I had before."

"Interesting."

"What does that mean?" she asked.

"I thought interesting was a better word than absurd. I'm working on my communication style."

Speaking of interesting, Clara wanted to say, but didn't.

"I should go," she said instead.

"Sweetheart, sell this mess and get back on track. You don't need to change a thing; you're merely . . . distracted. The Vienna Music Festival starts early November. You love Vienna."

She did love Vienna, but every word from his mouth felt like a trap.

"I've agreed to a one-night performance for charity tomorrow in San Francisco." Clara could have kicked herself the minute the words left her mouth. Why? Why did she still need to justify her existence to them?

"Oh, thank heavens. Your mother will be thrilled." A few more puffs of tobacco. "I mean, it's not Vienna, but perhaps you can parlay it into—"

"I'm hanging up now," Clara said.

Her father sighed. "One more thing before you go. Your mother wanted me to make sure you remembered—oh shoot, where'd that note go?" He shuffled through what sounded like papers. "There it is." He cleared his throat. "She wanted me to remind you that we love you. And she hopes you are using birth control. And even though you have these new people in your life, she wants you to remember you are our special girl."

Clara said nothing for a beat. "You had to write that down?"

"No. I wrote it down because I liked your mother's phrasing."

"Right. Well, thank you. I love you both too. I need to get back to—"

"Polishing banisters?"

Clara closed her eyes. "Goodbye, Father."

"Kisses." He always signed off the same way. Clara tossed her phone onto the table as if releasing it from her hand was enough to undo a lifetime of being told who she was and what she wanted.

Dylan came through the door moments later, and she practically climbed over the back of the couch to get to him. Throwing herself at him like her life depended on it, Clara held his face and kissed him, demanding more than she'd ever dared to ask. Drowning in the hollow of his mouth, Dylan tightened his hands at her sides and held on as they continued exploring one another.

"Book club must have been a hit," he said, when they finally came up for air on the couch.

Clara laughed, despite her mood. "It went well. They're fun and—" Emotion welled in her chest as she wrapped an arm around him.

"Hey." He lifted her chin, and she wondered if her panic registered.

"My performance is tomorrow," she said.

"I know."

"I have to leave at three o'clock."

"Okay."

"Tyler's helicopter is taking me."

"I know all of this, Clara. What's wrong?"

"I've never been this far away when I had a performance the next day." She shook her head. "I haven't even practiced with the current orchestra. Christ, do you understand how reckless that is? There are two new violinists." Clara knew she sounded irrational, but her father was toxic that way.

Dylan shook his head. "Did you want to—I mean, why didn't you practice with them?"

"Because I was here, and I've performed this piece with most of them at least a dozen times, but—" She put her face in her hands. "What am I doing?"

"Clara, breathe." Dylan carefully took her hands from her face. "Have you ever performed with an orchestra without prior practice?"

She almost smiled. She knew he was assessing, and completely unaware some things couldn't be understood from vital signs and visual cues.

Clara exhaled slowly and tried the truth. "I was relaxing, getting ready to watch *The Dark Knight*, and then my father called." She rubbed at the bridge of her nose, unable to put into words the anxiety or the anger. "I'm not sure how to do this"—she put a hand to her chest—"*and* that." She gestured toward the door with her head, still holding tight to Dylan as if he might tether her from washing away under her father's ugly words.

"It's one concert. You don't need to know how to do anything yet."

"I know, but it's like that world, and I can't—" Dylan shifted on the couch. "Please don't let go of me." Clara knew she sounded childish. She felt childish, which was also embarrassing.

She'd been so sure of herself, of her plan to take more control of her life and her career. She'd even considered that with enough work, she could have both worlds, but a part of her, the part now crumbling in Dylan's arms, always knew she wasn't allowed to stay. That they, her parents, her team, were always going to whittle away at the sense of self she'd found over the last few months. Clara had never been a pessimist, but she'd played this same tune for so long that it seemed impossible to change now without losing everything.

Before her grandfather's gift, there was an ever-growing list of doubts Clara conjured up daily. Being in Bodega, learning about people who came before her, getting the inn ready for people to enjoy even when she was gone, had fortified her sense of belonging. She wasn't unique, an outlier, untouchable. Not here, not with this community, and especially not with Dylan. There would never be an end to the list of doubts Clara conjured up. She'd been an adult long enough to know now, but being in this place that knew of her, knew her past more than she did, had her questioning the truth of so many things.

Dylan wasn't sure how to help, so while he figured out what to say, they ordered tacos and watched *The Dark Knight*. When the movie was over, he set aside her laptop and fell back on his training. "Okay, what's the largest, most stressful thing you've been through?"

Clara leaned up to look at him. "Are you assessing me again?"

"No. I'm trying to draw a parallel. If you tell me your pain threshold, we can determine how to better get through tomorrow's situation, but first I need to know your levels."

She seemed suspicious at first, but eventually said, "When I was fourteen, I performed at the inauguration."

"Okay, fourteen is young. Is this a big performance, this inaugura—Holy shit! Are we talking the presidential inauguration?"

She nodded, sitting up.

Dylan had mastered cool and unaffected over the years, but Clara was next-level sometimes. "Right. Okay. That *would* be stressful."

"Not really. Once I'm behind my instrument I'm fine, but I tripped. One of the Marines escorted me, and my heel snagged the

carpet. He held my arm. I didn't fall, but the people around me noticed and did the ooh and aah thing, like I was a child."

"You were a child." Dylan tried to imagine a fourteen-year-old
Clara.

"I was a professional musician." She pushed up her sleeves. "I
took the focus off the music and brought it to myself. I failed that
day, and I knew it. I was stressed from the moment before I started
playing and immediately after the last note."

"Were your parents there?"

She shook her head.

Who the hell were these people? What was more important than
their daughter playing for the President of the United States?

"They were in Switzerland. They called me later for the recap."

"Recap? Like after a game?"

She grinned briefly. "Kind of, yes. How I did. Where I was flat,
or my interpretation was unclear. They're astute at pointing things
out. Constructive feedback."

"At fourteen?"

"I was a different fourteen."

"I always thought I was a different fourteen, but you have me beat."

"How so?" she asked.

"It's a lot to perform in a place—"

She shook her head. "Not me. How were *you* a different fourteen?"

Once again, the tables turned, and Dylan wasn't sure how much
to share. After a few beats, he settled on the truth. "My mom made
things different."

"What was she like?" Clara asked.

He had never spoken about his mom—or lack of a mom—to anyone. He always changed the subject, even with people who knew
his story, but the way Clara asked made it seem like answering was
the easiest thing. Like there were no ugly answers or embarrassing
past he couldn't share with her. While Clara scrambled to take her
words back, Dylan put a hand on hers and searched for a memory
of a woman he rarely allowed himself to remember.

"She was . . . complicated. Unhappy, I guess. Drank too much, like my dad. She left." Dylan looked away. "I'm not sure there's much more to say."

"How old were you when your mother left?"

"Seven."

They sat in silence, and Dylan knew better, but still wondered if she was judging him. Maybe she was searching for a polite response. He hoped to God she didn't say she was sorry. He knew he'd said it to her, but it was the last resort of responses.

"I'm sorry," she said, soft like a breeze.

Dylan groaned. "Why? For what?"

She turned to face him. "I'm sorry that happened to you, that you grew up in a place that didn't feel safe."

Well, shit. That's why people said they were sorry. Okay.

He didn't have a reply.

"This book I'm reading has taught me that children can feel un-safe in a lot of different ways." She exhaled. "And why sometimes I feel like I was born an adult."

Even in the swell of his own memories and the discussion he'd just had with his dad about abandonment, Dylan's heart ached for Clara and the way she got when she talked about her parents. It was like they gilded her on the outside and forgot to care about all that was inside. His own childhood was full of adult responsibilities, but Tyler bore most of the brunt of their parents' neglect. His hard work allowed Dylan opportunities to screw around and be a kid. He wondered if he'd ever thanked his brother and how the hell he would even bring it up after all these years. Christ, these little chats with his dad were really starting to mess with him.

"That sounds sad," Dylan said, before thinking. "Missing out on being a kid."

Clara shrugged. "It's not. Just my path."

He had never heard it put that way, but she was right. Everyone had a path that included adjusting to the family they'd been born into. Clara's path seemed miles away from his, but he supposed in the end, everyone had struggle in common.

Chapter Twenty-One

Most days since she'd arrived in Bodega Bay, Clara felt free to figure things out. First asking questions about her family and then learning new things to protect the inn's legacy. Mixed in there were days she missed performing and others she dreaded returning to a life buzzing by at airplane speed.

Talking with Dylan last night after they watched *The Dark Knight* had helped erase the cruelty of her father, but Clara had always known she would have to face the world she left behind. Problems didn't simply solve themselves once a person packed up and left. Besides, there were pieces of her life that she wanted back. This evening would be her first professional performance in months, and a part of her wondered if she still had it, or if, as Kelly had said, the audience still cared. Maybe she was ruined for performing and would spend the rest of her days owning an inn.

Clara took a long shower and dismissed the idea of a life without performance, if only for the fact that she barely knew any other kind of existence. Anything else would be like starting over, and she hadn't worked this hard to throw it all away. Slipping into sweats, she walked down the hall to run through her pieces one last time before getting ready.

The performance started at six, which gave her plenty of time. San Francisco was forty minutes from "takeoff to touchdown," according to Tyler.

Once satisfied with her solo pieces, Clara brought her cello downstairs, and returned to the bathroom to finish getting ready. Plugging in the blow dryer, Clara realized it was the first time she'd done her own hair before a performance in years, possibly ever. Her hair was longer and sun-kissed now. A bit like her father's. She secured sections with pins. She'd thought about wearing her grandmother's clip, but a keen sense of protectiveness had her placing it back in the box.

A pin slipped from her hand, and Clara realized she was shaking. Was it possible the San Francisco Orchestra was poised in a packed theatre, waiting for the illustrious Clara Mar to land flat on her face? Zipped into her gown thanks to a gadget she'd picked up in an airport years ago, she paced the bedroom. This was absurd. She didn't get nervous before performances anymore. Music was her normal, her North Star, wasn't it?

After one more look in the mirror, Clara smoothed her dress, gathered her music, and went downstairs.

"Wow. You look . . . incredible." Dylan came through the front door, setting grocery bags on the entryway table. "That seems to be our word." He smiled. "How you feeling?"

"A little odd."

"You don't look odd." He stepped close like he might kiss her but hesitated, as if he didn't know where to start with the made-up version of her.

Clara glanced down at her nearly floor-length black dress and set her music binder next to her cello. Her entire life was built on timing, routines, and schedules, but now everything felt sporadic, like another surprise might creep around the corner.

"Thank you. I got ready too early."

"Do you want some food?"

"I'm not sure I can eat before a performance, and I'm all—" She gestured to her clothes.

Dylan checked his watch and grabbed the bags off the table. "I got sandwiches. Wait there."

Clara stepped out of her heels and set them by the door. As she put on her slippers to keep from running her stockings, Dylan returned with a button-up shirt and held it open.

"It's clean," he clarified, and if Clara's lips weren't red, she would have kissed him.

"I'm not sure . . ." She checked her watch to confirm she was ridiculously early. Slipping her arms into Dylan's shirt, she inhaled, and somehow what felt all wrong, righted, if only for a moment. She followed him into the kitchen.

Clara stood at the counter, careful not to wrinkle her dress. Sitting on the flight to Symphony Hall would create a crease, but nothing the crew couldn't steam out backstage before her entrance. Assuming she had a crew or a dresser. She had noticed mention of "support staff" in her contract, but it was the first time she'd ever asked to see a contract, so maybe she missed something. God, what was she doing?

Before she had a chance to panic, Dylan offered her the sandwich he'd obviously made a point of picking up for her "big day." It reminded her of their first evening together, after Mr. Hill delivered the news that changed their life. Dylan had fed her then too. He'd taken his time with her questions and even tolerated her falling asleep.

He was a good man, and Clara wanted to believe that, like Millie, she too could have both worlds—career and home—but at the moment she was overwhelmed by how much she'd never known about the workings of her career.

She was reluctant to eat, until he pulled out a dish towel with a flourish and tucked it at her neck before cutting the sandwich into nearly bite-size pieces.

"I don't know why I'm nervous," she said, carefully eating.

"Aren't you nervous before every performance?"

She sighed. "No. I mean, maybe a few times when I was younger, but I'm usually too prepared for nerves."

"Do you want me to come for moral support?"

She blinked, stunned at his offer.

Dylan was in jeans and her favorite sweatshirt of his, the blue one with the hole by his delicious neck, and she wanted to pull him to the couch, climb into his lap, and forget about this whole thing, but neither charm nor excellent conversation fed a career, especially not one like hers.

"I'll be fine," she said, hoping he didn't take her response as rejection. Before Bodega Bay, Clara had barely known how to mix performance and an occasional vacation. Managing a successful career on her own terms and a relationship with a man she adored was new and frankly terrifying.

Dusting the crumbs from her hands, Clara sipped some water, then rounded the counter to softly kiss Dylan. She would need to reapply lipstick anyway. When her tongue touched his, Dylan groaned, his arms at his sides like she was breakable.

"Don't forget to breathe," he said, when they pulled apart.

"I'll do my best." She stepped away and smoothed her dress.

Moments later, Clara walked down the porch steps as Dylan opened the door to his truck. He carefully put her cello behind the seat and held out his hand to help her inside before closing the door.

She placed her bag on the seat, scooted forward, and smoothed her dress again, a technique she'd learned before she was in the double digits that kept the dreaded dress-creasing to a minimum. Her performance preparation was completely out of whack, but apparently some things were hardwired. Clara glanced over to find Dylan staring at her.

"Ready?" she asked.

He cleared his throat and started the truck. "Sorry. Distracted."

"By?"

"That dress."

She smiled. "Seriously?"

"It's a great dress."

"It's plain black. Meant to blend in so the performance is the star."

"I don't care what it's *meant* to do. You look unbelievable in that dress."

"Thank you."

"Do you always carry your instrument, even on tour?" he asked, pulling through the gates of the inn and merging onto the main road toward the highway.

"On tour, my cello has handlers." She chuckled.

"Yeah?" Dylan glanced over.

Clara nodded. "They're good to her."

Clara was oddly nervous and struggling to anchor herself. She had a routine before every performance, and it never involved taking a helicopter, but she was learning flexibility.

"You've been to Symphony Hall?" she asked.

"A few times. Tyler was on a kick after I graduated from high school, but before I enlisted. I saw performances of *Star Wars* music, *Harry Potter*, and . . . something about a flute."

"*The Magic Flute*," Clara said. "An opera."

Dylan nodded. "Yeah, that one was rough."

She laughed and felt some of the tension ease.

"Tyler knows the creative director. I'm not sure if she's still there, but if you see Denise, they dated for a hot second."

Clara smiled. She wanted to stay in the truck, continue learning about him and the town she'd grown to love, but the days were getting longer. Summer would eventually arrive, and she would return from where she came. Everyone expected her to leave, so that's what she was supposed to do, right?

"Need any words of encouragement before I walk you up to that helicopter?" he asked as they pulled into a parking lot.

Clara shook her head, trying to breathe, but instead of continuing to question herself or doing one more relaxation exercise, she accepted Dylan's hand, stepped out of the truck, and kissed him. Easing back, she held his face. "Thank you."

Their eyes locked, and Clara wondered if he knew she loved him. Could he see it in her eyes? She thought she saw something every time he looked at her, but nothing made sense anymore. He wasn't asking her to stay past June, and she shouldn't assume. Lifting the hem of her dress, Clara walked up the ramp toward a sleek black helicopter that looked like something from a movie. Dylan followed behind and gently kissed her once more before the pilot promised to take good care, Dylan retreated, and the next thing she knew, she was in the air, reapplying her red lipstick.

Dylan watched the helicopter take off and wondered how she had lived at such a high level since she was a kid. He hoped he'd been able to put her at ease, at least a little. He had no clue what to say in preparation for something equal to the formality of that dress, but he imagined it wasn't the same pep talk his coach gave them before a big game, so he kept it simple.

He had spent most of his life in varying degrees of danger, but the idea of snooty music people dissecting every move and note seemed wildly intimidating. Dylan hadn't planned on going to the concert. He'd sent Clara on her way, back to her world and a job she seemed to love. But something about the look on her face last night and the stories about her parents had him flipping through his closet once he got back to the inn, until he found the one funeral-and-wedding suit he owned.

Her performance sold out weeks ago, a charity thing for St. Jude's. Tyler was on the board of St. Jude's, and they'd given him complimentary tickets. He had said nothing to Clara, never wanting to flaunt his connections, but he, of course, gave Dylan the tickets.

"In case, you know, you wanted to show up and be all romantic," Tyler had said.

Dylan had rolled his eyes and shoved the tickets into his pocket with no intention of thinking about them again, other than to slip them into Clara's scrapbook with the rest of her accomplishments.

Dylan didn't like classical music. He liked it when Clara played, but Tyler had dragged him to a few of these things when he was younger. They always seemed like a high-class dick show. Which rich guy was with which wealthy woman or in which car the shiny couple arrived and what jewelry she was wearing. No thanks.

While he wasn't ready to sort through the bulk of his feelings for Clara, he knew he didn't want her to feel alone out there under some spotlight. She said repeatedly that it didn't matter, but Dylan thought it might, so he showered, shaved, and was on his way into the city thirty minutes later with a tie loose around his neck and an overnight bag on the bench seat next to him, in case she asked him to stay.

He wanted to be there for her, whether or not she could see him. If she could sense someone who cared about her in the audience, it might calm some nerves.

Jesus. What the hell was happening to him?

Dylan could have called Tyler, asked for the same luxury transportation his brother had extended to Clara, but it wasn't worth the questions or tomorrow's gossip. Besides, he had plenty of time to get there. On the drive, he could figure out what he was going to say when he went backstage and surprised the hell out of her.

Checking his watch, Dylan figured he had time to stop for flowers on the way. Did people bring flowers to this kind of thing? The tickets started at two thousand dollars a pop. He was ashamed to admit he'd looked them up online. The last concert Dylan went to was Bella's jazz band in the school auditorium. He'd brought his almost-niece sunflowers that night, but Clara's thing was highbrow and flowers suddenly felt too simple. Besides, they weren't up to flowers and cards, were they?

An hour and a half later, he'd arrived way too early, so he grabbed a latte at Ground Town across the street from Symphony Hall. Sitting by the window, he imagined Clara inside. Was she still nervous? Dylan had always thought of himself alone, growing up on the economic fringes of a small town, but years had taught him he was never alone. And he'd probably never been *lonely* a day in his life.

Even though his father was a shit—a trying-harder-now shit, but still director of his and Tyler's sucky childhood in partnership with their absent mother—Dylan had people in his life. People that he knew cared and would miss him if he didn't show up. Levinson was one of those people.

Dylan had a feeling Clara didn't have that, that she was used to being center stage and all alone. Before he spun some crap about thanking Levinson by helping his granddaughter, Dylan reminded himself that people made choices in their life. Clara wasn't a victim. He chose to stay in the small town where he grew up. Her path, as she'd put it, was jet-setting and performing for thousands of people.

Her life wasn't his. That didn't mean she was lonely or needy— Dylan shut down all trains of thought and sipped his drink before he started questioning everything he'd done since rescuing her from that bookcase.

One more latte later, Dylan sat in the audience at Symphony Hall among the dresses and culture. He didn't feel out of place exactly. Well, maybe he did. He'd been to plenty of places outside his hometown. He wasn't a "bumpkin," as Rusty would say, but this wasn't his crowd. The orchestra musicians trickled onto the stage as the sounds of what Dylan assumed were warming up or tuning echoed off the walls. Eventually, they all took their spaces but remained standing, and the audience grew quiet. Clara's chair was in front, to the left of the podium in the center. Dylan recognized her cello.

A deep announcer's voice overhead warned about forbidden photography and welcomed everyone to the performance for a noble cause. More clapping for the director of this and chairperson of that, until the last guy walked on stage. Dylan's attention was on his program, reading Clara's bio, when the uptick in chatter drew him back to the stage. The guy with the stick looked familiar. Dylan scanned the program. Nope. He didn't recognize the name. But the yellow slip of paper stuck in the program read *Tonight we are honored to welcome Mr. Carter Sterling as our guest conductor.*

Dylan knew that name, but before he had a chance to absorb it, the audience was on their feet, clapping. Didn't they do all of this at the end of the performance? Standing, Dylan saw Clara enter from the opposite end of the stage, even more breathtaking under the lights. She clasped her hands together at center stage and bowed in thanks to the audience. Carter stepped down from his box, and Clara extended her hand. Tucking his stick under his arm, Carter took her hand with both of his and kissed her on both cheeks. It was kind of an air-kiss thing, but the crowd went nuts. Clara continued smiling as she took her place on stage with her cello.

All the musicians sat at once and the lights dimmed over the audience. Dylan must have still had his mouth open because the woman next to him leaned over, smelling of roses, and said, "It is such a treat to have them both here tonight, is it not?"

Dylan nodded and instantly felt like a fool. Or a pawn. That was more accurate, right? Clara Mar, polished and poised, was the queen of where she belonged, and he had followed her there in his only suit like an idiot. She wasn't alone. She was smiling and playing some game with the asshole king she'd asked Dylan to scare off. What the hell was going on?

Chapter Twenty-Two

At the last pull of her bow, Clara knew she still loved live performance and missed so much of the life she left behind, despite what was obviously some PR stunt concocted by her parents, her agent, or both.

At the standing ovation, Clara smiled, dipped her chin in a bow, and for the first time maybe ever, looked out across the audience—another group of people who showed up for her and from the looks on their faces seemed to think her capable of anything. Families, couples, and friends who had not forgotten her or moved on. They were a sold-out house on their feet shouting "Brava," and Clara was so grateful she nearly cried.

She'd practiced and sacrificed childhood to be on that stage right where she belonged. These people didn't care if she had a life too. They didn't want to know if she lived in a small town or took time off for vacation or even a baby. They'd never kept her from a life. The people behind the scenes had trapped Clara in self-doubt and absurd expectation. The audiences loved her music, and she prized performing for them over nearly anything else. No matter how big Carter loomed or how deep the lies, this, Clara thought, had stayed true.

Hand to her chest, Clara said, "Thank you," and nodded one last time before gesturing to the rest of the orchestra and exiting stage right.

Plunged into darkness, save the glow of a distant exit sign, Clara's heart pounded in her chest as the stage manager sent her back out for another curtain call. This time Carter handed her flowers and kissed her again on both cheeks before holding her hand up with his as the adulation she'd been so grateful for moments ago turned to a roar. Ripping her hand away, Clara walked off stage.

Her life, she realized, unzipping her cello case, would not change, allow for security or love, if she permitted the same behavior and continued as pleasant and placating Clara Mar. There was no break long enough or town remote enough to make the people in her life respect her as an artist and a person. She had to make the life she wanted, and that meant dealing with whomever put Carter on that stage, conducting her, of all things. But first, Clara gently lifted her instrument into its case and prepared for the inevitable.

"You were sensational, darling, per usual," Carter said, loud enough for everyone to hear.

Clara sensed his hand approaching her back, and she whirled on him.

"Do not touch me."

Carter stepped back, hands raised in mock surrender. "Jesus. Relax."

Clara smiled, removing all emotion from her voice. "Carter, I need you to hear these words." She leaned close, emboldened by her performances, her audience. "That performance was the last time you and I will ever be on the same stage again."

"Don't be ridiculous, we are—"

"Nothing." She shook her head. "We are nothing. Do you hear me?"

At his scoff she continued. "And I will make sure every contract I sign going forward specifically precludes you from working with me for the rest of my life."

"Working with you?" He grinned. "Aren't you adorable." Sliding a hand into his perfectly tailored pants, Carter tilted his head in that dismissive way that had silenced her so many times before. "Perhaps you are the one who needs to hear me, darling. No one tells me who or where I conduct an orchestra."

Clara knew people were milling about and tried not to relive the humiliation of her last talking down from Carter Sterling. She was not that woman anymore, she reminded herself. She did her own laundry. She ate ice cream from the carton, and she had deep roots in a lovely little town. Cowering now was not an option. So instead, she locked onto the darkness of his eyes as the backstage lights came up. "I will," she said. "I will specify for whom and with whom I work from now on. And every orchestra will agree to my caveat. Do you know why, Carter?"

He raised a brow, arms crossed now, jaw clenched.

"Because those people are here for me." She pointed to the orchestra still packing up on stage, her heart thundering. "They want to work with me. They'll listen to me because"—Clara swallowed all traces of emotion—"I am unbelievable. And so damn easy to adore."

Carter laughed, full and loud. "Someone's spent a little too much time on the farm."

Clara remained quiet as he attempted to make her small. "Are you finished?"

Dabbing at his eyes in jest, he nodded. "I'm not the one having a tantrum."

Clara zipped her cello case, lifted it to her shoulder, and made to leave.

"Darling," he said, blocking her way.

People began to gather now, Carter's adoring squad closing in to watch him humiliate someone else. Clara leaned in again.

"Have you ever heard of Jules Bartlett?"

His brow furrowed. "Clarinet?"

Clara shook her head. "Figures you wouldn't know her. Anyway, in the words of the great Jules Bartlett, get the *fuck* out of my way." She batted her lashes, and Carter, solidly stunned, stepped aside.

By the time the driver closed the door of the waiting car, Clara felt like she might hyperventilate. It was one thing to lean into

Jules's power to tell off Carter, but Clara was just getting started. There would be many more battles if she hoped to gain control of her life. She had been performing this way, following everyone's rules for so long, she wasn't sure what she'd learned in Bodega Bay would be enough to make real change.

Clara glanced out the window of the car at the buildings and nightlife of San Francisco. What she had with Dylan was real, tangible. It wasn't the dreamy love of her teenage imaginings or even the swaying promise in many of the pieces she performed. She and Dylan listened to one another, found answers together, and laughed. God, how the man made her laugh. Clara smiled in the back of the car as they pulled under the bulb lights of the hotel entrance.

Arriving in her suite, Clara unzipped her gown and slid it into her wardrobe bag. She removed her stockings and pulled on leggings and a sweatshirt Nikki had given her that read 'Love Is a Symphony.' Already feeling better, Clara put her heels into their bag and pulled the hair off her face.

Standing at the massive marble bathroom sink, Clara wiped off her makeup and allowed herself to hate her parents. It wouldn't last long, she knew. By the time she was moisturized, she would have excused their behavior to their upbringings or societal pressures, but for now, she hated them for treating her like some elusive thing instead of encouraging her strength, her ability to boldly compose a life of her own.

Clara splashed water once more before burying her face in the plush towel. A life of touring and bright lights was their dream before Clara ever had a chance to imagine her own. What if she'd wanted one school? A proper school, not tutors and piecemeal lesson plans? Would they have told her she was foolish? Probably. Clara had memories of wanting friends, birthday parties, and, on few occasions, a pet. All of it dismissed as "common" or "boring."

Putting on her eye cream, Clara acknowledged the guilt at thinking the worst of her parents and set it aside. She blinked in the mirror and put on some lip balm. She'd gotten through her first performance. Now she needed to learn how to ask for and get all the other things being in Bodega Bay had stirred in her.

Clara had been to nearly every major city in the world, but she'd never had a stranger wave at her at a coffee shop or a delivery guy call to ask if she wanted extra peppers. Bodega Bay wasn't Paris or New York. Their pizza was nothing of note, and the seagulls were not as friendly as they're portrayed in the movies, but the people, the inn, and Dylan made it unlike any place she'd ever been.

But how could she combine her music and this life she'd started? Running through the well-worn steps in her mind—calling her agent for advice, discussing options with her manager—Clara remembered those same people had put her on that stage with Carter. Maybe not directly, but they knew. She would need to do things differently if she wanted different results. Closing the room service menu, she suddenly knew where to start.

Dylan was out back following the electrical lines for the fountain in the hopes of figuring out why the thing wouldn't turn on. It was late. He was exhausted but couldn't just lay there in bed staring at the ceiling and wondering if the past few months had been another performance for her. So, he'd grabbed his gloves and gone out back to work on something he understood, something real instead of make-believe.

"Ridiculous," he mumbled to the late-night sky.

"What's ridiculous?" Tyler's voice parted the silence.

Dylan exhaled. "That you're sneaking up on me in the middle of the night. Don't you have a fiancée to annoy?"

Tyler was still in a suit, immaculate, in contrast to Dylan's dust and the chaos of a fountain that refused to work.

"I do. In fact, I was heading home and saw the back of the inn lit up like Christmas. What's going on?"

"Nothing. I'm busy."

"With?" Tyler asked.

"None of your business."

Tyler put his hands in his pockets. "Okay. Well, your girlfriend should be landing any minute, so I'll leave you to . . . this late-night fountain soiree."

Dylan furrowed his brow. "What?"

"Soiree. It's a party."

"Not that."

"Oh, Clara?" Tyler asked with bullshit confusion.

"I know her name, and she's not my girlfriend. High school's over." Dylan swallowed. "I thought she was spending the night. It's after eleven."

"That was the plan, but apparently, she had to get back to you. She called me and asked for a pickup."

"And you, of course, sent your helicopter?"

"Hey, I don't need your tone."

"Does it ever bother you that you sound like a grandmother?"

"No." Tyler smiled.

They stood in silence.

"What's up with the fountain?" He pointed.

"No idea. Rusty put in a new motor and can't get it to work."

"So, you're investigating in his stead?"

"In his stead? You *are* a grandmother."

"You're deflecting. Does this late-night energy have to do with Clara?"

"No. I want this thing done."

"Noticed your suit jacket on the couch."

Dylan furrowed his brow. "You just walked through the front door?"

Tyler nodded. "You went to her performance?"

Dylan ran a hand over his face. He was so damn tired of feeling. "Yeah."

"And?"

"And it was . . . right up your alley. Champagne, deep pockets, and . . ."

"And?"

"And her ex was the conductor. The prick who called me 'the help.' Who barged in and Clara just *had* to kiss me out of the blue so he would leave her alone." Dylan pulled off his gloves, giving up for the night. "That guy kissed her on the cheek before the performance and probably again once it was over."

"You didn't stay for the whole thing?"

"No. But I waited for intermission like a good boy. Wouldn't want to tarnish the Pace name." He snickered, anger roiling in his chest, and tossed his glove onto the grass.

Tyler's brow creased. "You know, her work world is probably pretty small. Did she know he was the conductor?"

"No idea."

"Did she know you were there?" Tyler asked.

Dylan shook his head.

"And you feel stupid."

"I don't feel anything." Dylan's jaw clenched.

"So you keep saying."

"Now might be a good time to start listening."

His brother said nothing. They stood in the dark of a backyard ten times larger and nicer than the one they grew up in, but Dylan still felt like he'd been caught doing something wrong and his brother was going to stand there until they figured things out.

"This was never going to work out anyway. It's no big deal."

Tyler stared at him.

"Quit doing that."

"What?" Tyler pulled his hands from his pockets.

"That pompous look you get when you think you know something I don't. You don't know everything. You get that, right?"

"Never said I knew everything. I'm just standing here."

"You are never just standing anywhere." Dylan gave up and walked toward the house.

His brother followed. "Don't you think she deserves a chance to explain?"

Dylan turned. "No. She doesn't owe me an explanation. I should have never gone. What she does and who she does it with are none of my business."

"If that's so, why do you seem so frustrated?"

Dylan sighed. "Why are you the way you are?" He went to the fridge, held up a beer.

Tyler shook his head. Dylan opened one for himself.

"Are you and Clara going to Movie in the Park next weekend?"

Dylan closed his eyes and exhaled. This was Tyler's way of continuing the conversation but moving off the shit Dylan wasn't willing to discuss. "What's playing?"

"*You've Got Mail.*"

"Christ. Does it always have to be a romance? Why can't we ever watch something like *It* or *Saw*?" Dylan washed his hands.

"Not sure those would go over well with the families, and Auntie N oversees the movies. She's all about—"

"Romance. Yeah, yeah, I get it. I'm sure we'll be there."

"So did you enjoy the performance?" Tyler tried again. "Clara's?"

Dylan sipped his beer, debating whether to answer the question. "Yeah. She was . . . incredible." Wrong word. The memory of them lying naked in the living room crashed over him. He was losing his mind. "I need sleep."

Taking the hint he was getting nowhere tonight, Tyler walked toward the door. Dylan grabbed his suit jacket and tucked it under his arm.

"This thing with Clara isn't what everyone thinks it is."

"If you say so."

"What?" He was flailing his hands like an idiot and knew Tyler saw right through him. "What does that mean?"

They both walked out to the porch, and Tyler turned to apparently give it one last shot.

"Look, I'm sure the inn and your differences make it . . . complicated, but you care deeply about this woman, probably love her. At a minimum, you two get along."

Understatement, Dylan thought but didn't say. "We do. We're having a good time, but honestly . . . she's not my type."

"Seems like it's more than a good time."

"Well, it's not."

Dylan heard the car door slam in the darkness, followed by a man's voice and footsteps up the walkway. Clara appeared in the glow cast by the porch light, Gus carrying her cello from the car. She stopped at the base of the stairs to the porch and tried to tip the guy who ran Bodega's hardware store and was now apparently her new BFF. Gus refused politely and looked between the three of them like he might be in trouble.

"I can take it from here." She sounded tired. "Thanks again."

Gus tipped his driving cap and was gone. Dylan wondered how much she'd heard and cursed Gus's electric car when her eyes locked on him. *Shit.*

"Hey." He stepped off the porch toward her. "Do you need help with that?"

"I do not." She lifted her cello onto her hip like she'd done it a million times. "Good evening, Tyler." She stopped on the porch. "Thank you for the use of your helicopter. It was a luxury, and I am so grateful."

"Evening, Clara." He grinned. "You're welcome. Anytime."

She hefted her cello and closed the door behind her.

"On that note." Tyler squeezed Dylan's shoulder as he passed to leave. "I'll leave you two to that *good time.*"

Dylan stood there like an idiot, replaying exactly what he'd said while he was trying not to say he cared about Clara. "Yeah. Thanks for stopping by." He tilted his head in goodbye.

"Be safe in there." Tyler laughed and was gone.

Dylan walked inside to face the consequences of saying too much. Not that it mattered who said what at this point. Dylan was covered in dirt, and Clara was off playing sophisticate with her asshole ex. As he'd expected, this was all about to go to shit anyway.

Turning from the locked door, he was surprised to see Clara standing on the stairs already in her pajamas.

"I thought you were staying in the city." Dylan shoved his suit jacket in the entryway closet.

"I was, but then I wanted to get back here and—" She shook her head.

"And?"

She took a step up. "Not as sure as I was on my way home." She tucked her hair behind her ear. "Did you tell Tyler we were *having a good time*?"

Dylan's back stiffened. "I did. Did you play kissy-face with your ex in front of a few thousand people?"

"I wouldn't call it that, but—wait, how do you—"

"I went to your performance."

"What?"

"I thought you needed someone in the audience, someone who—"

"Wasn't my type?"

"Right. I get it. You heard what I said to Tyler."

"Why didn't you tell me you were coming?"

"I didn't realize I was, but then I . . . did." Wow. So much for his big-boy words.

"I came back early." She swallowed.

"How's your ex?"

"He was not supposed to be there."

"Huh. Surprise, right? You two seemed friendly."

"I will be contacting my agent and manager in the morning."

"What's going on, Clara? One minute that asshole is kissing your cheek like nothing happened, and the next you're running back here."

"He was the conductor, Dylan. Not the conductor I thought I'd be working with, not the conductor on my contract for this performance, but still *a conductor*. He wasn't my ex on that stage. I played along because that is what people do in the professional world."

"Ah well, thank you so much for explaining the complexities of the professional world, Ms. Mar."

"Don't do that." She walked down the stairs and stood toe-to-toe with him. "Don't make me feel like I did something wrong. That is the world I work in, Dylan. You don't ruffle feathers or make a scene. You play your part."

"Got it." His jaw flexed. "Well, I'm glad I went. You looked"—*amazing, incredible, powerful and you are so damn talented*—"good up there under all those lights. And soon you'll be back at it full-time."

She shook her head. "I am making changes. That's why I'm here. To talk about things and figure out a way forward."

"A way forward for what?" he spit out.

"Us." She looked at him like it was obvious, like *they* were obvious.

Dylan's heart scrambled for solid ground, and he ran a hand over his face, as if that might help him understand the idiocy of any mutual path forward. "I need to get some sleep." He walked toward his room, the good guy and the asshole, as she'd called him, warring again. "You were fantastic, by the way. I mean, I left after intermission because the conductor is a dick, but you"—he faced her—"were incredible." He must be a fool, because despite what he knew, he still wanted to take her to bed and pretend anything was possible.

"Thank you," she said.

"No big party?"

"A reception and dinner." Her voice seemed to falter. "I didn't go."

"You needed to run back to your innkeeper responsibilities?" He let out a fake laugh and wondered why he didn't just walk away.

Clara shook her head. "I told you why I returned early."

"To discuss our path. Right."

"I came back to *you*," she said, her breathing faster as she stepped closer to him. "I'm in love with you, Dylan."

At his silence, she looked down. "So, I came back because I wanted you to know. I wanted to tell you."

Dylan felt nothing. It was almost like he was outside his body, disconnected. When she walked up the stairs, he turned off the light and went to bed. He needed a good night's sleep, but instead, he spent a few hours staring at the ceiling and questioning how the woman on that stage tonight could possibly love him. She didn't. She was mistaken. That was the only explanation.

Chapter Twenty-Three

*C*lara sat outside on the patio, trying to make sense of the new outdoor sound system she and Dylan had purchased back before they apparently no longer had a path forward. At his silence last night, she'd gone to her room and crawled into bed. Declaring her feelings was something she had never offered to another person; there was no way she was going to stand there and beg for acceptance too.

Unable to sleep last night, she got up early and watched the sunrise over the expanse of green lawn glistening with the remnants of early morning sprinklers before grabbing her laptop to hopefully find a YouTube video that would explain speakers in a way she understood. Rusty had offered to set them up, but Clara needed a distraction.

Besides, Rusty needed to continue troubleshooting the fountain. They'd replaced the motor twice and still had no luck. All the tile was done, and the pipes fixed. Her father's fountain was new and somehow still rooted in history. It wasn't working yet, but Clara had faith.

Pulling her feet under the blanket and cradling her mug of coffee, she realized she didn't want to leave.

She'd returned last night so excited to tell Dylan about putting Carter in his place for once and how she was taking her career in a new direction—one that would allow her to have a future with him and keep her music. For the first time in her life, she was in control. She wanted to share it all with Dylan, but he was so wrapped up in what he thought he saw or thought he knew, he'd completely blocked out that she loved him. Or he simply didn't feel the same.

If that was true and Clara had completely misread him, she would need to reexamine everything, because up until last night, it felt like their love was as essential as any base melody. It laughed with them on the couch at night. Held them close to the people in their town. Their love whispered to them in bed at night and had them smiling at one another even when things, like the fountain, weren't working. Clara's love for Dylan helped him feel safe and cared for. She knew it did. His love for her, whether or not he admitted it, gave her strength to be any version of herself she chose. It was a gift, and it was real. Which meant Dylan was either confused or hiding.

Clara wasn't prone to panic, but something like it swelled in her chest as she opened the sound system box and laid the pieces on the table. Watching the video about controlling the speakers with a tablet or phone, she wondered if Dylan had ordered an iPad for the entryway yet.

A few nights ago, they'd come up with a clever idea for guests. Upon self-checkout on the iPad, guests could take a picture and sign the guest book. The images would then download along with their comments to an electronic scrapbook and become part of the inn's history. *Bring the inn into the next seventy-five years.* Clara remembered her grandfather's words. What had been daunting when she'd arrived was an honor now. So few people received an opportunity to try something new or be a part of something bigger.

Downloading an app on her phone as the video instructed, Clara glanced into the kitchen. Still no Dylan. She wasn't sure how to get back to where they were before her performance, but she hoped this thing would blow over. She was confident they could find a solution, so of course, her mother picked that moment to call.

"Brava, brava, my darling girl. I heard you were sensational, and for charity, no less."

"Hello, Mother."

"Okay, what is with the cold shoulder now? Hate me if you must, but I will not apologize for the choices I made for *my* daughter."

Clara had barely slept last night. She barely had the energy for speakers, let alone another rehash of the obvious. "Your decisions were selfish. Let's leave it there."

"My decisions are no concern of yours, young lady." She cleared her throat.

Clara used to imagine her mother was fighting back emotion, but it was clear now even her emotions were contrived.

"Enough of this nonsense. I have not spent my whole life raising you, given you everything, for you to throw it all away."

"I'm not throwing anything away." Clara sat up. "And while I have you, what exactly did you give me? I mean, other than material things."

She scoffed. "You ungrateful little—"

"I am extremely grateful, Mother, you misunderstand. I'm simply curious about these sacrifices you like to throw in my face."

"For the last time, I did not keep the man from you." She was yelling now. "He died, for Christ's sake!"

"Right." Clara had not planned on this confrontation, not yet anyway, but she was suddenly unable to take one more piece of fabricated nonsense. "And was lying about your fling and my subsequent identity 'giving me everything,' or are you referring to all the love and attention you and Burt piled on me growing up?"

"Do not speak about your father—"

"Your husband," Clara spat, unable to placate for one more second.

"Fine. Do not speak about *my husband* that way. You may be off cavorting with the help these days, but you will respect my husband."

Clara exhaled, anger dissipating to indifference. The demand for answers from her mother waned the longer she was in Bodega Bay, the longer she forged her own life. Taking back her power somehow diminished her mother's cruelty.

"Please listen carefully, Mother." Clara's voice was calm and even. "I have given Kelly and Edward notice."

She scoffed. "You can't fire your agent and your manager."

"I can fire them, and I did. Last night."

"And where exactly do you think you will find new representation?"

"I have a friend who will—"

Her mother laughed. "I'm sorry. *You* have a friend?"

Clara closed her eyes, took in a deep breath, and let it out slowly. "I hope you will respect my choices. From now on, I will oversee my life and my career. If you can't—"

"You little bitch. I don't know who you think—"

"*If* you can't"—Clara pushed on despite the lump in her throat—"respect my decisions, I will—"

Her mother hung up. Clara knew she would. Never one to let anyone else talk, lest they ruin her performance, Bianca Mar didn't do the ugly bits of life. She didn't argue, sort through, or work out any issue. Instead, she simply focused on befriending another person from her entourage and forgot the complication ever existed.

Clara imagined that was how things went years ago with Christopher Levinson. Her father, too, was a casualty of her mother's callousness. For an instant, she wondered how her mother became the woman she was. If her toxic traits emerged from her own history.

Clicking on the YouTube video again and sipping her coffee, she decided she no longer cared. She was saving herself now.

Dylan swam the bay until his body collapsed on the small private beach tucked behind the inn, where he now sat, feet at the edge of the shallow waves crashing and retreating in that reliable rhythm he'd always found comforting.

As a kid, he'd been so intrigued by the inn. He got caught more than a few times attempting to jump the fence to discover the off-limit places only available to guests with enough money to spend their summers on the coast.

The inn's beach was beyond the south garden, down a planked path, and only accessible from the property. When Dylan was eight, he'd almost made it to the water when Levinson caught him and, probably tired of chasing his ass off the property, gave a scrawny kid a job. The old man still barred Dylan from the private beach, but he had a job.

That changed one Friday night a few weeks after Dylan's sixteenth birthday. Tyler and Drake had driven up to Berkeley for orientation and would be gone until Wednesday. Dylan arrived home from a football game to his father passed out on the couch and barely breathing. In a panic, he'd called Auntie N, who'd dialed 911. The paramedics arrived minutes later, turning Dylan's father on his side until he gagged, coughed, and eventually puked all over the floor.

Familiar rage rippled through him that night, bolstered by exhaustion from a brutal loss to an out-of-town team. Dylan left the house before the stench of neglect stuck to him as his parents' choices often did. Walking through town, he ended up on the bench in front of the inn at street level. It was late, and Dylan, spent from cursing his life and his luck, had fallen asleep with his backpack under his head.

Mr. Levinson must have found him the next morning when he came down the eleven steps to collect his newspaper.

"Breakfast?" he'd asked, gently swatting Dylan on the shoulder with the paper on his return through the gate.

Startled awake, Dylan pushed his over-long hair off his face, tossed his backpack onto his shoulder, and took the steps two at a time. They ate in silence that morning. Bacon, scrambled eggs, and white toast with grape jelly. Dylan hated grape jelly, but since nothing else was on offer, he ate it anyway. Levinson read the paper, and Dylan stared up at the canopy of trees. The contrast between his crappy house and the inn was sometimes painful.

That morning, Levinson tasked Dylan with trimming the growth around the path to the private beach and fixing the three planks closest to the sand that had come loose.

"When you're done with that, you can take a swim and rest in the sun," he'd said, like he was reciting a grocery list.

Dylan stood, bleary-eyed.

Levinson tossed him a sandwich and an apple. "You'll need lunch."

He caught them both, shoving them into his backpack, unsure what to say. It felt like a trick and the best idea ever, all rolled into one. As he stood waiting for Levinson to change his mind or joke that there was no way in hell Dylan got to spend the day on his coveted beach, the old man said, "Gus sharpened and oiled the trimmers yesterday. You should get going."

Now, sixteen years on the other side of that breakfast and still one of the best days of his life, Dylan sat on the same beach and closed his eyes. There was nothing but the sound of the water and occasionally the wind wrestling for space amid the morning marine layer. It was cold, and Dylan's body crawled with gooseflesh as he opened his eyes, pushed his wet hair from his face, and pulled on the sweatshirt he'd tossed over a rock on his way into the water.

He'd hoped the cold, numbing water would change him, wake his heart up to the realities of the situation, but nothing had changed. The stupid thing still wanted to run back to the inn and tell Clara he loved her too, with an intensity that scared the shit out of him.

Dylan understood brotherly love. He'd loved people in their town, and according to Tyler and Auntie N, he loved his father "on some level." What he had with Clara wasn't that simple. It was crushing, like waves much larger than the ones lapping at his feet now. These waves lured a man in with their sun-kissed crests and promise of work, laughter, and heat. This kind of love surrounded him and made him feel things he'd never entertained before, but Dylan knew how fickle the sea could be. It could turn and leave a man lost without a waypoint back.

He'd spent most of his adult life battling the sea to save lives. It was risky and had beaten him up. Levinson had again given Dylan a safe place to land, and loving Clara was a risk he was not willing to take.

What he said to Tyler was true. They *were* having fun, but fun turned to want, and want turned to need. Dylan didn't do *need* for more than a few hours. Ever.

Last night, when Clara said she loved him, need had Dylan wanting to exclaim, "I love you too." So, what? They could live happily ever after? Not likely. That kind of shit didn't happen to guys like him. An afternoon in the sun was allowed, a night of pleasure, but a lifetime with Clara? No way.

Dylan closed his eyes again. Slow breath in, long breath out. He'd given those instructions to other people thousands of times. People in distress had been his business. Hell, he thrived in trauma. Other people's trauma and his own.

Slow breath in, long breath out.

Dylan knew who he was and what he and Tyler had survived. He had structured his life accordingly. Falling in love with Clara Mar and her cashmere coat was not part of that structure. Survival had always been Dylan's primary goal. Levinson's will and his granddaughter changed nothing other than where he lived and how he made money going forward.

He stood, brushing the sand from the towel wrapped at his waist, now certain of his next move. He would roll back whatever feelings he had, give the inn the grand reopening it deserved, and hope like hell Clara returned to where she belonged. All of that seemed doable until he opened the back gate and found Clara dancing in her father's restored fountain, splashing water everywhere while Rusty laughed, collecting his tools.

They had finally fixed it. He smiled before reminding himself the fountain was one more check on the list, one step closer to June, and he needed to keep it together or he would ruin everything. A guy like him didn't get opportunities like this every day, Dylan told himself, stepping back through the gate and diverting his attention from Clara's laughter and celebration.

Flower beds and a party for the locals. That was all that remained before she left. And she *would* leave, he reminded the heart knocking at his ribs. When she did, he would have purpose, an inn to run, and a legacy to protect. If the current reservation roster gave any clue, Dylan would be so busy he wouldn't have time to miss anyone.

Chapter Twenty-Four

Clara hadn't spoken to Dylan for two days. She'd passed him a couple of times on her way to the backyard, and they'd glanced at one another like two people who thought they remembered the other but rather than take the chance, kept walking. She couldn't figure out if this was a holdover from her performance and Carter, or if it was that she'd told him she loved him. Either way, the silent treatment was maddening. What used to be the cozy inn they shared had turned into too much space, too many echoes.

Since she met him that first afternoon, they had always talked, even if it was awkward or painful. She wasn't sure how much more of this she could take, but she needed him to speak first. She'd told him how she felt, and he walked away. She wasn't about to ask what he wanted to do for dinner after that kind of snub.

With Rusty's help, Clara had secured all six outside speakers, and she was still ecstatic that they'd found a loose wire and finally fixed the fountain. It was Dylan's idea to put her father's coin collection into the bottom foundation of the fountain. The silver glistened through the sparkling water. It was a fitting tribute to a youthful life cut short.

Now, showered and back in her grandmother's yellow cardigan, Clara was grateful for the distraction of Movie in the Park. She sat with

Jules, Millie, Mrs. Branch, and Nikki on a large blanket as the sun melted orange into the horizon. Doran Park was a massive expanse of grass and hulking trees. Families, friends, couples, and more dogs than Clara knew lived in Bodega Bay gathered to watch a movie most of them had probably seen before. Like most things in this town, it was a chance to be together, relax, and even share some harmless gossip.

Clara had only seen two movies that weren't from a streaming service on her laptop. One was at the White House, and the other was in a movie theatre in Dubai. She decided not to share either of those stories with the ladies on her blanket, and instead simply said she'd never seen *You've Got Mail*. They were, of course, shocked, and assured her she would love the movie. Clara told herself she wasn't looking for Dylan.

"He'll be here," Jules said, leaning close.

"I wasn't—"

"Yeah," she said, "I'm not the best at side-eye either. But I have it on good intel"—she tapped her phone—"that he's coming."

"We're not speaking. Does everyone know that too?"

"Afraid so." Jules rarely candy-coated things.

Clara scoffed, turning the lid on the coffee she'd brought with her. "Honestly, I'm not sure why I care."

"Probably because you care about him."

"I do. I've made that clear, but he hasn't spoken to me since."

Jules nodded, sipping her giant thermos. "I've known Dylan my whole life. He subscribes to the first-to-speak-loses philosophy."

Clara sighed. "I'm getting that, but this whole thing is like . . . Prokofiev."

"What?"

"Sorry. I'm not making sense."

"No, you are. Is that a song or a piece? Do you call them pieces?"

"It is. One of the hardest pieces I've ever performed. The second movement of Prokofiev's Sinfonia Concertante, Op. 125."

"Is there a jackass male somewhere in there?"

Clara laughed. "No, but it is nonstop from start to finish with barely two resting points." *Much like her heart these days.*

"Yeah, that sounds a lot like Dylan," Jules said.

Both women laughed. Clara had never been in love before, but she loved him, wanted to make a life with him, but the wanting was frightening, especially when she'd spent most of her life being told she was one of a kind. With Dylan, it was almost unbearable if she was in this thing alone.

"People are rarely what they appear. I'm sure you know that, being a performer and all," Nikki said, not even pretending she wasn't listening to their conversation. "It's all about character arc."

"I'm a musician," Clara said.

"Right, but cellists are still telling a story."

"True."

"And the story isn't yours." Nikki leaned closer. "It's not your truth, it's an image."

"Also true, but interpretations allow some room for self-expression."

"My point is when people see you onstage, they think they know you, but they don't. It's the same for us non-artsy types. We're telling a story too, putting out what we want others to see, but keeping most of it for ourselves."

"Are you trying to tell me something, Nikki?" Clara glanced at Jules, who was now talking with Millie.

"I'm simply pointing out the obvious. Take me, for example," she continued. "Many people see me as this sweet bookstore type, but years ago, before he married Regina, I had a pretty steamy affair with Gus when me and my Harold were on a break."

Clara tried not to look shocked, but when all eyes turned on Nikki, she realized this reveal was new to them too.

Except for Muriel Branch, who rolled her eyes. "You slept with him once."

"One and a half times. Why must you ruin my scandal?"

The two friends laughed, and Muriel reached out to squeeze her friend's hand while the rest of their blanket sat slack-jawed.

"What?" Nikki said, adjusting the silk scarf at her neck.

"Are you going to give details, or is that it?" Jules asked.

"I don't nookie and tell. My point is, I may not seem like the kind of woman prone to a torrid affair—"

Muriel cleared her throat.

Nikki sighed. "Fine. Based on appearances, I'm not likely to make passionate love to a man one and a half times."

"I'm intrigued by the half," Millie said.

"We were interrupted." Nikki fanned herself.

They all laughed.

"This all sounds incredibly romantic," Millie said.

"It was. To clarify again, it was before he met and married Regina. I'm a bit of a tart, but I don't steal vegetables from another woman's garden."

"Why vegeta—" Jules said before seemingly changing her mind.

Nikki leaned back on her hands, the evening air flushing her cheeks. "He was a lovely man for a couple of weeks. I mean, he still is, but back then, he dumped me."

"Ouch," Millie said.

"Yeah. I got over it." She waved a hand. "Harold and I patched things up, but Gus, who seems like a big teddy bear, was not who he seemed. That's my point."

Clara bobbed her head in understanding, but still unsure what this had to do with Dylan.

Clara smiled as Tyler, Drake, and Dylan joined them, spreading out another blanket and putting two giant tubs of popcorn in front of everyone. Dylan sat next to Clara, legs extended and crossed at the ankles.

As the movie started, Nikki leaned over and whispered. "He's a softy, honey. True, he's built a hard shell around himself, but lots of heroes do that."

Clara tried to ignore the warmth of Dylan next to her. "He may be more of a heartbreaker than you know," she whispered back.

"Nah." Nikki reached into her bag and handed Clara a book titled *People We Meet on Vacation*. "Finding our way back is a common theme in love stories. I think this will be a good first romance for you." She winked and grabbed some popcorn.

"Thank you," Clara said.

"She doesn't read romance," Dylan practically growled, eyes straight ahead.

"Clara has expressed an interest, not that it is any of your business, Mr. Grump. I'm here in an advisory capacity," Nikki said. "Ooh, and heroines inheriting inns is practically its own subgenre, so let me know if you want a few of those too."

Clara loved this woman and wondered if reading romance was a key ingredient in Nikki's eternally joyful mood.

"You gotta stop peddling this stuff," Dylan mumbled.

"Oh, pish." Nikki leaned over Clara, poking Dylan's side. "Quit being such a cliché. No one likes a whiny hero."

Dylan closed his eyes.

"Well, thank you." Clara held up the book. "Now that things are slowing down at the inn, I will start reading. How much do I owe you?"

"On the house," Nikki said, still glaring at Dylan before passing the popcorn to Mrs. Branch and being swept up in the movie.

"Things are not exactly slowing down at the inn," Dylan said.

Clara looked over. "Oh, hello, Dylan. I wasn't aware we were speaking."

"We need to talk." He stood. When Clara looked up, he offered his hand. She took it and followed him toward the bay, away from the crowd.

"Romance? You're reading romance novels now?" he said, turning to face her.

"There is a famous romance author living right here in your town. You don't like romance?"

"I don't . . . care about romance."

"Obviously."

"Ha. Good one," he mocked. "Here's the thing, Clara. In less than a month, the inn will reopen, and I know we got . . . involved, but I don't think either of us is up for anything permanent. Ya know?" He hadn't looked at her once since he started speaking. "I'm sure you have performances to return to, and I'm happy to buy you out of your half when the time comes."

When he finally met her eyes, Clara understood everything. It was all right there in his tired expression. He *was* pushing her away, but not because he didn't share her feelings. Clara knew the look of being dismissed. This was something different. He needed her to leave because he *did* care. Dylan had always been reluctant to share his feelings, and Clara assumed he was private, but Nikki had been right again.

The man presently trying to roll back everything they'd shared since that bookcase, was soft and tender inside. He also loved Clara, and she didn't need a rescue show to tell her he was terrified.

"I mean, let's get real. You don't meet someone inheriting half an inn and fall in love. That doesn't happen."

Clara stood quietly, and Dylan couldn't seem to shut the hell up. The tables had definitely turned in the past few months.

"We are not long-haul," he continued. "You're passing through. You have a career, and your life is big. You're cashmere, and I'm not."

"I am not cashmere," she said. "I'm me." Clara leaned into him. "I *enjoy* cashmere, but Dylan, look at me." She took his face in her hands. "What if you *do* meet someone inheriting an inn? What if this is our chance?"

He closed his eyes. "You're going to live here? Better yet, I'm going to live in the city and make you dinner every night before your performances?" When he opened his eyes, she was grinning.

"That's a lovely image, but I can't keep eating before performances."

"Right." He took her hands from his face and lowered them, not completely able to let go. "Clara, come on. I know you say you want a place to belong, but I don't think you know where that is. You don't just pick a town and call it home. That's not how it works."

"How do you know that?"

"Because I was always a stopover, the help. I'm the guy you joke with, have sex with. I'm not a promise." He kissed her hands and let her go.

"I love you. I'm willing to change things, make different plans. I love it here."

Their eyes locked. Dylan exhaled. He was nodding almost involuntarily, like his heart was trying to take the conversation. He needed to pull this off, or she would convince him of all the possibilities, love him until she lost interest, and leave. Memories of her were everywhere around the inn, and dotted across a town he loved, but if he stopped now, he could turn it all around. Separate things out again, go back to the way he felt on that first day. It would take some time, but it was easier than the alternative.

"I'm sorry, but I don't," Dylan managed.

"You don't . . . love me?"

He shook his head, because he'd never get the words out again.

"Oh, Dylan." Her eyes softened. *Was that pity?* "Don't do this. I may have started off needing a place to land and you might have been the guy I joked with, but that's not who we are now. If you don't want a life with me, I will find a way to deal with that, but don't tell me you don't love me."

"We're different." He was trying anything now, hoping something made her back up.

"We are," she whispered.

"Good. Let's leave it at that."

"By 'leave it at that,' do you mean pack it up and get out of your town?"

"You're a cellist, Clara. You belong somewhere else. If you don't understand that now, you will eventually."

"What if I weren't a cellist? What if I was from, say, the next town over and—"

"You're not."

"But if I was. Answer the question."

"I don't know. I'm not up for questions right now."

"Do you know what I think?"

"No idea."

"I think we are a real thing."

When he made to argue, she held up her hand.

"We are different, but not where it matters."

"It all matters."

"I'm sorry." She made to touch his face.

Dylan stepped back, barely able to get a breath. "You have nothing to be sorry for."

"I do. I should have noticed it earlier."

"What?"

"You know we're real. That's why you're pushing me away. I'm in your space, in your town, and you can't let that happen."

"Don't screw with me, Clara. I'm not in the mood."

"I'm not meaning to. I've just been around people wanting me out of their way my whole life. You don't treat me like that. You don't touch me like you want me to go, Dylan. You are so rooted in this life that anything outside is a threat. You counted on me being some phony snob from wherever. You never imagined this." She gestured between them, and it seemed like she could see right through him.

"I scare you."

"You're wrong."

"Yeah?" She stepped closer.

He stepped back. "Yeah."

"Okay, then we'll go back to being business partners only. We'll run the inn."

"*You're* going to run an inn?"

"Don't do that." Clara shook her head. "Don't make me feel small."

Dylan wanted to believe her, wanted every word to be true. She loved him and would stay in Bodega. They would visit the city and have the best of both worlds. He wanted to believe that if he handed her his heart, his life, that she would protect it. But something inside of him couldn't let go of the idea that the depth of the way he loved Clara would eventually destroy him. No one of sane mind deliberately put themselves in harm's way unless they had a death wish, the same something whispered.

If he let her, she would make a complete fool out of him. And then where would he be? Sure, it was all love and caring now, but given time, he'd be some sad sop going from bar to bar, hoping to get rid of the pain.

Dylan closed his eyes. "Go, Clara. You have your life."

"And you have yours. Is that it?"

He met her annoyance and took his shot. "That's right."

"I love you. Does that matter?"

"Jesus, Clara. That's not the point." What the hell was it going to take for her to see that this would never work?

"Because you don't love me?"

"I can't love you."

"Oh, come on. What does that even mean?"

"You're not getting it." He held her shoulders. "I can't love you, Clara."

"Why not?" she yelled, pulling away from him. "What's wrong with loving me?"

Holy shit. The woman was going to break his heart straight down the middle no matter how this played out. Dylan's eyes welled, and on a blink, he wiped his eyes, shaking his head. "There is nothing wrong with loving you. You are . . . perfect."

She grabbed his shirt and pulled, anger roiling in her eyes worse than any storm he'd ever witnessed. "I don't want to be perfect. I want . . ." Her voice faltered. "My god, Dylan, do you know how lucky we are? Fight for us. Everything in that inn, our future, our history. How can you just—"

"Don't." He stepped away, swiped his eyes one last time. This ended now. "Do not lump all this together. *We* are not the inn. I've lived in this town my whole life. *I* am that inn. You are . . . passing through."

She swallowed. "I love you."

"Jesus Christ. Are you sure you love me, or am I the only normal person you know?" That one hit. Dylan saw the impact in her eyes.

Walk away, Clara. Please walk the fuck away.

She nodded, her expression pain and pride now. Widening her eyes to prevent any remaining tears, she squared her shoulders and did what women should always do when faced with an asshole.

She walked away.

Dylan exhaled and turned to the water. The wind drying the last of his emotion. They had a few weeks to get through, some flowers to plant, a party of all things, and then she'd leave. He'd done the hard part. He'd survived. The rest would be easier, he lied to himself, before walking to his truck and driving home to the only thing he had left.

The Garden and a Party

The flower beds have gotten away from me in the last few years. Please rein in the bedding and plant blooms a few weeks before the reopening so the front is welcoming. The soil is rich, but all celebrations need color. And finally, throw a big party for the locals before all the tourists arrive. I'm sure you've already found Edith's punch bowl and her Summer Spike punch recipe.

Chapter Twenty-Five

*C*lara spent the following week firming up what she and Dylan had titled "ancillary services" for the inn once it was open. Out front, Dylan and Rusty sorted flats of flowers and ground cover they'd ordered weeks ago from a nursery in Santa Rosa. Having never planted anything, save a few seeds with her science tutor, nine kinds of flowers proved out of Clara's depth, and she was no longer in the mood to learn new things, so she left the last task on her grandfather's list to the two of them.

Ancillary services were everything from room turnover and housekeeping to dog sitting for guests. They'd partnered with local businesses for everything except for the bed linens Clara ordered from Los Angeles, compliments of her inheritance fund. So far, everyone was set to provide services or supplies to the Inn by the Bay through summer.

Dylan recruited a recent culinary graduate who was working at Dough Bird to provide lunch and dinner at the inn. The menus were simple but delicious, and Clara ensured Edith's chili made the cut.

Continental breakfast would be a combination of inn-baked goods and early morning delivery from the Roastery, who would also supply the inn's coffee. Clara ticked down the master list. She supposed Dylan would bake on his own once she was gone. The pain of that thought had dulled over the last few days, but she still stumbled over notes and certain things they'd planned together.

She thought about telling Dylan she wasn't leaving. She still owned half the inn, but for that to work they would have to function as co-owners again. Clara knew that was impossible. Even if they worked something out, she'd never wanted to simply run an inn. She was getting excited about some version of a life where she and Dylan ran the inn together, as a couple, and she could continue performing in a limited capacity, but like some of the other items on the list, that plan was no longer relevant.

Needing a break from the what-could-have-beens, Clara minimized the spreadsheets and pulled up an email to review her preliminary performance schedule, compliments of her new manager. Tyler had put Clara in contact with an entertainment agency in San Francisco. A couple of interviews later, she had a new agent. After the same process and calling on references herself instead of relying on others, Clara hired a manager too.

She would leave next week before the party. It would be too difficult with everyone in her grandfather's inn knowing that she was leaving, so she'd spoken to Mr. Hill and given him instructions for her half of the inn and the remaining cash inheritance. He agreed to coordinate and authorized Clara's early exit.

So far, the only thing definitive on her performance schedule was a guest soloist spot for a three-part *Bach in the Park* summer series with the San Francisco Orchestra. Six shows total, which would leave Clara time to look for apartments and explore her new city.

Remembering how tired and alone she'd been when she first arrived in Bodega Bay, she would do everything in her power to never return to that version of herself. Dylan may not see her as permanent, but she had grown with this inn. She'd discovered things about her family—new and old.

She'd played music all her life, and she would continue performing once she'd found somewhere else to settle in San Francisco. As a soloist, Clara often envied musicians who belonged to an orchestra, but now she knew belonging, for her, came in her personal time. She had friends, had learned parts of a new business. The small, tender roots of her life were growing. She would plant them in a place of her choosing and never be uprooted again.

Clara would survive apart from the soil and sounds of Bodega Bay. The tinging of the boat masts, Jules on the harbor with the bellowing horns of the *Ginsburg* and the *Eleanor*. Laughter from the bookstore where Millie and Auntie N led lively discussions on romance. The buzz of conversation at the Roastery. Gus's stories, Rusty's corny phrases, and even her father's and grandparents' voices from that video were all part of Clara's symphony, the music of her life now.

Dylan may not be willing to work for their love, but this town had welcomed her with outstretched arms, and she was not letting them go. San Francisco was an hour-and-a-half drive. She would visit and find ways to stay in touch. Feeling like she might be again spinning a tale, Clara lay down on the floor of her grandfather's study with the remote for the new interior sound system. Selecting a song, she pressed play and closed her eyes as Handel's *Sarabande* filled the space.

"Knock, knock." Rusty's voice rang through the entryway. "Oops, sorry about that. Were you meditating or something?"

Clara got to her feet, surprised how relieved she was at the interruption.

"Nope. I was just . . . resting."

Rusty took in the room. "Sad music."

Clara nodded and hit pause.

"This place looks great, right?" he said.

Clara rested her hands on her lower back. "It does indeed. Thank you."

"Flowers are all arranged. Be back tomorrow with a crew to get all those beauties in the ground."

Clara couldn't think. The idea that they were nearly done sent a shock of panic through her that made no sense. She knew the plan, but her eyes watered anyway. She turned to put away the remote.

"That is"—she sniffed—"wonderful news."

"'Course, we're always around if something comes up."

She faced him.

"You're one of us now. Even when you fly back to where—"

"I'll be close. San Francisco."

Rusty grinned like it was his birthday and clapped his hands together. "Well, that's dandelions! Terrific news." He stepped closer to her. "Mind if I give ya a hug?"

Clara knew she would cry if he did, but in truth she needed a hug, so she agreed. Rusty carefully wrapped his arms around her, the warmth of outdoors and spice enveloping her until she squeezed tighter.

"Thank you," she said into his shirt.

"It was a joy." He pulled back. "A joy meeting you and being part of getting things ready for the reopening. Well, except for that darn fountain, right?"

Clara laughed, and despite the pain she knew would take a while to heal, she was so grateful to her grandfather, so happy to have met these people. Her life was truly changed for the better, no matter the damage to her heart.

After what seemed like a million questions from Rusty and not a lot of work, Dylan walked around the back of the house once Rusty left to "bid the fair Clara a goodbye." Dylan tried to tell him she would be around for another few weeks, but he was so upset to hear she was leaving that he barged up the porch.

Having slipped into the inn like the complete coward he was, Dylan took a quick shower and planned to get dinner out. He grabbed his keys off the bed, went back out through the kitchen, and ran right into Clara.

"Shit! Sorry." Dylan steadied her and himself. He'd done a decent job of keeping his distance, mainly to keep from feeding his stupid heart's idea that he was making the biggest mistake of his life.

Clara stepped out of his arms and stood at the counter. "I have updated the database and emailed everything to you."

She cleared her throat and Dylan realized he had not stood in the same room with her, looked her in the eye, for nearly a week. Before he'd ended things, he couldn't go more than a few hours without touching her. Progress, he thought.

"I've confirmed everything for the party," Clara continued. "I have given all deliveries your mobile, and they will be in touch when they're on their way next week."

She glanced out the window as if that was easier than looking at him. Dylan shoved his keys into his pockets.

"I am almost packed and will be out of the main suite by Wednesday."

"What?"

"I've arranged for housekeeping to get everything cleaned up Thursday morning. You have guests scheduled—"

"Clara, stop. I know the schedule. I thought you were leaving July one."

She shook her head. "I've spoken with Mr. Hill. Everything is in order, and I am leaving Wednesday morning."

"Before the party?" He sounded like an idiot. Like one of those people who ran their damn boat aground and just "didn't know what happened."

Her head tilted in confusion. "I have no desire to attend a party for the local community. Especially since you have made it perfectly clear I am not part of that community."

"I'm sure people will want to—"

"I will say my goodbyes privately." She walked toward the door but stopped. "You seem to do an excellent job avoiding me, so if I don't see you before I go, I will leave my keys on the entry table."

"It doesn't have to be like—"

She whirled on him so quickly that Dylan took a step back.

"But it does. It needs to be *exactly* like this." She was inches from him now, anger and pain spilling from her beautiful blue eyes. "And do you know why?"

Dylan said nothing.

"Because you're a coward." She practically spat the word.

"Oh, come on, Clara. Let's not do this. I was a decoy from the start. A plaything while you figured out your life. The help, if memory serves."

"I *never* called you that."

"You never corrected your ex either." Dylan didn't know why he kept pushing. She was leaving. Done. And somehow, every minute with her threatened his resolve.

"That's not fair," she said.

"Yeah, well, life isn't fair. You're leaving, so let's call this what it was, a fling. Kinda like your mother and your father. He was a local, and she was passing through."

Clara shook her head. "You're just pathetic and afraid. What is it? That you'll love me, and I'll leave? Is that it? Well, guess what, you're too late, Dylan. You already love me."

"I got wrapped up."

"In what? Loving me?"

"Your memories, your ex, your career, and your elitist crowd. Do you hear the common word there? *Your*. I don't want any of that in my life. You were right. You are too much. I don't belong in your world, and you don't belong in my town."

She laughed. "You don't get to claim this entire town. Bodega Bay isn't yours, Dylan. A lot of people live here. Many of them are my friends. I love it here, and I love this inn. And you know what? Good luck forgetting me, because I will be everywhere you look. That vase in the entryway? I bought it from your brother, along with the flowers, which will be delivered every week from the farmers' market going forward." She pointed to the window. "I picked out those curtains, I printed the labels in the study, and I helped fix my father's fountain." She sucked in another breath, and Dylan thought he might die if she said another word.

"I am part of this place, so believe whatever nonsense you need to make up, but do not tell me I am passing through and"—she pointed at him—"do not *ever* compare me to my mother."

Dylan leaned against the counter for balance. "I'm sorry." He was going to say something else, but she held up a hand and pressed it to his chest. Dylan nearly slid to the floor.

"Whether or not you love me, my heart will always love you. I may have to pack it away someday to get on with my life, but before I leave, I want you to know you were loved. Even if I'm on the other side of the world, or when I find my next best love, I will always love you, Dylan Pace, with my whole heart." She pulled her hand back.

He swallowed. Even the asshole version of him knew there were things he should say, but he couldn't speak.

"Now." She stepped back on an exhale. "Stay out of my way until Wednesday, and do not screw up my family's inn." Clara looked at him one last time and walked away.

Chapter Twenty-Six

The next couple of days were empty and quiet. Dylan was either finishing the flowers with Rusty, in his room, or away from the inn. He did as she'd asked and left her alone. It struck Clara how busy everyone got as summer approached. All the people who shared her life now had places to be—work, friends, and family. On her bad days, Clara believed she'd imagined it all, like a play or an extended performance. She'd imagined belonging when it was really just another temporary gig, and she needed to move on.

She walked downstairs to the smell of paint and furniture oils, and she saw everything was fixed and guest-ready, including the crooked switch plate near the front door. The porch was varnished to a new shine, and the bookcase was still in pride of place near the front door with two shelves now dedicated to romance novels of Nikki's choosing. Thanks to Tyler's marketing strategies, the inn was booked through September. Soon guests would enjoy the detailed craftsmanship of a time gone by, partnered with things like a new sound system and excellent Wi-Fi. Clara imagined the guest book filling up and the questions they might have about the inn, about the legacy.

Once again snapping herself out of memories that would never belong to her, Clara grabbed her bag and walked over to Jules and

Tyler's home to say goodbye. As she approached, Tyler swung open the door, laughing.

He noticed her and stopped short. "Clara. Hi, we were—"

"I'm still the champion," Bella called from somewhere in the house.

Tyler grinned. "A little friendly board-game rivalry."

"I can see that." Clara smiled. "Is this a bad time?"

"No, no. Come on in." He opened the door and gestured her into the warm wood and picture-covered walls of the home he shared with Jules and her daughter. "I'm already bankrupt. Monopoly."

"Huh. Good thing you seem to be winning at real life."

Tyler laughed. "Not always, but I'm not buying bad hotels, so that's something. I was going to get the rest of the stuff from the car. We were at the beach this morning."

"Do you need help?" she asked.

"Yeah, actually." They walked to the truck parked in the small gravel driveway. "Are you still leaving tomorrow?" he asked, turning to her.

"I am."

Tyler narrowed his eyes, and Clara noticed his were soft and warm compared to Dylan's sharper edges. They were clearly related, but like a remix, or two different interpretations of the same song. "Thank you for all your help," she said, swallowing the emotion she knew was all over her face.

Tyler put an arm around her and squeezed. "You're welcome." He handed her a bag with towels. "I heard you have a top-notch new agent."

"And a manager." She hoisted the bag over her shoulder. "Can I ask you a question?"

"Sure." He grabbed two beach chairs and closed the back of the SUV.

"Do you think it, us, was always about the inn? That I'm just imagining things?"

Tyler stopped short of the door. Possibly searching for a helpful response. For a moment Clara doubted her question but also oddly hoped he would reveal it was all a game. That his brother was, in fact, an asshole. It would be so much easier to walk away from an asshole.

"No," he said. "Dylan never expected that inn, and I know he never expected you."

Clara nodded.

"He does care. Probably too much. That was the real question, wasn't it?"

"I don't know what the questions are anymore. We seemed to have so much to say until we didn't." She shook her head. "I suppose silence is still part of a song." When she glanced up, Tyler looked concerned.

"Sorry," she said. "I'm just . . . never mind."

Tyler picked up the chairs. "You don't need to apologize. Things get complicated."

"That's it?" Clara asked, hoping to clear the cloud she'd brought to Tyler's evening. "That's your advice?"

"Oh, you're asking for advice now." He opened the door and gestured for her to set the bag in the entryway. "Advice. Let's see."

Clara could hear Jules and Bella in the kitchen.

"Who wants advice?" Jules called out.

"It's like the woman has bat hearing." Tyler smiled.

"I heard that. Who needs advice?" she asked again.

"Who do you think?"

Jules appeared in the living room. Bella, with her arms full of what looked like a bunny, gave a quick hello and was gone out the back of the house.

Jules smiled at her. "Ugh, I have no advice when it comes to my future brother-in-law. The guy is a royal pain in the ass."

Tyler laughed. "Clearly, we are all out of advice."

Jules pulled Clara into her arms. "I hope you're not here to say goodbye, because that is not happening." She pulled back, holding Clara by the shoulders. "I hate the city, but I will drive anywhere for you."

"Thank you." Clara wiped her eyes. She wasn't sure how she was going to get through all of this. Hopefully Jules was right, and she didn't need to say goodbye.

"Speaking of driving, do you need a ride tomorrow?" Tyler asked.

Clara shook her head.

"Driver?"

She nodded.

"Full-circle moment. You'll come visit, right?"

Clara hugged Bella and Tyler and walked out before she started to cry.

Jules ran out, and Clara turned.

"Their childhood was tough. Their dad wasn't the sweet recovering man you met. He was a handful. Not the best dad." Jules sighed and put her hands in the pockets of her shorts. "Anyway, Tyler and Dylan had each other, but there's damage."

"We all have damage."

"True," Jules said. "But some is worse than others."

"I don't know about that. Alcoholic father and a mother who abandoned him versus a dead father I never knew and a mother who lied to me."

Her eyebrows lifted. "You two *do* have a lot in common."

"Dylan doesn't see it that way."

"He's . . ."

"What?" Clara said, louder than she intended. "Please tell me what he is."

"Scared you'll leave. Scared he's not enough, we're not enough, and once you figure that out, you'll run."

"He wouldn't even talk about a path forward. I wanted to make it work, but he all but pushed me out the door."

"People have left him. His mom. His brother, to a certain extent, until he came back. Dylan has learned to push before people get too close. He's done it with Tyler, even in their adult life. Tyler's just . . . persistent."

Clara smiled.

"Trust is a hard thing to recover once it's lost," Jules said. "There's always this sense that you're being a fool, naive, and if you get smacked down again, you only have yourself to blame."

Clara must have looked impressed at the insight, because Jules grinned. "I have some experience in this area."

"Well," — Clara looked off into the distance in an effort to keep it together — "I tried. I don't know what else to do."

"Sure. I'm not saying you need to do anything. You've gotta make yourself happy, right?"

Clara nodded, and Jules pulled her into a hug before leaning back, still holding her shoulders. "I'll text you every day. I have some fierce men-suck quotes."

Clara laughed. "I can't wait."

Their eyes held before Jules nodded, squeezed Clara one more time, and ran back in the house.

Somewhere along the way, amid the papers and food, the memories and mud, Clara had learned to love herself. The loud noise of her upbringing and the opinions of everyone but herself had faded. She knew they would crescendo again once she ventured back into the world of performance, but one thing was different. She had Bodega Bay now. She'd missed out on her father and grandfather, but she knew these people, loved them, and in return, they'd strengthened her in a way she never imagined possible. It was in that strength, little by little, that she found her worth, her own power.

Dylan sat on a bench facing the bay outside Swept Away Books. The sun was setting. He usually loved a sunset, but Clara was leaving in the morning and this one felt like a fucking metaphor.

His father sat next to him. They sat in silence.

"I'm thinking about asking Nikki on a date."

"What?"

"Like maybe the next Christmas concert or the one after that."

"It's June."

"I know."

"Care to elaborate?"

"Says the kid who never elaborates." They sat in more silence, nothing but the bay and a couple of cars passing by. "Have you seen my ficus?"

"Is that the twisty tree by Stump's cage?"

"That's the one."

"Yeah, I saw it a couple of days ago when I stopped by to feed your oddly still-alive lizard when you were at that wellness thing."

"Getting big, right?"

"I guess."

"The key is this plant food I bought, and I clean its leaves."

He looked at his father. "Yeah, it looks good. What does this have to do with Nikki?"

"I don't want to start a relationship too soon. Even if she agrees to go out with me, we'll need to take it slow. But I've kept that tree alive, and Stump too. I'm optimistic."

"You like Nikki?"

"What's not to like? She's gorgeous, she has excellent fashion sense, and she reads."

Dylan nodded.

"Older-people romance is a trend. Did you know that?"

"I did not."

"It's next month's theme on her yellow bookcase. Apparently, a lot of readers want more mature romance."

"Interesting."

Either Dylan was delirious from lack of sleep, or the town he loved and its people had slipped into another dimension. Since when did his father date?

"You'll survive, you know?"

Dylan watched the bay.

"If you love her and she leaves. You'll survive."

He looked over at his father. The man who had been damaged and drunk most of Dylan's life, and a train wreck once his wife left for another guy was now giving advice. "Are you for real right now? What about the terrifying sirens?"

His father shrugged. "I was in a mythology period, but you wanna know what I've learned?"

Dylan took a fortifying breath. "Sure."

"It's not them who do the damage. The sirens or the woman we love, whatever. It's us."

He looked over at his once-frail father, now putting on weight and growing a beard. His eyes were so clear, Dylan again wondered if this was an alien-encounter kind of thing. "It's our fault. That's what you've learned."

"No fault. There's no fault. Risk, sure, but if it goes bad,"—his dad shook his head like he was arguing with himself—"man, that shit hurts, but then you have to let it go. If you don't, you do damage to yourself." He stooped to meet Dylan's eyes. "I did the damage. It wasn't loving your mom or losing her. It was me."

Swallowing back more crap than Instagram had advice for, Dylan looked away.

They sat in silence, the occasional car or group of tourists passing with ice cream or folded maps in hand.

"How do you stop it?" Dylan asked.

His father looked at him. "The fear?"

He nodded because if he spoke again, he was going to cry. And sober dad or not, Dylan was not crying in front of this man.

"Well, that's what I'm tryna tell you. No matter what happens, whatever you're fearing, even if it comes true and she, say, dumps your ass for a realtor."

Dylan snorted.

"You'll survive so long as you don't do damage to yourself. So, if you're gonna make it out the other side anyway, then what are you fearing?"

It felt a little schmaltzy, AA talk, but it was a new perspective, Dylan would give him that. Nothing Clara could do to him, to his heart, would be fatal. Kind of like that first jump into frigid water after months of classroom training. He needed to face it.

On an exhale, Dylan stood, not sure how to end this conversation. He went with the first thing that came to mind. A phrase he'd never once said to his father in thirty-two years.

"Thanks."

His dad made to hug him but stopped to check. Dylan hugged him back. When his father didn't let go, Dylan chuckled.

"I love you, son."

"I know. I'm starting to like you too."

"Like. Now there's something I never dared to dream."

Dylan turned to leave.

"I've got your blessing on the Nikki thing then?"

"My blessing?"

"Yeah, like, you're cool with it if I ask her out toward the end of the year, maybe next?"

"Dad, if Nikki's cool with this, so am I."

His father snapped his fingers, followed by a clap. "Hot dog."

"Take care of that ficus," Dylan said, waving a hand overhead on his way to his truck.

"Oh, I will," his father yelled after him, as the sun over the bay kissed the water and melted blue. Not the blue of Clara's eyes. Plain blue, and Dylan imagined everything would appear that way for a long time.

Chapter Twenty-Seven

*L*ights sprinkled the back patio and surrounding trees as the sunset peeked through the leaves and around the edges of the newly painted wood like fireflies ready for summer. Clara stood at the open window of her bedroom and marveled at her father's fountain, in the center of everything. He was kept from her but taken from so many who knew and loved him. Right as he got started, he was gone.

She supposed there were so many things in life like that. Moments, lifetimes, and everything in between. There were no guarantees. All anyone could do was cross their fingers and hope for the best.

When Clara arrived in Bodega Bay, she knew nothing about the people, running an inn, or her co-owner. She knew enough about Dylan now to love him. Of that, she was certain. But much like her father, some things were only for a time, a season, or in Clara's case, six months.

She meant what she said. She knew he loved her, but not enough. Despite all they'd experienced over the past few months, despite all the new things she'd discovered about herself, he wouldn't see her in his life. The thought hurt deep in her chest.

Clara could try again, beg him to accept her, prove to him she was absolutely right for Bodega, for him, but she was no longer the Clara Mar who'd arrived in January.

In honoring her grandfather's wishes, she'd learned about herself. He'd probably known that would happen all along. Clara liked to think of her grandfather that way. And because she never knew him, she could fashion him however she liked around the framework of pictures and memories he left behind.

Closing her last trunk, Clara pushed it out onto the landing and went to sleep. When she woke the next morning, her trunks were gone. She got ready and walked downstairs for the last time; her trunks were on the front porch and the black SUV that dropped her off the night she arrived was there again. This time the driver would take her to a hotel in San Francisco until she found a place to call home.

Clara had made the reservations herself, even negotiated a discount. She went into the kitchen, thinking she might see Dylan, but unsure what she would even say at this point. The kitchen was, of course, empty. Nothing but a wrapped sandwich with a C on the paper.

The man was trying to kill her. That was the only explanation. Shoving the sandwich into her bag before she could second-guess herself, Clara walked to the foyer and glanced at her grandfather's study one last time.

"Thank you," she whispered, then set her keys on the table and left before she started crying again. No matter where she lived, parts of Bodega Bay would stay with her, and she felt confident she'd left bits of herself behind too. She hoped she'd made her grandfather proud, and the inn would go on for many more generations.

Dylan opened one eye the next morning. *Hot pink. Shit.*

"Jules," he called, knowing she was laughing her ass off somewhere nearby.

"Be still," Bella whispered. "Mom said you love pink, and I'm al-most done." Her voice slipped right past his annoyance.

"I love pink," he mumbled as she straightened his hand again in a huff.

"It's a power color," Jules said from a place Dylan couldn't see because an eleven-year-old with glitter forbade movement.

"Can I sit up?" he asked.

"Yes," Bella said, dipping her nail polish brush like a pro. "Touch nothing. You're still wet."

Dylan somehow slid up the end of the couch to a seated position, and there stood Jules, sweatpants, Branch Fishing T-shirt, and a cup of coffee in hand.

"You did this?"

"Did what?" she asked, eyes wide with bullshit surprise.

Bella cleared her throat and gestured for his left hand. Dylan did as he was told because even he knew you didn't stop mid-manicure.

Jules snorted.

Closing his eyes and trying to forget that he'd crashed on his brother's couch last night because he didn't want to go back to the inn and watch Clara leave, Dylan exhaled slowly.

"You want breakfast? Not that you deserve it."

"What are you offering?" Dylan ignored her comment. He wasn't picking up that fight. It was too early.

"Banana bread or a peach scone, both from the Roastery."

"I'll take both."

Bella was blowing on his fingers now. Damn, the kid was cute.

"It's a good color for me, right?"

She smiled. "It is. It's new and called"—she turned the bottle—"Girls' Night Out."

Dylan grinned despite himself and glanced up at Jules, who mouthed "Girls' Night Out" while shaking her hips. The woman was ruthless.

"Okay. Now, this is super important," Bella said. "Keep to your-self for ten minutes." She grabbed his phone off the coffee table. "Password?"

Dylan gave up his four digits.

Bella tapped the screen before setting the phone down in front of him.

"When that goes off, you can get up."

"Wow. Strict." Dylan flashed his best diva face. He'd never known he'd had a diva face until he met Bella.

"Bells, let's clean up, or we're going to be late for lunch with Nana and Pop."

Bella gave her mother the thumbs-up and loaded her manicure supplies into a pink case before running off.

Dylan held up his hands. "Funny."

"I think so." Jules plopped herself down on the couch next to him. "Now that you're single and all. You know, I hear Gus has a cousin."

Dylan said nothing.

She sipped her coffee. "Do you want my advice?"

"No." Dylan watched the numbers tick away on his phone.

"Sure you do." She turned to face him. "Here it is. You have to ask people to stay. You gotta put yourself out there, balls in the wind, and ask." She sipped her coffee.

"That's it?"

Jules nodded.

"Thanks." Dylan looked back at the timer on his phone, smiling again despite his mood.

"No problem." Jules stood. "So, are you going to fix things, or can we expect you on the couch again tonight?"

The timer went off. Dylan tapped his phone and stood. "I'm going to eat your food, and then I'm outta here."

Tyler appeared with a pink sparkly backpack on one shoulder. "Hey, nice nails," he said before kissing Jules. And kissing her again. "Bells, let's do this!" he called toward the back of the house.

Jules pulled her hair back with an elastic and took Bella's backpack from Tyler.

"Wanna come?" Bella asked as she came down the hall. "We're painting pottery after lunch."

Dylan shook his head, hugging Bella as she wrapped her arms around him. "Thanks for the self-care," he said. "How much do I owe you?"

"First visit is on the house. It's a loss leader." She ran outside.

Jules followed behind, sticking her tongue out at Tyler before closing the door.

"Bella is already talking like you," Dylan said.

"She's a tycoon in the making. You okay?"

Dylan shrugged, grabbing breakfast from the kitchen.

"Hey, remember the night Levinson died?"

Dylan tilted his head. "I guess."

"I do. You called me from work, said you'd been to see him, and his nurse said it wasn't long. He had a sister who would be there by dinner. Remember?"

"Yeah."

"I asked you if you were all right then too, and you said, 'Why the hell wouldn't I be all right?'"

"Okay."

"You loved that man, and after we hung up, you went right into a double shift. He died that night."

"What's your point?"

"My point is that you've lived most of your life like you don't care, and you do care. You're too—"

"I'm not doing this." Dylan grabbed his phone and walked toward the door. "Thanks for your couch. You'd better get outta here. They're waiting for you."

Tyler followed him and locked the door behind them. "They're meeting me there."

They stood facing the bay.

"I love you," Tyler said. It was so simple, Dylan nearly cried. He glanced over at his brother.

"I want you to be happy." He bumped his shoulder. "She only left because you didn't ask her to stay."

"That's what Jules said too."

"Smart woman."

"Debatable."

Tyler laughed. "I'm telling her you said that."

"I'll deny it."

They stood in silence.

"It doesn't matter," Dylan said. "We've lived in this town long enough to know everyone leaves eventually."

"Better to not care and watch them go, right?"

Dylan shrugged. "You left."

"What?"

"Oh, come on. You left for the big money. Let's not pretend you stuck around."

"Is that how you see it?" Tyler put his hands in his pockets. "I left to make a living. What did you want me to do here, Dylan?"

"I'm not blaming you. I didn't need you to stay, and I'm glad you found your thing. Let's not pretend that people don't leave this place for something better. Mom did. You did. And at least in his mind, Dad did too. I've always stayed behind."

Tyler was quiet for a while. "I never realized that's how you saw things."

He shrugged. "This doesn't have to be a big deal. I'm good. You're good. You came back when Drake got hurt. That's what matters."

Tyler met his eyes. "But I didn't come back for you."

"Oh, cut the shit. Now you're being dramatic."

Tyler shook his head. "No. I don't think I am. You're right. I left for college, and you were alone here. Alone with Dad."

"I had friends. You called, and you came to visit all the time."

"I know, but it was still tough. And I was so busy thinking about ways to improve our situation that I never thought about making that better life right here. That you never wanted to leave."

"Yeah, well."

"No. Not well. You need to tell people what you want. We're not mind readers. Call Clara. Tell her how you feel and ask her to come back."

"What the hell does any of this have to do with Clara? She'll be back on tour. She's gone."

"Rumor has it she's not going on tour. She's limiting her schedule and looking to buy an apartment in the city."

"Must be nice."

"Don't do that."

Dylan tried to ignore the hope blooming in his chest. She was less than two hours away. He could ask, and if she told him to screw off, that would be that. "I'm not living in the city," he said, almost to himself.

"She doesn't want you to live in the city. She was willing to stay right here and run the inn with you."

"For now."

Tyler shook his head. "Man, you have to work at forever. No one stays with anyone forever if they think the person couldn't care less."

Dylan looked over. "I work."

"I know." His brother patted him on the back. "I'll leave it alone." He walked toward his truck.

"Did she tell you she loved me?"

Tyler turned back, a big, stupid grin on his face. "No. But you love her, or you wouldn't be fighting so hard to push her away. You need to feel, Dylan. You're missing all the fun." He climbed into his truck and was gone.

Dylan had worked a double the night Levinson died. He'd only been on the schedule for his regular shift, but Randy had a new baby and Dylan offered to take his shift. Looking back on it now, he must have known Levinson was going to die that night, and he couldn't be there.

Instead, he was at sea helping strangers. He realized now it was because he cared too much about the old man to watch him leave. Dylan had been at the inn that morning to help the nurse with firewood and lifting Levinson so she could change the sheets. Levinson's sister, who used to spend the summers in Bodega, was coming up and would be there by dinner.

Dylan sat with Levinson explaining the Wordle! app on his phone. The man was ninety-eight and still upgraded his phone at every opportunity and was more up on the new apps and games than most teenagers.

"The point is to dive in and try to figure out the word?" Levinson had asked.

"You get six chances. If you get to the end without spelling the word, you lose that round."

He nodded and tapped at his phone, glasses perched on his nose, hands steady for a man about to die.

What had started as grunts and chores had grown into friend-ship and, Dylan knew now, love. Levinson came into his life when he needed structure, something to count on. Tyler had Drake and two jobs. Dylan had sports and chores.

It was supposed to be spending money, a free lunch now and then, but much like his granddaughter, Levinson crawled into Dylan's heart and bloomed as love. Rain or shine, Dylan was at the inn. If his clothes were dirty from school fights or Tyler fell behind on laundry, Levinson would toss them in the wash while Dylan sat in the kitchen in a robe from the inn and read aloud some newspa-per article Levinson thought "every educated young man needed to know."

He and Tyler believed in Dylan, and because of them, Dylan be-lieved in himself. Why wasn't he there on the night the man died? Why had he intentionally avoided the inn that night, preferring to tend to strangers instead? Dylan never gave it much thought. He'd just never gone back. Chapter over, person gone. Done.

It hurt too much. He knew now. First his mom, then Tyler to adult life and the city, and finally Levinson. Sure, Dylan had the town, Aunt Nikki, and the Branch family, but Levinson understood things the sunshine warmth of his hometown liked to brush away. He talked to Dylan about things, life and loss, ambition, and being a good man.

Shit. Dylan had messed up. He had the inn all to himself now and didn't want it. Not without her. If life was going to be unpredictable anyway, joys and sorrows as Levinson's letter said, Dylan wanted a life with Clara. Hell, even if they ran the inn into the ground and he was stuck behind some desk somewhere, he'd be fine if he could come home to her and takeaway on the couch every night.

He was probably too late, but he needed to try anyway. What had Jules said? Balls in the wind. Dylan needed to fix this, needed to at least offer Clara a happily ever after. Climbing into his truck, he knew he would need to consult an expert, so he drove to Swept Away.

Chapter Twenty-Eight

*C*lara was in her dressing room after the final night of *Bach in the Park*. She'd thoroughly enjoyed the experience and hoped they would invite her back next summer. Her mother had not called in weeks, and of course, neither had Burt. Clara still felt pangs of guilt at being happier without them, but she hoped that would ease over time.

Having removed most of her makeup, Clara stood to change but stopped at the knock on her door, and like a favorite song rewound, she opened the door to her grandfather's attorney.

"Hello, Ms. Mar."

"Mr. Hill." Clara looked around like he'd appeared out of thin air. "What are you doing here?"

"I enjoyed your performance tremendously. May I come in?"

"I'm so glad. Yes, of course." Clara stood back while emotion she thought she'd packed neatly away over the last few weeks swelled, pulling her right back to that afternoon when everything had seemed so complicated and yet somehow was as simple as it would ever be. "Would you . . . care for something to drink?"

Mr. Hill shook his head. "I can't stay. I'm multitasking. Now that your performance is over, I am here in an official capacity to ask you to attend the ceremony welcoming your grandfather's inn to the National Historic Inn Registry."

Clara furrowed her brow and tried to remember where she'd left things. "I've sold my half of the inn, as you are well aware. When was the application submitted?"

"I'm afraid I was not privy to that process, but it would mean a great deal to the town if you were in attendance."

Mr. Hill pushed his glasses up his nose, and Clara watched for some kind of sign this was a joke. "As much as I would love to be there, I don't think it is a good idea."

"Understood." He nodded. "There is a slight wrinkle. The buyer of your half of the inn is making the sale contingent on your attendance."

"What?" Clara narrowed her eyes. "Dylan is the buyer. I wanted to give it to him, but you said I had to sell it, so my price was a dollar."

"Indeed. And I honored your wishes, but since you have yet to receive the dollar, he now has a contingency."

"Aren't contingencies on the seller's end?"

Mr. Hill raised a brow.

"I'm learning . . . about things."

"Yes. I can see that. This particular buyer-seller agreement is . . . tricky."

"He won't buy my half unless I attend the dedication?"

"Correct."

"And he can do that?"

"He . . . is doing it. For reasons only he can explain."

Clara sighed. "Of course. The great Dylan Pace mystery continues."

"He can be mysterious."

"Can I sell my half to someone else?"

"You could, provided my firm is—"

"Is given time for due diligence. I remember." Clara sat, removed more of her eye makeup, and stared at Mr. Hill in the mirror. "He all but chased me out of there. Why does he suddenly want this?"

"As I said, the Historic Inn Registry has honored—"

"We never submitted that application. There is no ceremony. This makes no sense."

"I do not have access to the particulars, but your grandfather leaving you half the inn didn't make sense either. Remember how confused you were the first time you sat in that room with Mr. Pace?"

"I do," Clara said, nearly choking on the memories she'd almost pushed to background noise.

Mr. Hill sighed, again adjusting his tortoiseshell glasses. "You know, it's been my experience that people often espouse the difficulty in leaving, closing a chapter. Goodbyes get a bad rap, but I've always thought goodbyes were easy."

He pulled out a handkerchief from his jacket and handed it to Clara, who didn't realize a tear had slipped down her cheek.

"Goodbyes are a quick plane ticket, a new city, or a new job. Goodbyes are letting go, often for good reason."

"Exactly."

"Sometimes though, goodbyes hang on small things, or pain, unspoken words even. Staying in those situations is where the work begins. It's tough facing things. Staying is difficult. Believe me, you grandfather knew that when he presented you both with this challenge."

"He doesn't want me. I tried." Clara wiped her eyes.

"Ms. Mar"—her grandfather's attorney cleared his throat—"I make it a point never to get involved in the personal lives of my clients. Bad business. But I can tell you that Mr. Pace has asked for your attendance."

Clara sighed, returning the handkerchief. "When?"

"Tomorrow evening. Six o'clock. I checked your website, and it doesn't look like you have any performances for the next three months. Are you taking a vacation?"

"I bought an apartment. I'm taking time to get settled."

"How lovely for you. A place all your own."

"Yes. It's about time, don't you think?" Clara stood.

"As I told you that first day, I believe everything happens at the right time." He smiled. "So, can the Inn by the Bay count on your attendance tomorrow evening?"

Clara closed her eyes. Jules had texted her last week asking how things were going. Millie called a couple of days ago to ask if Clara wanted to grab lunch the next time she was in the city. Clara had left Bodega Bay, but not the people. And she had promised to visit. She just wasn't sure she had the strength to return only to leave Dylan again. The last time, she'd shown up to an entire week's worth of performances with puffy eyes.

"Ms. Mar?"

But what if this seemingly fictitious ceremony was Dylan's way of reaching out? "I'll be there." Clara stood.

"Excellent." Mr. Hill extended his hand.

Smiling, she pulled him into a hug and quickly released him. "Thank you."

Mr. Hill smoothed his jacket, his expression full of the same emotion she'd seen when he read her grandfather's letter. Without a word, he tipped his head and was gone.

Dylan washed the dishes, cleaned up the back patio, and explained the checkout process for the three couples who would be leaving the inn after breakfast tomorrow.

"Everything is right there on the iPad?" Sylvia from Phoenix asked.

Dylan nodded, wished them all a good night, and immediately thought of Clara. The iPad was her idea; so many things were hers. Her parting words were right: she was everywhere. Dylan knew he was living in a hell of his own making. According to the psychologist Tyler hooked him up with once Dylan finally got off their couch, Dylan had "self-sabotaged" his relationship with Clara. Kind of like what his father said about abandonment, but a hell of a lot more expensive.

Not that he was complaining. He was learning a lot about himself in those sessions, and while the psychologist thought it was still a bit early for Dylan to jump back into a relationship, Dylan told him a woman like Clara came along once in a lifetime and he owed it to her to at least try. Standing in the kitchen eating ice cream, he hoped to God the grand gesture was truly the way to win Clara back.

"I don't need romantic fiction," he'd told Nikki. "I need a real concrete plan."

She'd rolled her eyes. "The energy I spend trying to convince non-romance-believers. I could run a marathon. Probably two."

Dylan had shut his mouth after that and listened as Nikki, using excerpts from romance novels, explained the "grand gesture" and the "grovel."

A few days after she left, Dylan was already more terrified of living without her than he'd ever been of losing her. Clara had never made a fool of him; he'd made a fool of himself, as Jules had so helpfully pointed out, using nearly all her four-letter words.

Maybe Clara would come back and realize he'd kept things running and want to be with him. Or maybe she wouldn't. Maybe she would say she had returned to performing full-time and didn't see a future for them anymore.

Dylan realized it wasn't about making her stay for his own needs, it was about making sure she knew how much he loved her, how much she'd changed his life. If she was going to leave, his father was right, Dylan would survive, but the idea of her out there in the world not knowing how much he loved her, wanted her, needed her? Yeah, that pain was too much.

"All done out there," Rusty said, rescuing Dylan from his thoughts. "Burnt out lightbulbs replaced, and new fountain light installed."

"Thanks." Dylan took one more bite of ice cream before returning the carton to the freezer and glancing out the kitchen window at Christopher Levinson's fountain.

"So, you think this is gonna work?" Rusty washed his hands and turned while he dried them. "Getting Clara back? You sure need to turn turtle on this thing, am I right?"

Dylan furrowed his brow. "Turn what?"

Rusty made to speak, but Dylan held up his hand. "Never mind. I have no idea if she'll forgive me. I said a lot of stupid shit."

"My money's on forgiveness." Rusty squeezed Dylan's shoulder. "Yeah?"

He nodded. "She already knows you're a great guy, it just took you a bit to catch up. Kinda like the tortoise and the hare."

"More turtles? Am I the hare in this story?"

"Nope. Tortoise is slower."

"So, I'm slow?"

"When it comes to Clara Mar, I'm afraid ya are." Rusty snorted. "I'm rhymin' without even tryin'."

Dylan laughed. It felt good, the laughter. And the optimism Rusty seemed to bring to every situation.

"I hope you're right," Dylan said, walking Rusty out the front door.

"Me too." Rusty climbed into his truck. "I miss her already."

As Rusty drove away, Dylan stood on the porch, looking up at the vast summer sky. When he'd first found out about Levinson's will, all he cared about was securing a new direction after his knee; now nothing made sense without her.

He wasn't sure how to fix things, so he closed his eyes like he had when he was a kid and made a wish. It had never worked back then, but Dylan was willing to try anything. Opening his eyes, he exhaled slowly, went inside, and turned off the lights.

Chapter Twenty-Nine

The next morning, Clara sifted through moving boxes, dressed, and climbed into the waiting car downstairs from her apartment. She'd spent last night trying to quiet the duet of thrilling excitement and wary restraint at the idea of seeing Dylan again. Seeing all of them, but mostly him. It had been nearly a month since she'd packed up her trunks and left. She'd closed on her apartment last week and finally unpacked for good.

An entire trunk was her collection of memorabilia and things she'd picked up on her travels. It was so nice to put her life on shelves, in the sunlight, instead of packed away. Her new agent was the right blend of involved and respectful of Clara's downtime. She was excited to find the balance, and possibly try writing some music. Much like the walls of her new apartment, there was room for growth, possibilities; and despite missing Dylan and Bodega Bay, she had never been surer of herself and what she wanted.

Now, she was heading back to the happiest time in her life under false pretenses. There was no registry, and Dylan could not make the sale of her half of the inn contingent upon whether she showed up; Clara had googled it. So why was she going, other than to honor Mr. Hill's fabrication and because he'd watched her performance in the park? Clara wasn't sure, but knew it had something to do with hope. She had always been a sucker for possibilities. Wasn't that what led her to Bodega Bay at the beginning of the year?

Clara listened to music most of the drive, hoping to calm her nerves, but as they pulled onto Main Street and past Swept Away Books, her heart sang. There were more people, even as evening approached. Dough Bird's expanded eating area was packed with people in flip-flops, and the Crab Shack had a line down the sidewalk. Clara touched the window as if that could bring her back, but she knew firsthand, life was rarely that easy.

Nikki ran to meet Clara when the driver opened the car door in front of the Inn by the Bay. Wrapping her in a hug, Nikki winked at the driver.

"Welcome back," she said, leading Clara along the side of the inn.

"Thank you. You colored your hair?"

Nikki put a hand to her vibrant violet locks. "It's temporary. Do you like?"

"I do. It's very South Beach."

"I love Miami. We should all take a girls' trip when it cools off. Nothing like Miami in the—"

Clara stopped before they rounded into the backyard. "Why am I here, Nikki?"

Nikki tilted her head in mock confusion.

"There is no National Historic Inn certification. Not yet. We never finished the application. And who has a ceremony at night?"

"Well, we wanted a time when everyone would be off work so we could celebrate."

Clara narrowed her eyes.

Nikki started walking again, holding Clara's hand. "You know in romance there's this thing called suspension of disbelief, which is loosely the willingness of a reader to ignore critical thinking to enjoy a story. Do you follow?"

"I think so."

Nikki opened the side gate and they walked along the brick path. "Now, you can't mess with the reader too much or they'll call baloney, but we let things like paperwork and even timelines slide sometimes for the magic." She splayed her hands as they came around the corner.

The back patio was lit with overhead pops of light. New flowerbeds were blooming with color, and in the distance, her father's fountain sprinkled under its own light.

Everyone Clara had ever known in Bodega Bay was there, and a few spouses she'd yet to meet. They cheered and hugged Clara as if this were a homecoming. She supposed it was. Gus handed her some punch. Clara sipped and knew it was her grandmother's recipe.

Millie updated Clara on her newest work in progress before Jules and Bella pointed out their handmade welcome back sign. Her eyes welled, and Clara was nearly overcome. She hadn't seen Dylan yet, but being surrounded by all the people she'd grown to love was almost worth the trip. Almost, she thought, as she scanned the crowd.

Everyone Dylan loved was on the patio when he walked through the back door from the kitchen. Everyone including Clara, who stood with her back to him, talking to Nikki, who winked at Dylan as he approached. Clara turned, and he nearly dropped to his knees. She hadn't even been gone a month. The reopened inn had only had four rounds of guests so far, but she'd missed out on the grand opening party and their first newlywed couple. Dylan added that to the list of things he needed to make up to her.

"Hey." He shoved his hands into his pockets to keep from reaching out to touch her. Christ, he'd missed her.

"Hello," she said, her expression a lot like the one she'd had on the first day they'd met. Guarded. Dylan cursed himself for every time he'd kept her at arms' length, made her feel like she wasn't the most amazing woman he'd ever known.

"We never finished the paperwork for the Historic Inn Registry, Dylan." She crossed her arms. "What am I doing here?"

He looked at Nikki, who shrugged. "She knew you were full of it, and she still showed. All great heroes grovel. Get on with it."

Dylan took in a slow breath and scanned the crowd as everyone grew quiet. Maybe this wasn't a good idea. Too late now. He wasn't screwing this up again.

"My imaginary friend was an otter," he said.

"Speak up for those of us in the back," Rusty yelled. "I don't want to miss a minute of this."

Dylan looked up at the stars and back at Clara, whose eyes were wide with surprise.

"His name was Billy."

"I can confirm that is correct," Tyler called out.

"Billy lived in our bathtub. I always kept a little water in there for him. I even made him a bed in our closet."

"Aww." The crowd sounded like a rushing wave.

Dylan swallowed. It was possible he would have a heart attack before this was over. "When my mom left, I stopped . . . believing in things . . . magical things. Until you."

Millie sighed. "Oh, that's perfect, Dylan."

Drake put his arm around his wife. "I think he's got this, babe."

"Right." She flinched. "Sorry about that. Go on."

Dylan smiled. "Thanks." He looked back at Clara, who was smiling, fingers twisting at the hem of her top. Dylan took her hands.

"I'm telling you this because . . . I'm not an asshole. I've just had some things happen and . . . the point is, when I met you, I started believing anything was possible and, you were right, I was scared." He was going to pass out. "And I know I pushed you away, that I hurt you." He pulled her hands to his mouth and kissed them. "I held so tight to this place, like I needed it to survive. I forgot to hold tight to you. But I'm working on myself."

Dylan let her hands go and wiped at his eyes, catching Tyler in the crowd. His brother nodded, eyes welling up too, and Dylan realized just how much damage he'd begun to heal.

"Me too," Clara said, stepping toward him. "I am working on myself too."

He held her gorgeous gaze. "I'm so sorry."

"I know." She nodded, taking in the lights and the patio. "You lit the fountain."

"I did that," Rusty said.

Clara laughed and wiped her eyes. "Thank you."

"My pleasure."

When she turned back to Dylan, he knew he would never get another chance. The fact that she was here instead of cursing his name in some high-rise spoke to the kind of woman she was, and he never wanted to be without her again.

He took her hand. "I love you, Clara. I've loved you for a long time, I'm just . . ."

"An idiot," Jules offered.

Dylan pointed in the direction of the crowd. "That. I was an idiot, but I love you. It was difficult for me to believe a woman like you would—"

"A woman like me would what?" Clara asked, falling back into their usual banter. "Run an inn with you?"

He shook his head.

"Love you. You didn't believe a woman with that much luggage would fall in love with you?" She stepped closer, put a hand to his chest. "You rescued me from certain death. How could I not love you?" she asked.

She put her arms around his neck and nodded. "I told you." Her blue eyes glistened with tears. "I will always love you." She put her hand to his heart. "I'll take care of it, I promise."

Dylan swallowed back so much he thought he might choke, before managing, "The joy and the—"

"Sorrows," Clara said through tears, and Dylan kissed her in front of a cheering crowd.

Easing back, Dylan met her gaze. "Clara Hildegard Mar, I can't guarantee you I won't screw up again, and I'm a verified pain in the ass, but I love you and I promise to bring you coffee in the morning and order the takeaway at night. I will fly, drive, take a boat wherever you need me to be, to support your career. And if you leave, I will follow you and beg you to come home. You are everything good in this jacked-up world and I want to wake up with you for the rest of my days, please—"

"Hot *dog*! Are you two gettin' married?" Dylan's dad asked, now standing at Nikki's shoulder.

"Don't start," Dylan and Clara said in concert, not taking their eyes off one another.

Everyone laughed, and Dylan shook his head. "Can I finish now?"

"Oh, sure," Nikki said, before shushing the crowd.

Dylan gently held Clara's face. "I love you. I will never find the right words to tell you how much, but I'll show you every day. Please stay."

Clara had never imagined falling in love. She knew love through music, but it had always seemed like some sweeping thing that required a cocktail dress and unrealistic expectations. She touched Dylan's face to confirm this was real, that he was real, and she said, "Yes," and the whole town erupted in applause, and she kissed him again.

This was her finale, Clara thought. The one she'd never knew she had until her grandfather changed everything. She and Dylan would work out the details, "off book" as Nikki put it, but Bodega Bay was her home.

"Where is the bookcase, by the way?" Clara asked.

"Storage. I couldn't look at it."

"Well, we're going to need to remedy that immediately."

"Yeah?"

"It's part of our story. Speaking of which, did you know Carley Rae Jepson has another song?" Clara touched his chest.

"I've listened to all her songs."

She smiled. "Honestly?"

Dylan nodded.

"Then you'll be familiar with where she says she really likes the guy."

"Pretty sure she sings 'really' a hundred times in that one." Dylan pulled her close.

Clara laughed and when they turned, everyone was silent.

"Oh, and I'm not selling you my half of the inn," she said into his neck.

"Thank Christ." Dylan kissed her again while the party erupted.

Clara turned to face the people she'd grown to love too, and knew that she was home. All those years of marveling at the ease of others making a life, and here she was, staying right where she belonged.

Epilogue

"Ladies and gentlemen, the incomparable Ms. Clara Mar." The crowd roared as Dylan stood in the wings, watching his whole heart walk on stage. Cello handlers—they were a real thing—met her center stage to make sure everything was adjusted.

It was hard to believe it was November, and even harder to believe he was in Vienna for Clara's last performance before they returned home to Bodega Bay to start preparations for their next hopefully-sold-out-again summer season.

They would be married next summer after Tyler and Jules. Bella was pulling double duty as flower girl for both weddings, and Mr. Hill would walk Clara down the planked path to Levinson's private beach where she and Dylan would "turn their HFN into an HEA," according to Nikki.

But first, before all of that, Dylan had never been prouder as Clara glanced offstage, her grandmother's hair clip glistening under the bright lights as she blew him a kiss, lowered her head, and, on a breath, began to play.

Thank you for reading *Stay – A Love Story*! I hope Clara and Dylan's story was worth the wait. These two did not cooperate at all and I think that's a testament to their strength. I'm pretty sure I went through more drafts of this story than any of my previous books. Clara and Dylan broke my heart, made me laugh, and we finally made it.

I hope you love this one as much as I do. If you do, please consider leaving a review at the book retailer of your choice, as well as Good-reads, to help other readers find this story.

Also, if you're not already, hop on my newsletter mailing list at: tra-cyewens.com to keep up with the latest news about my books.

Finally, thank you for the tremendous support. There are no words to express my appreciation. Keep reading for a peek at *Catch – A Love Story*, which is Jules and Tyler's story.

All the best,
Tracy

Chapter One

Jules Bartlett hosed blood off the bow of the *Ginsburg*. She was stress cleaning; everyone knew it and wisely let her be. As captain of both the *Ginsburg* and the *Eleanor,* she now had crew for these kinds of things. Twelve men in total at her command, but this morning she'd reached her threshold and needed to *do* something rather than give instruction. An hour into their morning run, her usual spot at the helm had been stifling, and by the time they'd retrieved the last crab pot, the often-entertaining banter of the guys was grating on her tired nerves.

Rather than taking her crap out on them, she'd handed the helm over to Skeet, her second-in-command, and was now mindlessly hosing the deck in a valiant effort to ignore everything save the water washing pink across familiar steel. The wedding invitation now resting soggy in the pocket of her bib overalls had arrived as expected. Spotting it, all sweeping script and fucking doves, on her parents' kitchen counter that morning beneath a bill from her daughter Bella's dentist, Jules would have feigned indifference had anyone else been around. But she'd been alone in the early morning quiet, and despite years of history that left her firmly planted in reality, the whimsical folds of expensive paper still crashed over the bow of her life like a rogue wave and knocked her off balance.

She was going to throw the damn thing away while her coffee was brewing but then thought better and shoved it into her pocket as if that would make it disappear. Jules no longer believed in that kind of magic, but she also had a habit of shoving trash deep into her backpack or her pockets in this case.

Hours later and thermos sadly empty, she was still wrestling with why something as harmless as the expected was messing with her normal and creating a sense that she was chasing some invisible clock like one of those stupid princesses tripping over their shoes.

"So, I know you're all Captain Ahab today, but you've gotta see this shot," Skeet said, coming to stand at her side. "The camera on these new phones is insane."

Jules turned expressionless.

"Ahab. The book. *Moby-Dick?*"

"I got the reference. Ahab was a man, and who's driving while you're here annoying me?"

"Fine, Captain Ahab-y." He chuckled like a clever child. "Mikey's driving. You told me to give him some time at the helm, and now's as good a time as any."

"So you can show me a picture?"

"Yeah." He swiped at his phone in that perpetually excited way he did most things.

Jules wanted to spray his face and his phone, but it was cold for March, so she refrained. Skeet lifted his phone to show her yet another picture of his puckered face air-kissing a crab. It was stunning that she often trusted this man with her life, her crew, and their clients.

"Why am I paying you for this?"

"What? The guys think it's my best work." Clearly disappointed by her response, Skeet put his phone away, pulled on his gloves, and rubbed his hands together for warmth. "You know, my social media skills are what business experts call a 'value-added benefit.'"

Jules laughed, oddly grateful for the distraction that was Skeet. "Are you listening to that podcast again? I thought we decided that guy was full of shit."

"That guy *was* full of shit, but this new one is—wait for it—*Million Dollar Mind*." He flashed his hands like a marquee. "It's gold."

Jules shook her head, the still-running hose now at her side.

"Don't judge. He's awesome. He's an entrepreneur."

"Oh, well, in *that* case."

Skeet shook his head and flipped his cap backward before the wind carried it away. "I'm not letting this negativity crush my dreams."

They stood in silence before Jules turned away to give the bait tanks one more spray down. An entrepreneur. Yeah, exactly what she needed. Jules had fallen for a smooth talker once in her life. She'd been lured in by promises of grand adventures, love, and acceptance before being tossed right back into the waters of Bodega Bay.

Six years wiser, she now spent nearly three hundred days a year on her family's fishing boats either bringing in catch or taking tourists on a menu of deep sea experiences. When she wasn't on the water, she was raising her daughter Bella, which meant she had zero time for bullshit, dreams, or million-dollar minds.

"They're pictures. A little bit of fun." Skeet made to take the hose, but Jules held firm, closing the bait tanks. "You do remember what fun is, right?"

She turned the hose on him this time, aiming for the face, but he held up his hands with a laugh, so she spared him again. "Now, *that* would've been fun."

"So crabby," he said. "Get it? Crabby? Maybe that should be today's caption—'Feeling crabby.' Or better yet, 'feeling' and then the little crab emoji. Yeah, that's good." Skeet nodded as if he'd discovered something revolutionary.

Jules wanted to appreciate his enthusiasm, but the veiled insult was one she'd often heard, and the invitation in her pocket whispered again.

"I am completely fun." Her voice cracked as if it didn't even believe her.

Skeet raised a brow.

"I don't need selfies to prove that I'm fun. Selfies are—"

"Fun, that's what they are. I've actually started calling them shell-fies. We've got our own hashtag and everything," he declared.

She shook her head. "No one wants this."

"Everyone wants this." He turned off the hose and began coiling it into the bow compartment. "We're in a competitive industry, and every little bit helps."

"Did the Millionaire Mobster tell you that too?"

"It's the *Million Dollar*— Oh, never mind. The point is we have over two thousand followers. We don't even have two thousand people in this town." He waved his hand across her line of sight as if presenting the approaching shore of Bodega Bay on a game show. "Branch Fishing, thanks to my mad skills, is steps away from becoming a global phenomenon."

"A *fun* global phenomenon."

He nodded. "Laugh now, but you'll thank me."

"I will not. Check that loose starboard dock line and tell Mikey he can throttle down."

Skeet sighed dramatically and did as he was instructed.

In what felt like an instant, he was back at her side. "I hate your crabby mornings."

Jules unzipped her jacket.

"Are you pissed I ran the lines when we were only hauling in pots?"

She shook her head. Skeet always baited the lines for rock fish even when they only went out to collect. It never bothered her. They usually sold whatever they caught to the restaurants, or Grant, Skeet's husband, made the world's best fish stew. Not that her parents, who also owned The Crab Shack, needed to know about Grant's otherworldly talents.

"I'm not... crabby or Ahab-y," she finally said. "I've got things on my mind."

"What kind of things?"

"That pinging thing when we throw the *Eleanor* into reverse. I'm thinking about that, and Bella's play is tonight. Things."

"I'll get *Eleanor* into the boat doctor next week." If Skeet knew she wasn't telling him what was actually on her mind, he didn't let on.

Jules nodded and instructed the rest of the crew to prepare the dock lines as she returned to the helm, Skeet still at her back.

They rounded the breakwater, the morning's sunrise a burst of tangerine and a welcome reminder that the envelope in her pocket was not a big deal by comparison. The ocean made her feel small, which, while frightening when she was younger, was a helpful reminder when she returned home six years ago.

Small meant her problems back then were small too. That no matter how massive the pain seemed in those first few weeks and months, it was a speck, a drop in the collective well of struggle so many people survived every day. The ocean gave perspective, her father explained one night.

"Do we honestly have that many Twitter followers?" she asked Skeet.

"Instagram."

"Is that the one with the pictures?"

"Yeah. Do you have the app?" Skeet asked, confusing her renewed calm for renewed interest. "Give me your phone."

Jules pulled off a glove with her teeth, the other hand still on the wheel, and gave him her phone.

"Damn." He tucked his own gloves into his back pocket before passing the admittedly older model iPhone between his hands like an ancient artifact. "Does this thing even have a camera?"

"Yes, it has a camera." She reached to take it back, but he was faster.

"This is sad, Cap. Don't let Grant catch you with this. Neglecting upgrades is blasphemy in our house."

"Yeah, well, it works just fine for me." She managed to snatch the phone and shoved it back into her pocket. "Upgrades are not my religion."

Still smiling, Skeet radioed their approach before they returned to silence, shoulder to shoulder, watching as Bodega Bay welcomed them home for the thousandth time.

"That's not a phone." The man couldn't help himself.

"Well"—Jules signed the logbook he held in front of her—"at least I'm not kissing crabs so people will like me."

"True. You're not kissing crabs or anything else," he mumbled, returning the logbook.

He inhaled to speak again.

"Could you please quit critiquing me and go do your job? Get me off this boat so I can drink more coffee and take my kid to school."

Sensing her limit, as he often did when he was driving her nuts, Skeet saluted and joined the rest of the crew on the bow as they brought the *Ginsburg* to the dock and watched as the *Eleanor* followed close behind.

After stuffing her coat through the strap of her backpack and running through her checklist twice, Jules handed things over to Skeet and thanked the crew on both boats for jobs well done.

Hopping onto the deck, she made her way toward the parking lot, debating if she had enough time to stop for coffee before meeting Bella. Jules started her truck and realized she'd have to tackle the next hour caffeine-free. She'd survive. She always did.

Tyler Pace had learned to juggle when he was thirteen, working at the only grocery store in Bodega Bay. He'd started with walnuts, and by the time he left for college, he was deftly tossing lemons for Mr. Beaman and their patrons in the small coastal town where he grew up. Working at Beaman's had been a bright spot in an otherwise dimly lit childhood. Juggling taught Tyler so many things, not the least of which were hard work and practice. A good juggler needed both. Practice had given him something to focus on and a way to entertain his brother Dylan when their parents' fighting drew out the neighbors, the sheriff, or both to the Pace front yard out of "concern for the children."

Tyler and Dylan, younger by less than a year, were often found sitting out back on their dilapidated deck. Dylan would count to see how long Tyler could keep whatever he was juggling in the air until the storm of their parents' anger and excess passed.

Hard work and its connection to money came early to Tyler too. Adding any job he could find, either before or after school, initially kept him and his brother in snacks and shoes that fit. Once their mom left for good, his extra money helped pay the mortgage on their small crappy house while their dad sunk deeper into the bottle.

Tyler met every setback and learned more every time he dropped literal and figurative balls until the day he left for Cal Berkeley, the only major university willing to give him a full academic scholarship. He earned a double degree in economics and marketing, worked endless hours to pay for things scholarships didn't cover, and applied every algorithm for success until he had made more money than he could ever spend. He was a machine back then, driven at first by the fear of ending up like his parents and eventually by the power to effect change with what he'd learned—what he had earned.

Now, years away from Beaman's, Berkeley, and several courses of expensive therapy, Tyler leaned back in his chair, lacing his hands behind his head. The unopened email glared at him bold from the otherwise orderly inbox of his laptop, and he understood, maybe for the first time, that no amount of practice, hard work, or juggling could change his past.

"Are you sleeping with your sweet elderly neighbor and buying her water heaters in exchange for homemade cookies?"

Tyler was already grinning as he glanced up at Addie, his assistant, leaning in the doorway of his office, one high-heeled foot resting behind the other and a plastic wrap-covered plate in her hands.

"Guilty. Who told?"

She held up the plate and walked across his office. "You must be quite the neighbor." Her dark eyes lit with humor as she set the cookies on his desk.

Tyler inhaled. "Walnut chocolate chip. My favorite. And for the record, I didn't buy her a water heater." He closed his laptop, more than happy to leave the email right where it was for now. "But I did teach her the art of negotiation. When that didn't work on her son,

I showed her how to buy a laptop, set up Wi-Fi, and purchase her own water heater."

"Sounds like you fixed him. Is there anything else I need to know about you and Gertrude?"

Tyler checked the time and reached for his jacket. If he didn't get moving, he would be late for his favorite eleven-year-old's school play.

"No, I think her cookies speak for themselves." Sliding into his navy suit jacket, Tyler peeled back a corner of the plastic wrap and offered Addie a cookie. She shook her head. He tugged his cuffs into place before biting into his own cookie and relishing two of his favorite things—butter and chocolate. Gertrude did bake a mean cookie. Or he was a complete sucker for all things dessert.

Addie handed him a few folders. "Okay, well, those cookies are, as you already know, from your adorable neighbor Gertrude, who told me you, and I quote, 'liberated her from her evil son who is hell-bent on putting her in one of those old lady homes.' She also wanted me to let you know she's ordered your Christmas present from Lithuania. And that the next time you're at the apartment, she needs you to show her how to create a Bitmoji."

Tyler widened his eyes and finished loading his leather messenger bag. He had nine minutes to get upstairs. "She told you all of that? Wait, did she drop off the cookies?"

"No." Addie rewrapped the plate. "She had an Uber driver deliver the cookies. But"— she held up a finger for effect—"she was skeptical that the 'young man' would deliver her cookies, so she called me to confirm."

"Got it." Tyler popped the remaining bite into his mouth.

"We had a twenty-minute conversation about how you are her hero and some lucky person should snatch you up. She then asked me if I was single and sounded downright disappointed when I told her I was married and my two kids would miss their father if I threw him over for the 'adorable' Tyler Pace."

"Gertrude does like to chat." Tyler fastened his jacket button. "And play matchmaker."

"That she does. Lovely woman." Addie leaned on the desk. "Her son, on the other hand, not so much. He called shortly after Gertrude hung up. I told him you were tied up for the rest of the day but would return his call tomorrow as priority one."

Tyler made to answer, but Addie held up her hand. "To which he said, 'tell that meddling prick to quit filling Mom's head with ideas about being powerful.' And that if the two of you were sleeping together, he was calling a lawyer. I informed him you would not be calling him back."

Tyler removed his glasses to clean them on the cloth he kept in his suit pocket. "That would be Randy. He's always accusing me of sleeping with his mom."

Addie cringed. "Seriously?"

Tyler nodded and put his glasses back on. "He's an interesting man."

"I sensed that." She checked her watch. "Four minutes."

Tyler slung his bag over one shoulder, and put his phone into his pocket.

"Today's mail is scanned and on the H: drive," Addie said, running through her usual mental list before the elevator dinged and the doors opened to rooftop level. "Flowers are waiting in the helicopter. Anything else before I leave you?" She held the elevator doors open.

"Not that I can think of at the moment, but I'm sure I'll email tonight."

"Okay, well then"— she gestured with mock demure—"they're ready for you, Mr. Pace."

Tyler shook his head and stepped off the elevator. "Never gets old, does it?"

"Nope." Her eyes glinted. "Be safe up there."

"I'll do my best." He made his way toward the double doors that led to the helipad, cookies and conversation almost cancelling out his earlier edge.

"Ooh, one more thing. Did you get a chance to read that email from your father's doctor? They called earlier to follow up, and I wasn't sure what to say."

And there it was. Tyler was at the top of his building, one of three he owned in downtown San Francisco. He was about to climb into a helicopter he also owned, and somehow all it took was a mention of his dad for Tyler to revisit that dirty-faced kid the school principal used to buy lunch for when his stomach growled so loud the other kids in class made fun of him.

Well versed in managing nearly everything, including his emotions, Tyler glanced back. "I did, but I need to review in more detail. I'll follow up directly. Thank you." He smiled before facing Newman, Pace Capital's helicopter pilot, who was patiently waiting at the door of the 525 Relentless. This was his reality, he reminded himself on a slow exhale. "Have a good night, Addie."

"You too."

Pushing through double doors to the helipad, Tyler gently rebuked Newman's efforts to take his bag and climbed inside the sleek black machine. There were several factors to consider when buying a helicopter—distance without refueling, interior details—but Tyler would admit only to himself that the model's name, Relentless, had sealed the deal before he even knew the damn thing could go over five hundred nautical miles on a single tank.

Relentless. Yeah, he liked that word.

Newman announced his standard greeting as they lifted off the top of the Pace Capital building and banked left out of the city.

Resting his head on the plush leather seat, Tyler checked his phone before setting it face down on the table in front of him, determined to enjoy the colors of dusk instead of obsessing. He managed a whole thirty seconds before flipping the damn thing over and tapping the email that read "Marvin L. Pace Test Results, Diagnosis, and Treatment Plan—Confidential."

You can find *Catch – A Love Story*
at all major retailers to continue reading.

OTHER LOVE STORIES BY TRACY EWENS

Premiere
Candidate
Taste
Reserved
Stirred
Vacancy
Playbook
Exposure
Brew
Smooth
Tap
Blow
Catch

Acknowledgments

I would like to thank:

Sarah at Lopt & Cropt for helping me believe in this book even when I wanted to give up.

Erin Tolbert for her proofreading eye, her joyful sense of humor, and somehow making everything work.

Erin Willard for her insightful guidance, warm words, and finally explaining ellipses.

Every reader who has read, reviewed, or sent me an email about one, or all of my books.

Michael for wiping my tears, dusting me off, and sending me back out there. I love you.

Tracy Ewens is a recovered theatre major who writes contemporary romance.

When not working on her next book, she drinks copious amounts of tea, prefers an exit row seat, and reads well past her bedtime.

www.tracyewens.com